CHAPATTI
OR CHIPS?

Thirty-two year old Nisha Minhas lives in Milton Keynes with her partner and two cats. She is currently working on her second novel.

CHAPATTI OR CHIPS?

NISHA MINHAS

**POCKET
BOOKS**

LONDON • SYDNEY • NEW YORK • TOKYO • SINGAPORE • TORONTO

First published in Great Britain by Pocket Books, 2002
An imprint of Simon & Schuster UK
A Viacom company

1 3 5 7 9 10 8 6 4 2

Simon & Schuster UK Ltd
Africa House
64-78 Kingsway
London WC2B 6AH

www.simonsays.co.uk

Simon & Schuster Australia
Sydney

A CIP catalogue record for this book is available from the British Library

ISBN 1-7434-3045-X

Typeset by SX Composing DTP, Rayleigh, Essex
Printed and bound in Great Britain by
Cox & Wyman Ltd, Reading, Berkshire

For the love of my life, Dave.
∞0X9!

Acknowledgements

To my brilliant agent Lorella Belli at Laurence Pollinger. Thank you for all your support, hard work and valued input. For being more than an agent. I'm indebted.

To Kate Lyall Grant, my editor. A massive thank you for all your encouragement, skill and kindness. You're a gem.

Thank you to everyone at Simon & Schuster who worked with the book behind the scenes.

And especially I want to thank my other half, Dave. Without you, I'd still be on page 1, word one, 'Rumour'. Without you, there would be no book. Without you, there would be no us. Without you . . . our house would be tidy.

Chapter One

Rumour has it, the USA intelligence agency listens in to everything we say through their covert surveillance systems. Listening in for keywords such as 'bomb', 'president', 'assassination', 'Monica'. Some men have this ability when talking to women. Just waiting for the keywords like 'SEX', 'PINT', 'FOOTBALL', ignoring everything else with a clever look as if they are truly interested.

Dave sat back in the squashy cushioned armchair in Florelli's coffee shop. For thirty minutes he had been half listening to the posh woman sitting opposite, waiting for the keywords, watching her pretty little face. It was one of those coffee shops which, although very much outside London, pretended it was slap bang in the middle of the West End; though it was actually in the heart of Buckinghamshire. Dave hated the pretence and pseudo yuppiness, but he loved their home-made apple pies. Seven pictures – *The Wonders of the World* – all framed in chrome, adorned the indigo-coloured walls, with one more, entitled *The Eighth Wonder of the World?* – a picture of Florelli's coffee shop. There was a long chestnut bar surface as you entered on the left, with about ten blue soft-topped chrome bar stools for the quick-grab-a-sarnie-and-coffee sort. In the main carpeted area, dark blue sofas and sofa chairs hugged around small tables, frequented by the self-styled would-be entrepreneur sort, with their laptops, hands-free mobiles, briefcases, *Financial Times*, all looking like they'd been cloned, all swimming fiercely in the sea of finance, trying desperately to climb the ladder of success, and all leaving big tips that they probably begrudged paying.

'So, what do you think?' asked the pretty-faced woman in her late twenties, sitting opposite Dave, wearing a navy two-piece Ralph Lauren suit.

'Uhm, sorry, what was the question again?' he said, puffing on his fag, trying to look interested, but trying harder to work out whether she had on either stockings with suspenders or just plain old tights.

She examined him: piercing blue eyes, short dark brown hair, good looking, a bit rough with his earring, but dressed extremely well. 'I said, what do you think of Monet's *The Japanese Garden*?'

Dave gazed up to the ceiling with its whirring fan, and tried to come up with the best words to describe Monet. 'Well, I've got to be honest, it looks like he painted it in a rush.'

Monet in a rush. Hardly the arty-farty answer she wanted. Maybe she wanted something a little quirky, like: 'Monet lived the life of a human but had the mind of God.'

He knew better than to judge a woman on first appraisal, especially when he was feeling horny. But sometimes a window to the future bagged his attention. This one, with her long, never-ending, silky, slender legs, short-cropped streaked blonde hair, sweet innocent smile and pouting kissable lips, he could see, ten years from now, dumping off her two bratty kids at some posh-nosh private school, meeting up with Fanny Adams at some scone-and-cream festival and then mixing it up with the local rowing team down the Park's Rotary Club with cocktails and fritters, leaving her lawyer hubby catching up with his paperwork inside his secretary's knickers.

Dave was watching her now, her mouth moving, the words just silent whispers. 'God, this is so boring,' he said, not realizing that his thoughts were coming out loud – loud and clear.

Droning on and on about Monet, Picasso and Vincent Van Gogh, listening to her pronounce her Ps and Qs correctly, and watching her sip her cappuccino with her little pinkie out to one side, all in aid of what? Just so Dave could get his leg over with the pretty-faced snobby woman. That was about the size of it. Sex.

She stood up in refined disgust. 'I beg your pardon? Well, it was nice talking to you. I just remembered I've got an appointment. Goodbye.' And if this was a phone conversation, she would have slammed the phone down.

Dave smiled at her anger. 'Ciao.' It sounded like 'cow' though. 'By the way, Claude Monet's *Waterlilies* painting looks muddled and out of focus

3

up close. I reckon he was pissed when he painted it.'

She turned her nose up at him in disdain, yet failing to conceal her surprise that he knew Monet's Christian name, and masterfully stalked out into the rain in her high heels, leaving the faintest of perfumes amongst the boisterous smell of ground African coffee beans.

Dave put his feet up on the small round coffee table. His Nike trainers squeaked on the wooden surface and one of the middle-aged waitresses, in her blue apron and matching baseball cap, gave him a look. He smiled back and pointed for a refill in his coffee cup. Grudgingly she obliged. He was a paying customer after all.

'Thank you,' Dave said, watching her refill his cup.

'Would you like anything else, sir?' she asked, holding the coffee jug.

'A smile wouldn't go amiss.'

She huffed and walked off.

He looked to the etched window, 'S'ILLEROLF', and watched the rain begin to pelt on the pane. People outside began to walk faster; some opened their umbrellas, some used newspapers, some got wet. A little gang of shoppers harboured from the pouring rain under the blue coffee-shop canopy, clogging it up like cholesterol in an artery. The warmth inside and the cosy rinse of light. It reminded Dave of being twelve, doing his paper round while everyone slept in their warm beds – until he banged their gate shut – and rushing back on his chopper to the warm seclusion of the newsagent's shed, where his good boss would be serving hot chocolate to those boys who finished their rounds early. The secret was in only delivering papers to the moaners and chucking

4

the rest. Always Dave would be first back, putting his feet up, and enjoying the hot chocolate while all the other paperboys suffered in the darkness and rain outside. He got the sack after four weeks. One person even claimed that she only found out about the new Prime Minister three weeks after he was elected, because of Dave's lack of papers.

The frosted glass door burst open and Dave's feet suddenly came off the table. Fuck Picasso, he thought, now *that* was a work of art! Nothing abstract or muddled or even rushed about *her*: she was plain and simply beautiful. Very slim. Straight shoulder-length black hair with a hint of brown, astonishingly pretty, light brown skin, exotic, but then she would be – she was Indian. Some women had already begun to bitch about her before she had even stepped three feet inside. And the men made pathetic attempts, in front of their female companions, not to notice her.

She put her black canvas bag down on the side of the counter. 'Just a straight white coffee, please,' she said, in perfect English.

Dave watched her head move up to the big blackboard on the wall behind the serving area. He could almost sense the tension as she decided whether she should or shouldn't order a dessert. He willed her subconsciously to take the apple pie, take the apple pie, take the apple pie. Then she peered down to the glass counter with its selection of croissants, iced buns, apple pies, scones and cheesecakes. She decided against it and pulled out her purse from her bag.

Dave casually wandered over. 'I'll pay for that,' he said, and placed a scrumpled fiver on the squeaky clean surface top.

She turned to the side and looked at Dave's face, then she checked him up and down. Designer clothes, smelt gorgeous, very good looking, let the man pay. 'Thanks. So kind.'

'I'm sitting over there.' He pointed to his table and walked off.

The waitress glanced at the girl and shook her head from side to side. She smiled in return and followed to the table 'over there' with her coffee and his change. She sat down on the opposite sofa chair, crossing her long legs and sliding her fingers through her wet hair. 'Hope you don't pay for everyone who walks in.'

'Only the ones with skimpy skirts and high heels.'

Naina eyed her short black Miss Selfridge skirt and Dolcis high-heeled shoes. She wondered whether, if she took them off, he might throw in a chocolate-chip muffin as well. She noticed the smudged red-lipstick-stained stub of a fag in the glass ashtray and wasn't surprised. 'Sex, football and pint,' she delivered, very clearly and quite loud.

Dave smiled as a few people turned round.

She continued, 'Now I've got your full attention, Dave . . .'

'Naina, I've told you only to use those three words in an absolute emergency.' He stubbed out his own fag in the ashtray. 'You keep teasing me.'

To date, Naina and Dave had had four arguments, about five walks in the park, twenty-five coffees and a few apple pies between them; plenty of chats, friendly kisses, friendly cuddles, friendly pecks on the cheek; they had become very good friends, who had surfed just above the salty waters of passion, but never had they fallen right in.

Two very different people from two very different lives. He, a twenty-five-year-old owner of a gym. She, a twenty-three-year-old group manager of a large insurance company. He drove a BMW. She caught the bus. He had been in a police cell more than once. She watched *The Bill*. He lived on his own. She lived with her parents. But, but, but they both loved the apple pie. They had met over the pie. The only piece of pie left in Florelli's. Dave had seen her at the desserts counter that day contemplating the mouth-watering, crusty, warm, oozing piece of pastry. He had told her that there was someone outside trying to get her urgent attention. She went out to find them, and when she returned he was scoffing down the thick apple chunks at the counter, desperate to get it all in his gob before she returned. He still remembers it as the best piece of apple pie he ever ate. That was a year ago. And still to this day, he claims that there *was* someone out there, and still he claims that he didn't know she wanted the pie. If he had known that she wanted the pie – because he was such a gentleman – he would not only have let her have it, but would have paid for it himself.

'I had a horrible morning,' Naina whinged, now wishing she smoked, as it was one of those comments that looked perfect for lighting up a fag, blowing out a smoke ring and sighing. 'I hate working there sometimes.'

'I don't know how you work in an orifice anyway,' he said, gazing into her Galaxy-brown eyes.

'Office, thank you.' She laughed and kicked him hard on the calf.

'Same thing. Anyway, why don't you take the

afternoon off, and I'll keep you company?' He paused. 'You can even dry your wet clothes off round my place if you want. I don't want you catching a cold.'

'No.' The 'No' was refined, chiselled to perfection. A firm no.

It had to be a no. She had told him many many times. She didn't mind sharing an apple pie or the odd plate of salty chips or even the occasional secret, but not his bed. She wouldn't share that. Not that she didn't think he was attractive. The problem was that she knew him too well. He had even summed himself up to her once, during one of their honest chats with each other: 'I'm a bastard. I use women, then dump them, and if I had half the chance I would do the same to you.' Naina was grateful for Dave's honesty, yet she was not willing to be so honest in return. There were too many things he would never understand.

Dave continued regardless, 'Naina, there must be times when you're lying next to your boyfriend and you're thinking about me.'

Naina's manners took a turn for the worse, as she nearly spat her coffee out. 'Never, Dave. Ever.'

'Shame. I think about you all the time when I'm with my women,' he remarked in his pretend hurt voice. 'I have this dream. Hear me out and don't put that face on.' He leaned in closer. 'All the men on the planet are dead, except me . . .'

'Forget it, Dave. That is so kacky.' She laughed. 'This is just going to lead to sex talk, isn't it?' Naina was suddenly annoyed. She flopped back in the chair and shook her head.

'Well, when I'm with my women . . .'

That was the problem with Dave, *women* not *woman*. Naina could even imagine him at eighty-five, arthritic, and strapped to the operating table, asking the nurse for a quickie before the anaesthetic kicked in. Commitment was void. Three dates with the same woman, in Dave's books, and he might as well be married to her. And marriage – well, that was just for insecure people. God, how he loved saying that to married couples.

Naina twiddled with her damp hair, twirling it round her slender fingers. 'Dave, you talk so much—'

'La la la do do do doobie do, la la la do do do doobie do.' They were interrupted by Dave's annoying mobile tune. He grabbed it from the floor under his seat and glanced at the caller display. 'Hello . . . Who's this? . . . Oh, Donna, hello . . . Fine. You? . . . Good . . . Tonight? Yeah, I'm free . . . I'm in a meeting . . . Yeah, boring . . . Okay, I'll see you tonight.' He switched off his phone, smiled to himself, then turned to Naina. 'Sorry about that.'

The coffee shop was still quite full. She didn't need to be here, entertaining Dave, keeping him amused in her lunch hour, watching his wandering eyes sizing up any beautiful woman who walked through the door. Sometimes she just wanted a normal everyday chat with him and quite often he could hold a conversation, he could be a good listener and sometimes he could even be quite deep and sensible. This, however, was not one of those days: his hormone levels were too high. Every other word was twisted into an innuendo regarding sex. He needed help.

'Dave, I've got to go back to work. I'll catch you next week.' She stood up.

'She's just a friend, Naina,' he said, looking up, putting on his adamant expression.

'Why the fuck would I care who she is? See you next week.' Naina picked up her bag, straightened her skirt, kissed him goodbye, then left.

He watched her walk out. He regarded her as a good friend but was willing to lose all that for one good shag. But the point was, and this really irritated him at times, if she was such a good friend she would give him his shag. That was another woman he could not understand. Dave had a simple motto: Don't try to understand women and you'll never have to pretend that you can. He looked around to see that the waitress had taken his earlier advice and was now smiling like a Cheshire cat. 'Ciao.'

Panic suddenly struck in. The massive chrome clock on the far wall struck 2 o' clock. Shit, he had told Liz that he would only be gone half an hour to fetch the wine. Praying she was still in his bed, he snatched his phone, keys and fags, left a tenner on the table, then ran out to his forty-grand black BMW 540i sport, parked on a double yellow line, and sped off back to his luxury flat in Stone Valley, not even bothering to pull the ticket off and using the word 'fuck' at every other gear change.

Sweating and breathing hard, he slammed the flat door shut and walked into the bedroom as casually as a sweaty man could. He couldn't believe it. Liz was still there, in his bed, half-dressed in her lacy bra and knickers, watching the Ricki Lake show on his massive 41-inch satellite TV.

'Sorry about that,' he puffed.

'Did you get it?' she asked, raising her perfectly

arched eyebrows. 'The wine?'

'Yeah, I left it in the car, back in a second.'

Ignoring that 'woman' look they gave sometimes – the one that said all men are useless – Dave legged it down to flat number one and banged on the door. The old couple downstairs were always in: He was right. The wooden door opened.

'Sorry to disturb you, but have you by any chance got a bottle of wine? I'm entertaining upstairs, with a lady friend, and I forgot the . . .' he winced, 'I forgot the wine.'

The distinguished-looking old man in his tartan slippers and green cardigan, pipe in mouth and a copy of *Horse and Hound* in his hand gave a knowing nod, disappeared for a moment and came back with two bottles, red and white. Dave took the white, thanked him, ran up the stairs, kissed the bottle, and walked back in, pleased with himself.

He half danced across the pine floor into the enormous kitchen and returned to the bedroom with the wine, wine opener, two glasses and a special 'Dave' smile. Already his top was flung aside, showing off his muscular body with its perfect six-pack – he did own a gym after all. Switching the television off, in the middle of Ricki's advice to 'kick him to the kerb', he launched himself into the springy bed and joined Liz. A quick tickle in the right places, a quick list of compliments and that look of Liz's anger soon dissolved.

Just enough time to drink the plonk, see to Liz's needs, change the bedsheets, have a shower, and then head on out to meet Donna, leaving Liz crying and wondering why her deep green eyes, ample bust and long legs weren't good enough any more. 'You're just not my cup of tea, Elizabeth', was all he'd said. She was dumped like a used tea bag.

Later: 'Donna, you are so beautiful. I've been thinking about you all day,' said Dave, kissing her on the lips, as she sat down on the leather seat in his car.

'Thanks.' She blushed. 'What have you got planned for tonight?' she asked, smiling at him.

Dave totted her up: 9 for looks, 9 for body, and 2 for personality, he wasn't sure about emotion, he'd have to wait until he finished with her for that. She seemed the blubbering sort, but luckily in his glove compartment he had a box of man-sized tissues ready. 'I mean it, you look gorgeous.' He paused and took her hand. 'What about a quiet night in, with a bottle of wine, just you and me.'

And that's what they did. Come to think of it, that's all he ever did on his dates.

While Dave was enjoying his Friday-night-women binge, Naina was lying on top of her bed, in the near darkness, crying her eyes out. She was supposed to have been given more notice than this, she could have prepared herself, programmed her mind. Now all she could do was try to take some comfort from her younger sister's arm and her whispering voice, 'Naina, please don't worry.'

Sometimes Naina hated being Indian.

Chapter Two

Who the fuck's she? thought Dave, referring to the mound next to him in his king-sized bed. A red sequinned dress lay discarded on the floor along with one matching red strappy sandal. An empty bottle of white wine stood on top of the pine chest of drawers. A deluxe Scrabble board, half-filled with tiles, sat neatly on top of his stereo in the corner, and the cream-coloured curtains had been left open, admitting the Saturday morning sunshine.

No matter how the evening before had gone – even if it was explosive – if drink were involved, his memories were gone. Trying to recall what had happened was often as futile as it was pointless and a waste of time. It would be like trying to look at the midday sun on a foggy day. For, come morning – and it didn't matter who it was lying next to him – it was time for her to go.

Careful not to move the mattress too much, he

crept out of bed, pulled on some boxer shorts and went to the kitchen, leaving her fast asleep. Here was the point of having a large fitted kitchen when you were a single man: one cupboard full to the brim with old shoe and trainer boxes; one cupboard for his lagers, stocked and well-stocked at that; magazines stuffed in two out of the three main drawers; a few empty cupboards just in case, and one medium-sized cupboard for everything else. The silver Smeg fridge, its trays removed to fit in more Carlsbergs, left just enough room at the top for butter, a tomato and bacon. And it was with these ingredients that he would be making the mound in the bed her farewell bacon butty.

Six slices of best smoky bacon were laid under the grill until that wonderful smell began to disperse throughout the kitchen, through the hall, up to the ceiling and into the smoke alarm. With the bell ringing, he slapped a wad of Utterly Butterly on the thick-cut bread, tossed on the sliced tomatoes, threw on the crispy cooked bacon, squeezed out the ketchup and pressed down the other slice of bread. He licked his lips. Too good to give to her, whoever she was, but from experience he had learned that a good bacon butty always cushioned the blow of being told: 'I'm not ready for a relationship right now, I'm on the rebound and it's just not fair on you. You're a lovely person and I wish we could have met at a different time when my life wasn't so screwed up. Eat up.' He neatly, diagonally, cut through the sandwich, after making himself one, placed them on a dinner plate and came back through to the bedroom with his Dave smile.

She was sitting up in bed, awoken by the smoke alarm. He passed her the plate and she smiled. 'Thank you, Dave.' She seemed shocked, surprised, never before had a man made her breakfast. So sweet.

Dave looked at her: not bad, not brilliant, passable. He'd blame the drink. Her blonde hair impersonated a mop, her black eyeliner had given her the Ozzy Osbourne look and half her face was creased with lines from the pillow. He'd have to blame the drink. He eyed the Scrabble board in the corner. He figured as much, drink and dirty Scrabble always led to an Ozzy Osbourne look-alike in his bed.

'Do you know my name, Dave?' asked Ozzy, staring down at her yummy bacon sarnie.

He thought about it for a while. The odds of guessing it right were one in a thousand. Normally slappers had only two syllables. 'Ka-ren?'

She clambered out of bed naked (not a bad body, he thought) and walked up to him, looked him squarely in the eye, and slapped him hard round the face. 'I'm a fucking vegetarian, you bastard.'

Unbeknown to Dave, after finishing with Donna, he had sat with Chloe in the pub for the remainder of the evening, pretending he was a vegan, pretending he had been on marches and demonstrations with his banner of 'Meat is murder', and even sat outside a pharmaceutical company claiming he would hunger strike if they didn't stop testing on the rats. All that, to get his leg over with her. That was about the size of it. Sex.

Dave rubbed his cheek as Chloe dressed. Now the 'quorn' and 'soya' on the Scrabble board made sense. God, if they were her dirty words, it must have been a crap shag, he thought.

'I thought you were different,' she screamed. 'I thought you understood me, I really thought you cared about animals. You're sick, you are. Sick!' She stormed out and slammed the front door.

After showering, changing the sheets and getting dressed into his gym clothes – black baggies and white Crazee Wear T-shirt – he set the burglar alarm and headed down the one flight of stairs and out through the main entrance. The flats, four of them altogether, were built to the design of a mock Tudor house. Black and white wooden timbers criss-crossed the outside frame giving a sense of grandeur and prestige to its exterior. Dave's footsteps crunched on the multi-coloured gravel as he walked towards the old barn-converted garages, opened the lock, and pulled up the black metal garage door. Inside the garage it was dark and switching on the light still did not make it appear. Where the fuck was his forty-grand car? The last he remembered of the night before was dropping off Donna, making his apologies and finding out that she rated 1 for emotions after all, as she cried like a new-born baby all over his leather car seats, Versace top and copy of *Men are from Mars, Women are from Venus*. And after that, just empty space, no recollection at all. He punched in a number on his mobile.

'OOzing, mate. Where was I last night?' he asked his friend Froggy.

'OOzing. Where are you now? The police station?'

'No, outside my garage, my fucking car's gone. I can't remember where I left it.'

They both laughed. 'What was that veggie like?' Froggy asked.

'Who, Karen? Didn't like my bacon sarnie. Bit of an old boot.' They laughed again. 'Seriously, where was I? I need to get to the gym.'

'Down the Nut and Squirrel.'

'What, my end or your end?'

'My end.' Froggy paused. 'Forget it, Dave, it's Saturday morning, I'm taking Sandra shopping.'

'Cheers, mate. I'll catch you later then, you tart.'

Fifteen minutes later, Dave paid the Greek taxi driver the £4 fare. Four pounds well spent, he thought, as he pocketed Stavros's cheque for the one-year membership fee he had managed to persuade him to take up, after a sneaky comment regarding the size of Stavros's waistline, and walked up the side road to the Squirrel. Sure enough, his car was there, on the yellow line, waiting like a loyal dog, with the added bonus of yet another parking ticket. It was getting to the point where he even knew from the handwriting which traffic warden had written it. Bitch. He pulled off the ticket and stuck it on the car behind. If his day was going to be wrecked then so would the driver's of that beige Volvo.

'Still the same Dave, I see,' said a woman's voice behind him.

The hairs on his neck twisted and contorted. He knew that voice; he thought he'd seen the last of her; he thought he had got rid of her. He turned around to face her after putting his Dave smile on.

'Hello, Lucy, looking good. How are you?' he said, trying hard to hide his concerns.

The short story is this: Dave was supposed to have married her. He was caught in her parents' bed with her and convinced the father that his intentions were good and he wanted to marry her, even though he was only twenty-one. Before he knew it, a wedding was fully arranged and the week before the wedding, he left for Tenerife for six months with his mates, where he partied every night to forget her. One minor point was that he forgot to let Lucy and her parents know. Lucy was devastated. Lucy had therapy. Froggy thinks Dave's postcard sent her over the edge: 'Wishing you well from Tenerife.'

'I'm very well, thank you. I got married last year and I'm expecting my first child later this year.' She looked down to her flat stomach, proud as punch, then back up to Dave. 'Still being a bastard?'

A few weeks in therapy and some positive thinking, gets herself up the duff by some truffle head. Who'd she think she was?

'Where did you conceive? In your dad's bed?' He laughed as she smacked him round the face, a bit harder than Chloe's smack but not as hard as Donna's.

'You *are* still a bastard. All you've got is looks and money and nothing else. You'll never amount to anything. You'll be the sad one sitting there at fifty with no wife, no kids, no life, only you and your biceps.' Her lips quivered with anger. 'I actually loved you, Dave, but now I see you for what you are, you coward.'

'You didn't love me. And I could stand here all day listening to your apologies, but I'm running a little bit late . . .'

'I . . . was . . . not . . . apologizing.'

'Well . . . you . . . fucking should have been.'

'You left me standing at the altar. You left me—'

'Yeah, I've heard it all before.' Dave lit a fag. 'Did you not wonder why? And before you answer, here's a few clues: nag nag nag nag nag.' He paused. 'Oh yeah here's another: nag.'

'You don't take anything seriously, do you? Life's just one big party for you, isn't it?' Lucy fixed him with a cold stare. 'One day you're going to fall down and I want to be there to see it. And believe me, Dave, that day will come, and there'll be no getting on a plane and running off to Tenerife for you then.'

Ahhh, Tenerife, thought Dave. It brought a smile to his face. Tenerife saved him from a life of hen-pecking. The first time he saw Lucy he thought he'd died and gone to heaven. The second time he saw Lucy, he *had* died and gone to heaven – it's just heaven, that day, happened to be hiding inside her silk knickers. It was wonderful; she was prepared to try anything, no inhibitions whatsoever. Let's do it in an open park, in the middle of the night, he had suggested. Okay, Dave, she'd replied. Fantastic. What about in the Open University library, upstairs in the medieval section, he had begged. No problem, she'd replied. Underneath dual carriageway bridges, back of taxis, cinemas, swimming pools, fairs . . . what about in your parents' bed, he had asked. No problem.

'Dave . . . Dave . . . Dave,' she screamed, from her parents' bed.

'I'm trying, I'm trying,' he yelled.

'What the bloody hell is going on?' shouted Lucy's dad.

It was here that Dave's passion for telling lies took a sharp turn. 'Ah, Mr Roberts. Have you heard the good news?' Dave said, pulling himself out of Lucy. 'Your daughter and I are to be man and wife.'

Mr Roberts loosened his grip on his briefcase. He loosened the grip on his grimace as Dave lunged out of bed naked, wrapped himself in Mr Roberts's robe and shook his hand gruffly. 'Congratulations, Mr Roberts, I am going to be your son-in-law, and Dave's the name.'

Lucy just stared. Then she spoke. 'We both love you, Daddy.'

And the lie was sealed. Harder and harder it got as the wedding approached, Dave's lies becoming as thick as soup, Lucy getting excited and falling in love with Dave, and Dave wondering why he didn't have the courage to tell Lucy he didn't love her, never loved her. The thought of shacking up with Lucy for the rest of his life scared the pants off him.

Peterborough passport office heard a very disturbed young man on the phone about a month prior to Dave's and Lucy's expected wedding.

'Passport. Listen. I need your help. I have been caught in a posh man's bed with a posh man's daughter and I decided to do the posh thing: propose. Anyway I need to get out of this country for a while, let things cool off a bit, you know? See the world. I cannot marry her. Do you understand? I need a passport. I need a passport fast.' Everything was sorted and the line went dead.

Just as Lucy's heart went dead when the light from the sun disappeared on Lucy's and Dave's wedding day, and the realization that Dave would not be turning up began to shine.

Boarding the plane at Luton airport with his five

mates, Dave congratulated himself: 'I am free.' And here he made a promise never to get within sniffing distance of an engagement ring again.

Now, a few years later, Dave stared at a pregnant Lucy.

'Anyway, Lucy. I wish you well,' he said.

'You don't wish anyone well. All you think about is yourself. All you think about is what's in between women's legs. All you think about is . . .'

Dave held his hand up. 'Lucy, leave it.'

She spat at his car and walked off.

Dave turned round to see a few shoppers staring at the scene and talking amongst themselves. 'You nosy fuckers! Get a life, you sad fucks.' He climbed in his car, jammed it into first, skidded off and headed to his gym. Women. Who needs them? Especially mental women.

The journey from the pub to the gym was straight, if not slightly sanctimonious, and always fast. The new roads of this thirty-year-old city covetously gripped the tyres and yelled out from under the tarmac, 'Faster faster faster.' And Dave sped on faster, curling round the flower-dressed roundabouts, one hand on the steering wheel, the other free for fags or gestures. It was always a mad sprint.

He stopped at Shenley roundabout, held up by two lost out-of-towners whose family would never see them again. He waited patiently. Poor things. Same ol' story no doubt: asked at the petrol station how to leave this town, to be told 'Turn left.' And as Dave watched them signal right, then turn left, he chuckled. Serves you right for calling this place 'Concrete City' – now you're stuck here, like trapped wind in the intestines of Milton Keynes along with everyone else, all waiting for this new town's accent to develop. Milton wrote *Paradise Lost,* but was this lost paradise Milton Keynes? Time would tell.

Over another landscaped roundabout, down the quick V3 dual carriageway that bridged the wide fishing lake of Furzton. Past thousands of green fir trees like upside-down pipe cleaners claiming the air space, and on to a tasty piece of fast road – the H7, Chaffron Way. He changed up gears. Yeah, you may be stuck here, he thought, but you have to admit, you're beginning to fall for the place. With its young attitude, its growing business, its cleanliness, lakes and its beautiful women. Especially not forgetting the concrete cows grazing in the fields.

Twelve dizzy roundabouts later, Dave pulled up outside his gym in Linford Wood, checked out his cheeks in the car rear-view mirror and quietly thought to himself while burning a fag. He thought back to all the women he had made cry. If he lined them all up down some road, side by side, anyone would think that a boy-band member had been shot dead: he smiled. Then he thought about all the women he had brought to orgasm – tonnes: he chuckled. Then he thought about all the lies he'd told just to woo women: he laughed. He sat in his car laughing. His final thought was how many slaps he had had. If people could hear them all together, anyone would think that Michael Flatley had just given his finest performance: he felt sorry for himself. Mellow thoughts required mellow music, so he pushed in a R.E.M. CD and reclined back in the heated cushioned seat, listening to 'Losing my Religion'.

Voices from outside broke his doze; whipping up his eyelids, he was treated to the sight of two bodybuilders, bronzed by the bottle, both in stars-and-stripes baggies, one with a bandanna, the other with a weightlifting belt round his waist. Both entering Dumbbells Gym as if they were so big they had to walk in sideways. Dave smiled – if only they knew how stupid they looked: one even had a tattoo saying 'Born to Train' on his shoulder. Next week, who knows, his mate might have one announcing 'Born with a Brain'.

Where the clientele of Florelli's coffee shop were characterized by their designer suits, laptops and London-speak, the gym's members were marked by their tight buttocks, firm waists and desire to better themselves through rigid diets and caveman training regimes. Dave sat back in his car, admiring two leotard-clad women both snapping back their lycra from their bottoms almost in unison as they entered the gym. However, one thing he had learned over the years was never to become too familiar with the customers – leave that to the staff. To be the boss meant just that, 'To be the Boss'. One that put his foot down, one that customers respected as having the final word when it came to the gym, and one that under no circumstances went to bed with any of the women who worked out there.

He blipped the car alarm, put on his Dave boss face, and entered. The entrance greeted you with first a few potted rubber plants, then a smell of protein shakes, vitamins and energy drinks, then the smiles of two fitness instructors with their red and black Dumbbells' uniforms. If you glanced to the right as you entered, you would see a whole room draped in mirrors and filled with steppers, treadmills, rowers, bikes, walkers, and TVs with MTV playing in the background. This section was the cardio section and normally swelled with people trying to burn off that loose tyre. Down at the end, under an arch, was a sprung wooden floor, more mirrors and a step-aerobics class in full swing. Through another arch to the left was the free-weight and machine section and yet more mirrors. This was where the fight was going on. Oblivious to the staff, two bodybuilders with too much testosterone, too much ego and too many steroids had not taken too kindly to a snide remark regarding the size of their bodies in relation to the size of their heads, and also more importantly in relation to the size of their penises. Dave looked at the monitor behind Steve's head.

'There's two people wrecking my gym,' he said, pointing to the CCTV, obviously not too pleased.

Steve the manager nervously looked at the black and white screen to see a loose 25 lb dumbbell shoot across the floor, followed shortly afterwards by another. The body arrived a split second later, followed by the two bodybuilders. Before he could turn round to Dave to tell him how sorry he was, he could see Dave on the monitor grabbing one of the bodybuilders round the neck. The other bodybuilder kicked over one of the adjustable incline benches like a spoilt child and grunted out some quotes he had picked up from a gorilla. Within the space of ten minutes everyone had apologized to everyone else, everyone had received their warning: 'Next time you're banned', and Dave sat in the small office, with his feet up, smoking a joint, wondering why he had a gym in the first place. Wondering why this day had turned out so shit. But, like most things, even shit is relative. For if Dave thought his day was slightly shitty, he should have seen how Naina's was panning out. How does that old record by Bryan Ferry go? 'Walk a mile in my shoes.'

Back at the depot, Rose and Joan watched the door open and Maggie lumber in.

'What are you looking so pleased about?' Joan asked Maggie.

'Me?' She tossed her hat onto the table. 'I got that horrible man.'

'Who?' asked Rose.

'You know. That disrespectful man who thinks he's so smart. You know, the one who gave you the finger the other day?'

'Oh, that bastard.'

And all three traffic wardens laughed.

Chapter Three

Naina knew that when she got married she had to be a virgin. She didn't know who she would end up marrying, but one thing she did know and that was that her husband would expect her to be pure and untouched by another man. She also knew that the man she would marry, she would not love.

After crying herself to sleep the night before, Naina awoke to the sound of her own heart thumping. A day that she had dreaded had arrived with a bang. Judgement day comes to all Indian children, whether they like it or not. They fool themselves into thinking that it's years away, and then, as with Naina – BANG! – it arrives. It was her destiny from the moment she was born, and nothing really prepares you for this day. The day your parents introduce you to the man they have chosen for you to marry.

On the journey from Milton Keynes to Dagenham,

while the February sun shone down on the congested M1 motorway, Naina was reminded of the rules she must follow to impress her future husband, Ashok. They were: keep quiet until spoken to, smile, best of manners, do not laugh, do not cry, and if in doubt, look at the floor until spoken to again. Naina was sure she would be looking at an awful amount of floor today.

The family car pulled up onto the gravel drive set in front of a huge Victorian house. Dad turned off the engine and stared behind at Naina. 'See, now I bet you're pleased we put the car through the car wash. No good turning up to a house like this with bird-shit on the bonnet.'

Mum looked at her husband and shook her head. She then glanced back at Naina. 'Now, remember all we said. First impressions are lasting.'

Sonia, Naina's fifteen-year-old sister, squeezed her hand.

All four crunched up to the front door and were greeted by a man with a white turban, big smile and industrial garlic breath. Strewth.

Dad introduced the family to Ashok's dad and they were led through the hall and into the living room where more introductions took place. And where more assessments took place. Naina could feel the full weight of high expectations as Ashok's mother and two sisters scrutinized her like a set of judges would a gymnast: was Naina pretty enough for Ashok? Was she the right weight, height, shade of skin colour? Would those small hips be able to sustain a few pregnancies? Did her hands have calluses, meaning she worked hard, or were they soft, meaning she was lazy? Most importantly: would she do as she was told?

They all sat down awaiting the arrival of Ashok. Sonia peered across at Naina and an undercurrent of apprehension swept through both pairs of eyes. Naina looked so Indian dressed in her satin shalwar kameez. A burst of lavender decorated with silver diamantes, beads and painted thread-work, an artificial diamond choker round her neck, matching earrings, a bracelet, and a pair of six-inch high-heeled sandals finished her off and turned the English Naina to an Indian Naina.

Finally Ashok arrived and sat directly opposite Naina. Their eyes met for the very first time. They looked at each other for a short moment, until Naina turned away, slightly embarrassed. She stared down at her long lavender nails. If she stared to the left she would meet with the approaching stares of Ashok's family; if she stared to the right then it was her own family staring back, and if she stared ahead it was Ashok. So, she stared at her nails. Even though she had only glanced, his good looks were very apparent. These swift glances at men, as quick as a blink, were something all Indian girls were very good at.

Naina's dad, in his royal-blue stiff turban, was speaking in Punjabi, in a low rumbling voice to Ashok's dad, in his white soft turban. He was basically a salesman selling his product – his daughter. The only difference being that she did not come with a five-year warranty or a thirty-day no-fuss-return. And as salesmen are known to exaggerate, so too did Naina's dad. She had become an expert in the kitchen. The tidiest Indian girl this side of the Raj. Never known to complain when a job needed doing. She would make Ashok the perfect wife and supply him with an abundance of children.

Mum gave Naina a discreet look. She had inquisitive and intelligent eyes that seemed to perceive the fragility of the moment. She placed a slim finger on each side of her shapely lips, pushing them upwards, trying to coax a faint smile from her daughter. And Naina responded with a falsie: a smile let down by her watery eyes. Who would want to marry a grumpy daughter?

Dad's voice was rising and a deaf person might think that the two fathers were quarrelling, Dad with his arms crossed in a threatening posture, his black beard jutting forward, and Ashok's father with his two clenched fists and shuffling feet, also with a beard, twice as long as Naina's father's. But they weren't arguing about beard length, nor about who could shout the loudest nor who had the jumbo turban. In fact they were not arguing at all. They were convincing each other.

'Those relatives in India think we've forgotten our ways,' Dad spoke loudly. 'We're more Indian than they are. We may not have elephants and drums at our weddings, but,' and Dad raised his finger like a soldier saluting, 'but, we send our daughters off with good dowries that we've worked hard for.'

'Yes, yes. And my relatives –' Ashok's dad raised his black, bushy eyebrows to the heavens '– Oh, jealous. So jealous. They drive around in their scooters, flagging down the rickshaw wallah and we . . . we drive Mercedes. But we took the risk. We got on the plane. We came to this country. We made a life. We . . .'

Mum watched on, her pretty features lifted as her smile thickened. Listening to her proud husband and his never-ending stories of life in India compared to England was something she never got tired of. Sonia yawned.

Naina looked up towards the two pictures decorating the walls. Both framed in polished golden wood; one was of Guru Nanak – the first Guru of Sikhs, and the other of the Taj Mahal in all its glory. The pristine white sofa that she sat on, up straight and dignified, seemed too posh for her, she thought. And how the hell did they keep it so clean? The room was large – massive even, and spoke of great wealth. Like the two red and gold antique churns, one in each corner, and the marbled fireplace with ivory statuettes of great Indian elephants on either side. Like the mahogany display cabinet with its crystal-cut glass figurines. Like the two brand-new silver Mercedes cars parked on the small, oval, stone car park, which had greeted them on arrival in their red family Ford Mondeo.

Naina had often wondered, dreamed, of what it would be like to feel a *man*, hold him tight, kiss him and caress him and make love to him. She had wondered what it would feel like to lie with a man, while he touched her and spoke to her softly. Would Ashok answer her dreams?

In the carefree days of school and college, in the unchaperoned world of the playing field or lecture theatre, Naina had occasionally succumbed to her curiosity; she had tried 'men', or rather 'boys', *behind her parents' back*. A quick kiss here or the odd snog there. Jake, then Adam, even Danny, had all groped and felt their way round Naina's body as far as she would allow. Some girls in her class obviously allowed more, and Naina had seen them surreptitiously flicking through the Argos catalogue looking at 'Mamas and Papas' baby buggies. But as Naina reached the age of twenty, shedding her teenage years, anger, spots and Duran Duran, she realized the folly of lustful thoughts. She accepted that Indian girls had to be respectful of Mum and Dad and all of India. 'Stay clear of the men,' Dad would say. 'Your body is a sacred temple,' Mum would add. 'You're getting fat,' Sonia said. And so came the lies.

Men had approached her, asked her out, sent her Valentines, flowers, chocolates and even the odd cuddly toy. But never, ever, had she even come close to going against the Indian ways and traditions again. She couldn't. It would be like sticking a knife into her family's heart. It was so much easier instead to lie to the men who asked her out, to tell them she already had a boyfriend and explain that she loved him. And all this, the lies, the explanations, had been told again and again to one man in particular over the last year: Dave. But, no matter how bad she knew Dave was, and she knew he was pretty bad, out of all the blokes that she had met through work, pubs and clubs, he stood out. He was the only one who gave her sexual feelings, who turned her on, who made her dream of what it would feel like to have him inside her. He was like a naughty cream cake: you know you shouldn't eat it, but it doesn't stop you looking at it. It doesn't stop you wanting just a bite, knowing full well that probably every beautiful woman in the vicinity has already had a slice, or a lick, or a taste. But it wasn't just Dave's cream that Naina wanted. Sometimes she saw the real Dave. The Dave who was ambitious, intelligent, and understanding. Most importantly Naina felt that he was very protective of her. A few months back, she and Dave had gone for a quiet drink or two at the Ship Ashore pub. Two blokes, who had obviously drunk too much, grabbed a bar mat each and knelt in front of Naina, pretending they were praying to Mecca. It was quite funny, even Naina laughed, until Dave came up behind them and told them they were facing the wrong way. To which one replied, 'Tell that to curry girl, she seems to be enjoying it.' And then it all went wrong. The police were called . . . He was very protective. Naina couldn't help but like that rough element in Dave. That unpredictable edge. The one who would slam her down on the bed and show her a good time, if she were to let him. The one who would not let women walk away from him until they were totally satisfied. The one who she knew she should keep away from, but couldn't. He was everything she liked in a man. But never would she tell him that and never would she tell him that she was having an arranged marriage.

The two fathers decided that Ashok and Naina should be permitted to talk to each other alone for a few minutes in the dining room next door. Naina's dad seemed to be getting on well with Ashok's dad, which normally means both families are happy. So Naina followed Ashok into another large room, with a thick fluffy burgundy carpet and a never-ending mahogany table with matching chairs. More Indian pictures filled the walls and the smell of an aromatic incense stick hung heavily in the air.

Ashok pulled out a chair for Naina and sat down beside her. They both opened their mouths to speak at the same time and then both laughed in embarrassment. Naina nodded towards Ashok to go first. He spoke in English, to her relief.

'You are very pretty.'

'Thank you,' she replied, sweeping the floor with her eyes. She hated being complimented on her appearance. It made no difference, as far as she was concerned. Looks were just the packaging, it's what's inside that counts. And, sad as it seems, with an Indian marriage the packaging is very important, hence the salesman next door.

'You look different to the photos your father sent,' he said. 'Prettier actually. Not that you didn't look pretty in the photos, but you know how some people look worse in real life; well, you look better.' He shut up then, embarrassed at his not-so-clever remark.

'Anyway, how old are you?' she asked, quickly changing the subject. For some reason she was not nearly as nervous as she'd thought she would be. In fact, if anything, she felt in control and confident. This could be the man that she would marry, and in this short space of time she wanted to find out as much as she possibly could about him.

'Twenty-four. And you are twenty-three?'

Naina nodded yes. 'Have you got any hobbies?'

'I really don't have much time, with the business, but I do like to take a run when I get the time. What about you?' He looked at her, trying to read her mind, trying to fathom out whether she liked him or not.

'I enjoy reading good books, mainly horror novels, Stephen King, James Herbert, that sort of thing.' She

33

paused. 'I like anything to do with horror or the occult.'

Ashok's face dropped slightly and his eyes lowered to her nails, maybe expecting black gothic nail varnish.

Now was not the time to mention cybersex and how she and Dave sometimes spent a whole afternoon trying to fornicate with someone else's soft-drive, turning it into a hard-drive.

There were a few seconds of silence until Ashok spoke. 'Am I the first man your parents have found for you? Or have you seen a few?' He paused. 'You don't have to tell me if you don't wish.'

'No, you're the first. To tell the truth, I only found out about you last night, my parents had kept it a secret, and I was a little bit—' Naina stopped, thinking maybe she shouldn't be telling him this and changed the subject, yet again. 'If we got married, would I be allowed to go out to work?'

He tilted his head to one side, frowned slightly, and took his time answering. 'If we got married, I would want you to be happy, so the choice would be entirely yours.'

Naina glanced at him. He seemed decent, honest, shy, but he wasn't turning her on. Maybe they fitted these shalwar kameez with a minute lining of lead, keeping those sort of feelings out, she thought. Or maybe he wasn't her type. What would have happened if she had met him in a pub? Would she have given him a second look?

'I suppose your parents gave you the big speech of how to behave in front of me, just like my parents did?' Ashok asked.

Naina smiled and nodded.

He continued, 'Well, I'd rather you be yourself. Then I can see the real you. I hope that doesn't sound too rude.'

'No, not at all. Same goes for you.'

This one meeting could determine whether or not little Ashok/Naina kiddies would be running around the planet ten years from now. It was quite a frightening prospect. A strange feeling knowing that sitting right in front of you might be the very man that you would have to get into bed with and make happy. A strange feeling knowing that he might be feeling the very same way about you. A strange feeling that right this second you might be losing any control that you might have over your future life: what you wore, what you bought, what you said, what you did.

Naina watched Ashok stand up and walk over to the patio doors. His shoulders were quite broad and his maturity seemed broader. He seemed very determined to let her know that he was not quite the Indian cliché of a husband-to-be. The one who eyed you up and down and paid more attention to what you could do with a Moulinex food processor or a John Lewis knitting machine than to what went on inside your head. Ashok seemed beyond all those old-fashioned ideas. He seemed caring and not a servant to his parents' rules.

'Come and see the back garden,' Ashok suggested, talking into the glass, then turned around and smiled. 'And don't worry, I'm not going to mention how lovely it would be for our twenty-three children to run around in it.'

Naina walked across smiling and began to relax

some more. She stood next to him and peered out to the huge boundary of tall oak trees that fenced in a spectacular green lawn. A large pond, about twenty feet from the patio doors, reflected the tree branches, and a few large goldfish dozily swam in the gleaming water.

Ashok spoke. 'I have never done anything daring you know. All around me, even at university, my friends would all have these fantastic adventures planned out for them. They would ask me what I wanted to do after study and I never really knew.' Ashok glanced to Naina who stared at the pond. 'What about you? You must have dreamed of something that you could do with your life.' And then he whispered the next bit, 'Without the bloody parents looking over your shoulder.'

They laughed again. Naina found herself warming to him a little. Whatever she had expected was not this. Whoever she had expected was not him. He seemed so nonconformist. Most of the Indian guys she'd heard about, met, had nightmares about, were so wired up with what their parents wanted, you would think that they hadn't a brain for themselves. But Ashok did. He seemed intelligent. In fact the list of his qualifications would probably need a qualification to understand. He was also direct, laying his cards on the table, opening his personality up. In fairness, he did seem like he was being himself.

And Naina tried ever so hard to do the same. 'Well, I only ever really wanted to be a—' And then she stopped. Dad's famous words between junctions 10 and 9 on the journey up here came back to her: 'You must never, ever tell him what you wanted to be when you left school. I'm serious. They will put you in a straitjacket.'

Ashok stared at her, waiting for the completion of the sentence.

'Well, I always wanted to be good at a sport,' she lied. 'But, to be honest, I never really put my mind to it because I always knew my arranged marriage would put a stop to it.'

'Well, maybe we could join a club. Something we've both never done and then we can look like rookies together.'

Ashok slid open the patio doors and she followed him onto the wide wooden decking. Naina shivered slightly at the cold weather.

Ashok continued, 'Okay, what would you say you hated in a man? What, if you married me, would you dread that I did?'

Naina, slightly shocked at this question, thought for a second before answering. 'Well, I would hate it if you lied to me; if you were unfaithful to me, and, as we are being honest with each other,' she looked into his eyes, 'I would hate it if you stuck up for your mother over me.' She paused. 'What about you?'

Ashok nodded. 'Okay, me. Well, I would hate it if you kept things to yourself, afraid to speak up.' He rubbed his forehead, thoughtful, then looked up. 'Actually, forget all this talk about hate. What would I like? I would like us to be able to feel comfortable around each other. You know? Be able to go out to the cinema, meals and abroad. My parents do nothing, just like most of my relatives. They sit at home, talking about—'

Naina interrupted, 'India?'

37

They both laughed. The word 'India', when used by Indians, at certain times, can tickle quite hard. Just as the word 'England' when used by the English can tickle quite hard when talking about winning the World Cup. Even qualifying brings a giggle.

It was a weird feeling. All Naina's life, she'd been warned, 'Stay clear of men, they are only after one thing.' So here she was with a man, chosen for her by her parents, with whom she might have to do that *one thing*.

She looked at Ashok and thought: I really want to like you and it's a shame, but you're not the one I want to do that one thing with. Admittedly he was nice, good looking, even funny; but he just didn't have that ooooomph. He didn't give her that feeling in the stomach where all your nerves seem to meet to discuss which part of your body you want the man to ravage first. Maybe, after a bottle of whisky, he might get past the ooooo. But, he'd never have the full ooooomph. Only one man had the full ooooomph, as far as Naina was concerned, and right now, he was probably ooooomphing another woman. Lucky bitch.

After twenty minutes or so, Ashok and Naina returned to the living room, amongst the chitter-chatter of the families. It had been decided between the two fathers that unless a major row had broken out in the dining room next door – something which would never happen – Naina and Ashok would be man and wife in six months' time. Unfortunately by no means would they be allowed to meet each other on their own. They would meet again for their engagement in two weeks' time and the next time they would see each other would be on their wedding day.

It was as simple as that. Naina had made her parents proud and she would just have to forget all that nonsense about falling in love. Indians don't do that.

So, going back to shitty days, it's safe to say Naina won hands down this time.

Later that evening, Naina went to her bedroom crying, yet again. In six months' time, she would be Mrs Ashok Chandileriery – she couldn't even pronounce the name. It was as if her whole life had been put down on some map, and from here on out, there would be no more surprises, she knew exactly where she was heading and she also knew what she would be leaving behind. Her elder sister, Sumita, had married this way, and so had many of her Indian friends and cousins. They all seemed happy. So why was Naina crying?

Sonia appeared at Naina's bedside, crouched down and tapped her on the shoulder. 'Do you believe in reincarnation?'

Naina peered across to her sister's questioning eyes. She sobbed, 'I don't know, I've never really thought about it. Why?'

'Well.' Sonia paused. 'I do. If you carry on crying like that, you're going to come back as a snotty hanky.'

Naina laughed.

Sonia smiled – that was the reaction she'd wanted. Then, taking full advantage of her new 'comedian' status, she continued, 'A snotty hanky, tied up in some Indian man's topknot.' She stood up. 'When I come back, I've requested I come back as the Father, the Son and the Holy Ghost,' she opened the bedroom door, glanced back, 'of Lucifer.' And giggled down the stairs.

With Sonia and her parents safely watching *Blind Date* on the TV downstairs, Kiran, her younger brother, out with his mates, Naina wiped her eyes with the back of her hand, pulled out her Nokia mobile and phoned Dave, typing in his pseudonym 'Gloria'. If she was caught phoning a man, she would never be able to talk her way out of it, so her voice was kept down low. Dave was Gloria, albeit with a suspiciously deep voice.

Dave was in his car, proceeding to the Squirrel, when the phone rang. 'Hello.'

'Hi, Dave, it's Naina.'

'Naina, I'm driving, let me pull over.' He skidded onto a lit-up Esso garage forecourt and turned the stereo down. 'I was just thinking about you.'

'Cut the bullshit, Dave.' She shook her head. 'Have you been drinking?'

'Not yet, why? Do you fancy coming out for a drink?'

'No, not tonight.'

'Where's the boyfriend?' he asked, looking at a fat man who had just come out of the garage hugging a 2-litre bottle of diet cola, chocolates, crisps and biscuits, using his belly as a food tray.

Naina ignored the question. 'Can I ask you something personal?'

'Sure.' Dave was intrigued.

'If you found out that one of the women you've slept with was pregnant, would you marry her, even though you don't love her?' Naina asked, sitting down on her bed.

'You're not up the duff, are you?'

'No, I just want to know, would you marry her

even though you don't love her?'

Dave inhaled his fag and thought about it for a moment. 'No, because it would never work, you need love to make the relationship work.'

Naina was quiet for a while, she could hear the *Blind Date* music coming from below with her dad's voice echoing above it. She took in Dave's words, 'you need love to make the relationship work.'

'What's your definition of love?' she asked, slightly shocked to have heard the four-letter word come out of his mouth. He never spoke of love.

'Naina, have you had an argument with your boyfriend? Because this is too much for me on a Saturday night.' He paused. 'Unless you want to come out for a drink with me and I'll explain all about love to you, I'll even throw in a demonstration for free.'

'Well, I'll pass on that, thanks all the same, but, last question. Do you think that you can grow to love someone after you have married them?' She could hear him fiddling around with something, otherwise there was silence. 'You probably think I'm a bit batty or I'm on drugs or this is a weird Trivial Pursuit question, but . . .'

'No, sorry, I was just looking for some chewing gum. Okay, what's the problem then? Why the questions? Something is obviously screwing you up.' He popped in an Orbit. 'Look I was going to go out, but if you want to meet, I can pick you up.'

'No, no, it's okay; thanks though. Maybe we can talk Monday morning?'

'Monday's fine.'

'I'll take the day off and meet you round yours. About nine okay?'

41

'Well, you'll have to keep buzzing, I'll probably be in bed.'

'Okay, thanks, Dave. I'll see you Monday. Have a good pint, or ten.'

Dave placed the mobile back on the dashboard, turned up the stereo, did a U-turn, then resumed his journey to the Squirrel. He passed through the high street, where the pubs were already full and people spilled out onto the pavements. His thoughts were still gently probing his mind: love, women, Naina, commitment, ahhhh.

Churning up the gravel he skidded into the pub car park of the Squirrel. And there she was: unbelievable even in the dim shadow of the pub light that was dancing on her luscious curvy body, standing there with her two (not-so-nice-looking) friends. They might as well just call this place heaven, he thought as he parked the car. It didn't occur to him, not one little bit, that anyone else would be having a chance with her, she was his, a foregone conclusion. She would be going home with him tonight. Getting out of the BMW with his Dave charm smile, he began to put his pulling plan into action.

Chapter Four

Many people have favourite sounds: the drowning noise of angry waves crashing on the shore, or maybe the birdsong on a fresh spring dawn, even Beethoven's Moonlight Sonata, all wonderful sounds that play and pull on the chords of our emotions. But Dave's was a richer tone of sound than all those blended together; his was the sultry sound of a beautiful woman's knickers as they're gently eased off her slender legs – the sound of heaven. And even heaven had its differences, every woman was totally unique. Some, he would compliment, lie and listen to, just to hear that rewarding sound of her silk knickers falling to the floor at the end of the boring evening. With others, all it would take was a McRib and then she'd drop her Oxfam hand-me-downs before he'd even finished his salty fries.

Dave ambled across the pub car park, greeted all three but only held the gaze of the pretty one.

Somewhere that chilly night a constellation was missing two of its stars; for her eyes were like beautiful starlets of blue, and as Dave entered the warm crowded pub, he thought, if there was any justice in this world, then she would be in his bed tonight.

His local felt so good, it felt like home. A huge screen for football and boxing took pride of place at one end, with smaller screens dotted around above the wooden tables and chairs. The stained bar curled round in one massive horseshoe shape, with six or seven bartenders, dressed in black T-shirts, frantically trying to keep up with the thirsty demands. The light polished wood flooring – sometimes cleared for Karaoke evenings – bore the scars of one too many Elvis Presley skids across the floor and blue-suede-shoe tapping. But there was no Elvis tonight – a new King was in town.

Dave, dressed in an Armani Neptune tight blue T-shirt which matched his eyes, black combat trousers and Nikes, located his mates and some of their girlfriends making much noise around one of the corner tables. He brought over his orange juice and joined them, while lighting up a fag and, in his eyes, lighting up their lives.

'OOzing.'

'OOzing.'

'OOzing.'

'OOzing.'

'You're all so pathetic. Why don't you start growing up?' suggested Sandra – Froggy's girlfriend – looking around the pub.

Ignoring her, 'On the pull, Dave?' asked Matt,

spotting his lonely orange juice amongst their lagers and spirits.

'I've already pulled, mate, I'm just waiting for her to realize it,' Dave responded.

A harmonious look of sympathy passed between the girlfriends – for the woman – whoever she was.

Dave sipped his sweet BritVic orange juice, chinking the ice, deep in thought. If he wanted to shag the beautiful blonde standing outside the pub, his mind had to be crystal clear and his delivery of compliment after compliment had to be timed to perfection, a complex ballet of words. He needed all the oratorical skill of a bee talking pollen out of a flower. Bear in mind, he didn't yet know if she was thick, intelligent, or even if she came from Liverpool. Adapting the flow of conversation to appeal to her level was the key to success. If she was intelligent, then he would talk of Monet and Picasso. If she was thick, then it was sausages and beans. And if she came from Liverpool, then he would just smile, walk away and order himself ten pints and a packet of pork scratchings.

'Found your car then, mate?' shouted Froggy, turning to the gang. 'Can you believe he lost his car again?' They all laughed.

A few more lost-car jokes later, Dave leaned back on the wooden chair – balancing on its back legs – and noticed Diane, Matt's girlfriend, singing away to one of the songs playing on the jukebox, 'La Isla Bonita'. God, that would annoy him normally, but not tonight, he was going home with the beautiful blonde and Diane could be Madonna if she wanted to be, as long as she didn't sing along with 'Like a Virgin'. He hated hypocrisy.

Sandra watched Dave light a ciggie. She'd seen this man light so many. Seen him juggle his women around. Watched him dart under the table a few times. Even once got caught up into phoning a woman for him. He seemed to live on a permanent high. Yet, try as hard as she could to dislike him, she couldn't. The first time she'd met him, three years ago, she'd found herself hypnotized by his midnight blue eyes. He had this carefree attitude, 'Take me as I am', and she did once. Shagged him behind Froggy's back. It was like crack, she was hooked straightaway, but her supplier didn't want anything more to do with her, he'd got what he wanted and he left Froggy's patch – so to speak – alone after that. She couldn't even share with him a secret gaze from time to time, a knowing nod that they had shared something for one night, for now he looked at her like a blind man would a painting – he saw nothing. And she hated it. From woman to woman, he moved like a wandering gypsy. 'Never more than three dates,' he would say. 'Commitment is a lonely word if you have no one to share it with,' he would say, even though she never quite understood what it meant.

She watched him now, involving himself in the commotion of pub life: the smells, wit, and noise; his eyes flicking impulsively to various corners, various women. Lost in his own world, his own naked world of the opposite sex. He glanced at her, and as always she gave a hopeful smile, and as always he glanced away, thinking, possibly, about the one woman who hadn't quite got caught up in his women-trawling net. Naina. Sandra hated her, despised her. Why? She was both pretty and kind, a man's wet dream, and there was nothing Sandra could do about it.

Sandra yelled above the bellow of noise in the pub, 'Dave, still holding a torch for—'

'Who?' he interrupted, not really paying attention.

'Naina,' she replied, dragging out the 'Naina' like a mop on a dirty floor.

Maybe Naina should be added to Dave's keywords, sex, football, pint, because his attention was immediately seized, aimed entirely at Sandra now. The single word, Naina, flipped out a memory like a horsewhip to his mind. Not of the last time he saw her, or the sound of her voice an hour back, not the time when she slammed the door to Florelli's in his face. No, this memory, now etched in his mind, was when he first *really* saw her, after he had eaten the apple pie, after he had walked to her table and bent down to tell her how lovely and appley it was. Her face, so beautiful, so perfect; he wanted her in his bed.

'Dave, I'm talking to you,' Sandra said, throwing a peanut at his chin.

'Naina's got a boyfriend, we're mates, end of story, this is boring me, Sandra.' He looked away, glancing at the footy, keeping an eye on the score, then back to Sandra, who still stared at him, but now with a jealous false smile, a smile that said, 'Don't pretend with me, Dave, I'm a woman.'

Froggy snatched back his lager before it hit Dave's lips again. 'All it is, Sandra, all it is, is, he can't get her to bed. All his sensitive talk with her, all his bollocks, doesn't wash with her and he can't handle it. So, he's always going to be this way until he gets her.' Froggy paused. 'Which will be never, 'cos she's got sense, she can see right through him.'

Dave had been pulled into this argument one too many times of what he would, could or wouldn't achieve with Naina. The so-called 'experts' on human philosophy – his mates. Ha! Some women made you beg or crawl, some set goalposts that got forever wider but, in the end, it all boiled down to one simple fact – orgasms. He'd read somewhere that you could actually stare a woman into an orgasm. He had tried it once – frigid bitch. But with Naina, there were no goalposts, no making him beg or crawl, just plenty of flirting and it was driving him nuts. There had to be a way to hear her heavenly sound – the sound of her knickers coming down, down, *down*.

The whole pub was now sheathed in an aura of glowing joy – the joy of being pleasantly pissed. A little hamlet of beer, song and the odd opinion on who should have done what with a passing shot or strike at goal on the big ol' screen. A chorus of 'Offside' rang out, as a flustered bartender came to the OOzing table, and passed Dave a pint of Stella. The lager dripped down the glass on to her hand.

'I've made you all wet, haven't I?' said grinning Dave, taking the drink.

'From the blonde lady sitting over there,' she spoke awkwardly, her face flushed red. And she pointed to the table by the jukebox. Dave peered across, raised the glass to the blonde beauty – the one he had had his eye on – kicked his chair out and stood up.

'I'm off to pork Cinderella. Behave yourselves.' And Dave crossed the heaving mass of jolly people, grabbed a chair beside her and put out his hand. 'Dave.'

'Hello, Dave; I'm Kelly.'

'Cheers for the drink; where's your two ugly sisters? Joke.' Dave lit a fag, passed her one; she declined. Kelly, what a wonderful name, like water from a waterfall. Blonde, slim, sexy, deserving of a sonnet, deserving of attention and if she was really lucky, deserving of his bacon butty; she was already giving him a hard-on.

Kelly assumed the embarrassed, side-headed stance. 'I don't normally do this, you know, buy a drink.' She paused. Dave was taking it all in his stride, smoking away: carry on, Kelly. 'My two friends, they're sitting over there.' And she pointed, but he didn't bother to look.

Dave just loved women who came on to him, it was like he was in a boat and he didn't even have to paddle. They did all the work. And besides, with women like that he couldn't do a thing wrong. He'd already noticed she couldn't look him in the eyes, couldn't hold a stare, nervously adjusting clothing that didn't need adjusting, playing with the beer mat, *squandering* all that energy. But you could say she had a reason: he was very good looking. More than passable, far more than probable, one hundred per cent hunk material and her stomach churned like a whisk. But as far as Dave was concerned, his looks might get him initially noticed, but after that it was his charm that enticed them in and entitled him to hear his favourite sound in the world. He honestly believed that.

He gulped down his Stella, letting the lager chill the back of his throat. They talked in various tones. Sometimes serious, sometimes playful, all the time Dave trying to fathom the best angle to get inside her knickers. The pub was now heaving, you could hardly breathe, and the noise level was almost deafening. So deafening, in fact, that Dave had to be sitting in very close to hear what Kelly had to say. And he *did* want to hear what she had to say. He did want to hear about her and all her interests, her dislikes and likes, her favourite colour. He wanted to hear it all. Even though it bored him shitless. But he knew that in order to get in her drawers, he had to be a good listener; women just loved that in a man.

'So Kelly, what d'you do for a living?'

A wry smile accompanied her next comment. 'I'm a physicist.'

Alarm bells rang in Dave's head. Oh dear, brainbox here. Monet talk was out, Stephen Hawking was in. This babe, this immaculate creation, this top-notch totty, was an Oxford grad. And would he be able to cope?

'A physicist?' he repeated, raising his eyebrows.

'Yes. Also, I'm very interested in cosmology. I work in the Open University here in Milton Keynes.' She sipped her lime Bacardi Breezer.

He lit another fag. 'Cosmology?' This just gets better, he thought. 'The universe, wow. So you must be really interested in the new revelations that the universe is expanding far quicker than once thought. I mean, all this talk about dark matter and not enough to hold the universe from expanding forever. And those scientists get their big ugly Hubble Telescope, put the wrong fucking lens in, and find *this* out, it makes me so angry.' Dave frowned and put on his slightly upset face.

Kelly, quietly startled, smiled and moved in closer

to Dave. 'Oh God, you do know about cosmology, I'm impressed, normally people are totally lost.'

And he did know things, he was well read, but, as so often is the case, he knew a little about a lot. He stole half of his knowledge from *New Scientist* and filed it away in his mind in a box marked 'Knicker Wrench' for days just like this. On the other side of the coin, and this one was a well-kept secret from everyone, he also subscribed to both *Woman* and *Woman's Own* to read the problem pages and find out what a woman really wanted. And it hadn't taken him more than a few weeks of reading to establish: a woman wanted fucking everything.

It soon became apparent that Kelly would not be lowering her panties for him that night. She seemed the wining and dining sort, the dinner and dance sort, the flowers and choccie sort. Dave could just tell. So without further ado, he jotted down her number and sincerely promised to call her, then hovered over to his mates.

'Dave, you're all alone, could it be that you didn't pull tonight?' Half-drunk, Froggy then nearly collapsed on the floor laughing.

Dave sat down, lit a fag. 'What a fucking waste of time, what a waste. That's it, I'm getting pissed. See that one over there.' He pointed to Kelly. 'She's gorgeous, she's got the body we all dream about, and yet, she's so boring. She's a physicist of all things.'

Froggy steadied himself on his seat, then retorted, 'At least we'll all get cheap condoms then.' The table rocked with laughter.

Dave shook his head. 'You tosser, Froggy. Not a pharmacist, a phys— Oh never mind.'

Dave was in a bad mood. Maybe it was because he hadn't managed to pull. On a Saturday of all nights.

A few pints later, after a few more wisecracks about Dave and his empty bed tonight, a stunning brunette, with silky smooth legs, a ravishing bright red dress that curved in and out of her body using her slim hips for detours, arrived only a foot away from Dave. The table stopped in mid sentence. Matt, Froggy and Andy stared with dribbling minds and Sandra, Philippa and Diane all cast a jealous eye to each other – 'Bet they're implants.'

Her soft voice began, as she touched Dave on the shoulder. 'Dave.' He turned and smiled. 'You are a loser. You may have looks and money but you are a nothing!' And she removed his pint glass from the table, poured the contents over his head, and removed his smile. 'A user and a loser, and I don't know what I ever saw in you.' And wiggling her hips, she walked away.

Dripping, Dave turned back round to his laughing mates. 'That's bang out of order that is, *bang* out of order. If I remember, I gave her what her husband couldn't.'

Naina's dad had favourite times: 6 o'clock, 7 o'clock. And his most favourite, 10 o'clock. News time. North, east, west, south. But when Dad watched with that look of intensity of his, anyone would think he was watching the *Newsi*. North, east, west, south and India. Anything about India, and breathing would stop. 'Shut up, India is on the *News*.' Dare anyone to breathe.

It was 11.15. *Newsi* over, and Naina unobtrusively

slipped into the living room to the sound of Nusrat Fateh Ali Khan chanting in the background, building up to a crescendo. She sat next to a sleeping Sonia on the sofa, careful not to destroy the Qawwali peak. Mum, cross-legged on the floor, in her old salmon pink shalwar kameez, was in her own rhythmic world of slitting and salting the spiky karelas for the following day's dinner and barely noticed Naina's arrival. It was winding-down time in the Indian household.

For some.

Naina's brain needed bleeding, and she wished she'd gone for that drink with Dave. Which would have led to getting drunk with him, which would have led to her raising her skirt up to him, which would have led to teasing him. Anything to escape from the day's events. Anything to forget about Ashok. Two days ago Ashok didn't even exist in her world and now. . . now he was going to be part of her for the rest of her life. And the rest of her life had started when Mum and Dad had asked Sonia to fetch Naina from her bedroom yesterday evening. It had begun with an order:

'Sit down,' Dad had ordered.

Mum nodded her head for Naina to do as she was told. She hated these spur-of-the-moment chats. What was it this time? Too much make-up? Coming in too late? Not helping Mum enough? God she hated . . .

'We've found you a boy. He lives in Dagenham,' Dad began.

. . . God she hated being Indian sometimes.

Dad continued, 'His family are well respected. And it's all arranged for you to meet with him and his family tomorrow.' He threw a few plump sultanas in his mouth, pulped them up, swallowed, then voiced once more. 'They've got their own family business making shirts.'

Mum spoke, the hammer came down, Naina was condemned. 'Your dad has conversed with his father many times. He sounds perfect. Right age. You'll be the first girl he meets. They sound very interested in you. Balbir, his massi, saw you at Neelam's wedding, she talked highly of you to his father. Very highly.' And Mum smiled her seal of approval – if Balbir spoke highly, then no higher accolade existed – and she twisted her long ponytail into a bun.

In that one minute, Naina's heart changed continents and it beat with pure Indian blood as the western tourniquets loosened. Blood distilled from a thousand years of tradition and made more viscous by the hopes and expectations of her mum and dad. She couldn't be seen to be sad. She couldn't allow her weeping nerves to give way. And it was the hardest thing she'd ever done, trying to remain relaxed in front of her parents; while inside she was falling apart at the seams, trying to restrain the reflex to jump up and run away. This wasn't an ordinary world. This couldn't be happening.

Not in Milton Keynes.

Naina wondered what her prospective husband was called. 'What's his name?'

A snatched glance between her parents, like, oh yeah, we forgot to mention that bit. And as soon as Naina knew his name, she pondered what an Ashok would look like. The chances were pretty slim that he would resemble her dream man. The chances of

Ashok having blue eyes were nil.

Trying to sound more enthusiastic than sulky, Naina forced out the words, 'I'll wear my lavender suit . . . shall I?' Mum nodded and Naina smiled as she walked out of the room.

The tears were rolling before she'd hit the stairs, and in her bedroom the water shed like a burst pipe. She was drowning.

Drowning in a tradition that was filled with a billion tears. Who was she to question it? She was Indian. All Indians married this way. It was a done deal from your first breath. In India, where you breathe Indian air, you know no different. In England, breathing English air, being an English-born Asian, you know it is different; different watching life, love, freedom. And never being allowed to join in.

Naina stood at the bedroom window. The night was as black as soldiers' boots, as she peered upwards to the burning stars of Orion. Unmoving there, all confident with his shining sword. She pushed open the glass and took in the cold February air. This wasn't about blame. She couldn't blame her parents for coming here and risking it all to make a better life. She couldn't blame her parents for gripping hard at the slippery rules of tradition, as ten thousand miles of distance tried to pry their hands from its clasp. And she couldn't blame her parents for showing her this new world and what life could be like. Life for an English-born Asian.

She returned to her still-warm bed. God, this was worse than she imagined it could be. She wasn't ready for marriage. Shacking up with an Indian man of whom she knew nothing. Trying hard to love him.

Having his children and obeying his rules. Kissing goodbye to all that she was, leaving her soul fluttering in the temple rafters with all the other Indian girls' souls. Souls that had seen their personalities dissolved by the third verse of the Lavan Hymn (Sikh marriage vows), and their virginity stolen by the third unwrapping of the wedding sari. She wasn't ready to become chained.

But she wasn't ready to hurt her parents either. If she refused to marry Ashok, it would cause too much pain. And she couldn't live with their pain. So she had a choice. Pains or chains. And that's why she gave a shallow shrug and a lacklustre smile and left her parents organizing the rest of her life.

Nisha Minhas

56

Chapter Five

Pretty looks were about as loyal as a hungry cat. All it took was one measly spot, or one late night, or a king-sized Snicker bar, and they were off. I'm out of here, you're on your own. Naina had been crying most of the weekend, she felt about as pretty as Quasimodo and if she wanted sanctuary, then Dave's flat probably wasn't the best place to head.

The rickety rusty shutter of the secondhand record shop '33s to 78s' banged up precisely at 9.00 a.m. on Monday, and Naina pushed out a sigh at the sight of her reflection in the window. Puffed-up eyes, a home-knitted cream woollen jumper, black jeans and trainers. Scruffy. Normally she took great pride in her clothes with her countless outfits, matching nail varnishes; and even matching underwear (not that anyone ever got to see it). But today, scruffy. And as if to punctuate the look, the strong wind wrestled

with her hair, blowing it this way and that, but mostly
blowing it in front of her unhappy face. The only
saving grace, if any, was that she did smell nice due to
the perfume samples she had just attacked in Boots
like someone at a wine-tasting session: Chanel no. 5,
Georgio, Opium, Contradiction, Eternity and lastly
Paco Rabanne for men, all wafting away from her.
She was never good at making her mind up and began
now to feel quite nauseous at her perfume bouquet
garni.

Naina watched a withered leaf being chased by the
crying wind as she stood on the red bricked path that
led to Dave's abode set snug in Stone Valley
Apartments, and her Indian side wanted to turn back.
Up in that top epicurean flat, a sex-mad man was
waiting and her pulse quickened. It quickened at the
thought of him wanting to do things to her. It raced at
the idea of them alone in his bedroom. It fired on all
cylinders at the thought of doing this most un-Indian
of things. It was the mother of all things un-Indian –
being with a white man, and her two best friends had
both warned her not to fall. Leena her Indian friend
and Kate her slut friend.

Since the early days, since the daisy chain days of
Sir Frank Markham school when all three eleven-
year-olds would sit on the just-cut grass of the playing
field and weave the threads of a friendship on spindles
of Bananarama, *The Lost Boys* and Swatch watches,
a pattern had formed that would last for ever. The day
they had become friends stuck out in Naina's memory
like a cherry on a cake. Kate had the coolest shoes in
the school. They were 'Lush'. Naina remembered her
walking round the classroom like she owned the joint;

wiggling her bottom, flicking her blonde hair, smiling, smiling and smiling some more. For God's sake it was only a pair of shoes. Naina soon wiped the smile off her face. Tripped her up and sent her flying. Leena clapped. The friendship had begun.

'I'll get you at lunchtime, you bitch.' Kate had hissed, struggling to her feet.

'We'll be waiting . . . won't we, Leena? Outside the science block, be there, 12.05.'

And lunchtime arrived; 12.05 came and went. Three young girls could be seen crying in the head-mistress's office. Their parents would all be informed. Two detentions later, a thousand multicoloured lines of 'I will not fight ever again, I am a lady and ladies do not fight' later, and the three were as tight and in one piece (and just as skinny) as Indian cricket stumps when playing England.

And that was half the problem. Naina already knew what each of them would say when told of her forth-coming marriage to Ashok. She needed perspective. Leena, although not one to abide totally by all the rules, was Indian, knew the score and would be realistic. Her words might well be: 'Jeez, you knew this day would come, accept it like we all do and while you're at it, stay well clear of Dave. I mean it, Naina.' And Kate? Her advice would be tainted with a different set of truths: 'Naina, you only live once, make the most of what time you've got left and, while you're at it, stay well clear of Dave. By the way, I love what you've done with your nails.'

And Dave. Well, he would just tell her straight. He would be fair. He was perspective. And he certainly wouldn't be adding the words 'stay well clear of

Dave'. And if she got nothing more out of going up to that flat with the sex-mad man than a few laughs and smiles, then so what. It would take her mind off Ashok for a while.

Her pulse quickened again and she walked up the path.

Dave was asleep, snoring on his cold, tiled kitchen floor. It was an absolute tip. A Domino's Pizza box was under his head – presumably as a pillow. Empty lager cans and fag ends strewn about, a dustpan and brush containing what seemed like two glasses worth of broken glass, washing-up everywhere, and a full sink of egg noodles floating in dirty water.

Naina buzzed the intercom from the main entrance. Thirty buzzes later, the entrance door unlocked and she stood on the plush blue carpeting of the lobby. Two cushioned armchairs and a small round table sat down the far end near the stairway, and either side of a couple of tall potted rubber plants were the doors to flats one and two. The top floor matched the bottom, except the entrance had a 'Fire Exit' sign above the door. Fresh new smells of paint and newly laid carpet breezed the air, revealing the fact that this was a new building. There would be a fifty-fifty chance of guessing which was Dave's flat, if it wasn't for the dead give-away that edged the odds in favour of flat four – a shining brass plaque with *Nisi Dominus Frustra* engraved in old English calligraphy.

Naina hoped that Dave was in a sensible mood. There was no point in praying, though. Her God was Indian and would tell her to go home and accept her wedding to Ashok. Dave's God was the managing director of Durex condoms, and would advise Naina of the first commandment – to shag any bloke at least three times a day, so his share prices would climax. So, she crossed her fingers instead and knocked on the dark blue-painted door.

The door flung open. Naina stared at Dave. He looked both Nainas in the eyes. A piece of salami sausage hung off his brown out-of-control hair. What looked like ketchup was smeared on his cheek, and his rose-gold earring was half coming out of his ear. She ignored what was stuck to his sleeping willy.

Naina laughed and walked in. 'Dave, put some clothes on please, please.' She quick-stepped across the wooden pine floor to the mammoth deep blue sofa set to one side of a large open fireplace. She sat down, not on, but in the sofa to await Dave's return. The place was messy but clean. The first time she had come here, she'd been shocked at how well decorated and expensively furnished it was, and amazed that he could keep it so clean. Then she met the Argentinian cleaner.

Amazement never lasted too long with Dave.

Cleaners never lasted too long with Dave either. But Ruby was a home-bred Argentinian and had dealt with worse: six kids, fourteen grandchildren and a stubborn husband. She thought the world of Master Dave, keeping his flat tip-top twice a week; flapping around in her oversized Nikes, baggy Armani tops, and skin-tight Dumbbells Gym shorts; scrubbing the skirting boards, dusting the furniture, mopping the floorboards, and general maintenance. She had one rule: 'I donta flusher your looer . . . after a number tooer.' And she charged double time for clearing up after parties.

'I'll get you a coffee, Naina. Sorry about the mess,' yawned Dave, then headed out.

A huge bong was set on a psychedelic Persian rug in the middle of the room. You would marvel at the tackiness of it – it was shaped in a mould of a three-foot-high naked woman – if it wasn't for the expert craftsmanship. Four or five glass ashtrays, full, surrounded it like ancient worshippers and empty lager cans and wine bottles littered the wooden floor. You'd think a bomb had hit the place, but Naina had seen it worse. It smelt like an Amsterdam pub. She looked to the shelf above the fire. And there it was, as always, on top of the fireplace, centred perfectly, awaiting the next poor sucker to read it. A card that on the outside said 'Thank you', picturing a cute little bunny playing with a dormouse. On the inside, it read 'I'm going to kill you, you nosy bitch'. Dave could normally tell which women had read it when he was out of the room, by the look of terror on their faces when he returned. Oh how he loved his games. It surprised Dave how nosy women really were, and Naina was ashamed to admit that she, too, had fallen for it the very first time she'd been to Dave's flat.

She walked to the French doors, opened the heavy curtains, and looked out to the gardens. Trees, and thirty shades of green bushes, on a crisp-cut emerald lawn stretched way back to the distant countryside, giving the place a dreamy isolation. A church steeple seemed to balance on the tree line; this really was a private world. Last summer, in the silent heat, sitting on the cast-iron bench underneath the huge old weeping willow tree, Naina and Dave had spent whole days, hours and hours, idly chatting until darkness sneaked up on them and closed their conversation down for that evening. He had been so honest with her about his life, his women, his dreams; and the more he opened up, the more polished he became in her eyes. Other people only ever got to see the tarnish; he had let her see another side to him. The side that she had fallen for. Yet, even though she felt compelled to return the honesty, to tell him about her arranged marriage, she was afraid that doing so would maybe lead to sympathy. And sympathy was something she *never ever* wanted.

Slightly concerned that the flat was deathly quiet and not a sign of coffee, Naina marched across the floor, down the short hall, and pushed open the door to where she expected she might find him. He was asleep in bed, snoring his head off, his bum in the air. It was the bum bit that did it, that made her so angry, so spitting with fumes that she just wanted to pick up his stereo and smash it on his head. Then she looked at the bum again. Pretty damn cute. And that made her even more angry. She walked out, back into the hall, back into the living room, still fuming: he was supposed to be helping her out today.

Naina had never fallen over a Buckaroo before. She went head first across the floor and into the safety of an armchair. *FUCKAROO!* Picking herself up, trying to look cool, she angrily kicked the plastic donkey across the floor, smashing it into a glass cabinet full of PlayStation 2 games. The loud crash was satisfying and Naina momentarily smiled, then furiously picked up her Liz Claiborne bag, ready to leave. Then, like magic, Dave appeared – still naked.

'What the fuck was all that racket?' he asked, now appearing slightly more awake.

'Lucky it wasn't your head. I'm going. I'll see you whenever.'

'Hang on. I thought we were going to have a chat. I'll get the coffee; sit down. Two sugars? You look nice by the way,' he said, sparking up, eyeing her up and down. '*Very* nice.'

Dave's voice had a certain tone, flirty. She prayed that his willy didn't rise up, especially with the Rizla paper still stuck to the end. She hadn't taken the whole day off work to visit a slob, and she hadn't come here to smell the booze and fags, and she definitely hadn't come round to see to Dave's sexual needs.

'You're a right turn off, you know that?' exclaimed Naina.

'What?'

Naina dropped her bag, her eyes flicked him up and down. 'Is that really the sight women have to put up with in the morning?' She paused. 'No wonder they always slap you before they leave. I feel like giving you a good slap myself.'

'I'd prefer a massage.'

'The answer is NO. And for the next hundred sexual innuendoes it's still NO.'

Dave smiled, possibly imagining all hundred sexual innuendoes. Then he collected his breath. 'Back in a moment. I'll take a quick shower, then we can talk, sense-ibly.' He walked off.

The opulent bathroom was fully kitted out like that of a health club changing room: a corner bath with steps, bidet, toilet, walk-in shower, two fitted cupboards and a rack of fluffy, soft, perfumed towels – the sort of towels you dream about. Oh yeah, and a Jacuzzi. Small blue and purple mosaic tiles covered every square inch, and a pile of fitness magazines stuffed in the toilet corner completed the decor. The light switch fan vroomed into life, just like Dave did, as the power shower hit his sleepy face, washing away yesterday like it never even came. The plughole tried its hardest to swirl away the salami and, without a thought, Dave prodded it down with his big toe. Then wondered what the hell it was, hoping it wasn't something dubious. Ten minutes later, he was back to his sparkling self, clad in perfectly ironed designer clothes and confident corona.

He handed Naina a large red coffee mug, plonked himself next to her on the sofa and lit up a fag. 'Naina,' he sniffed the air. 'What perfume are you wearing?'

She knew his game. What did he care what it was called? Any perfume would make his loins go boing. 'It's called Ashok. You say it with a French accent, *Ashoque*. Why? Do you like it?'

'It's lovely. ASH-cock. And French, blimey.' Boing!

Naina swallowed her laugh. She glanced at him; it was a miracle what a shower could do. He personified 'good looking'. Sometimes she just felt like going over and kissing him full on. Imagining his arms enveloping her, imagining his hands moving up and down her body, imagining her senses becoming dizzy as she wandered into the shining blue of his eyes. Imagining every fine detail.

'So, Naina, do you want to just talk about things for a while until what's bothering you slips out? Or shall we go straight to the point?'

They did this sometimes: gently easing the other one out to talk about what was eating them up.

'I don't want to talk about it,' Naina replied.

'Okay, we'll talk about something else.' He dragged on his fag, watching Naina peel her lavender nail varnish off with her nails. 'Froggy was round here last night. Him and a few others. He logged on to one of those websites, you know, where the women will do anything for you—'

'Yes, I know, I don't think I want to hear this either, Dave.'

'Anyway, this dirty cow comes on the screen asking him what she could do for him, so Froggy asked her to put her clothes back on, she was revolting . . .'

Naina laughed. 'Okay, I'll tell you what's bothering me.' She focused on the bong, not quite sure of what to say. 'I got engaged at the weekend, I'm getting married in six months . . .'

'Fucking hell, Naina, marriage is for insecure people, how many times have I told you?' He sparked up another fag, forgetting the fag still smoking in the ashtray. 'Anyway, if you want to get caught in the doom and gloom of a bitter marriage, swamped in misery, all I can say is congratulations.' He leaned over and kissed her on the cheek. 'So why the long face? You should be happy, shouldn't you?'

Naina felt as if she was exposing herself. She stared at the French doors. Rain pelted against the double glazing like little liquid balls of glass. What had seemed like a good idea on Saturday, when she was feeling low, now seemed like madness. She couldn't possibly go into the whys and what-fors of the Indian way with Dave. He would never understand. How could he? She didn't even understand it herself. Plus, she'd worked so hard in convincing him that she had a pretend boyfriend – she'd look a little bit stupid. That would never do.

'Oi, mute girl,' Dave uttered.

Still no response. The hurling rain was hypnotic and Naina's thoughts were magnetized outwards to the silent splashing and sploshing. Her days were numbered. Even this, sitting here with Dave in his flat, would all be a dusty memory come wedding day. And by then she would be so Indian, even the dust mites would be wearing saris. And Dave, he'd be on beautiful woman one million and six.

He watched her sitting there with a face-ache. This *had* to be one of those moments when a man should know what was bothering a woman. And Dave normally knew the answer to that one: men. Toe-rag men. Men like his stepdad.

And he recognized that face of hers, that hidden trouble, her struggling smiles concealing other emotions. And he guessed it had something to do with that phone call on Saturday night: 'Do you think that you can grow to love someone after you have married them?' Surely only someone not in love would ask such a question. But up until now her boyfriend was the bee's knees, the crème de la crème, the master of love and boycotter of the boring missionary position. He was perfect. And her love for him, so she said, was robust, unshakeable. And he sounded like a right tosser. But still, the weird phone call questions.

Fluttering around in his head like a few loose loft pigeons were some old thoughts. Thoughts he'd brought up with her before. And it made him think again. Those pigeons were all shitting at once.

He nudged her. 'Is it an arranged marriage? Is that why you're fucked off?' And he sealed his comment with a big salivary Columbo stare, and posted it in her open mouth. Sorted!

'Just because you watch one documentary on the BBC about arranged marriages, you think you know it all.' Naina screwed her face up. 'I've told you before, I'm not having an arranged marriage. If you must know what the problem is, it's timing and logistics.' She looked at Dave. His eyebrows were two question marks. 'I knew he was going to ask me to marry him – he loves me. But . . . it just took me a little by surprise when he told me he's already booked everything for six months' time. Because he's romantic like that. Unlike you, Dave.'

He didn't know whether it was the closeness of Naina, her anger, or the cosy weather, or even the ASH-cock perfume, but he wanted to take his clothes off and ravage Naina's insecure body right there and then. She was obviously having pre-wedding nerves. He'd been having them himself for ten years. She needed something to take her mind off things for a while, poor girl. And who could blame her really? Look what happened to Dirty Den and Angie in *EastEnders*, it was enough to scare the confetti right out of you. Then you've got all these relatives at your big day, pretending how happy they are for you, knowing full well that their own marriages turned out to be a big heap of shi— No, it made sense to stay single. But here he was worrying about Naina and her problems, when really he had a huge problem of his own: he hadn't had a shag in two days, not since

Karen the vegetarian. He should really get out more. Then, get a grip, he told himself, he was here as a mate and a mate he was going to be. He turned to Naina and then . . .

'Dave, I shouldn't be doing this.' She lunged across and kissed him passionately on the lips.

A good friend would push her away, and say, 'No, Naina, you're getting married, you're just feeling a bit down,' he thought, as her tongue danced in his mouth. He feebly pulled away from the embrace.

'Look, Naina, this is wrong, the sheets aren't clean.' He just couldn't say the words that a good friend would. He tried, God damn it, he tried.

Naina had often thought that when it came down to the crunch, she would be out of tune in the sexual department. But she wasn't, she was in total harmony, enjoying every second. And how she had dreamed of putting her hands over his body and feeling all his muscular contours. But this was not a dream. It was fun. Exciting fun. And then *he* took over, *he* became in control, she was now out of her depth and at the mercy of him. And she loved it for a moment, one sweet tantalizing moment, just seeing the power of his masculinity. Then, just as quickly, she became scared. Like she'd swum out too far; the undercurrent was going to sweep her away. She was reassured by his eyes which told of only softness towards her. But what lay behind those eyes? A sex-mad maniac?

The left side of Dave's brain – the side that was devoted entirely to sex, to getting inside a beautiful woman's knickers – began to steam into action. Here he was, with the woman who always said no, and his lips were firmly pressed up against hers. The enormous risk in pulling away to get the condoms was that she might come up with that stupidest of stupid women's clichés, 'Sorry, I can't.' The condoms were in the bedroom, so he pulled her up, still kissing, and, walking backwards, began to negotiate the room, still kissing, all the time thinking to himself, 'I can't believe I'm finally going to fuck her, I'm going to make it sooooo bad.'

Pictures of her dad talking to Ashok's dad emerged in Naina's head, and she gently pushed them away. But somehow, she couldn't find the willpower to push Dave away. She had never felt this way before. Burning feelings of pleasure hurled from spears of pure bliss stabbed through her nerves like a heavenly war. She felt like a virgin whore.

Naina knew of dyslexic people, getting their letters all mixed up, but she had never thought that a parallel existed in the world of unclothing until now as she watched Dave frantically try to pull off his clothes in the wrong order, as he fell head over heels in a mad rush, pulling his Armani boxers off before he had even removed his trousers. She laughed out loud as he scampered around on all fours, trying desperately to look like a man who knew what he was doing. 'Give us a hand, Naina, I'm stuck.' He didn't look very cool.

Dave finally untangled his shorts and trousers and in a mad fit of anger threw them at the big-screen TV. Recovering his composure, he came over to Naina, smiled his Dave sexy smile and began to kiss her neck; she could feel the hardness through her jeans of what Dave often referred to as his 'next of kin'.

A promise of excitement lay beneath his diamond sharp blue eyes and a chill passed through her. Why did he have to be so sexy? Naina felt he was about to turn her life upside down. She had dreamed of him wildly making love to her, and the feeling of what he was about to do was spinning her around inside. She wanted to let go of all she had known; all those harsh rules; all those frustrating feelings of save, save, save. She couldn't be saving herself for Ashok, a man she didn't know, when right in front of her was the man she wanted to give it all to.

Her hand moved down to his cock and felt its warmth. She could hear her inner voice yelp, 'It's huge.' And her thoughts right now were unforgivable: she wanted his cock as far inside her as possible. She couldn't be save, save, save for Ashok. Don't Indian parents know anything? Women don't like saving, they love to spend.

'Oh, my God, it's—' Naina nearly complimented Dave on his manhood. Then thought better of it. 'It's circumcised. Wow!' She knelt on the wooden floorboards.

Dave peered down smiling. 'Tidy job, hey?'

She glanced up to Dave standing above her. 'BUPA?'

'Nah. NHS.'

Naina opened her mouth and put her lips around his cock, listening hopefully for words or moans of encouragement that she was giving him a top-notch blow job. If it deflated in her mouth, she would die on the spot.

'Hang on.' Dave pulled away. His eyes frantically scanned the room. 'It's here somewhere.' He stretched across and grabbed it off the stereo speaker, tossing it to the floor.

Naina glanced down. 'What's that?'

'What do you think it is? I'm only thinking about you and your knees.'

Naina rested her knees on the blue satin cushion or, as Dave called it, 'Gobble Gizmo'. He seemed to be enjoying it. But her thoughts were filled with worry. Was she doing it right? Would he compare her? Was she supposed to be humming?

Afterwards, Dave pushed Naina gently on the king-sized bed. He pulled down her jeans, manoeuvring his hands up her long legs. Kissing her passionately all the time, he began to slide her knickers off. Oh that sound again. Dave's favourite sound in the world.

Never before had a man seen Naina, let alone touched her, down below. And here was the problem. Any second now, he would know that this was her first time. All those occasions she had explained to him about her fabulous lover, all those key sentences she had used, like: 'I would marry him just for his sexual prowess,' and 'If I died tomorrow, I would die satisfied.' And all the trouble she went to, to send herself those text messages from her pretend boyfriend. All with various sexual undertones. All shown casually to Dave. All parried off with his usual chivalrous charm, 'Naina, only a real wanker would call himself BIG boy. And I mean that literally. Change your phone number, he sounds like a right weirdo.'

Dave's warm hands began to tease her, not too close, but close enough. And then . . . Naina pushed him off and gave the cliché: 'I can't, Dave.'

Dave looked around, he was hearing strange noises again, sounds like 'NO'.

'Naina, but I thought . . .'

'That's the trouble, you don't think. I told you I was engaged.' Her black knickers came back up with the worst sound in the world. 'That's all you think about, sex, sex and sex. Does our friendship not mean anything? Does it mean nothing to you? Does it mean nothing to you that this, this, what we are doing here may screw up my relationship with my husband-to-be? If you were a friend you wouldn't have taken advantage of me. There was obviously something upsetting me and you, you stick your lollipop in my mouth.'

Dave was flummoxed. This was beyond the realms of reality. He stared. Lollipop??? Naina looked bleakly at him. His tongue, which had earlier seemed so keen on giving her a thorough tooth polish, now seemed tied up in knots. 'SEX, PINT and FOOTBALL, now answer me,' shouted Naina, getting off the bed and chucking his clothes at him.

Dave thought for a minute, then nearly had to slap himself, he knew better than to try to understand a woman. They were so touchy.

There was an article he had read once in *Woman's Own*. It was about how to make your first time with a new partner really special. He returned Naina's glare. She could do with reading it herself, this wasn't very special at all.

'I'm only a man, Naina. Not a fucking mind reader.'

She sneered at him. 'What d'you mean by that?' She zipped up her jeans.

'Remind me again, who came on to who here?'

She sat on the bed and began tying her trainer laces

up. 'That's not the point, the point is, I was feeling low and you took advantage.' And she huffed. 'Typical.'

If each of our emotions had a volume control then Naina's 'guilt' would have been rocking the rafters just then, blasting in each ear. What the hell had she done? What was she thinking? This man would sell his own mother just to look up some skirt, and Naina's mother would be so ashamed of her. She'd never be able to look her in the face again.

'I'm sorry, I did take advantage.' He pulled on his T-shirt and walked round the bed to face her. 'But, there's obviously something wrong with your fella, if you're here giving me a blow job.' He looked her in the eyes. 'In my flat.'

'Pardon,' Naina spat.

'I said there's obviously something wrong . . .'

Naina stood up, returning the gaze of those enticing blue eyes. 'I heard.'

'I'm only telling you the truth.'

'Well, I'll tell you some truths.' Naina's voice grew louder. 'You know what you are, you hurt women, you walk over them like they are nothing, you screw people's lives up, you have ruined – what? – seven marriages or is it eight? Who knows, you're such a liar. You're a pig. I hate you and I wish that I had never even met you. I don't think you're a very nice person at all.' With that, she stormed out of the bedroom, grabbed her bag, and violently slammed the front door.

'See, I told you,' said the old man in the flat below. 'Come and take a look.'

Ivy struggled over, using her walking stick, and peered out at the departing Naina. 'I wonder what he does to them? They always come out of there crying.'

The old man put his arm round Ivy's waist. 'But he's always so polite, he even offered me a smoke once on that huge pipe he keeps up there.'

The old couple stayed at the window, watching a lonely figure crying halfway across the gravel car park in the pouring rain.

Dave helped himself to some dejection and pity. He picked up his computer scanner and threw it across the bedroom, hitting the far wall, scraping the blue paintwork, cracking on the floorboards. He then took a short run up and kicked it, finishing it off. 'Scan that, you fucker!'

Six messages flashed green on his answerphone. He pressed erase, without listening to any, then looked towards the messy living room. Next time he had a get-together at his flat, it wouldn't be just bring a bottle and hash, it would be bring a bin liner too. Clear up your own frigging rubbish.

He sat. Smoking inside and out. Grey smoke for a grey day. He couldn't believe he had been that close and now Naina was gone. A whole year, waiting as patiently as a chess player, and he let her just slip away. Teases him, then shoots off, most likely to her boyfriend/fiancé, probably in his bed now, making noises that he should be hearing – where was the loyalty in that? When those scientists finally unravelled DNA, they would find the 'teasing gene' in women, probably dressed in some little mini see-through cytoplasm dress. One small chromosome for man, one giant leap for man's peace of mind. And peace of mind? Dave had none.

He stubbed out the fag in the volcanic ashtray and listened to the heavy rain pelt down for a few minutes, wishing he'd paid a little bit more attention to what Naina's body had looked like rather than concern himself with tensing his muscles and looking 'muscly'. He wondered where Naina's boyfriend was going wrong. With a woman that beautiful, you'd have to be a right donk to mess up. He obviously wasn't satisfying her, that was blatant. What did architects know anyway?

Ego was low. Down-hearted and down-trodden. He knew of only one way, one way only to lift the gloom that now tormented him.

'Melissa, hi, it's Dave. Fancy coming over? I've got the day off. I really miss you . . . Great, I'll see you in ten minutes . . . Oh yeah, wear that, I love you in that . . . I'll tell you now, though, the place is a bit of a tip . . . Okay, bye.' Dave placed the receiver down, smiled. Dave was back.

Just time to change the sheets, have a shower, and write Melissa a little poem – she loved his poetry. He searched for clues that told tales. He opened the French doors to extinguish Naina's perfume, washed the lipstick-stained coffee mug, and sprayed some deodorant round the entire flat. Dave was back. He didn't need the likes of Naina telling him where to stick his lollipop.

Chapter Six

Melissa's brand-new red Saab pulled up outside and Dave whistled to himself. Nice to see that even at short notice she had made the effort. Everything tied in superlatively with 28-year-old Melissa, from her stylish designer two-piece suit, to her knee-length suede boots and not forgetting her perfectly manicured nails. You wouldn't have been surprised to see her on the cover of a glossy magazine flaunting her beauty, she looked like she had been put together by a professional stylist. He stood almost panting at the door waiting for his mistress of sin to shimmer through the entrance.

But sinners never shimmered, they shuffled, with a guilty gait, making only polite talk, getting down to business and then shuffling back to their husband with a grocery bag full of his favourites and moaning what a hectic day they'd had. That's what Dave appreciated about Melissa: her polite talk, her lack of personal inquisitiveness, her lack of interest. And anyway, he never liked talking about his personal life, especially his childhood – he'd shut the door on that one a long time ago, slammed the door in fact.

Some people look back on their childhood as a huge fresh open garden, running wild with adventure. Dave looked on his as a waste ground swamped with rubbish. How do you tell someone that you had a bastard of a stepdad who treated you like shit? How do you tell someone that your mum betrayed you, and your real dad, when you cried for help, ignored the cries?

The flat door was already ajar for Melissa and he waited, sitting casually on the sofa.

'I knew you would call, eventually,' stated Melissa doubtfully.

Dave admired her long golden-blonde hair and thought, 'So did I.' She always smelt so good, possibly a little too much perfume, but good nevertheless.

'Coffee?' He jumped up and headed towards her, planting a kiss on her already proffered cheek. 'Sorry about last time, Mel, I honestly forgot the time.'

Melissa smiled. 'Never mind; I know what you're like, Dave.' She paused. 'Since when did you make coffee? But now you've offered. Yes, I'd love one.'

He stubbed out his fag, reluctantly walked to the kitchen and grinned to himself; then saw the mess in the kitchen, thought, 'Sod the coffee, I'm not her sodding tea-maid.'

'Melissa,' he shouted, sneaking his head round the corner. 'Shall we forget coffee?'

With a cheeky face such as Dave's the mere fact that

he had offered was more than enough. 'Thought it was too good to be true, you making coffee.'

'You didn't come round for coffee, did you?' He took her by the hand and led her to the bedroom.

He began to patiently undo the tiny material buttons on her pastel pink cashmere cardigan; it looked so itchy, and he flung it over his left shoulder like jumble sale stock. To keep the symmetry he flung her skirt over his right shoulder. And he was pleased to see that she had worn just what she had said she would underneath: nothing. Before long they were both rolling around the large bed, heavy breathing, heavy petting and the occasional softly spoken dirty word.

Two minutes later, Melissa abruptly stopped doing what she was doing.

'What!?' Dave asked. He hated it when women's foreheads creased up, it normally meant sex was over.

'I think there's someone at the door,' she whispered, her creases now like a rippled pond.

Knock knock.

'It could be my husband,' worried Melissa.

'Yeah, right.' Dave got up, plucked a discarded wet towel from the wooden floor, wrapped it round his trim waist, and shot out to answer the door. He chuckled to himself in the hallway, 'Your husband, yeah right, like I care.'

He swung open the door and froze.

Inside Dave's mind, Danny Zuko from Grease *waited for moments like this. Moments when Dave looked 'uncool'. Danny in his leather jacket mocked . . . Dave told Danny Zuko to get out of his head, this was damn serious. He was up shit creek.* Somehow he composed himself. 'How did you get in?'

'The old bloke downstairs was coming out and kindly let me in.'

'I hate it when they do that. What's the sodding use of security when they do that? It really pisses me off,' he moaned. And they stared at each other for an uncomfortable second or two.

'Sorry about earlier, I don't know what got into me. Sorry about taking it out on you, I've come to make peace.' Naina pushed the door, passed Dave and walked into the living room, wondering why he was standing in a towel.

Dave slowly closed the door. Like it or lump it, he had to deal with this some how. Naina had only been gone an hour, and it struck a chord even with Dave as looking bad, if she found Melissa here. That could cause a problem in the future when he tried to get Naina to lower those knickers again. Today he was on the verge of something special with beautiful Naina; he felt a bit like Louis Pasteur must have felt on the discovery of penicillin or Captain Scott on the edge of those icy things; he was sure they wouldn't have let a Melissa stand in their way.

Dave had already applied the sadness face. 'Naina, I'll put the kettle on; sit yourself down. I've been thinking about you since you went. God, I felt so bad, you know. Sorry for . . . I'll be right back.'

He eased the bedroom door shut. 'Melissa,' he whispered, 'I can't believe it, it's your possessive husband. Don't make a sound. Can you believe he followed you here? Can you believe it?'

Melissa sat bolt upright on the bed. 'You're jok—' Dave's hand covered the rest.

'Shhh, he'll hear. Don't worry, I'll sort it all out.

80

Just stay here. The best thing is for you to hide under the duvet just in case.' Dave threw the blue quilt over her, praying that it might muffle Naina's voice if things became too heated next door.

He quickly chucked on his gym baggies and Gravity Force top whispering, 'Melissa, your husband doesn't deserve you,' clicked the bedroom door behind him and waltzed into the living room, carrying his black Nike trainers, and his well-practised apologetic smile – he *had* to get rid of Naina.

'Sorry, Naina, I just got a call on the mobile, there's a problem down the gym, I've got to shoot out.' He sat down on the edge of the sofa chair and began to slime his way into his trainers. 'Can't leave those morons five minutes without them saying: Dave, we need you down the gym, Dave this, Dave that. God, Naina, I don't know why I bother with it sometimes, I really don't. I'm a fool to myself, always taking on too many things at once, but I suppose it pays the bills.' Lies lies lies.

Naina sighed, a bit disappointed. She really wanted to sort this out. She felt so bad: she'd had no right saying those things to him, and it was she who had come on to him. 'Dave, sorry I said those things to you, I shouldn't have, my brain sometimes just goes into—'

'Don't worry about it. Can we meet later? Tonight maybe?' he asked, standing up.

Naina stood up as well. 'Tonight's fine. What time?'

'Six?' Dave came forward, put his strong arms round her. 'Look, sorry, I did take advantage and I shouldn't have. But I'm really in a rush. Do you want me to pick you up later?' The hug was warm and generous.

'No, it's okay, I'll meet you here.' She picked up her bag. 'Actually, could you give me a lift to Silbury Boulevard?'

Dave tried to retrieve a file under 'More lies and cop outs' from his brain.

Loading . . .

Loading . . . . . .

Loading . . . .

But before the information fully downloaded, Melissa fumbled in, his wet towel wrapped round her delicate frame, out of view of Naina, but in full view of ZX81 Dave.

System error . . .

Dave threw his mobile over his shoulder and dropped his car keys to the floor; the metallic sound had a finality to it that bit into his brain. He slumped back on the sofa chair, hand on head, and resigned. He'd been doing so well. At this point he wished he was abseiling down the inside of an active volcano, anything but this. Naina was prone to read too much into things. Women were so touchy.

Melissa's eyes wandered round the room, searching for her husband whom she was bravely going to confront. Suffocating under the duvet, she'd decided that now was the perfect time to tackle him, while Dave was there, rather than on her own later: Dominic had been known to become violent and there was even a risk that he might cancel her credit cards.

The large room was now a theatre. 'Dave, where's my husband, and who is she?' And the acoustics were perfect: clear, audible, spine-chilling.

'I'm sorry, Naina, I cannot explain,' Dave said, giving Naina his shamed face.

Naina turned to see Melissa standing there, with a look of confusion. Slowly her head turned back to Dave, still with his feigned look of shame. And she stared at him in disbelief. Pulses of information were shared between them and their eyes locked as one. Suddenly his crystal blue eyes were all murky and stagnant, his gorgeous looks had taken on the appearance of a leftover mouldy lump of cheese, and his manner, his charm, his wit, had all merged to form the shackled pig dump that he was.

Melissa was just background noise as Dave stood up to approach Naina. 'Naina, are you thinking what I'm thinking? She's a bit on the old side for me? Bit of a bimbo? Erm, no, I'm not very funny, am I?'

Naina walked up to him. 'I'm thinking that she's too good for you.' Then whacked him round the face as hard as she could. 'Don't you ever call me again and you can stick your apple pie right up your lying arse!' She then offered some advice to Melissa. 'Get out before he wrecks your life. Do you know he slept with seven women last week?' Then Naina stormed out, leaving the door wide open. She didn't want to hear his excuses, she was gone out of his life.

That went well. Dave rubbed his cheek. She had one good right hook; it bloody hurt. The background noise of Melissa began to surface.

'What's she mean, seven women, Dave?'

'You can shut up. You come here all married up and try to lecture me. Think about it, woman, which one of us is in the wrong? I suggest you go and look at your wedding photos and think what a mess you've made of your life,' Dave said with a certain amount of contempt.

'But where's my husband, Dave?'

Chapter Seven

Leena – Naina's Indian friend – was shoplifting in Boots when she received the call from Naina wanting to talk about a lying bastard. Leena had been known to come home with three carrier bags full of totally worthless items, just for the thrill of it; the adrenaline rush of being caught was her ultimate turn-on, but the thrill of slagging off Dave was even better, and she rushed over *à toute vitesse* to meet her friend in Florelli's coffee shop.

Naina sat in the prime spot by the open fire on one of the huge blue sofas. A spitting-hot mug of hot chocolate and a piece of steamy apple strudel (not apple pie) floating in homemade vanilla custard sat before her. She wore a thoughtful expression shaded with betrayal. She wasn't yet a sunken ship, but she did feel a wreck, although the hairdryer in the Ladies and a quick refresh of make-up somehow seemed to put some wind back in her sails.

She crooked her head up over the back of the sofa and glanced round the busy coffee shop. Anyone would think that the entire world was run from inside these walls, with the amount of important phone calls and business meetings going on. Some bloke dressed in a dark jade suit stared across at her from a far table. He dashed a smile; she tried not to sneer and just looked through him like glass. Like glass: that's what all men seemed right now – weak and transparent.

Time and time again her parents had told Naina, lectured, threatened her: 'Keep away from men . . . it's not our way. We may breathe the same air and have the same coloured blood, but our cultures do not mix. You must never forget where you came from, your roots, your traditions. Just because a man plants an acorn in a foreign country doesn't mean it does not become an acorn tree.' That's what Dad would say, in Punjabi, while Mum nodded in agreement, knitting. And sometimes he would follow it up with: 'Anyway, Indian men are the best looking,' and Mum would miss a stitch.

After a few minutes, Leena arrived and tapped her on the back of the head, shaking Naina away from her morbid Ashok thoughts. She walked round the sofa, kissed Naina on the cheek and handed her seven Revlon lipsticks of various colours.

'S'freezing out there.' Leena leaned into the fire and warmed her thieving hands. 'What's that bastard Dave done this time?' She sat back next to Naina. 'Like your perfume, what is it?'

It was a bad link – Ashok, you say it with a French accent – and it forced out Naina's frustrated tears. 'I'm getting married in six months, Leena. I only met him on Saturday, I just don't think I can do it. But I can't hurt my parents, I just couldn't do it to them.' The tears fell heavier and Leena placed her arm round her friend. She understood: her parents had also found a husband for her, in India, and were just waiting for him to finish his doctor's degree and then they would be married next year. She too would become a wife to a man she neither knew nor loved, just like all the other Indian girls. It was fate. Hearing of Naina's forthcoming marriage was never going to be a surprise. But it proved the futility of any western ideas of love and romance that may be lurking around in an Indian woman's mind. It proved that it would happen to them all. Even Naina.

'What's he like?' Leena asked softly. 'Do you sort of like him?'

'Sort of, seems okay, lives in Dagenham. Mum and Dad love him. It's just six months, Leena; I can't get my head round it. No time to get fat.'

They both laughed. Leena scooted off to get a coffee and Naina watched the way her long black curly hair bounced like springs. When they were younger, when life was one big merry-go-round, Naina used to weep with jealousy over the length of Leena's dark locks. But unaware to Naina, Leena used to weep with jealousy over Naina's astonishing pretty face. So Naina grew her hair long and Leena became obsessed with make-up.

Leena returned with a frothing cappuccino dusted in chocolate. 'So what's Dave done to upset you?'

'I gave him a blow job this morning.'

Like wind-bellows, Leena's mouth blew off the top of the cappuccino leaving a frothy mound sinking into the carpet like a shrinking Casper the ghost. 'Jeez, you slag,' she spat, dumbstruck.

'I just can't believe I lost control like that. It even sounds so dirty.' Naina felt disgusted with herself. Only two days before, she had sat talking to her future husband. Prying out what they could about each other, making her parents so proud. Today, she had swapped her dignity for two sore knees and a free lesson in bastard men. 'Dad's turban would fly off in anger if he found out.' They laughed.

The glass door to Florelli's burst open. Dave, with an element of chutzpah, walked in, smart and sickly smooth. He smiled over to the young waitress and tipped his hand to suggest he wanted a coffee brought over to that table. *That table* happened to be situated just behind Naina's. And, just behind Naina's, one could hear every damn word she was saying.

Dave narrated to himself: 'And in he walked, to his kingdom, as cool as a cucumber. What have we here? Oh my goodness, is that Naina? And she's with another woman: Leena the thief. I must not interfere, that would be dead rude.'

Dave sneakily sat back on the blue couch, resting his Nikes up on the table and relaxed. The young waitress brought over his coffee and he mouthed 'Thank you' to her and watched her tight bottom wiggle away.

'Jeez, I still can't believe what you did, Naina. Is he big?'

Dave waited with baited breath. The answer would determine whether he wanted a friendship with Naina any more. Someone laughed out loud, rudely drowning out the response, leaving Dave clinging on to every subsequent word for clues.

Leena sipped her cappuccino. 'What's his body like? What did it feel like to put your hands all over him? Did you squeeze his bum? Was it firm? I bet it was. All that gym training he does . . .'

'Leena!' Naina paused. 'He may have a lovely body, but who cares when he treats you like shit. You know what happened? I went round and there was already some slag there.'

'You're joking, and you still went on your knees?' There was nothing better than finding out your best mate was morally retarded; she couldn't wait to discuss this with Kate.

'Noooo, that was after, after I ran out of the flat. Don't you listen?'

Naina explained everything again. Twice. And Dave still didn't manage to hear whether he matched up or not. He was tempted to shout over, 'Just tell me, am I huge or what?' but he didn't want to blow his cover.

Dave was highly amused; he couldn't believe that Naina and Leena could talk about him for so long. He was slightly disappointed when the subject changed as he especially wanted to find out why Hannibal Lecter had more sensitivity than himself, and he was on tenterhooks wanting to know whether Leena was going to buy the beaded black DKNY handbag or the lilac sequinned DKNY handbag. After all, the lilac one did go extremely well with her Lello Bacio sandals, but on other hand the black one matched her new black Punjabi Textile Indian suit . . . God, women talked so much shit. And then . . .

'I still can't believe I'm going to marry Ashok. He's

just not my type, if I'm allowed a type.' Naina stretched her arms back, just missing Dave's head. 'He's my parents' type for God's sake. I'll probably end up stabbing him on our wedding night.'

Dave was confused. Naina's husband-to-be was named after a perfume. ASH-cock with a French dialect. Weird. For an infinitesimally small moment he was sort of jealous. Why couldn't they name a perfume after him? Then he remembered *Cool Water Davidoff* and he smiled. It was more macho being named after an aftershave. ASH-cock sounded like a poof.

There was an interlude of silence for a few minutes while Leena exited to the Ladies. Naina stared at the crackling fire, watching the flames turn and twist in their own melody of orange and red, the fire folding into itself like molten cake mix, and for precious moments she forgot all her problems, all her lists of worries.

Leena returned, saw the back of Dave's cowering head, but registered nothing. 'Naina,' she said quietly, sitting down. 'I take it you're still intact for Ashok?'

'I am, but I nearly wasn't this morning. I was that close, but I came to my senses. Good job really, because Dave's such a pig.'

'A gorgeous pig though, hey?'

They both laughed.

'La la la do do do doobie do, la la la do do do doobie'. Dave frantically turned his mobile off, but it was too late. Naina knew that annoying tune anywhere, and it was coming from just behind her. She stood up and stared at Dave open-mouthed, stunned.

'Hello, Naina. How are you?' Dave enquired. 'Hello, Leena, looking lovely as ever. What have you stolen today?'

Leena sprang up, joining Naina in her mini symphony of astonishment.

'Did you hear it all? Were you listening? And don't you dare lie to me.' The questions by Naina were coated in prickly rose thorns; her eyes swallowed Dave's smug look and spat it out like hot acid.

'Just tell me, was it big? Was I big? I need to know, I'm dying here, Naina,' he asked, ignoring her scorn.

Leena laughed.

'You want to know how big you are?' There was authority in Naina's voice, almost as though she were dealing with a delinquent child. She shouted in disbelief, 'You want to know how big your willy is?' She pointed her long fingernail directly at Dave's now worried face.

Suddenly the world's problems could wait. Everybody wanted to know how big Dave's willy was. Everyone. Including the waitresses who Dave had been so rude to over the years and including a few of the businessmen that Dave had threatened if they didn't give him their parking space.

'Your willy was tiny!' she thumped out. 'And that is the truth, isn't it, little boy?'

Giggles. Lots of them. Naina wasn't laughing though.

Dave stood up. 'Right, you've had your say, now mine. Listen to this everyone, like you're pretending you're not, you nosy wannabes.' Dave looked round at all of them, not even slightly embarrassed. 'Ask her what she spent the twenty-five quid on, for giving me a blow job this morning.' And he smiled at her. '*Et Tu Brute!*'

Almost severe silence, except for the swishing of the dishwasher and one man who could be heard on his mobile: 'Ring back later, this is excellent, there's an argument going on here. Cancel my next appointment!'

An apt quote from a film would be 'Time to die' from *Bladerunner*. Naina had never been so humiliated in her life; her face burned hot as embers. Like a mass of pigeons waiting for their next crust of bread, the Florelli's crowd perched on the edge of their seats, almost urging Naina to cut him down with her next comment.

Naina collected her bag, then stepped towards Dave. He waited for the slap. But instead she whispered in his ear, 'Hope you catch VD, you bastard.' And grabbing Leena by the arm, they both subjected Dave to a 'witch' stare, as they left the stunned coffee shop.

Dave put his feet up, squeaking his Nikes. Women were so touchy, it was like they were on one massive period. Those customers lacking in coffee shop etiquette carried on staring, while the rest returned to their newspapers, laptops and pretence. Stress was the biggest killer of them all, so Dave lit a fag to calm himself down. There had been a moment just then, he thought, a very sexy moment, when Naina passed beyond normal anger and entered some sort of psycho mode. What a turn-on. Such rage, such pent-up frustration. If she could just channel that energy into something constructive, like sex, then they would both benefit immensely.

Amongst the litter of widened pupils still centred on
Dave, were those of a round-faced man with skin as
coarse as leather, staring from the bar stool. He
typified Dave's pet hate in people – he was
judgemental. A wanker of sorts. He spoke through his
nose, looked down at you through his nose and
pretended he didn't even pick his nose. Dave had tried
chatting to him a few times, only to have the man
lower his *Times*, sneer through his pores, and almost
wave him away with a gesture of his eyes 'go away,
commoner, shoo shoo'. And then everything changed
when he saw Dave's forty-grand BMW; he bought
Dave a coffee, he brought out his relic of a smile and
tried to fuel up some friendly banter to which Dave
replied simply: 'Fuck off.'

And still the man stared. Possibly thinking he had
been right about Dave the first time and the man was
a 'commoner'; rich, maybe, but still common,
someone who hadn't been born with a silver spoon in
his mouth.

The man in the jade suit, the one who had been
eyeing Naina earlier, walked over to Dave, sat himself
down opposite and coughed. Dave glanced up.

'You know, I think the way you treated her was
disgusting. There was no need for that,' he stated.

'And you are?' enquired Dave, blowing fag smoke
in the air.

'I'm Peter Duckworth. I just think you treated her a
little unfairly.' He paused. 'She was crying earlier,
before you walked in, she seemed really upset.'

It was like a bolt from a crossbow. For some reason
the thought of Naina crying didn't amuse Dave like it
normally would when a woman shed tears. In fact, it

felt wrong. And the joke that seemed so hilarious at the time – talking of blow jobs in front of thirty people – well, it wasn't so funny now. It was cruel and he knew it. Sometimes he forgot that Naina wasn't one of his male friends, where embarrassing each other was the key to a lasting friendship. Naina was the only woman friend he had ever had, his closest friend (if he admitted it to himself) and now he had lost her. He jolly well knew there had been something bothering her this morning, but all he could think about was getting in her knickers and taking advantage. And all just for sex, that was about the size of it. Sex.

He picked up his mobile and keys and left, leaving a fiver and a grateful look to Peter Duckworth. He had to think: what would Danny Zuko do for Sandy? How would he make things right again? Dave didn't have a Rydell letter-sweater, he couldn't take Naina for a spin down Thunder Road, but he could buy her flowers. One hundred pounds' worth should do it.

He sauntered thirty yards up the road and entered Buds and Vases florist shop. Why not call it Man Done Wrong shop, he thought, as he viewed the vast selection of bright tulips, dafs, roses and all those other strange flowery poncy things. And what the hell were cuddly toys, silver keys and baskets doing here? And then he saw her, hiding behind a green bushy thing: long champagne-blonde hair accentuating her leafy-green eyes. A smile so sweet, with teeth so white you needed factor 10 sunscreen, and a pair of breasts that he couldn't have hand-picked better himself. A Goddess. His Dave smile appeared and he was pleased to note that even in the foliage it worked a treat, because ten minutes later he left the shop with 'the goddess's phone number, two free sachets of plant food and a bag of pot-pourri. He had forgotten the flowers.

Chapter Eight

Naina's throat was as dry as Tutankhamun's bones. She'd been slagging off Dave that much with Leena. Non-stop for four hours.

She jiggled the front-door key and let herself in. Smells of garlic, ginger and onions bathed in her nose. Hindi music twanged and twinged from the living room, and upstairs Marilyn Manson rasped and screamed from the bedroom she and Sonia shared.

Her eyes shied away from the framed oil painting of Guru Nanak glaring out from the canvas, hanging above the radiator. It was just a painting, but it looked almost real enough for his arms to reach out and grab her, reminding her of her Indian duties. Sucking on a white man's lollipop did not qualify.

In the living room, Mum sat with her slippered feet on the sofa, in her mauve sari, knitting a pale blue jumper. Hands quicker than the eye producing row after row of complicated knit-work. Dad in his reading glasses wandered the *Financial Times*, his blue turban sitting next to him on the sofa like his best friend. They both gazed up as Naina entered.

'I don't want dinner, I'm going out,' Naina announced, in Punjabi.

'But –' Mum straightened up in her seat '– I made karelas, you love them.'

Naina stared for a breath. 'I'll microwave them for breakfast. Okay?'

Dad prodded his glasses up his Roman nose and viewed Naina with his normal suspicion. 'You make sure you don't go out with boys, you make sure you don't talk to them.' His eyes flicked sideways to Mum. 'Microwave karelas?' Then back to Naina. 'They'll bloody explode!'

'When are you going to learn how to cook for Ashok? They expect you to be able to cook—'

Naina interrupted her mum, 'Next week, promise. I'll learn how to make dhal.'

As Naina walked out she heard her dad say to Mum, 'She's got to learn more than dhal, they can't live on just dhal, they'll get the runs.' They both laughed.

Mum and Dad came from India – their motherland – in the sixties. They herded up their belongings, took a deep breath and plunged right in, hoping for the best, not knowing quite what to expect. Some things they liked: the fresh air, open space, freedom. Some things they hated: the weather, no family and skinheads. But they muddled through and realized that bringing up the children in England would give them a good education and the opportunity for a richer life, so they stayed. But in their hearts they didn't feel welcome. They felt more like visitors, guests, that at any time they could be booted out. Dad would say, 'We'll never quite fit in. You do know that, don't you?' and four sets of children's questioning eyes would all stare to Mum and Dad hoping Mum and Dad were wrong. Parents can be wrong, can't they?

Naina climbed the stairs two by two, opened the bedroom door, walked to Sonia's bed and pulled back the red duvet to find her sister admiring her glow-in-the-dark *X-Files* T-shirt. She then turned down the music a notch.

'Naina, look what I made,' said Sonia, now standing and pointing to the thing hanging round her neck: a necklace consisting entirely of chicken wishbones tied together with catgut and painted glossy black.

'It's lovely Sonia. You're wasted.'

'Ta.'

The medium-sized square bedroom was heaven and hell. Sonia's side was painted white with red handprints and strange hieroglyphics in black. Each handprint had a spear piercing the palm and out of each wound burst forth the lyrics of Marilyn Manson songs. Sonia was fifteen now; a few years ago, she had come home with a letter from the headmaster explaining that Sonia's behaviour was not normal for a healthy ten-year-old girl and that she frightened all the other kids with her strange imagination. Dad had written back saying that the headmaster was only picking on poor Sonia because England lost to India in the cricket.

Naina's side of the bedroom was overly pink on the

Chapatti or Chips?

walls with cubes of various sizes scattered randomly and painted in light red and dark pink to give them a 3D effect. The idea was pinched from *Changing Rooms*. Her pine wardrobe, jam-packed with clothes, was colour coordinated. Summer wear, winter wear. Dark clothes and light. Shoes of all descriptions filled the space on the bottom. Bags, scarves, gloves, and other accessories were on the top shelf. This was one huge wardrobe. Huuuge and well organized.

'Where're you going?' Sonia asked, watching Naina holding up her little blue flimsy dress.

'Pub, with Leena and Kate. I'm going to get totally slaughtered.'

'Keep your legs crossed, unlike Kate.' Sonia giggled.

Naina gathered up her inventory of bottles, potions, bath salts and sachets, and walked into the bathroom. She turned the fat golden taps, locked the door, and soon became lost in steam. Two hours to get ready. Just enough time to condition her hair, moisturize her skin, wax her legs, pluck her eyebrows, dry her hair, and apply her make-up and nail varnish. Her longest record was five hours to get ready. All that just for a stinky McDonald's. The hot water ebbed up and down the bath as she used a big foot sponge to wash down her skinny legs, and every now and again she bit into the orange sponge, sucking upon the water and angrily spitting it out in memory of Dave. She wouldn't be showing her face in Florelli's again. Dave had made damn sure of that. Little boy! She wished he really was a 'little boy', then she could say it with conviction.

Naina was stunning in her little blue flimsy dress. High-heeled strappy sandals showed off her toned slim legs in all their elegance, emphasizing her tiny waist and hips. Her hair was piled high, leaving a few curls dangling. She was a babe and she was ready, finally.

A loud jarring knock on the front door.

'That'll be Kate.' Naina grabbed her long black going-out coat. 'See ya later, Sonia. I'll try and be quiet when I come in.'

'Ta,' mumbled Sonia.

Naina's going-out coat was a godsend, keeping her skimpy dresses well hidden from her parents' eyes. Not that her parents were the strictest of Indians – some made their daughters keep to shalwar kameez and trousers, and some never even let their daughters out at all – but if they could see what Naina wore sometimes, she'd be housebound until marriage.

She walked slowly down the stairs, careful not to break her neck on the heels, popped her head in to say 'goodbye' to her parents, and answered the front door.

'Go away,' she snapped, annoyed.

'You look gorgeous. Where're you off to?'

Naina jumped out through the door, and closed it quickly behind her. 'Dave, I'm not in the mood.' Each word was backed up by a snarling gesture from her turned-up mouth: rabid.

The porch light cast two long shadows halfway down the path, until it blended with its relative – the night. The air, laced with winter chill, buckled the lips and goosed the flesh, leaving those who had little sense and dressed in just a tight white Armani T-shirt to show off the biceps, shivering. Dave.

'Look, Naina, I'm really sorry. I've been a right prat.' He looked her up and down. 'Can you believe those earwiggers listening in to our private conversation? Fucking cheek.'

'Dave, I'm warning you, if you don't get off my drive right now, I'm going to smash your car up with that brick.' She pointed to the brick in question, to consolidate her threat.

He picked up the brick lying innocently near his Nike and handed it to her. 'Go on, I deserve it.' He smiled.

Naina held the weighty slab, and stared at the tempting BMW parked rudely half on their drive and half on Dad's lawn. She walked up to the car, brick raised in a threatening posture. What was she doing holding up a brick? She had to get him out of here, and fast. Behind the confines of the closed living-room curtains were her strict parents, and if they were to spot Dave, all hell would break loose.

'Throw it, Naina, throw it hard,' Kate remarked, walking up the path.

Dave glanced over his shoulder to see bitch Kate arrive. For such a bitch, she looked pretty sexy. Shame. Even in the pitch black her pink false-fur coat lit up the entire driveway like a mountain of fairground candyfloss.

Kate stood next to Naina, planting her chunky black boots on the concrete, and kissed her cheek. 'Tell me pig's not coming with us.'

'No chance,' Naina replied, tossing down the brick to one side of a quickly moving Nike.

'Kate, you look nice. Are you ill?' Dave enquired, sparking up a fag.

'Not really, little boy,' she replied, laughing, and pinched her thumb and forefinger together.

Dave smiled, highly amusing. It would be so easy to retaliate: he could even hear his inner voice heckling him to do it, 'take the mickey out of Kate's coat.' But he was here to apologize to Naina and that's what he would do.

Dave grabbed Naina by the hand, gently pulling her to one side, away from bitch Kate's radar ears and lip-reading mouth. 'Naina, I'm really truly honestly sorry, I screwed up big time. I don't want to lose you as a mate, it was only a joke.'

'Dave, I don't think you realize that I really hate you at the moment, but—'

He kissed her on the lips. 'Thanks, I knew you would understand. I knew you'd turn the other cheek.' He wondered what colour knickers she was wearing – he guessed, skimpy lacy racy red – just as he always wondered – rain, sleet or snow, club, pub or funeral, whenever he faced a beautiful woman, he wondered about her particular mode of 'fanny transport'.

Naina's face dropped, and before she could pick it back up again it was too late. Kiran, her brother, who had just seen Dave kissing her, walked up the short path, stern and Indian brotherly.

'Whose car's that?' he demanded.

Dave invested in a few moments' thought. Whoever this bloke was, he seemed jealous of his car. 'Mine, 0 to 60 in—'

'You're in our drive. And *who* are you?' Kiran asked, eyeing Dave inhospitably.

Dave opened his mouth to be extra rude (and his mouth could be very rude, it was like a dank dungeon of insults, each one chained up until a moment just like this arrived), but before he could say anything,

Kate butted in, grabbed Dave's muscular arm, dropped a smoochy kiss on his lips and said, 'He's my little boyfriend, Kiran. And don't worry, he's nothing to do with Naina, she's still respectable. I'm the slut here – in your eyes.'

Kiran humphed, gave Naina a look of 'I'll speak to you later' and told Dave to move his car, he wanted to park his Beetle. Dave sniggered. Pushed aside by a Beetle.

Kiran's off-white Beetle chugged and spluttered onto the driveway like a slow cue ball sending off Kate's purple-blue Corsa one way and Dave's black BMW the other. Dave had hit 85 m.p.h. before he reached the end of the short road away from Naina's house in Shenley and away from the howling woods that backed on to it. Once when stopped for speeding by a policeman, in a desperate attempt to fool PC Randel, he had quickly spat his Orbit chewing gum on to his hand and slapped it on his Nike trainer, wound down the window and said, 'Thank God you caught me up in time, officer, my trainer was stuck to the accelerator pedal, look.' He received points and a fine. The fine was slightly more than expected for a mild offence, possibly for the added word of 'Tosser' as the policeman wrote down his details.

'I am a brick, I am a wall,' thought Dave, listening to a CD, as his car veered up into sixth gear. A cocoon of warmth, smells of leather and Davidoff aftershave. 'And my brick cannot crumble.' The car skidded round a tight corner, round another, then into the car park of his gym. 'And my wall is hard as diamond.' He cranked up the handbrake, switched off the engine, then lit up a fag.

The illuminated sign of Dumbbells cast an eerie blue glow, and the echoing sounds of pumping iron clicking and clanging together inside could be heard through the thick walls like a late-shift chain gang. Dave popped in a Travis CD and reclined the seat. It had been a strange day: nonsensical. Strange how Naina had got engaged but obviously wasn't happy about it. Strange that she had given him a blow job. Strange she told thieving Leena that Ashok was not her type; if she was allowed a type, she'd said, he was her parents' type. Strange how Naina remained 'intack' for Ashok – whatever that meant. And even stranger when bitch Kate kissed him, pretending she was his girlfriend in front of Naina's brother. Dave *was* confused. He blew out a smoke ring which tickled the windscreen, then dispersed. And why had Naina been crying? Why hadn't he just listened to her that morning instead of listening to his dick? And why had Naina never before mentioned that her boyfriend was called Ashok? She had told him that he was called James King or, as she sometimes said, 'Jimmy K', and he was a top architect. Women! He'd never understand them. Drama queens, that's what they were. They've got vibrators, what more do they want?

He looked to the sign saying: Dumbbells Gym, and remembered the day, three years ago, when he'd watched the workman climb the metal stepladder and drill those twenty-four bolts into the concrete blocks. To Dave it didn't read 'Dumbbells Gym', it read 'Fuck you, Dad.' Or rather, 'Fuck you, Stepdad.' Maybe not the nicest, most polite honour to label on your replacement father, but things had never been right between them from day one. And Dave could still remember day one like it was yesterday, the day his new dad replaced his old. A bad day.

He'd been nearly six. Mum in her newly dyed blonde hair had been frantically cleaning the three-bedroom council house for a month. She was wearing a red and blue cotton dress. Dead pretty she looked. The happiest he had seen her for ages. Then *he* walked in. Large brown suitcase in one hand and a bunch of flowers in the other. Sideburns, flares, Brylcreem and Brut – eat your heart out, Starsky. Mum kissed him on the mouth and Dave knew right then that Starsky was his new father. Dave stood there, insignificant, in his white oversized karate suit. He tied up his green belt tight, and wondered how many faraway places Starsky had been to, to make his suitcase so tatty. When Mum disappeared for a few moments into the kitchen to fetch him a pre-chilled lager, Starsky bent all the way down, took hold of Dave's ear and spoke quietly into it with hot alcohol breath: 'You will never be my fucking son, get it? You little twerp,' and he twisted the ear and stood back up. When Mum returned, he said, 'Wendy, what did you say your boy was called again?' 'David,' she replied, and Starsky kissed Dave on the cheek and remarked, 'Handsome little blighter, ain't he?'

Still Dave stared at the luminous sign.

Chapter Nine

Whisky was like a skeleton key unlocking all of Kate's inhibitions. Outside the Squirrel, sitting in the Corsa, she passed round the 500 ml bottle and Naina and Leena both took a swig, letting the fiery tipple scrape down their throats. Eyes squinting, mouths contorting, bodies quivering. The taste was rank, but the effect was bliss. The perfect aperitif to an evening of girlie talk. And the three girls descended out of the car, giggling already, and walked hand-in-hand to the pub entrance.

Leena, dressed in stolen designer wear of indigo satin trousers, black cropped top and trainers (out of habit, for her quick get-away), pushed open the pub door, to the sound of Blondie's 'Tide is High'. A group of filthy-clothed builders ogled, as the three made their way to a table well away from their gawping eyes; and the girls sat themselves down on the wooden chairs.

'Let's just face it, we all look gorgeous,' said Kate, provoking their laughter. She pulled out her Marlboros and handed Leena one. 'Are you sure you don't want one, Naina? You're going to die from our smoke anyway.'

Naina declined; she'd never had a fag in her life – joints excluded – and she was going to stick to it. Kate had always been going on about how she was going to quit when her hair started to go wiry but, as things stood, that would never happen; Kate's blonde bob always looked glossy and healthy and was accounted for by the diet of liquidized avocados that she weekly massaged into her scalp.

Naina, desperate for alcohol, stood up. 'I'll get the drinks; usual?'

They nodded and she made her way across the wooden floor to the bar, side-stepping the small clusters of people just standing like door wedges with their pints, grins and nodding heads. MTV played Moby on all hanging screens, and his little head bobbed and weaved about the stage as he picked up every single instrument he could find. Such energy. As Naina reached the shore of the counter – Nirvana – her name rang out from not too far away.

'Naina, Naina, over here!'

It was Froggy. Slowly she walked over to their rowdy table, annoyed that she hadn't managed to get a drink. 'Hi,' she said, with a weak smile.

'OOzing.'

'OOzing.'

'OOzing.'

'OOzing.'

'OOzing.'

107

Five of Dave's mates, three girlfriends, but thank God, no Dave.

'I wish you lot would just grow up,' moaned Sandra. 'Hi, Naina, how are you?' she asked, squirming in her seat like a viper, irritated by Naina's good choice of slag rags.

A chair was kicked across by Matt for her to sit on. 'Sit down, Naina; who're you with?'

Naina forced a smile at Sandra, sat down, and looked at the drinks on the table, mesmerized by them, so desperate was she for some alcohol. 'Kate and Leena, they're over there, can't be long.'

'Bring 'em over,' suggested Froggy. 'The more the merrier.'

'Yeah, bring them over. Bring some beauty into my life,' Jingle dreamed.

'Yeah, Jingle, like they'd be interested in you, you ugly twat,' said Froggy, then laughed, ducking from the beer mat.

Naina stood up. 'I'd better get back, I'll see you later.'

'Hang on, I'll come with you.' Sandra picked up her purse. 'Drinks anyone?'

Stupid question. Sandra and Naina dug their way to the bar and waited in the bustling queue. Moby was still strutting his stuff; everyone was still shouting; so the music goes up, so the shouting goes up and in the end the pub is just one massive decibel.

Sandra spoke clearly though, right in Naina's ear, with a sting. 'Sit on the fence too long, Naina, and you'll get splinters in your crotch. You either like Dave or you like your boyfriend, you can't have both!'

Chapatti or Chips?

Naina turned to Sandra. 'Well, Sandra, putting that it's none of your fucking business aside for a moment, I don't particularly want Dave. You never know what slags he's been with, do you, Sandra?'

Sandra's face was taut, suppressed with rage. 'Just as well, let's face it, he's only after you for a cheap shag.' She ordered her drinks, then turned back to Naina. 'Anyway, he's popping in later for a pint, I'm sure you'll want to pop over yourself to prick-tease him for a second.' And Sandra left before Naina could even reply, giving her a bitchy smile that seemed designed perfectly for her bitchy face.

Naina could just imagine Dave now, nearly bashing the pub door down as he entered, basking in a smile as wide as Southend pier – before the fire – clocking all the pretty women, working out which ones he would be shagging in the next few months and then sitting down with his mates, screaming at the top of his lungs, 'OOzing' and insulting as many of them as he could before he fell in a drunken heap. What an evening to look forward to! She'd avoid him at all costs. She was here to get pissed and drown her sorrows over Ashok, not for Dave to stand on a pub stool, hush down his audience and shout out how Naina had gobbled him off this morning.

Naina returned with three pints of Stella, three doubles of vodka and orange, three Bacardi Breezers, two aching arms, and a pissed-off look that cracked up Kate.

'What now?' she asked, laughing with Leena.

'That pig's coming. I'm going to blank him. I just can't seem to get rid of him today,' replied Naina, tucking herself in under the table.

'Who? Little boy?' More laughter.

The noise in the pub was gathering momentum, trying to keep up with the alcohol consumption. The gangway separating the two sides of the pub now swelled with people, intermixed with small trains of two or three women weaving through, tunnelling their way to the Ladies for a top-up and an empty-out. Leena, nearly drunk already, picked up her Streamers bag and slung it on the table.

'Avon calling,' she sang and poured out the items from the list of make-up Kate had ordered.

Kate rummaged through the pile. 'But where's the mascara, Leena?'

Leena considered herself a pro; leaving out an item was a sackable offence. 'Sorry, Kate, I'll nick you two tomorrow.'

'Cheers, Leen.'

Naina watched them, the alcohol producing emotions she didn't want to feel right now. She'd been trying to drown her sorrows away, but they'd popped back up with little life jackets on. She'd often thought of what would happen on her wedding night. Once all the guests had gone, once all the laughter had died down, when all the camcorder batteries had run out, and day had turned to night, she'd be left with a stranger, standing in his bedroom, alone with him. Scared. Knowing that his hands would soon be touching her. When he stepped towards her to unravel the red and gold wedding sari, she would have to let him. She would have to let him undress her and she would have to give her body away to him. Her wedding day was a day she dreaded.

She couldn't keep the tears in any longer.

'I hate being Indian,' she babbled, while an unsteady Leena put her arm round her and patted her back, noting that Naina had drunk nearly all their drinks. Big teardrops lingered then fell on to Naina's blue dress, blotting and spreading. Laughter in the background from strangers, music from the loud speakers drumming and vibrating, chitter-chatter from a hundred voices and drink orders yelled from one end to the other. All that. And still not enough to drown out, 'OOzing' Dave had arrived, followed by five more loud 'OOzings'.

Naina's stomach felt like someone was churning up eggs with a blender and her heart played Beethoven's 9th. Kate heaved up her lungs and shouted out 'Little boy!' and fell back on her chair laughing, joined by Leena, then Naina.

But while Naina was laughing on the outside, her insides were crumbling; western and eastern ideas battling against one another. It was as though she was torn in the middle. Parents, tradition and culture on one side. Liberty, love and lust on the other. She wished she could talk to her mum, she wished she was closer to her mum, but Indian girls never get too close to their mums, because there are certain things that 'you just don't talk about', like fear of arranged marriage, fear of that first night, fear that he might turn out to be a bastard; and they certainly don't talk about love and lust. Oh yeah, you just don't go round telling them that you've got the hots for a white, womanizing pig.

Kate stood up to see if her voice had travelled and quickly sat back down again. 'You'll never guess what, Naina, he's with another woman!'

Naina stood up, then down as quickly. 'She's sickly gorgeous.'

Leena stood up, then down. 'Jeez, where's he find them? They're always so pretty.'

The three immediately turned bitter and sour, and started slagging off the woman.

Dave sat down. 'I'd like you all to meet Danielle.' She was soon introduced to the table.

The story of how he'd met her was simple: she worked on the Clinique cosmetic counter for House of Fraser. He walked up, noted her name-tag and said, 'Danielle, can I ask permission to think about you tonight, please?' She fell for it, she took his number, and it was she who was thinking about him that night; he'd forgotten all about her.

She'd already been forewarned by Dave that his mates made up the most horrendously outrageous stories about him and not to take anything seriously. She sat in close to Dave, a little nervous, a little shy. (This will teach you, Dave thought, I wanted sex, but oh no, you wanted to meet my mates.)

'You're a pretty little thing,' admired Jingle.

Dave shot him a look. He knew things about Jingle. Disgusting things.

'Are you married?' asked Froggy, his mousy hair glistening with gel like dew on grass, and his wide green eyes centred on Danielle.

'No.' She looked at Dave, who shrugged.

'It's just that the divorce rate in this town seems to be rising, that's all.' Hysterics from Froggy and a few other giggles. Then, 'Sorry, it's the drink talking.'

'Maybe you've had enough, Froggy, hey?' Dave

said, raising his eyebrows for him to stop whatever he had in mind.

Froggy ignored the look. 'I see you're not drinking, Dave. Feeling lucky tonight?'

'Ignore him, Danielle, he's just a waste of space,' shrugged Dave, lighting up a fag.

Dave viewed the table: his mates. His five Hillthorpe School buddies. In his heart, one day, he knew all this would be gone – you never see six buddy biddies together (unless they're senile, lost in Blackpool). So what would break them up? he wondered. In a way, they were almost like family, although if anyone ever dared say there was any resemblance between Dave and Jingle, they would need a dentist pretty quickly; they'd spent holidays abroad together, leaned on each other, had Christmas together, shared the same police cell. Just like a happy family.

The pub was awash with noise. Heaving with people. Discussions of footy, girls, private parts, boasts, promises, and lies. A whole swathe of chitter-chatter being spurred on by the volume of alcohol being consumed. A semi-conscious person could be seen dragging a heavy wooden chair across the floor, apologizing to everyone in the way, apologizing to chairs. Struggling with the directions, struggling with the balance and struggling with the giggles.

Naina arrived at the table occupied by ten people. Seven seemed joyfully pleased to see her. One appeared gutted – Sandra; one seemed indifferent – Danielle; and Dave, Dave was in shock. Naina pushed her chair in between Froggy and Philippa, sitting directly opposite Dave. She was plastered.

Incoherent noises came out of Naina's mouth, until she finally managed to pronounce a sentence. 'See that one there.' She pointed at Dave.

This has to be good, thought Froggy. Please let this be the night that Dave falls down, thought Matt. Don't forget the next bit, *please*, Naina, thought Andy. I think I love you, Naina, thought Jingle. Make him cry, thought Pete. She hasn't got it in her, thought Dave.

Naina's arm was swaying and Froggy helped her point in the right direction before she continued. 'See him, that good-looking pig, see him. I caught him with a naked married woman this morning. An hour after I'd already given him all a man could possibly need. One woman a day is just not enough for some men.'

Like death, the table was silent. But for one second only. Then it was too much: they were crying with fits of laughter, at Dave's expense. Danielle, white as talc, could only look for reassurance from Dave's eyes. But it was not there. With his head nestled on Diane's shoulder, he was laughing with the rest of them. Danielle picked her bag up and left the pub on her own – unnoticed.

Naina continued in between giggles, rolling her head round to face Sandra. 'And *you*. I know you hate me. It's mutual, Sandy. Your little secret's safe with me. Never fear, Naina's here. Ain't that right, big-ears Dave? I won't . . .'

Dave stood up, suddenly not laughing, friendships were at stake here, good ones. Telling Naina of his betrayal of Froggy over Sandra had obviously not been such a good move and Dave's heart, the one that was supposed to beat at 100,000 beats per day, suddenly felt like all his beats had just come at once, driving his worried blood round his veins like an outraged Ebola virus. 'Come on, Naina, let's go. I'll take you home.'

'I'm not going with you, I hate you, Dave. Remember?'

A bewildered table watched with a mixture of curiosity and apprehension. Sandra was still hanging on to Naina's last words. Froggy didn't understand. Matt had privately sussed. Jingle still loved Naina. And Dave, he took hold of Naina's hand, pulled her gently from her chair, and they both walked away from the table that was now scorched with one massive question mark.

Chapter Ten

Never is it so easy to change worlds as when you walk outside a pub on a cold winter's night. From crowds to solitude, light to dark, chitter to teeth chatter.

Dave and Naina crunched across the pub car park in silence; Naina was sulking at being taken away from her party. It was like a fridge out there, aching the bones, freezing the toes, and reddening the cheeks.

Inside the car it was invitingly warm and the engine purred to life, lighting up the dashboard and waking up the stereo. Dave switched the CD off, lit up a fag, and looked at Naina. Never had he seen her this way before. Never had he seen her this drunk. And he wondered. He wondered if he was to blame, he wondered if he had lost her – lost his best mate. He put his arm round her.

'Naina, I know you hate me, but tell me what's wrong.'

Naina felt the tears drop before she even knew she was crying. Her emotions, her feelings, her common sense, all kaput. 'I don't want to marry him, but I've got to.'

Getting married was stupid enough, Dave thought, but getting married when you didn't want to was utter madness. He wiped away her tears with a man-sized tissue. The box was nearly empty, a fact that was duly noted by Dave. 'Come on, why have you got to marry him?'

The leather seat heaters were definitely worth the extra money. Naina had once argued with Dave for a full hour over the waste of money spent on in-car seat heaters. But she appreciated them now as she grabbed another tissue from the box and gave a hearty blow. 'Because I'm fucking Indian, and that's what we do. I think I'm going to be sick.'

Naina had never seen Dave move so quickly, he was round her side of the car before the end of the word 'sick'. A few moments outside, a few dribbles, a few peas and carrots, and an awful amount of liquid, and she felt a little better. It didn't matter how classy, posh or well brought up you were, there was no way of looking elegant when puking. The Queen might well rest on her satin kneepad, hold on to her gold-rimmed toilet, but when it came to the crunch, even she must retch like a wild animal. And then: 'One puked.'

Naina sat back in the car and laughed.

'What?' Dave queried.

'I hope I didn't wreck it for you and that . . . that bitch.'

'Danielle? No, she was too clingy for my liking.

117

She was getting overly possessive. She even asked me my surname, can you believe her?' Dave shook his head. 'So, you were saying about not wanting to marry this guy, ASH-cock?'

Naina rolled the perforated white tissue round her fingers. 'Can't we talk about this some other time? And his name is Ashok.'

'Okay. Why don't you come round to my place for a few hours to sober up? I don't think you'll want your parents seeing you like this.'

In an affectionate way, Dave liked Naina's parents. Never having met them, he'd only gleaned a picture from the crusts she sometimes threw his way: a sparkle in her eyes when she spoke of her mum and her little foibles, a snigger and a shrug when she told of Dad's tantrums if the chapatties weren't absolutely round, and she would raise her eyes to the roof and flutter those long lashes when she told of the strictness that followed them round the house like a rule book on legs.

But Naina's rules were coated in love, cotton wool, for her own protection. And Dave's rules, well, where do you start?

He hated his parents. A stepdad who became a tyrant and a mother who watched; between them both they had ripped his emotions up and kicked the child right out of him – literally. A favourite trick of his stepdad was to come to Dave's bedroom and declare that in a few days' time he was going to be punished for something. Dave would ask for what, and his stepdad would laugh and say: 'I haven't decided yet.' Belts, sticks, fists, anything that ended in an 's' really, except 'happiness'. It could be that his shoes weren't lined up straight, or the cereal box flap wasn't securely shut, or the weather, but most of all it was because Dave looked the spitting image of his real dad. Mum couldn't bear to look at him, despised the little things he did that reminded her of the man who had one day packed his bags and taken off, leaving her to bring up his kid alone. The same kid that grew up and talked about his past to no one. Naina had asked him a few times about his parents, only for him to reply, 'You look gorgeous, Naina, fancy a shag?'

The headlights blinked on, and the car slowly drove out of the pub car park and on to the main road in Midsummer Boulevard, the alloy wheels catching the streetlamps' reflections as it cruised down the V7 dual carriageway. Naina stared out through the side window, watching the bedroom lights in people's houses rush past. Cosy, warm, and safe.

Dave played thought solitaire, leaping one idea over the other, trying to disregard the junk. An unshakeable image began to appear in his mind. Naina in a beautiful white wedding dress being dragged to the church by a few weighty henchman, and forced to take the vows by the demon Ashok. The car jerked up a side road taking a short cut to the flats. Then a jarring thought: maybe she was pregnant and her parents were forcing the issue of marriage. Christ. She shouldn't be drinking like that when she was due any minute. Or, maybe – and these thoughts were like movements in water: slow, deliberate and awkward – maybe it was just that old cherry, blackmail. Maybe Ashok was blackmailing her. Maybe once she had been a prostitute and Ashok had found out – that was it! James King – Jimmy K, was the pimp, and Naina was an old pro. It all made sense now. He could see where she was coming from, poor poor lass. The car pulled into Stone Valley car park. He looked across to Naina. Her head was rocking, clutching at sleep briefly, then awaking again. Pissed and peaceful. An Indian beauty. An Indian . . . hang on. It might have been dark outside, but inside Dave's head it was sunrise; warming daylight. He'd remembered something she had once said. They were talking about Bollywood movies. Naina had laughed and said, 'They're all the same, boy meets girl, falls in love, yeah right, and they live happily ever after. They're so false, I hate them!' Dave had replied, 'But you're into all this love shit, aren't you?' Dave was confused back then, but not now; it was making a lot of sense.

Inside the flat, Naina removed her thick coat, threw it on the floor and noticed that the cleaner had been. Immaculate. She clomped over to the sofa in her high heels and huddled into the huge blue cushion, waiting for Dave to light the open fire.

With a twist of newspaper, four fire-lighters and a generous spray of barbecue liquid – guaranteed to light first time – whoosh; the crackling heat soon invaded the large living room, melting away any cold edges that the central heating hadn't quite reached. Dave handed her a chunky, fleecy white skiing jumper and a glass of water to sip. She sat there, still drunk, watching him go through his routine: closing the curtains, dimming the lights, kicking his Nikes off, lighting a fag and listening to his messages.

'You bastard, Dave.' A woman's angry voice.

'Dave, only Steve. Nearly run out of banana protein powder. See ya tomorrow.'

'Pick up the phone, you lazy git.' A bloke's voice.

'Dave, it's Sara. I don't know if you remember me, you gave me your number about a week ago. Anyway, can you ring me? It's 4676382.'

'Dave, Frog, need to speak to you pronto. I tried your mobile but it was off.' Froggy's flat voice. 'Call me any time, however late.'

Naina felt the guilt cascading through her. 'Dave, I didn't mean to say that to Sandra, I feel awful. D'you think he knows?'

Dave sat close to her on the sofa. 'No use worrying about it now, maybe he deserves to know what she's like, and what an absolute bastard I am.'

Naina looked at him through fuzzy eyes. 'Really?'

'No, don't be daft, I'm shitting myself. He's my best mate. I've done such a shitty thing. This is definitely a no no in all our books; never dip your wick in anyone else's candy pot.' He leaned back and put his hands behind his head. 'A definite no no. We made a solid pact.'

Naina watched Dave listen to the messages three more times, trying to make out whether Froggy's voice sounded angry.

'It's no use,' he said. 'Even when he wishes me happy birthday, he uses the same tone as when he told me his nan had died. Shit, he knows.'

Naina lay back on the comfortable sofa, watching the silver, gold and green Christmas decorations softly dancing to the rising heat. She allowed a smile, February and no one had taken them down. Sack the cleaner. Her eyelids closed down the evening for a few moments and noises of Dave in the shower began to subside into nothingness. With him, it felt like he could cram a whole hour into a minute. A life matching even the fastest roller coaster. And the mellowing thoughts of him being faithful only to her were gently soothing, but also far-fetched and light years away. But still, she liked him – however mad that seemed. More than popping bubble wrap, more than putting ear-buds in her ears, more than a good day out, more than a friend. Why did he have to be such a pig?

'Naina, you can come and scrub my back if you want,' Dave shouted out. Naina smiled. He'd never change.

She nestled back into the soothing warmth, rubbing her bare legs of their numbness. The booze was beginning to fade and her wits were slowly returning. Then she got angry. Like an over-heated pressure cooker ready to explode. Little fists of fury ready to scrape down his body, inflicting wounds. Then getting salt and . . . now now.

Dave sauntered in, dripping all over, a white towel round his tight waist. 'Looks like you're feeling better.' He noted the anger in her eyes.

'I'll tell you what really annoyed me about today, David.' She approached him, he took a step back. 'You.' She tried to balance, pushed over the naked bong. 'You embarrassed me in Florelli's.'

Naina looked at him. If you could take away all the lies, then what you saw was what you got. Dave never pretended he was something he wasn't, never cared what other people thought. And all the women would probably agree that when he was with them, he made them feel extra special – five minutes prior to dumping them. He had even said to Naina once that if she ever had a car crash, then he would miss her. Sweetie. She didn't know whether to take it as a compliment or not.

'You're cheaper than a parking ticket, Naina. Twen-ty-five quid. Bargain!'

Naina laughed, tried not to. She didn't want to encourage him, seeing that he was only half wearing a towel, an earring, necklace and Davidoff after-shave. And his smile, a smile that was soon upgraded to a grin, when he saw her looking down at his bulge – his mogul. She quickly stopped, stepped back-wards, wobbled unsteadily and nearly fell over.

His hands caught hers. 'I knew I was big, Naina, but I didn't think it would topple you over.' And their eyes swept everything aside for a moment, inviting each other in, daring each other, both searching for signals to continue, while they stood only a breath away. She put her arms round him and kissed him. Her long fingers coated in electric blue nail varnish worked their way down his chest and over his stomach muscles, speedily removing the towel. His 'large' lollipop was on Defcon 5 and ready for battle.

'Let's go in the bedroom,' Naina suggested, pulling off the white ski top. 'If it's vacant.'

'The sheets are clean. Don't worry, there won't be any surprises.' He removed her flimsy dress, watching it fall to her ankles, and stood there admiring her smooth, dark olive skin. She was more beautiful than ever. How? He didn't know.

Naina lay back on the bed wearing nothing but a

smile. Dave lay beside her, held his hand over the bulb for a minute, then turned off the bedside lamp, and ripped open a glow-in-the-dark condom.

Chapter Eleven

The smoke alarm sounded, echoing throughout the spacious flat. The crispy bacon sandwich was ready. Dave cheerily ambled into the heated bedroom, wearing just a pair of red boxer shorts, pulled the cream curtains apart and let the bristling sunshine in. Naina squinted her eyes open, vague and confused. Her long hair matted like a wolf's arse, make-up smudged on the white pillow-case, eyes red and bloodshot. And her mouth was parched with stains of last night's drink. She looked like a troll, a troll with a massive hangover.

'I've made you a bacon sarnie. You look fabulous, by the way.' He laughed as he placed it on the stereo.

'What time is it?' Naina asked, massaging her eyes.

'Gone eleven.'

'Shit, I should be at work.' She flung the duvet back. Dave smiled, raising his eyebrows, and she quickly pulled it back again – her modesty not intact.

He picked out a topaz blue Ralph Lauren T-shirt from his Mr Ben's wardrobe – a designer outfit for every occasion – and lobbed it at her. 'Wear that.' It landed on her dishevelled head.

Naina swiped it from her face. 'Tell me you didn't, you know, to me last night. Please tell me you didn't,' she pleaded, down-spirited, fumbling the XXL T-shirt over her head. Old stock T-shirt – made his biceps appear too small.

'You don't remember?' he talked into the wardrobe. A smile as wide as a coat-hanger emerged. Then, like a true expert of facial dressage, he hung a look of pained concern on his face and turned to her. 'How can you not remember?'

The cramped pub of the night before she pictured with great clarity: the over-powering noise, Leena and Kate, the jealousy when Dave arrived with that tart, Sandra's face when she nearly spilled the beans. Then the cold, the drive back to Dave's flat, the warm friendly fire, then – nothing. Absolutely zero. Zilch!

'I don't remember anything.' She watched him standing in the doorway.

Dave stepped towards her, dived down on the bed, hooked his arm under the wooden frame, and pulled it out, smiling like a smug magician. 'You don't remember this?' he asked, referring to the tiny JVC silver camcorder now clasped in his hand. 'Get dressed and we can watch it, see if that jogs your memory.' He stood up.

What a worm. 'You taped it?' It was a question, a

statement and a threat all in one.

Dave tossed the mini camcorder in the air, it landed with a proud thud in his paw. 'Yep, all on 8mm. Something to show your grandkids, hey?'

Naina thought about it for a second: coming home to her mum and dad. Dad fuming, 'I wanted you to be a doctor, or a lawyer, but you turn out to be India's first female porn star. Ashok will be so disappointed in you.'

'Naina, you were the best shag I've had in years. You were un – fucking – believable.'

That was it, Naina's tear ducts exploded. He put the camcorder down. What had he said now? Women. He sat down next to her; her sobbing was uncontrollable and he tried to share the grief. Nature had done women an injustice, Dave thought, they should come fitted with little windscreen-wipers on their eyes since they were always crying about something. Then as he watched Naina's long curling eyelashes flick away a hanging tear, he thought that maybe nature already had suitably equipped them.

'Naina, I'm sorry, I was only having a laugh. I didn't pork you. I was close but I didn't.' He turned her head towards him with both hands to try and make her understand: he was telling the truth.

In the heat of the night, in the passive void of darkness in the bedroom, when Naina had lain there naked and wanting, telling him to stop doing his *Star Wars* impressions and stick it in – 'Luke, I am your father, feel the force' – he had seen the light. He was shown the way, guided. He would be one shitty mate if he shagged her now when she was out of her skull, so he had slept all alone on the sofa, quite pleased with himself, feeling almost self-righteous with his new-found self-control.

It reminded Dave of the self-control he used to possess as a kid: Nan had come to stay once for the six weeks of the school holiday while she recovered from her bad rusty hip. All the time she was there, each week she would pop in some ten pences and five pences into a little ceramic NatWest piggy bank on the fire-ledge for him and his two half-sisters to spend at the end of the long summer holidays. By week five the piggy was quite heavy, and with Starsky's claw hammer, Dave was about to break the pig and nick all the money for himself to spend on Refresher sweets, liquorice and acid drops – his favourites – when he was guided, and shown the light, by Stepdad's hand across the back of his head. He had shown self-control then, when he refused to cry in front of his four-year-old and two-year-old sisters.

Naina wiped her tears on the T-shirt. She had to believe him, it was the only way to cope. She had to believe a man who kept a large yellow book labelled 'Handy Honeys', listing which lies he had told which beautiful woman. Dave's jolly little comment of 'You wouldn't walk for a week if I porked you,' did not soothe her mind, as she headed into the shower. The hot spray of the power shower eased her hangover, hosing down the skin, flushing away the remnants of last night. She had no magic answers ready, just the usual lie for when she didn't come home. Kate. Kate put her up. Her parents would triple-check with Kate, Kate would lie through her teeth, and Naina would be lectured: 'All it takes is for you to pick up your mobile and ring us. You never have your mobile on so we can't ring you. You know how much we worry.'

Naina stood ready to leave, hair damp, face on, waiting for Dave to locate his car keys. Her heel tapped with no particular rhythm on the wooden dining-room floorboards. A small picture, framed in cherry-stained wood, hung inconspicuously on one of the claret-coloured walls – almost like it didn't even want to be seen. Inside the glass frame a single, crisp fifty-pound note sat mounted on black backing. Above the banknote, in Dave's flowing handwriting in silver ink: 'If you need this, you've failed.' Sometimes there was depth to his character. Sometimes kindness also. As she stood in last night's clothes, now immaculately ironed by Dave himself, she wondered why he hadn't done what was automatic for him last night, what was programmed in his genes. She wondered why he hadn't shagged her.

'Found them.' He jangled the huge bunch of keys. 'Naina, I know you're in a rush, but can I ask you something?' he added.

She nodded.

'If Ashok's not right for you, then you shouldn't marry him, whatever the reason.' It wasn't a question, but still.

'Promise I'll tell you why I have to marry him, but not now, I'll ring you. But Ashok is right for me.' She made for the front door, ignoring Dave's laboured look of confusion. He followed her out, resetting the burglar alarm and they both descended the steps to the ground floor, only to be greeted by Froggy.

Naina and Dave stared at him, like they had just discovered a new species of animal: Froggy appeared windswept, lacking in sleep, unshaven and unwashed. Perturbed. A distant bell tolled from the church in the countryside, a tuneless ringing. Sandra's pendant – a gold St Christopher ingot, Froggy's pride and joy – was absent from his neck.

'Hello, mate. Rough night?' Dave asked, setting himself up for the punch. He was about to say 'OOzing', but thought better of it.

Froggy's tired red eyes focused only on Naina. 'Naina, tell me what you meant last night, about—'

Dave interrupted. 'Mate, she's had a crap night. I'm just going to take her home. Don't worry, I'll fill you in later.'

Naina shuffled to the main door, full of guilt. 'S'okay Dave, I'll get the bus.'

Thanks *a lot*, Naina. 'Sure?' Dave's question sounded like, 'Please don't leave me here, I need at least a good half-hour to think of something believable.'

'Sure.' Naina stood on her toes, kissed Dave on the lips, and whispered, 'Sorry, Dave, thanks for everything, call me.' Half-smiled at Froggy and left.

Dave watched her leave. Like a slippery fish swimming away from a net that he was well and truly caught in. He shut the lobby door and looked at Froggy where he stood on the plush blue carpet.

'I'm telling you, Froggy, you look like shit. I think the best thing is for you to take a shower, I'll make some coffee and we can talk.'

Froggy followed Dave up the stairs, like a lost lemming, still in last night's pub clothes. 'She's having an affair, mate, I know it.'

Dave fumbled with the flat-door key, pressed the wrong code to the alarm four times, told the old man below to stop yelling and finally punched in the correct code, before the security company had time to phone through to the police.

'Have a shower, mate, I'll just phone security.'

Froggy was in a faraway place, not even listening, wondering when and where Sandra had done the dirty. Wondering why. All those little things she said to him meant nothing now. Lip-service. Three years together, happy years he thought, and now, all gone. Kerboom!

Froggy slouched on the sofa, listening to Dave on the phone, as he talked to security: 'Yes . . . Sorry . . . I know . . . My password . . . Yes . . . It's Smelly Jelly . . . Sorry again, bye.'

Froggy almost laughed.

Dave clapped his hands together like an announcement. 'Right, Frog, let's sort you out. All this nonsense.' He threw him a fag, and plonked himself on the sofa chair. 'Tell me everything, mate.' His black Nikes rested on the glass table.

Froggy lit up. 'No, *you* tell *me*, mate.' He paused. 'She said, ask your best friend Dave, he knows everything.'

Dave thought back to when he was shagging Sandra, her feet by her ears, in Froggy's bed. She had yelped and screamed out, 'That was the best orgasm ever. Can we do it again?' But Dave had said, 'Where are your morals, Sandra? He's my best mate, I've known him since I was six; I told you once, and once only.' As he left the room he then said sneering,

'What are you, some sort of lowlife?' And slammed the front door on his way out, tossing the condom in next door's bushes, feeling totally guilt-ridden.

Dave also thought back to the pact that Froggy, Matt, Pete, Andy and he had made when all five of them were fifteen years old, gagging for a good time and anxious to sleep with many many women. They had all shared willing Deborah for about four months, taking it in turns. Passing her round from week to week like a present from heaven itself. Then Debs fell pregnant. It could have been anybody's. A meeting was held and they decided to lay the blame on Jingle, their newest friend, who hadn't even shagged her. He was all too willing to take the blame, as it proved all the rumours wrong: that he was so ugly he would remain a virgin for life. But God spread its wings that summer, for with Debs it was a false alarm. The five mates who had been through so much, made a pact. Never *ever* sleep with someone else's woman. It was risky, it could have torn their friendship apart. A few years later they improved the rules. Not only was it risky, it was also morally wrong. As far as Dave knew, only he and he alone was the traitor to a pact soldered during their youth, and it was with these thoughts that a confession nearly spilled out of his mouth.

'Froggy, I've got something to tell you.' Dave put his hands to his head, brushing through his short hair. 'I should have put you right about this a long time ago.'

Froggy let his fag ash up, until it fell to the floor. His nerves felt as cremated as the nicotine that now dusted the rug. 'So tell me then, Dave, I'm shitting my pants here. Who is he?'

Dave's fragmented honesty now took a respite; he would be nuts to tell the truth so he followed the first rule of adultery – lie through your back teeth.

'It's no one, it's Naina, she's jealous of Sandra, she talks about her all the time, how pretty she is and her fantastic body. She said those things last night just to cause trouble for Sandra.' The lies were queuing up. 'Can you believe it? Jealousy, hey, it can wreck friendships.'

Froggy mulled over the words. 'But Naina's so pretty, she's like a model. Sandra's pretty but nothing like Naina, not even close. I can't believe Naina's jealous over Sandra, it doesn't make sense.' Froggy drew a long breath. 'Nah, it's something else.' His eyes swigged the fag smoke and became watery.

'What does Sandra have to say?' Dave threw in quickly.

'Nothing. After you and Naina left the pub, I asked her what Naina meant by "your little secret's safe with me" and she got up, telling me to ask you, you know everything, and she chickened off to her mother's and I haven't spoken to her since.'

Dave scrounged around his lying mind for a good one, something concrete and believable. 'And that's it, you think she's having an affair over that? You're fucking mental, Froggy, she loves you, she'd never have an affair, it's just girls being bitches, that's all. They've never liked each other, can't you feel the bad atmosphere when they're together?' Dave appeared angry at his make-believe world he had just invented. Very angry.

'I suppose, but why go round her mother's?' Froggy asked, taking the bait but not liking the taste.

'It's a nesting thing. When things are rough, they fly to their nest, haven't you read *Wom— New Scientist*?'

'It's got to be a man, Dave. She's not the sort to get upset over a snide remark, even if Naina was stirring. And I do know she hates Naina, she's told me, but I've got a bad feeling about this.' Froggy grabbed the ciggie packet and lit up.

'Look, Froggy, all I know is this: when Naina sobered up this morning she felt awful for stirring. She said that Sandra had been getting on her nerves last night.' Dave lingered on a puff of his fag. 'I mean, look at the way Naina spoke to me, mate, she wrecked my date with Danielle. Naina should just keep off the booze, I've told her. One day she's going to hurt someone.' Dave's eyes shrank and his disturbed face emerged.

Froggy needed convincing. Three hours' worth. A lot of time. But Dave would do anything for a mate. Dave had heard that if you clench your bum cheeks together then you can fool a lie detector test, but at the moment, his bum cheeks were anything but together, he was crapping himself. Unsure whether Froggy was seeing through his charade, unsure whether Froggy was playing a game back, it was mental torture and it was the first time in Dave's life that he was glad to see the back of his friend when he left. Time was caving in on Dave on this one.

He picked up the phone, dialled; the answerphone clicked on. 'Sandra, it's Dave, just a quick message. Froggy does not, repeat, does not know. Tell him

134

that Naina was stirring because she's jealous of your looks. I suggest you give him a blow job tonight.'

He soothed his face with an accomplished smile and cracked open a highly deserved can of cold, honest Stella. Sorted!

Chapter Twelve

Next Day.

In Dave's own way, he admired Stephen W. Hawking. Even though stuck in a wheelchair, the guy still managed to have an affair with his nurse. Top man. He was also very clever, thought Dave, as he tossed aside *A Brief History of Time* which he had just sped read in Florelli's, in preparation for his date tonight with Kelly the physicist: the boring one, with a name like a waterfall, the one he had met in the pub three nights ago, the one who was about to be entertained. Move over, Einstein, a new theory was about to arrive.

Kelly lived in a smart little place in a cul-de-sac called Walnut Tree, not too far from the Open University. Rumour had it that a big black panther stalked these parts, using the wide, open green fields as its hunting ground. Yeah right, thought Dave, like I'm scared. His car smoothly rode the dark road, lights on full beam shinning up and down the brick walls on either side of the through-road that led up Walnut Tree estate.

Wearing black combat bottoms, tight white Versace T-shirt showing off his adequate biceps, Nike trainers, Davidoff, he stepped out of the car, picked up the colourful bunch of mixed flowers from the back seat and knocked on the glass-panelled door.

Kelly answered wrapped in a smile, fiercely beautiful in her short ruby-shaded tight dress. 'No bra, but no nipples? – strange, thought Dave, then the cold air hit and they tweaked through, making him feel a whole lot better.

She spoke. 'I know we said we would go out, but I thought it would be nice if I cooked us a meal. Is that okay?' She closed the door gently behind him, thanking him for the flowers.

Dingy, thought Dave, as he sat down on the ivory-coloured-throw-covered sofa. 'Sounds lovely. Mind if I light up?'

She passed him a white ceramic ashtray with black printed Chinese symbols, and left to fetch some wine. (First rule of optimist: If she brings you wine, you're staying the night). He checked his back pocket for condoms; this was the fifth time he'd checked since leaving his flat. A paranoid optimist. He didn't quite know what to expect on the inside of a scientist's house. Possibly a few test tubes or the odd Bunsen burner, maybe some graphs on the wall, or a cabinet with mysterious coloured bottles marked 'Vaccines'. But this place had a strange 'Chi', almost clinical.

On the magnolia walls a few large pictures of . . .

he stood up to see . . . a dragon, a tiger, a turtle and a funny-looking thing jumping out of a fire: a phoenix, it said underneath. In one corner a smoking sweet-fragrant incense and in another a trickling, noisy water fountain.

Kelly returned with two wine glasses and a bottle of house white wine. 'I'm into Feng Shui, hence all the Chinese paraphernalia.' She passed Dave a glass, poured in some veeno, and rested the bottle on a small glass table by the sofa.

Dave sat back down. 'Feng Shui. Earth, wind, water and fire?'

'You're too much, you are, you know everything.' She smiled and sat in close to him.

This was already a success. Time to impress her even more.

'Kelly.' He looked into her shining eyes. 'Not quite everything, tell me about yourself. I would love to become an expert.'

She giggled. 'Me? No, I'm boring.'

Yeah, you got that about right. 'Don't put yourself down like that. You're gorgeous and intelligent, and by the smell coming from the kitchen you can cook too. Hell, Kelly, come on, drink that wine, let's enjoy ourselves, put some music on.'

Kelly pressed in a CD. Looked over at Dave, smiled. 'I think you might like this.' And sat back down next to him.

It was f-ing boring classical, and if he wasn't mistaken it was Chopin. 'You thought right, Kelly, like poetry from heaven, ah Chopin.' He gulped down some wine. If she put on a ballet video then he was out of here.

'It's Bach,' she corrected gently.

'Yeah, Bach, lovely.' Dave cringed. How did he make that life-or-death, nit-picking mistake? 'Yeah, actually you're right, it is Bach. I was only listening to this melody a few days ago.'

She twirled her blonde hair around her index finger. A jumbled bag of nerves, sitting so close to him. He was her ideal-looking man from *GQ*, with a ruggedness she more than approved of. And also, so sweet, after she tells him he know's everything – what does he do? Just to make her feel better he pretends he doesn't know Chopin from Bach. Sweet.

'I hope you like Indian, Dave, I sort of took a guess. You do eat meat, don't you?'

'Sounds lovely, I love Indian food.' His smile was cemented to his face. 'Have you ever been to India?' He was running out of things to say that wouldn't lead to Quarks, Feng Shui or Chopin.

'No, I'd love to go, so mystical. What about you? I bet you've been.'

A problem with Dave – and he blamed this on watching too many politicians on TV – was that he could never admit to not knowing, doing or seeing. He would rather bluff his way through, risking hemming himself in with lies, than admit to someone: 'No'.

'India? Just the once, for six months. I went to find myself. I stayed in . . . Delhi. Beautiful country, absolutely beautiful.' Dave poured out some more wine and lies.

'So, did you bathe in the Ganges?'

'No actually, you'd be surprised, but the hotels out

there are pretty well equipped, they had showers and everything.'

Kelly laughed. 'You're so funny, Dave.' She sipped her wine with her little pinkie sticking out. 'Tell me about the temples, you must have visited that famous one. What's it called?'

It's called the Kingdom of Boredom; you live there, Kelly, it's your fucking house. Dave stood up. 'Can I use your loo?'

'Of course, top of the stairs on the left.'

He legged it up, locked himself in the lime-green bathroom, dropped the karzy lid down and sat. Matching green bog-roll, green towels, toothbrush, sponge, Palmolive soap, green flowers in a green vase. For Christ's sake, he'd feel guilty doing a brown poo – good job he wasn't doing one.

From the toilet seat he dialled Naina's mobile.

'Naina, it's Dave,' he whispered. 'Where are you?'

'With Leena and Kate.'

'S'all right for some. I'm stuck here with a right boring old bat.' He turned on the silver taps for extra noise. 'Naina, tell me, what's the famous temple in India?'

'There's loads.'

'The one you swim in.'

A pause. Swim? In a temple? 'Dave, are you smoking hash?'

'No, quick.' He flushed the loo. 'Come on, Naina, think. A shag depends on this.'

Another pause. 'Oh, I know which one you mean. It's called The Snozzley Snozzley Temple. Have you got that? Snozzley Snozzley.'

140

'Are you sure?'

'Dave, who's Indian, me or you? Now go on, have a nice shag, bye.'

Dave legged it back downstairs, sat down, composed his smile. 'You were saying, Kelly, about a temple?'

'Yes, you must know it, the famous one.'

Dave scratched his head, thinking hard, kicking off the turf on his mind. It had to be buried there somewhere. If he wanted to make a fool of himself he could definitely come up with something better than Snozzley Snozzley, something like, Batman and Robin's Cave Temple. Then it came to him: a shudder of neurones twitching, a sparkle of relief. 'Oh, you must mean the Golden Temple of Amritsar. Oh yes, very beautiful, so dynamic and dramatic. You know they say if you steal some of the gold, you will be cursed with blindness.'

Kelly smiled, still avoiding his eyes, fearful of blushing, then stood up. 'I better check on dinner.' She walked out.

Dave leaned back on the sofa. He saw the reflection of his smile in the glass table. Cute. Things were going very well indeed. Although Kelly was a monster of boredom, she was also a scientist, and he was desperate to shag a scientist no matter how many brain cells died in the process. He thought to get her in the bedroom, he would need to talk of the vast cosmos and all its mystery. In order for her to remove her dress, then there was only one thing for it: the Theory of Relativity. But in order for him to get in her knickers and shag her, then it would have to be talk of 'super strings' and 'chaos'. Complicated stuff, but he was more than capable, however boring it was. That was about the size of it. Sex!

Leena and Kate both fell back on the bed laughing. 'Tell me again, Naina,' begged Kate.

'The Snozzley Snozzley Temple. I think he bought it,' Naina replied, almost wetting herself.

Kate's flat – Bitch HQ – was small but homely: modelled on a picture she once saw in a homes magazine, even down to the pasta machine that she still didn't know how to use. The three girls sat on the double bed with a bottle of red wine, a photo album of their school days, and a tampon spliff. Mixed love songs played on the CD, mixed love songs they all knew, and they sang their hearts out, slowly getting pissed and high. Snozzley just tipped them over the edge.

To Kate and Leena, Naina was metamorphosing before their very eyes: where before she would have a drink, now she would get drunk. Before she would talk about men, now she blew them. To Naina, six months was all she had before her life sentence with Ashok began. And consequently her sensible side had grown horns, and there was no telling what she might do next.

In a way, Kate loved the new change in Naina. For years she'd felt frustration for both Leena and Naina for the Indian strictness. Felt that they were missing out on the fun of teenage years, which definitely included rampant boys. Kate had a simple rule that she had always stuck to with good effect: what the parents don't know, won't harm them. Simple. She had given up trying to talk her Indian friends out of having an arranged marriage years ago. Maybe not being Indian and not living with the pressure that they were under, their way of life, was something Kate would never grasp, but her duty as a friend was to lead them astray as much as possible before they married and ended up with a man so straight and slick flick, you'd think he was walking with *Granth Sahib* in his back pocket. But as for going astray, Naina had sure picked a foul-mouthed, dirty-talking, sex-mad, lying, womanizing thug of man to go straying with. But he was very good looking, so she was partially excused.

'Naina, so now you've had your first taste of a man, what d'you think?' asked Kate.

Naina answered, lying back, looking up at the ceiling: 'I think without women, they're so sex mad, they'd end up shagging each other.'

They all laughed.

'So, will you be sending Dave a Valentine's bomb then?' asked Leena, passing Naina the joint.

Naina drew on the tampon spliff. 'Knowing my luck, it would blow up in my face.'

And here it was, Dave's name, always creeping into conversations like a shadow that won't go away, even when you've turned out the light. A man who had run away from his own wedding, wrecked eight others, the man who had lied and hoodwinked his way into as many women's knickers as he could, the man who, when she asked what his dream in life was, replied: 'I would love to get all the ten past winners of *Mastermind*, invite them into a room and when they were inside, blow them all up, shouting, "You're not so fucking clever now are you?" But Naina still liked him, badly. And Ashok? No. All she could think about was Dave.

Kate pulled a Waitrose carrier bag from under her Ikea bed. Supplies. Twiglets, crisps, biscuits, choccies and a brand new bottle of Smirnoff. Leena stood in front of the full-length mirror and did her only joke, as Naina on cue chucked her the salt and vinegar crisps.

'Oh I couldn't possibly,' Leena pronounced in her posh voice, and pointed to the mirror. 'I'm watching my figure.'

It wasn't funny the first time, let alone the fifteenth, but they still laughed like idiots, in between gulps of vodka, munching, spliffing and something they had looked forward to all evening – slagging off Kate's new magazine featuring the top hundred most beautiful women.

Outside, on Marshworth Road, opposite Kate's flat, an off-white Beetle sat insignificantly in the pitch dark. Kiran – Naina's eighteen-year-old brother – dressed in his warmest clothes, lay in suspicious wait. His view, slightly concealed by the overhanging sycamore trees, was still ample enough to take in all aspects of the entrance and the top two windows of Kate's flat. He shivered and rubbed his cold hands together, blowing on them with his warm breath. Kiran was a very patient Indian brother. He would sit there all night if he had to just to make sure Naina was not secretly seeing a man, to make sure Naina stuck to the rigid path laid out by her Indian upbringing. Cars brushed passed him, gently rocking the Beetle with turbulence. He could see silhouettes: heads and arms, waving and swinging through the pale yellow curtains in the flat window up top. A tape played in the stereo, The Beatles' *A Hard Day's Night*, and he thought back to the man in the expensive black BMW on their driveway who he had seen kiss Naina on the lips, holding her hand, too cosy. The tape clunked over, a few crackled noises. (He had taped from vinyl, the only true sound, he thought.) He remembered Naina at school, coming home one spring day with a birthday card, which read inside: 'Love from your boyfriend Greg.' Next day at school Greg was brought to the closed canteen by Kiran and some older Indian boys, and explained with a fist to leave Naina alone. Kiran sometimes wished she wasn't as pretty as she was, as men's heads did turn, and when men's heads turned, their dicks soon followed. So he waited.

'I want you to tell me again that you have never trained as a chef; I for one don't believe you,' Dave said, patting his mouth with a Chinese symbolized serviette.

Kelly giggled shyly. 'Honestly, it's from a book, I swear.' He was so lovely: not only was he good looking, but he was also extremely intelligent, full of compliments, and so polite. She had a good feeling about the two of them. 'Now for sorbet.'

Sherbet ice cream, naff. 'Lovely, my favourite. Kelly, you're something else.'

Kelly cleared the Chinese symbolized plates away from the fake oak dining table. Dave offered to help as quietly as he could, almost a mumble under his lips. But she heard, refusing his offer, telling him he was a guest.

After the lemon sorbet they sat back on the sofa – time for Dave to make a move – but instead Kelly pulled out from a wooden Chinese symbolized black and red cupboard, a Chinese symbolized padded photo album, of a holiday in . . . Dave hazarded a guess – China?

Dave's morale was getting low. There was only so much more of this he could take, before he got hold of a Chinese symbolized chiffon scarf and strangled her with it.

He pointed to one of the photos: 'Is that you?'

'Dave, you are so funny. No, that's the Buddha.'

'La la la do do do doobie do, La la la do do.' Dave jumped for his mobile, saved from the photo of Kelly standing by a huge yellow and red Chinese carnival dragon. 'Hello.'

'Hunky boy, it's Naina. Can you do me one big favour?'

'Go on, Snozzley, let's hear it.' Dave glanced at Kelly and shrugged.

'We've run out of Indian hay. Skunky boy, hunky boy, please. I'm round Kate's, please.'

'No way, Snozzley, can't help, sorry. I'm with a beautiful woman right now.' He winked. 'So, bye bye.'

'No, no, Dave, please, hang on.' A pause, giggles. 'You know you are so gorgeous, so sexy, big, big, biceps, please.'

'No, sorry, Snozz, got to go.'

'Okay, hang on. What if I were to give you a blow job, would you come?'

'Snozz, I always cum when given one of those.'

Flirty laughter. 'You know what I mean. Would you come here now, with the stuff? And I promise I will give you one tomorrow.'

'Hold on a mo.' Dave turned to Kelly. 'Kelly, I know it's rude, but I've got to pop out to my gym, is that okay? I can always tell them no, but it's pretty urgent. I can be back in forty minutes, is that okay? It will give enough time for that delicious meal to go down.' She smiled, and nodded yes. Dave returned to Naina on the mobile. 'I'll be there in fifteen minutes. I'm going to have to dock this out of your wages though.'

'Dave, you talk so much shit: "It will give enough time for that delicious meal to go down." She's not falling for that shit, is she?' He laughed. 'See you in a few minutes. I'm round Kate's, remember.'

The idea of running an errand for a blow job was highly appealing, a turn-on even, especially in the middle of a date with a beautiful woman – even if she was boring. And he stood up, kissed Kelly on the lips – giving her an appetizer for tonight – and watched the thermostat on her face finally break as she began to belch out heat from her scarlet cheeks.

'Kelly, could I take that CD of Bach to listen to on the way? And I know this sounds soppy and all that, but already I think it will remind me of you.' You boring cow.

Kelly was taken aback and blushed even deeper. 'Of course, Dave, make sure you don't drive too quickly on my account though.'

Yeah, right, Kelly, like I'm going to speed to get back to you. 'I'll be dead careful. And can we continue looking at those photos when I come back?'

Fifteen minutes later Dave had already collected the gear from his gym safe, and was travelling to bitch Kate's with Guns n' Roses blaring out of the speakers. Kelly's CD was safely flung on the back seat.

Kelly had better not sneak in a shit when I'm gone, he thought, turning through the roads that led to Kate's flat hiding away on the outskirts of Tinkers Bridge. Just a few house lights left on, like the last numbers on a bingo card, and Dave pulled up in the deathly quiet street of Kate's address, parking neatly next to her Corsa. He honked the car horn. A curtain twitched upstairs and after a minute the front door opened with Naina half-cut, in just her long night T-shirt, goose-stepping up the small path to the edge of the road in her bare feet.

Dave opened the car door, got out, and greeted Naina by the gate post.

'Hunky boy, well done, hunky boy. Where is it?' Naina glanced to Dave's empty hands.

Banging on the window above made them both look up to see Kate with her breasts pressed up against the cold window, like two car airbags. Must be strong glass, Dave thought.

Naina continued, shivering, 'Come on, hunky, give us a kiss then.'

Dave smiled at her, with a Waitrose carrier bag on her head, he guessed she was drunk. 'Snozzley, I brought you two lots: The Force and Fire of Smaug.'

Naina kissed him, arms wrapped round his neck. 'My hero.' She kissed him harder, then on the neck, then lifted up his T-shirt, flashing his abs to the window above which caused more banging on the glass. 'My hero, Dave.' She stepped backwards, wobbling. 'Where is it then?'

Dave smiled and looked down to his black combats.

'Bad boy.' Naina rummaged inside his bottoms, feeling round his boxers.

'No, Naina, in my pocket.' He pulled out the two small cellophane bags and placed them in her hand, not letting go. 'So, what time are you coming round for this blow job, Naina?'

'After work. Pick me up from my office at 4.15, and I'll wear something nice and sexy for you. Something in red, something lacy, something mouth-watering.'

Dave let go of her hand, kissed her on the lips, and said goodbye, watching her amble back up the path, giggling and swaying to and fro. He chuckled, returned to his car and drove back to Kelly's – to China town.

Kiran aged a year. He felt like one of those UFO spotters who had finally seen a flashing light. He didn't know whether to believe. He didn't want to believe. But he knew what he had seen. She had her hands in his pants, they kissed, arms entwined, his sister with that, that rich white thug. She looked a disgrace, out in next to nothing, drunk, behaving like a slag. Mum and Dad must never know about this; he would have to sort this one out himself. He knew exactly what he had to do to put an end to this. Naina would be marrying Ashok in six months, even if he had to drag her to the temple himself. And this bloke in the BMW would wish he had never met her. He picked up his Nokia, dialled a number, and spoke in short, angry sentences, emphasizing one point in particular: no one ever messes with an Indian girl and gets away with it. Especially a white fucker like that.

Chapter Thirteen

The February snow fell like sherbet, then marshmallows, from God's winter candy shop, until it was thick enough to coat the entire high street in its perfect white velvet, and thick enough to cover the double yellow lines painted on both sides of the road. The black BMW sport edged quietly over to the roadside, its alloy wheels pressing down on the virgin snow, and snugly parked like a sleek panther. The electric window slid down, a fag was tossed out, and the orange glow sizzled as it was extinguished, its nicotine life snuffed out.

Dave tiptoed across the creaky snow, leaving a trail of small 'ticks' from his Nike trainers. The cars crawling past seemed quiet, as though wearing slippers, and the stillness of the normally busy town was a welcome change, almost like alien territory, and the few shoppers wrapped in their winter shawls, gloves and coats, looked *almost* alien. Those who did stop to talk, talked of one thing – the weather.

Dave kicked his feet, shook off the snow and shivered into Florelli's. He sat himself on one of the sofas, ushered over a waitress and lit up – he had a bitch of a headache. The middle-aged waitress walked slowly over, took his order and walked slowly back. She dreaded Dave coming in.

Florelli's Valentines

Picture an open fire.
Picture romance.
Picture fine food.
Picture Florelli's.
£12.00 per person.

The pink leaflet, printed on glossy paper, surfaced a memory: a line of girls from his school, all queuing up outside the school gates, to receive their first French kiss, from yours truly – Dave, the best-looking boy in school, who had just found out the *real* use of his tongue. It was to be his Valentine gift to them all – except for the ugly and fat ones, and Emma (she had an awful skin rash).

'OOzing.' Matt arrived, dressed in about three jumpers, and sat down opposite Dave. 'Sorry I'm late, mate.'

Matt with his blond hair and blue eyes could quite easily be mistaken for a good-looking Scandinavian, until he spoke. Dave and Froggy had first met him at a community club for under sixteens, where they used to call him Midwich Boy until they found out that his parents always bought him the most up-to-date electronic games. He was recruited from then on. And from then on, he went from electronic games to computer games, and finally landed a top job at a computer company writing software. He was extremely intelligent. A bit of a whiz.

'OOzing,' Dave responded, putting down the leaflet.

'You're looking rough, Dave.' He lit up.

The slow-footed waitress returned with Dave's coffee and was told to go and fetch another one with a warmed apple-pie slice.

Dave stubbed out his fag and slid over the ashtray to Matt. 'Rough? I'm fucked. I've never worked so hard for a shag in all my life.'

Matt laughed. The waitress looked to the ceiling – it was starting already. All that man ever talked about was sex, nothing else.

Dave continued, 'Kelly the scientist, you saw her the other day, stunner.'

Matt nodded, he knew the one.

'I was round hers last night. She bored the shit out of me with ying and bloody yang. Then she showed me every single photo of her entire boring life.' He lit up another fag. 'It was a nightmare. She went on and on and on, until I couldn't stand it. I was getting really sick of her face. She's got this sort of smile when she thinks she's about to stun me with something funny.' Dave shivered at the thought. 'Some poor sod will have to marry that one day.'

Matt laughed. 'But you did shag her, though?' He stirred in the sugar in big wide arcs like the turns on a Tibetan prayer wheel.

Dave blew out a smoke ring for effect. 'She was like a Brillo pad, mate.'

Matt shook his head. He did enjoy the company of Cro-Magnon man but sometimes Dave's mind seemed just too many evolutionary jumps away from civilization.

The slight overhang of Florelli's window ledge was accumulating snow quickly enough that every time the door banged shut, a small cascade fell to the street pavement below. Flurries of snowflakes targeted the window as if clamouring for the warmth of the coffee shop inside. And the entrance carpet became soggy and darker like a spreading inkblot.

Matt, forever the tactful, decided to ask the question that would lead to the question that had been pressing on his mind ever since Naina's drunken speech: 'So, you finally got Naina into bed?'

Dave seamlessly moved from confident to defensive. 'One-off. Naina made a mistake. Anyway it was only a knees bent, mouth stretched, ra ra ra.' He picked up the food menu and pretended to scan for tucker.

'Was Sandra a "one-off" as well?' Matt paused. 'Come on, Dave, it was obvious what Naina meant; Sandra did a whitey. I've never seen you panic like that, mate.'

Dave's fingers drummed on the solid square table. 'I made a mistake, Froggy and her weren't even serious at the time. I was going to tell him a few days later, but I couldn't, I would have looked like a right bastard.' Dave's eyes seemed to narrow.

'What's new, *you are a bastard*, and what? Froggy never even suspected a thing?'

'Never, I wouldn't do that to him.'

'But you did.'

'Metaphorically speaking. Anyway, it's the past now, her and him seem to be getting on okay, it would be wrong to wreck their relationship just so we could all have a huge giggle at their expense,' joked Dave.

'S'not funny, mate.'

Dave nodded his head. 'I know, it was shitty.' He paused. 'Real shitty.'

Matt was standing as judge and jury, as so often was the case. If ever there was a moral issue, then Matt held all the cards and most of the answers. 'Dave, hate to say it, but you're going to have to tell him. He will find out, and I don't mean metaphorically.' He looked to see if Dave was paying attention; he was. '*And* he deserves to know the truth, he deserves to know what you did and what Sandra did. You know I'm talking sense. I know you know I'm talking sense.'

And Dave did know. Matt was a good buddy, an anchor of sorts. He was the kind of man that you could find yourself thinking: If Matt did it, then it's okay. Matt would never betray one of the OOzing gang, so it quite clearly was not okay.

Matt liked things logical, even his friends. You could say he was almost binary. What Dave had done disturbed the flow, it needed sorting; friendships always needed sorting. Matt remembered back to a time when, after a month in the OOzing gang, certain people – Dave – were getting impatient with him. Decided he needed sorting out:

'Right, Matt, you little upstart, it's about time you broke some fucking rules, either that, or you're out, your choice!'

A week later, all six were arrested, handcuffed, and brought to the attention of the Magistrates. Handling stolen goods. But it didn't matter, it was a proud moment for Matt, he was now officially 'in'. Back then, Dave was all-powerful, almost invincible, contumacious. Until Matt began to see through his charade, his smiles, his rebelling and his backchat (and his shaved head, earring, cut-off T-shirts).

One day stuck in his mind: he'd come knocking for Dave on a balmy summer's day. Dave's mum answered: 'The little shit's run away.' And she slammed the door in Matt's face. Matt found him at the wood that overlooked the back of the council houses. And he saw Dave cry for the first and only time.

'What's wrong?' Matt asked, husky and sincere.

Dave glanced up, his back resting against the mouldy green bark of a holly tree, wiped his sore eyes on the sleeve of his navy sweatshirt, careful not to scrape his eye with the metal popper on his leather wristband. 'I hate them, I hate them both.' And Matt sat down beside him.

They both stared outwards until Matt spoke. 'Did he hit you again?'

'I forgot to bring the milk in. He grabbed us and started bashing me round my head.' Dave sniffed. 'Then me mum, she told him to stop, she said, "If you must hit him, make sure you do it when the baby's not asleep. I've told you before, Jack, his screams wake the baby," so he took me outside and beat the shit out of me in the garden. Jack-a-fuck-in-ory.'

Matt swore on his life, he would never tell anyone about Dave's tears. And that was the last time Dave had ever opened up to Matt. Years later, Matt once asked him what had happened to his real dad and Dave replied: 'He found himself a better son.'

Matt delved into his apple-pie slice. Dave watched.

'Just like women, hey, Matt? Apple pies. Sometimes you want to take your time with them, and others, you just want to woff down.'

The conversation had had its peak, and after that it descended to general mate-to-mate talk. Dave thought back to the last comment he had made to Froggy: 'Mate, if she is having an affair, you and me will hunt down that fucker and rip his eyes out.' Sorted!

The red and white plastic sealed envelope flapped like a caught bird trapped on his car window. Dave ripped off the parking ticket and walked down the slippery path, hunting down the Sasquatch-traffic-warden-bitch, looking for footprints of size 14 in the snow. At the bottom of the street he saw her. Yuck.

'Margaret, isn't it?' he enquired, sidling up to her big frame, eyeing her CD-sized glass lenses from sideways on.

The formidable head turned to greet him. 'It's you. You were parking on a double yellow, again. You must have money to waste.' Her smile was frozen in place.

Dave stuck the ticket on her wide forehead. 'Now go and wax off that horrible moustache!' And walked back to his car, scraping off the build-up of snow on his windscreen with the back of his credit card.

Driving was hazardous in drifting snow. Bumper-to-bumper hold-ups at certain roundabouts and the odd clapped-out car on the side verges. One huge roundabout seemed to keep the snake of cars waiting for ever and Dave peered out to the slopes in the distance, watching a group of young kids screaming down the side of the hill on an old orange bread crate, a sledge – or, as Dad used to say, toboggan. He smiled: make the most of it, he thought, you'll soon have to grow up. Then gave a finger to a passing motorist for nearly sliding into his car.

The 4.00 p.m. sky on the horizon was tinged by a picturesque red glow that turned this otherwise boring busy road into a postcard beauty, and finally Dave eased up the gears on to the deserted side road and drove up the short cut that would lead to Naina's office.

Standing, leaning against his car, he struggled to light a fag, and watched the main entrance to the three-storey blue-mirrored-glass building – 'Saviour Life Insurance' – his cold breath and smoke funnelling out like one large exhaust.

A whole mass of umbrellas, coats, scarves, gloves and boots left the entrance, all in an attempt to protect the bosses and their entourage from the arctic bite. Naina, after visiting the Ladies, donned herself in her thick black Dolce & Gabbana winter coat – covering her short black skirt and berry fitted shirt – braced herself for the freeze, and opened the heavy glass door. Her knee-high leather boots sank two inches in, and she felt the cold whistle up her coat. Her two office friends grabbed an arm each, and the three headed towards the pick-up point outside.

'Corrrr, he's a bit of all right,' began Sally. 'Bit of a dickhead though, dressed in only a T-shirt. But I wouldn't mind his arms round me, I'd soon warm him up.'

Office giggles.

'He's gorgeous, I wonder which bitch he's picking up. I bet it's that no-they-are-real-Helen,' muffled Natasha through her woollen scarf.

Office giggles.

'The bitch he's picking up is me,' Naina stated.

Office bitch stares.

'Where d'you find him!?'

'He found me, we're friends,' Naina corrected. Then, saying goodbye to her two colleagues, she smiled towards Dave, and walked over to him, careful not to slip.

Like snowflakes, each kiss is unique. The two stood amongst the winter debris, holding on to a kiss that was warm, friendly and secure.

'You *are* wearing red lace under there, I take it,' Dave presumed, trying to undo her coat.

'Stop it, Dave. And yes, thank you for asking, I have had a good day, thank you.'

The doors to the BMW slammed shut, and Dave began a pleased-with-himself smile that would take them all the way back to his place in Stone Valley, whilst they listened to Eminem's 'Stan'.

Kiran pumped down the accelerator and skidded up the road following the BMW. It was as though all flavour had been removed from the day. He could hardly believe just how right he had been. This bloke driving up the road at 60 m.p.h. with his sister in the side seat was taking something that was not rightfully his. Kiran had *only*, and emphasizing *only*, lain in wait for her at her workplace, because there was a temptation to doubt all his inner fears. A temptation to doubt that his sister was really stabbing India in the back. But, as he tried to keep up, as he banged his hand on the steering wheel, he realized that now was the time to stop waiting and watching what might happen, now was the time to put a stop to it. Naina would not shame the family, and this man, this parasite of culture, would pay the steep price.

Chapter Fourteen

The big stubborn willow trees in the gardens round the back of Dave's flat looked like huge exploding fireworks, frozen in time, and planted firmly in a stretching springy mattress of white foam. Apart from a few trails of cats' paw prints, the canvas was blank.

Thhhhump! The snowball hit Naina clean on the head. She refused to acknowledge it. Thhhhhump! The second snowball hit Naina clean on the head.

'How old are you, Dave?' Naina brushed down her hair. 'Do you want to build a snowman, little boy?' she asked mockingly.

Naina watched him lob another snowball at the hanging willow branches, watched the snow fall like confetti and, like chameleons, the branches change from pure white to greeny brown.

'I'm freezing, can we go inside? There'll still be snow later for you to play in,' she said, rubbing her hands.

Inside the fire roared, spitting contempt at the cold, as little chunks of smoking wood buffeted the fire screen in front. Dave joined Naina on the sofa, kicking his Nikes across the pine wood floor. He sparked up a fag and watched her stuff down three chocolate biscuits without pausing to breathe, or dropping a crumb. She then stuffed in two more, and guzzled down the rest of her coffee. Manic Street Preachers played nearly unnoticed in the background.

Apart from the bubble and spit of the fire and the CD, the room seemed starved of noise, until Dave broke the grip on the near-silence. 'So, Naina, tell me about this arranged marriage!' Fire flames flickered in his eyes.

Naina stood up. She'd thought she was here for a blow job? Damn! She presumed Dave's directness was an acquired taste, for presently it tasted like bitter saag, and she departed to the loo, flabbergasted. Inscribed on the chrome toilet-roll holder were the words: 'If you're unsure, wipe some more.' His grossness was not an acquired taste. A few moments of general pondering, and she returned, wishing she had a brain that could lie on tap – i.e. Dave's.

'Did I tell you when I was drunk?' she asked, sitting back down.

He re-lit his stubborn fag. 'To be honest, Naina.' She sniggered. 'To be honest, *Naina*, it was a few things: listening in to you and Leena, and the odd thing you said when you were drunk.' He paused. 'I suppose, if you really want to know, it was finding out that Ashok was your parents' type and not yours, and possibly the bit about murdering him on your wedding night.' He chuckled.

The first time Dave had asked Naina about arranged marriages, he found himself facing a ferocious rottweiler, snarling and snapping out the words: 'Just because I'm fucking Indian does not mean that all those clichés are true: arranged marriages, corner shops, curries every night, Kama Sutra, watching *Gandhi* on video, watching Gandhi perform all sixty-four positions of the Kama Sutra, a thousand people living in one house, a thousand people fitting in one car, bhangra, Bollywood, bindis, bangles and bollocks!' Seething. 'Oh yeah, and us using an aubergine as a bloody dildo!' Understandably Dave had rarely brought the subject up again, although he made every effort to keep at least one aubergine in the kitchen cupboard from that day on. Maybe if Dave had bothered to check what an aubergine looked like then he wouldn't have been sitting there with a three-foot marrow in his flat.

'You shouldn't have been listening to mine and Leena's private conversation. You're a pig, you are.' Naina turned her head away. 'And now you throw that conversation in my face. Ooh, lowlife.'

'Seriously, Naina. Tell the lowlife pig, are you having an arranged marriage? Am I right?'

And quietly Naina thought, her eyes drawn to the colourful fire. One dry log seemed to burn into the next, the fire eating them up quicker than Naina had eaten the biscuits. The warming glow of the soft red, orange and yellow darting lights echoed off the walls, almost in a language of its own, foreign and mystical. It was a good question. Was she having an arranged marriage?

Naina spoke. 'Dave, you'll look at me differently if

I tell you, besides, you hate talking about marriage and parents.'

He shuffled in his seat, dragged long and deep on his fag. 'Granted, but this is not my wedding and not my parents, so . . . just fucking tell me,' he said, with ironic frustration.

They laughed.

Naina lowered her voice. 'Look, I will tell you, but can I ask you one question first?'

He nodded yes.

'Why don't you talk about your parents?'

And Dave was up, walking around the room, agitated. 'I suppose I don't want people to look at me differently either. I'm not a sympathy scavenger, and sometimes past is past.' He momentarily stopped burning a trench in the floorboards, then began walking again. 'And really, I am ashamed of them.' He flopped back down next to her; she took his hand, sensing the hurt in his voice. 'From the age of about six, my stepdad used to beat the shit out of me for no reason, while my mother, my mother just watched. She listened to me crying and did nothing. Looking back, I sometimes think she actually—' He clammed up.

Naina felt Dave's dread, and a shiver treacled its way down her spine. She couldn't even begin to understand: her parents had never laid so much as a finger on any of their children, no matter what.

Naina's voice said nothing, but maybe her eyes did, for Dave continued, 'My real dad left for another woman, and Mum got shot of all his stuff, binned it all, including wedding photos and the ones with me and him together. Chucked the lot. But she couldn't get shot of his son, so instead she—' And as though the two subjects were mysteriously entwined and without a change in tempo, Dave changed the subject, like switching from *EastEnders* to *Brookside*. 'So, tell me about this arranged marriage.'

It was as though Dave's reclusive past had clambered out of the darkness for just the briefest of seconds, into the bright, attentive light of Naina's sympathetic ear and then crawled back inside like a restless Gollum. There was more to Dave than met the eye, and more to his past that he wasn't telling; Naina wanted to find out about both. She also wanted to reach over and hug Dave. Most of all she wanted to reach over and hug the poor scared kid he had left behind. But he wanted to know about her now and she wanted to tell him.

Naina viewed history for a second: a great, sprawling family tree; generation upon generation had been married this way – the arranged marriage way. And it worked, she saw that it worked; her whole family was proof of that. Begot begot begot, and here she was sitting on top of that tree, overlooking the deep roots of her own family, with doubts.

'Yes, I am having an arranged marriage.' She paused. 'I'm only allowed to see him twice before we marry, which isn't a problem. All my life I've known about this and I've programmed my mind for this, and I thought I could handle it. But what I didn't foresee,' Naina focused on the picture over the fire – a massive enlargement of the chariot race in *Ben Hur*, 'was that I would fall for another man. If I don't have this arranged marriage, then my parents will disown me.

And that's what's screwing me up, not the arranged marriage, but this other guy.' And before Dave's hormones marched to battle: 'And it's not you, Dave.' But it was.

He smiled. 'So, Jimmy K, yeah, that's the other man, and Ashok's your, your erm, parents' ideal man.' Dave began to roll a joint, deep in concentration, his eyes on the black block. 'Look, Naina, you can't let your parents choose your partner, and parents have no right to give you ultimatums: "If you don't do as I say, we disown you." It's you that's got to live with him, not them.' He licked the king-sized Rizla, and looked up. 'If they want you to be happy, they'll respect your choice.' And he sparked up the spliff.

Before this, Dave thought only one word didn't go with 'married' and that was 'happily', now here was another, 'arranged', that made even less sense than happily. To him it was black and white.

'It's your life, not your parents, they've had their—' He was interrupted by Naina's mobile ringing. Her eyes lit up with a start.

'Hello . . . I'm round Kate's . . . Yes, I am coming home tonight . . . Yes, Kiran . . . Well, you can check if you like . . . Oh go away!' Naina cut him off, then quickly dialled Kate. 'Kate . . . Who? . . . What? He asked you out . . . You said no? . . . Anyway . . . I'm round Dave's . . . Yes, his clothes are still on . . . If Kiran phones, I'm with you . . . He just might . . . He just phoned me . . . Okay, thanks, Kate, bye.'

Dave smiled at Naina. 'You're getting as bad as me, all those lies.'

And Naina smiled to herself; he hadn't heard the

half of it. She still had to tell him Jimmy K didn't exist and what 'intact' meant. And if he was really lucky he might eventually get to know that she had never owned a horse, her parents did not have a villa in France, Sonia, Sumita and herself had never auditioned for *East is East*, and she hadn't got a black latex sari which she only wore on Baisakhi.

And the two friends continued chatting in front of the blazing fire, waiting for a Domino's Pizza, while the weather outside growled and gritted its teeth in a noisy temper.

Kiran replaced the cordless phone in its holder and looked across to his two Indian friends. 'She's with that fucker, I know it.'

As though all India's respect was at stake here, the three hunched over the small dining-room table in Kaz's house in Bletchley, like a committee, deciding the best way to serve the cause – the Indian way. Nass wanted the lights down low, so just the whites of their eyes showed – this was serious – and he'd also seen it in a Bollywood Mafia film.

'Who'd e fink ee is, innit?' said Nass, his eyes white as white.

Kiran nodded his head. 'This is so bad. My sister! Why the fuck couldn't this white piece of shit stick to his own women, hey?'

'Innit, ee's messed, big up. The man's going down, nuff said, kill him, innit.' Nass twisted his blue baseball cap so the lip faced behind. His get-up was supremely streetwise: huge baggy oversized T-shirt, trousers that would fit the Nutty Professor, more gold than what went down with the *Mary Rose* and enough aftershave to require a sign saying Flammable. So far he was the only member of the 'MK bhangra, hip-hop, rapping, Punjabi, dissing crew'. But he was still recruiting.

Kiran jumped up and flicked on the lights. 'Nass, stop trying to fucking sound like a black man, this is dead serious here. This is my sister we're talking about. You can't just kill him, innit, you idiot.'

Nass was slapped on the head by Kaz. 'Dope.'

Kiran began his moody look: brooding and discerning, saved for the worst of times. 'We've got to find him and warn him off and tell him not to mess with our Indian girls.' He paused for effect. 'And if he doesn't listen, we get more people, until he does.'

Kaz nodded in agreement. 'How are we going to find him? Follow Naina?'

'No, I want to leave her out of this, I want it so he just disappears from her life. I'll sort her out separately, don't want to scare her, she might run off with him.' Kiran slammed down his fist and the table juddered; Nass copied him. 'He drives this brand-new BMW, forty, fifty grand, we wreck it.' He slammed his fist again; Nass copied. 'I still can't get his smug look out of my head. It's fucking freezing out there right, and he wears the tightest T-shirt you could imagine just to show off his muscles.' He paused. 'That's how we find him. Find the gym he trains at and we find him, simple, innit?'

Nass shuffled in his seat; his thick gold chains rattled. 'Wot, ees arms as big as wot, like, big as me head? Or wot, like big as me foot, when mees kick im in ees head, innit. Big up.' He laughed.

Kaz smacked Nass on the head again. 'Dope.'

They all looked to each other. This man with Kiran's sister was nothing more than a glitch in their lives. Kiran stood up. 'We start tomorrow, at the main gym in town, Dumbbells, innit.'

'Yes, Dave, you did hear it right.' Naina had a fleeting look of impatience.

'Tell me again, slowly.'

Naina stood up, dragged on the spliff, nodded her head. 'I have not had sex before.' She sank back into the sofa. 'Exactly which bit do you not understand?'

'The bit between the age of eleven and now, that bit,' he said, stuffing in a slice of pizza.

'Look, der brain, we've got to save ourselves for the marriage. We are not meant to have boyfriends. So, who exactly am I meant to be – how did you say? – "shafting"?' She sipped her lager. 'If there is any doubt, they get a doctor in, and he checks our hymen, so we don't risk it.'

'This is ludicrous, what about your natural urges? It's almost illegal.' He lifted up his tight white Armani T-shirt, stared down to his stomach muscles, smiled. 'Phew, thank God they're still there.' And threw in the last pizza slice. 'I really don't think you can shock me any more tonight, Naina, and I thought I was open-minded. I suppose that's why there aren't condom machines in Indian restaurants.'

Naina laughed, stretched across, and hit him. She wondered about him sometimes.

He carefully studied her face. He couldn't be sure, but now that he knew her sweet wrapper was still on, there was definitely something missing from her persona: she had a sex-starved look. The sort of look he'd expect from a kid in a classroom full of pupils all saying they've been to Disneyland and that one kid saying: 'I haven't.' It wasn't fair. Naina deserved to go to Disney. Naina deserved to be taken there. She needed the ride of her life.

'Naina, are you sure you're a virgin?' he asked sternly, almost like he was reprimanding her.

She huffed. 'For God's sake, Dave. It's not the end of the world if you haven't slept with someone. There is life outside sex, you know.'

He mumbled, 'Life, Jim, but not as we know it.'

Naina stood up. 'Right, I'm off. You're being very childish. I didn't sit here for the last few hours telling you about this arranged marriage, my pretend boyfriend – and don't you dare snigger again – and no sex just for you to—'

He grabbed her hand. 'Sorry. It's just . . . sorry.' Her face softened and she sat back down.

'Look, Dave. This isn't my choice. I'm doing this for my parents.'

He put on his 'I understand' face. 'Oh I see. No problem. Hope your parents appreciate what you're doing for them. It's fucking ridiculous.' He kissed her on the cheek. 'Why can't parents keep their fucking nose out of things? I've got clean sheets next door. But, oh no. What's the point . . .'

'Actually, Dave, I should get going really, I'm knackered, I need an early night. On my own, in my own sheets.'

He stood up. 'I'll give you a lift, give me five minutes to shower.' Just before he hit the doorway, he turned. 'Does sex in the shower count?'

As Dave showered, Naina snooped in his bedroom.

She hated being so nosy but she couldn't help herself. It was like she heard voices in her head: open me, look here, under the bed, in between the pages, look for clues (clues for what?). Exactly, she found nothing.

It had been a strange day. She removed her boots and lay back on Dave's ever-ready bed, her focus muzzled by the stormy cloud of a strong spliff, and her mind wandering down dangerous avenues, again. God, she did get those urges he was talking about. Okay, he was good looking, and unpredictable, and sexy, with a lovely body, and those blue, blue eyes, and . . . oh . . . God . . . another urge.

He burst in. 'What about masturbation? Tell me you masturbate, *please*.'

Naina laughed and stared at this man wearing only a pale blue fluffy towel, hair dripping, illegal. Gorgeous gorgeous gorgeous, with a smile that could lower the tightest knickers. She had to get out of here before she did or said something . . . too late . . .

'I did wear red lace you know, for you.'

Boing!

She continued, 'It's awkward wearing a G-string all day, for nothing.'

Dave walked to the side of the bed and looked down at her. 'Show me!'

'Help yourself.'

He jumped on the bed, discarding the towel as his warm hands began to undo the small buttons on her berry top. She arched her back so he could remove the shirt and chuck it to the floor. He slid her skirt down. She was wearing black, he smiled. He wanted her more than ever now, knowing that no man had ever made love to her before. He hadn't even known until

171

today that untouched women over the age of seventeen existed (apart from certain politicians that is). Their kissing became more heavy and intense, and his hands began to pull down her knickers – his favourite sound in the world.

'Naina, do you want me to continue?' he spoke softly, kissing her neck. It hurt him to ask, but it amplified his sensitivity. And sensitivity frayed many a woman's knicker elastic.

'I want you to, but,' she rolled across, 'I can't.' And searched for her knickers. 'Horrible, aren't I?'

Dave sat up. 'No!' Her anxious eyes searched the floor. 'These what you're after?' And he threw her the knickers which hadn't even left his hand. He hated sensitive men. He wouldn't be going down that nicey, nicey route again.

He watched her snap the G-string from the air and slip back into it. It was a 'Hamlet' moment. Leaning across the plump mattress, he grabbed her unwilling hand, as she sat there in just her bra and knickers, refusing eye contact.

'Naina, look at me.' She glanced across at him. 'It's no big deal.'

'I can never just enjoy myself. I can't get that Indian hold out of me. So it is a big deal.'

Dave lit a fag. 'Forget you're Indian for a minute. What do *you* actually want?' His eyes glittered.

She focused on his screen saver (an ape waving a bone above its head, from the film *2001*). 'I want the bloke that I was telling you about to love me.' And she wanted to get out a megaphone and shout in his ear, 'The bloke is you, Dave,' but she couldn't, because he'd get out his even bigger megaphone and shout,

'I'm off to Tenerife; you're getting clingy, Naina.'

'Naina, you get one life. You don't want to look back on your life and wonder "what if." He dragged on his fag. 'You said he doesn't even know you exist, so make him, go for it. He sounds like a bit of a shit to me, though!'

Naina stared at Dave. 'He is a bit of a shit.'

Chapter Fifteen

Above the seats of Dumbbells toilets there are signs: 'You may weigh less now, but that doesn't count, go and train harder' – Dave's idea. The mirrors in the fitness area are designed to make you appear slimmer – Dave's idea. The mirrors in the bodybuilding section are designed to make you appear wider – Dave's idea.

It was early, 11.00 a.m. Dave sat with his feet up in the Dumbbells' office doing nothing – Dave's idea. One tall red metal filing cabinet was allocated to the corner: a stand for the portable colour TV. A large black desk – home to a computer – with an executive black leather swivel chair in front. No windows, one door. Dave's hideaway.

He watched the CCTV monitor that kept an eye on the gym, while smoking a fag and flicking through the pages of the latest *Muscle Media 2000*. He'd seen some strange goings on in this place: blokes catching their ponytails in the equipment and crying out for help; people stuck under weights too heavy for them; flare-ups between overactive men; some of the worst chat-up lines in history, and some of the ugliest men that nature could find with *the* most gorgeous women. And women who were so big and muscular they looked like men – and scared him witless.

A sharp knock at the office door; Froggy walked in, 'OOzing,' with a less crestfallen face than the last time Dave had seen him.

Dave glanced up. 'OOzing.'

Froggy plonked himself down on the chair opposite, dressed in his grey BT overalls. 'Can't be long, I've got the van outside.' He swiped one of Dave's fags. 'S'freezing out there.'

Dave dropped his feet off the desk, tried to display a casual look. 'So, how's things with Sandra? Sorry I haven't phoned, but I thought I'd leave you two lovebirds to sort it out.'

Froggy had played second fiddle to Dave's understanding of women ever since the early days at school. No doubt about it, Dave was way ahead of his time. Bringing in words like 'tantric' and 'multiple' to the classroom while the other lads played conkers and Top-Trumps. Things seemed to come easy to him.

Dave donned an expression of concern. 'Fickle, women, aren't they?' He paused as Froggy nodded. 'So what's the story?'

Froggy leaned back in the chair. 'I think it was her hormones, mate. She said she didn't know why she acted like she did. Things are sweet.' And Froggy held a secure smile. 'Sweet, mate.'

And now Dave's guilt, which had been residing in a

small air pocket in his brain, hissed out, leaving a small amount of room for smugness to seep back in – after all, he had got away with shagging his best mate's woman.

Dave began, 'You and Sandra are like –' he looked to the ceiling to think of an apt word, '– I've got it, Froggy, you and her are like a bulb and a filament. She's the bulb but without your filament she never lights up.'

They both cracked. Dave was such a good mate.

Watching Froggy waste BT's time, seeing how happy and relieved he was over Sandra, made Dave wonder about Matt's advice. Maybe the best thing was not to tell him, to sweep it under the carpet. What good would telling him do? And if Sandra could put up with Froggy's measly 30 watts when she'd tried Dave's 100 watts, then he wasn't going to wreck their relationship.

Dave gave Froggy the safe combination, and let him scurry round the floor of the heavy metal, looking for loose skunk seeds to roll that elevenses tonsil tickler. It was a quiet relief to see Froggy back to his normal self, leaving Dave's cerebral nuts and bolts to wander back to last night.

Flourishing within Dave's mind was a fresh field of thoughts. Big, ripe, ready-to-pick corn, but without the required tools to pick them. Naina had said some things to him last night that baffled if not intrigued him. For example, what right has an Indian man to demand of his wife that she must give birth to sons? *The Indian way.* Even the way she said it sounded restrictive and orderly, as though it weighed down the shoulders from the moment you were born into an

Indian family. With Naina, he could discuss anything: she was like an open hearth, ready to warm him with her point of view. He looked to Froggy, his best mate. He could discuss beer and Frazzles with him, but anything more than that, and Froggy had this habit of laughing in his face, explaining: 'Dave, loosen up, you're getting too heavy.' Maybe if Froggy hadn't – and Dave had warned him of the consequences at the time – sniffed all that glue back then, he might now have a fairer grasp on life outside the pub. As it stood, Froggy was useless. The phone rang.

'It's Naina. Are you busy, hunky boy?'

'Never too busy for you. Funnily enough, I was just this second thinking about you.' He smiled to Froggy.

'Cut the bullshit, Dave, I need to ask you something. Is this a secure line?'

'This isn't the fucking FBI.'

She giggled. 'You said I should do what pleases me, I think you're right.'

'You're not pleasing yourself at this moment, are you?' He winked to Froggy.

'I'm putting down the phone, Dave.'

'No, no, seriously, you're looking very beautiful today. I love what you've done with your hair today, stunning.' He paused. 'Anyway, you were saying about pleasing yourself.'

Froggy laughed and Dave grinned.

Naina continued, 'Hunky boy, I want you to fuck me.'

'Play it cool Dave,' Danny Zuko said. 'But don't let your chills go multiplying.'

Dave's grin was gone, and he swivelled the chair to evade Froggy's ears. 'You want me to fuck you?

177

Why?' And he couldn't even believe what was coming out of his own mouth. It didn't matter why, it never mattered before, why now? He hated being inconsistent. He would never be able to trust his mouth again.

Naina deliberated. 'Because I've thought about this. I'm not saving myself for some man I don't even know. At least if you shag me, then I know it will be brilliant – going by your own boasts – and you won't make a big deal about it, no strings attached. So?' She hadn't been expecting 'Why?', not from Dave. Maybe 'How many times, what position, I'm coming over now' but never 'Why?' If she had, then maybe she would have said, 'Because life is for living not just existing. I fancy you rotten, you dirty filthy man and I need to get you out of my system and then think about Ashok. Plus, you're the one who told me to go for it, so if it all goes wrong, I blame YOU!' So she said, 'So?'

He'd dreamed about hearing those magic words from Naina, mulled over different scenarios of how those words might come up: maybe after she'd drunk too much, maybe after a little heart-to-heart chat invoking some sort of bond, or even in a fit of anger, throwing him against the wardrobe and teaching him a lesson. Never did he think it would be over the phone on an unsecured line. A whole year he had been trying to get in her knickers – desperate at times – thinking of all the sneaky ways that would make her open her legs for him. He'd even thought of ridiculous ways that didn't even bear thinking about now: like being honest, for example. Now, she wanted to use him, use his body that he had worked so hard for.

Hours and hours in the gym. All those women he'd practised on, now she wanted to use him. Dirty cow.

Dave continued, 'So, *you* want to fuck *me*. What about this other bloke you like? The shit? And what about your fiancé?' He looked to Froggy who mouthed 'Dirty cow!' Dave smiled and nodded yes.

Naina huffed. 'Forget about him. Forget about them both. So, do you want to or not?'

'Say the time, say the place, I'll drop everything. I mean it!' Pulse quickened, a sip of his Red Bull. 'I fucking mean it.'

'Okay. Day after tomorrow, Valentine's night.'

Another sip of Red Bull, some trickled down his chin onto his Armani top, it didn't matter. 'You want me on Valentine's night? It's lucky for you I'm not booked up this year.'

'Bye, hunky, I've got to go. Valentine's night then. My boss is giving me the eye, bye.'

Dave swivelled back round with a grin so big and deep, Froggy nearly fell in. Then, as if he had a fuse inside, he stood up and punched the air, 'YES!' He exploded.

'How d'you do it, mate?' Froggy asked, tucking into another of Dave's fags. 'So, who's this beautiful woman?'

'Can't even remember her name, mate. Months she's been begging for it, months. Listen to this, I laughed when she showed me, she's only gone and got a tattoo with my name on it; honestly, mate, she's got it bad.'

A knock on the office door. Steve entered, all pumped-up biceps and pumped-up smile. 'Dave, have you got some off-peak cards? All right, Frog?'

Dave handed him some orange cards. 'Looking good, Steve, looking goooood.'

Steve stood, soaking up Dave's comment. He had to admit he did look pretty damn good. Every night in front of his bedroom mirror he admitted it there too. Biceps and triceps to die for. 'Oh yeah, I know you said hold your calls, but I didn't think you'd mind me putting Naina through.' And he closed the door behind him.

Froggy smiled. Made out he didn't click. He couldn't wait to see Naina and ask her all about this tattoo with Dave's name on it. And who would have thought Naina had a fiancé. That in itself was worth drinks all round. But not only that, she also had another man on the side – a shit. And now she steams the sheets with his best buddy, Dave. Three men, one woman, no wonder she and Dave connected. They must go like the clappers!

Froggy stood up. 'I should get going before they sack me.' On the way out: 'Pub, tomorrow night, usual?' He couldn't stop grinning.

'See you there.' And the door slammed shut. Phew!

Even though it was only morning, outside peak-time hours at the gym, weights could be heard crashing away beyond the door and the thumping of feet from the step-aerobics studio. Some people of normal disposition, who outside the gym walls wouldn't say boo to a goose, would find themselves within the walls of Dumbbells yelling at the top of their voices to their training partner: 'Come on, one more rep, no pain no gain, dig it dig it dig it!' Dave upped the volume on the TV, drowning out the gym atmosphere.

But he could remember a time when he listened through his office walls and heard nothing. No members, all his savings spent, heavy loans, and fingers crossed so hard you'd think he was arthritic. And he wanted to remember the generously poor past he had had. It comforted him to know that not everyone could succeed, because everybody would otherwise. And as he worked throughout his youth, whilst many played – saving every penny from his self-employed fitness training – he knew a big stodgy future awaited him. And he couldn't wait to meet it. And his past, well, it could stay there as far as he was concerned, he'd never got on with it anyway.

'You're the biggest waste of talent this school has ever seen' – Mr Perkins, year head.

'You're a loser, just like your real father' – Mum, years 10 through 16.

'It's you again' – Buckinghamshire Constabulary and the Magistrates, years 11 through 16.

'You're no fun, always working, why won't you spend some time with me for a change?' – girlfriends, years 16 through 19.

'I don't give a fuck that it's bleeding, put your hand out there, boy, you little shit, before I hurt you like you've never felt before.' – Stepdad, the wonder years.

Yeah, the past could fucking well stay there. Dave looked around his office. He got his dream, even though it had brought with it many nightmares. Maybe he just needed someone to share it with. Maybe.

But a rolling stone gathers no moss, and he never

rested on his laurels. Two old sayings to describe the same thing: Dave still worked hard, in between sex pint and football, and if the good life ever bailed out on him, he never wanted to look back and declare, 'I could have done something about it.' So he worked.

Three hours later, Dave glanced at the massive pair of sky blue underpants on top of the lost property box beside the safe. If the owner ever came back to reclaim them, then Dave would personally see to it that he found out how to use a washing machine – filthy animal. 'What the hell am I still doing here?' he thought, and picked up his keys and phone and headed out.

Fifteen minutes later, three Indian misfits cruised into Dumbbells, all dressed in fitness gear. Steve the manager looked up as they came in.

'Can I help you?' he asked, drying the blender with a red and white chequered tea towel.

Kiran glanced at the main gym area. 'Nice gym. We're thinking of joining. We were recommended by this bloke – do you know him? – wears designer clothes, big arms, drives a smart black BMW.'

Steve placed the blender down. 'You must mean Dave, he owns the place. Did he tell you the prices?'

Kiran, Kaz and Nass exchanged a look underlined in hate. 'No, is he here? He said something about putting us on a special routine so we could all have big arms like him.'

Laughter, including Steve's. 'Yeah, that *will* be Dave. Well, you've literally just missed him, he's in later tonight. About 9.30, but I could help you out though.' Steve posed his arm. Muffled laughter from Nass, until elbowed by Kaz.

'No, we'll come back, thanks anyway.'

The three left the counter. Kiran looked around the gym one more time – he hated Dave even more now. Nass tried to rectify his error for laughing at Steve's biceps on the way out: 'Me finks da man got legs for his bleeding arm' innit.'

Steve did not understand a word.

The three departed in a red sooped-up Cavalier, driving through the grey slush from yesterday's snow. The extra-large chrome exhaust could be heard in the next estate and vibrated the car like it was from the cartoon *Roobarb and Custard*. Nass flipped his baseball cap back the right way, showing off the logo 'NEC, Mela Mela'.

'Must be Guru Nanak's shining down on us, innit. We found him well quick,' Kaz said grinning, as he floored it down H3 Monks Way dual carriageway. 'Rich white bastard, innit.'

'We come tonight for him, while he's in the gym. We wreck his car, and then we wait for him. We'll have to bring some more guys though innit, just in case. He's going to wish he never met my sister.' Kiran looked round to their nodding heads.

Naina held the hand mirror up to the back of Sonia's head so she could see the reflection in the dressing-table mirror. 'See, Sonia, the hair is all in place, there's no bald spot.'

'Sure? There were clumps on the floor. That bitch Melinda, she fights just like a girl.'

'Sure,' Naina confirmed.

She lay back on the patchwork quilt. She'd just found out that the huge Sikh temple and hall had been booked for her and Ashok's wedding. Her depression would have dissolved a Prozac factory: there was a finality to it all that didn't bear thinking about . . . but think she did. Every time she tried to kill off her dark thoughts, they would reincarnate themselves, returning even stronger and scarier. Phoenixes of Indian tradition with wings that couldn't be clipped.

With a hand that seemed glued to a troubled chin, Naina lay on the bed, wondering if she should consult the powers-that-be? Should she dare see what messages lay hidden in the supernatural world? Exam results, driving test, even the cricket scores for Dad once, all these premonitions had been forecast by her Tarot cards, and she wondered if now was the time to ask them again. Did she really want to know her destiny?

Reaching up to her massive wardrobe, she pulled down a deep brown wooden box, the size of a shoebox. The decorations – elephants trunk-to-trunk round all the edges and, in the middle, a picture of a typical Indian village scene with women in saris, cows, goats, and children – all carved to a degree of painstaking perfection that probably stole a month of work from an expert craftsman for a measly 20p. It had been a present from her gran whom she had never even met. Inside, Naina had lined it with finest black felt, a cushioning for her Rune-stones and Tarot deck.

Sitting cross-legged on the beige carpet, Naina shuffled the Spanish Tarot cards. Sonia paid little attention. Twenty-one cards were laid out in the Pyramid Spread, determining Naina's past, present and future. The peak of the Pyramid, her outcome, showed Three of Swords, suggesting delay and difficulties lay ahead. Another card to the right, her distant future, showed Two of Swords, warning of trouble due to someone else's actions. She wished she hadn't bothered now, her life prospects were summed up in one word: *bleak*.

'Staying in tonight, Naina?' Sonia asked, logging on to the Internet.

'Yeah, I'm getting an early night,' she replied, carefully putting her traitor cards away.

Sonia had her own web page: 'Generous Pain!!!' A whole site developed by herself and her two gothic friends, devoted entirely to Marilyn Manson. Sonia's friends were named at birth Lucy and Katrina, but preferred to be called Damnation and Destruction, respectively; Sonia was just plain old Death.

'Ah, twenty-seven e-mails.' Sonia, beaming, looked to Naina now lying on the bed. 'Twenty-seven; it must be because of the lyrics that I wrote for a suggested song.'

'What song, Sonia?' Naina's head rose a little, then regretted it as Sonia was already standing above her with the printed lyrics.

'Read that and weep, my untalented sister.'

My Chosen Fear. By The only . . . Death.

> *Internal pain, I beseech you.*
> *My bridge is rotten and lame.*
> *Inner domain, I seek you.*
> *So I fall into your flame.*

'Lovely, Sonia, you're wasted.' Naina lay back, not reading verses 2 through 20.

'Ta, your loss.' Sonia turned back to the computer, and continued to tap away.

Downstairs in the hall, Dad could be heard boasting on the phone – on the extra line they had had to have fitted because of Sonia and her Internet obsession – to his older brother in Slough. Blowing his own trumpet on how well he had chosen for Naina. How Ashok was from a decent, well-respected family. Dad didn't really need a phone, his voice was that loud. And for some reason, when phoning long distance, to places like India, his voice would shake the foundations of the house. The agonizing part for the rest of the family was when he slammed the phone down and still carried on just as loud, repeating exactly what had been said on the phone, at least twice.

Naina's parents were over-excited at the prospect of marrying her into a rich, prominent, honourable home. It was like they had hit six numbers on the lottery when Ashok agreed to marry Naina. The bonus ball was when Ashok's dad had come back with the date of the wedding. There are no rollovers on the Indian lottery.

'Fucking ace!' muttered Dave to himself. He had never taken that corner at 65 m.p.h. before, especially in sludge. His car spun and skidded into his Reserved for Gym-owner spot, and the electric window hummed down. He threw out a fag end. It was 9.30 p.m.

Dave hopped out and walked inside the nearly deserted gym. He ordered Steve to turn the music off, to discourage any gym-rats, and bagged up the money, stuffed it in the safe, and collected half an ounce of hash. Dave and Steve waited for the last people to collect their training bags after letting the other staff go.

Bold as brass, Kiran walked up and down the BMW, rubbing his index finger down the fine lines of the car. It would be a mistake to let his impatience get to him now. He would have to wait just a little while longer. Whispered calls for him to get back in the blue Transit with the four other Indian men distracted him; even from where he stood, the only thing he could make out was Nass's one gold tooth, like a sovereign of treasure in the black pit of night. He returned to the thick heat of the van, and sat at the front next to Kaz.

'It's a beautiful car, I can't wait to trash it,' Kiran said with envy.

The van bounced on its suspension from the internal laughter. Then silence, as the white bastard appeared at the entrance. Kiran willed the other man to go away, and yet again Guru Nanak obliged as Steve walked past the Transit, not even registering it, and crossed onto the road that led away from Linford Wood. Dave was on his own now. Just him, and the five Indian men wanting justice.

The electric shutters wound down slowly, and Dave watched hoping the burglar alarm would not be activated as it sometimes was by the rumbling metal and gears. Finally the lip of metal clanked to the cold concrete floor.

He was well and truly locked out.

'Dave.' A voice behind him.

Dave, startled, turned round as far as the arm

round his neck would allow. His windpipe was crushed by a tight locked arm in a thin woollen jumper. If it was not for the pain, it almost tickled.

Instinct threw his head back, butting a fleshy nose, and his right Nike shot backwards, bruising someone's calf.

'Get hold of him, he's struggling.' Another voice.

Dave felt grabbing, like an octopus of arms pulling him downwards, pushing on his head, pushing him to the wet floor. But before he had time to study the tarmac in great detail, he was lifted up again by two strong sets of arms and hoisted before whoever this was who was trying to kill him: maybe it was Tracy's husband, or Michelle's boyfriend, or Katie's husband, or Lisa's boyfriend, or Shelly's fiancé, or Anna's husband, or Jane's husband, or Becky's boyfriend or even Penny's bisexual girlfriend (she was a bit butch he later found out).

'Oooff.' Dave was punched slam in the stomach, and his face became tight. Voices were streaming over his head, all panicky, all in a fever, all excitable, all except one. Kiran.

The blade shone like a goblin's. A four-inch jagged dagger, perfect to stick into a white man's flesh and paint the dull steel a glorious red.

'You keep your white fucking hands off Naina, she's ours!' Kiran spoke with clenched teeth, wielding the knife inches from Dave's taut throat. Little sweeping movements of the cutting edge swayed from side to side. 'She doesn't belong to you.'

The five men in black balaclavas closed around Dave, his arms held uncomfortably behind him.

Another voice, edgy and defined. 'Why don't you

stick to your own women? Our culture doesn't mix with yours. We don't treat our women with disrespect. We don't go round having affairs, we don't hit them, we don't leave them to bring our children up on their own and we fucking don't divorce them when we're sick of them.' And the nervy voice trailed off, angrily, to be replaced by Kiran.

'Tonight is a warning; next time we'll kill you.' His pupils boiled like black tar and the statement was unequivocal. 'Keep away from Naina!' And the blade brushed across Dave's throat, almost delicately in contrast to the thrusting force of Kiran's hate. He hated everything about this man. He hated that this man, this white piece of shit, had touched his own flesh and blood – his sister. 'Smash his car up!'

Dave crumbled as the four began to scrape the car paintwork with a car jack, the knife in Kiran's hand still unwavering against his throat. They kicked and attacked the car like a hated foe, puffing with exertion, and slowly the car was destroyed. A gleaming BMW devoured by hate and turned into a worthless piece of junk.

Then they turned their attention to him.

Yet another voice. Calm, direct, straight to the jugular. 'You white people call us Pakis, yet you try to steal our women. You hate us, but you needed us when we came from India to do your dirty work. But we are a success and you show your jealousy through your ignorance.' He spat in Dave's face. 'And now you want us out. You have no honour, no pride, no family values.'

Dave never saw the sign, or heard, but all five men knew that now was the time to lay into him. A hail of punches, scattered all over his body. Frantic clenched fists and tight jaws, bruising and pounding him. A muddle of pain sweeping through, until it finally stopped – leaving only his face untouched. Kiran's warning to the posse had been clear: 'Avoid the head and face, we don't want a dead gorreh on our hands. Innit!'

'Next time, we'll finish you off!'

They left him on the ground, climbed back into their idling Transit van and casually drove off – honking their horn. The last thing Dave saw was the saffron-coloured Sikh flag – the size of a bed sheet – being waved out the back by someone with a gold tooth.

Chapter Sixteen

Three hours later.

'Cup of tea?' Sandra asked, propping a flowery Laura Ashley pillow behind Dave's back.

'Brandy and a bag of peas please,' he whimpered.

Froggy turned to Sandra. 'I don't think we've got peas.' He looked back at Dave. 'Will mini pizzas do? Or waffles?'

'Anything, mate.'

It was 12.30 a.m. Dave lay back on the orange sofa in Froggy's and Sandra's house, milking it. The walls were mandarin and cream, furnished with a handful of framed posters of West End musicals: *Chess*, *Cats*, *Phantom Of The Opera* and *Miss Saigon*. A pack of frozen mini tomato and mushroom pizzas now lay on his stomach to ease the pain, and a quiet evening in, watching *The Perfect Storm*, had been put on hold to play nurse to Dave.

Froggy lit up a fag and passed it over to Dave. 'Sandra,' he yelled. 'Do you think Blockbusters will let us keep it for another night without a fee?'

Dave sniggered, hurting his bruising.

Sandra launched herself through the door. 'Froggy, you are so selfish and stingy. Your best mate lies here and all you think about is your £3.75 DVD. Dave, here's your brandy.' She handed him the drink and sat opposite him on the orange armchair. 'We got the film with our Sainsbury's reward voucher anyway.'

Sandra was the epitome of house-proud. The two-bedroom semi-detached, with its leaded windows, perfectly manicured garden and hanging baskets, was everything Sandra had wished for since the age of twelve when she used to coordinate her doll's house with the precision of a top designer. Inside, small bowls of pot-pourri, vases of fresh flowers, and little ceramic aromatherapy burners invigorated the small homely abode with a rush of warm summer smells. Then Froggy would take his trainers off.

After the Transit had departed, Dave had phoned Froggy and then the police. His statement was simple: 'No, I have no enemies, everyone likes me, and I found the car wrecked when I came back from a short jog round the outside of the gym. I didn't see or hear anything.'

'Who do you think it was?' asked Sandra, tying back her blonde hair with a scrunchie.

'I don't know. All they said was keep away from Naina.'

'And are you going to stay away from her? It makes sense. They sound dangerous.' Sandra held her breath waiting for Dave's response.

'No, of course not. She means a lot to me.'

It takes roughly thirty-six muscles to smile. Ten of Sandra's failed to work as her face dropped like a wet towel. 'Even if they kill you?'

Froggy, who had no shame and was munching on one of the half-defrosted pizzas, decided to speak. 'Fucking hell, Sandra, talk about overreacting.'

Sandra's hazel eyes were scornful. 'Overreacting? I'm not the one who goes round accusing his girlfriend of having an affair.' She stood up. 'Am I, Richard?' And she stormed out.

Dave tried to shrug, but excruciating pain interfered. 'Cheers for picking me up, mate, I appreciate it.'

Froggy lit up another two fags, one for himself, the other he passed to Dave. 'I still don't understand why you lied to the police.'

'Look, I didn't even want to call them, but I had to for the car insurance. If I told them the truth, then Naina would be involved and then they would question her, and then I'd be putting her in it.'

'How, though? How would you be putting her in it?' Froggy seemed confused.

Dave dragged on his fag. 'Froggy, just like you tell me secrets and it's only between you and me, well Naina's told me something and she's got my word I won't tell anyone. So, sorry, mate.'

Froggy nodded his head, he understood. He knew his elastic-band secret was safe with Dave. How he used it as a noose to prolong his erection. He knew the time that he and Dave were handcuffed and arrested at the age of fifteen for putting a chainsaw to Mrs Dewberry's apple trees when the Dewberrys were on holiday, and how he had *cried* all the way to the police station, was safe with Dave too. (All the Dewberrys had said to the young Dave and Froggy was: 'When we are on holiday, make sure you don't steal our apples, you little tikes. We've counted them all and we will know.') And they did know, when they had returned to see four apple trees felled in the garden with a little note: 'Count that, you fuckers!'

Dave sat up, lifting up his top to admire the colourful bruises that were now blossoming. 'It was probably all caught on camera, you know. I told the filth the camera was a dummy.'

'You're joking?'

'No, I'm going to look at it tomorrow. But I don't want Naina to know any of this, okay? And tell Sandra not to breathe a word to anyone, especially Naina.'

As Froggy and Sandra soundly slept upstairs, a shadowy figure in the downstairs living room could be seen doing press-ups, rubbing himself up against a sofa arm, holding on to the Laura Ashley pillow with one arm and with the other balancing on the floor raising his hips up and down.

Finally, he slumped back onto the sofa, smiled his Dave smile, exhausted. 'I'm going to be okay, it's going to be all right, I'll still be able to perform perfectly on Valentine's night for Naina.'

Dave couldn't sleep, so he got up, and checked out the shelves for some pornography. There was none. Sandra was changing Froggy. So he sat quietly in the darkness, smoking a fag, waiting for the Nurofen to kick in.

The few stealthy noises of cars passing late outside

the window, the deep rasp of Froggy snoring above his head and the buzz of the fridge freezer in the kitchen next door. Someone else's house. Jesus, how did Sandra put up with that snoring?

So, today he'd been warned off Naina by a bunch of Indian men in balaclavas – nice touch. Sermonized to by an Indian preacher, then gobbed in the face – nice touch. And as the van sped off, a last comment by a gold-toothed mouth: 'Steroid abuser, innit!' – nice touch. Dave's thoughts spun on their axis, becoming dense and heavy. Naina was right, Indian men did not want their women straying. Why not put a chain round their women's necks and be done with it? A twenty-two-carat gold chain – nice touch. He had kept his mouth shut during his ordeal. It wouldn't have done any good to say, 'I love Naina's exotic brown eyes. I love the way her brown-tinted black hair falls down her beautiful Indian face. I love the feeling I have when I see her naked brown skin brush against my white body. And most of all I *love* the way our cultures mix when we stick our tongues in each other's mouths.'

He looked to the ceiling. That fucking snoring.

Chapter Seventeen

'**O**Ozing.' Followed by four 'OOzings'. Friday night, pub time.

A message had gone round the mobiles that Jingle had pulled last night and was bringing her down the local that evening. Apparently she was, quote: 'Out of this world!'

Dressed in his Armani tight white T-shirt, black jeans, Nikes and Davidoff, Dave, with his two pints of dreamy Stella, pulled over a chair and joined the expectant crowd. He was going to get slaughtered tonight. No women, though: he was going to save himself for tomorrow night with Naina. He was especially going to forget all that he'd seen on that CCTV video tape, for now.

Oasis played on the loud throbbing speakers, 'Don't Look Back In Anger', and the pub was beginning to swell already. Football was on the agenda. Man U against Liverpool, and a small shoal of red jerseys swam up to and back from the already swamped bar counter. A large chap, possibly 24 stone, sat crammed into one of the wooden chairs, folds of bum poking through poles of the chair back like huge swollen saveloys. On the back of the shirt 'No 7, Beckham'. Next to him, and maybe this was a coincidence and maybe it wasn't, sat a small, skinny woman in a Spice Girls T-shirt.

'Pete,' Dave shouted, 'tell them that joke about the woodcutter and his axe.'

Pete looked around, the drink was flowing, maybe this was a good time to tell that joke. So he did.

Nobody laughed at all. No one. It wasn't even funny and Dave knew it.

'Shit, isn't it?' Dave pointed out, laughing to everyone, clenching his painful stomach.

Suddenly the pub went pink. Bitch Kate had arrived in her pink fake-fur coat and coming in right behind her was Naina.

'Oi, Naina, Kate, over here,' shouted Froggy. Sandra killed him with a smile.

The two pushed their way through the bustle, Kate's coat collars wiping away most people's sweat. Four lethal stilettos swathing through the crowd, like stabbing tent hooks. Attracting not very wholesome stares from partly drunk men willing to forget the football for a moment for a taste of Naina's body. Her tight, figure-hugging, backless deep-purple dress complimenting her spectacular curves and dishing out IOUs to the fantasies of many men.

'Where's the thief?' asked Matt.

'Leena is away for the weekend,' replied Naina, totally ignoring Sandra's presence.

Dave's and Naina's eyes connected with each other for just a blink. But that blink was a mini conversation in itself. How are you? Fine, you? Fine, you look nice, Naina. Thanks, you look drunk, Dave.

'Sit yourselves down, Jingle will be here with his bird any minute,' Andy suggested, shunting up his seat.

'Kate and I—'

Kate interrupted, 'Yeah we'll stay for a few drinks, won't we, Naina?' Took off her fur coat, nearly sat on Pete's lap, and pulled over another chair for Naina.

Naina hung her heavy coat on the back of the chair and sat in between Kate and Diane, feeling slightly depressed. She'd only come to discuss her dreadful wedding with Kate, get drunk, then go back to Kate's. Now she had to put up with a rowdy table all waiting for their thrill of the evening – Jingle.

Andy took the drink orders and walked off.

A veil of smoke lay over the pub like early morning mist over a lake. Great football clichés could be heard, like 'we're on the ball, we're on the ball' and 'vindaloo vindaloo'. And between 'come on, if you think you're hard enough' and whopping great belches, was the continuous background noise of 'Who's next?' from the bar.

Froggy gave a heart-warming smile to Naina. 'Naina, thanks for the card. You didn't have to, but Sandra and I was well pleased.' Froggy looked from Naina to Sandra, prodding his girlfriend's ribs gently. 'Weren't we, Sandra?'

'It was lovely, Naina, and the poem was beautiful. So talented you are, really.' Sandra squeezed out a fake smile. And Froggy gave her a hug for trying.

Naina forgave herself for being confused, she hadn't a clue what they were talking about. 'Card?'

Dave cut in like a whippet. 'Naina, I thought it was extremely decent of you to apologize for your drunken behaviour the other night and if I'm not mistaken I think this whole table would like to give you a small round of applause.' He started to clap, and reluctantly the rest followed. It had taken Dave a whole morning to sneakily write that poem, one of his better ones, he judged – he thought it had an air of Kipling about it. He lurched over and planted a kiss on Naina's cheek saying, 'I'm so proud of you.' She wanted to kill him.

And why had Dave written a poem on Naina's behalf?

Dear Froggy and Sandra,

There are so many colours that
I could have been.
You see me as brown, but really
I'm green.

I'm envious, Sandra, I feel like a fool,
of your looks, of your body,
I'm jealous of it all.

So I bitch, and I struggle to make you
look bad. I want what you've got,
what I have is sad.

So next time I'm nasty, and next time I'm sick,
my permission to you pretty Sandra

is reach out and kick.

And when we get older
when looks matter not
I thank thee, I thank thee
for the friendship we've got.

I am so sorry for getting pissed and trying to cast
doubts on your solid relationship. Please forgive me.
        Yours enviously, Naina.

The answer: to save his butt. Keep his friendship with
Froggy. The letter and poem should clear up any
doubts in Froggy's mind of Sandra's fidelity. Naina
was bound to understand. She was doing something
admirable, letting herself look a fool, to keep his
friendship alive with Froggy. Very admirable. He'd
make sure Valentine's day was special. And all for
sex, that was about the size of it. Sex!

Naina gulped down half a pint of Stella, making a
mental note to ask Dave the story behind this card she
had supposedly written. She peered through the lip of
her pint glass at a smug-looking Sandra. She then
glanced across to Kate who was immersed in some
heavy flirting with Pete, running her fingers through
his hair and giggling, whispering, 'Pete, you look just
like a younger version of Kevin Costner, only much
more handsome.'

Naina watched Dave smiling towards the other side
of the pub. And when he smiled, his whole body
smiled with him. It had to be a beautiful woman. But
there was no way she was going to look, no way.
Maybe just a glance, a little turn of the head, pretend

to watch the football screen to see if Man U had scored. Naina subtly twisted her head. Man U had not scored. Dave had. The beautiful woman at the far end was pouting her lips and beckoning him. Hard luck, there is no way Dave will be coming over, my little blonde bombshell, thought Naina, because Dave is having sex with me tomorrow. She turned back. Dave was gone.

Bastard.

Naina tried hard to do away with the sums. This was no time for maths. Just because she would be Dave's 100,000 and third lover, and he only her first, didn't mean anything, it didn't matter, did it? She grabbed Kate's beer and gulped. Heavy hops sank to her stomach. But it did matter. What if he didn't even take into account that this was her first time? What if he laughed at her? What if he kept mentioning his other conquests and comparing? And what if he wanted her to do yoga, and what if he turned round at the end and said, 'Cheers, you were fucking useless but at least I can say I've shagged you now!' Dave returned, still smiling.

As if the whole table was on stilts in wet mud, it began to sink into a drunken stupor of stupidity; getting louder, filthier as it sank lower and lower. Even through partially drunken eyes, however, Naina could fathom that Dave's clenching of his stomach every time he laughed at someone else's expense was an indication that all was not quite well.

'Done too many sit-ups, Dave?' Naina asked, concerned, running her index finger round the rim of one of her empties.

Froggy intervened like a good drunken mate would.

'I love this man. He did seven hundred and ninety-eight and a thousand sit-ups last night. I said, Dave, if you could just do two more then you will be on six hundred million, one-handed as well.' Froggy put his arm round Dave. 'A right little amusement arcade, aren't you?'

Kate burst out screaming, damaging one of Pete's eardrums. 'Yeah, an amusement arcade with the smallest joystick.'

Laughter. Many hands beat the table. Beer spilled, ashtrays hopped, Dave snarled at bitch Kate. And then the snarl moulded to a smile, and the room seemed to go extra still and quiet, noises now just vibrations: Dave had finally seen an angel.

Wingless she moved, graceful and surreal, a perfect beauty. Speechless, Dave watched her as she began to float towards him. Her holly green eyes like crystals of the purest stone, enticing, captivating, and passionate. And then she was there, long tanned legs astride, standing directly within his tunnel vision. She was naked . . .

'Everyone, I would like you all to meet Melody,' announced a very proud Jingle. 'Sorry we're late, we were looking for some charcoal tablets.'

The general thought in most people's mind was: 'What was an ugly fuck like Jingle doing with a beauty like her?' Stunned table and a strange little noise.

Somehow two more seats were found and the new couple sat down as close as two Twix, while everyone shuffled along to make room. They were already quite at home holding each other's hands, and Dave's initial thought, that Jingle must have got himself an overdraft to pay for her for the night, was ruled out. Wow!

Naina watched Dave. She could see his 'Porn' look. Pathetic.

A strange little noise.

'Melody, reminds me of a song.' A few female laughs. 'Sorry,' Dave continued, 'So, when was the last time you visited an optician, Melody?' More laughs. 'No really, I'm damn serious.'

A strange little noise. Dave looked under the table. 'What the fuck is that noise?'

Jingle turned a deeper red, and glanced at Melody, then at the table. 'Melody has a medical condition.' Melody urged him to go on, tell them. 'She can't stop breaking wind, her bowels leak.' Had Jingle learned nothing over the years about his mates?

Laughter was to be expected, and laughter is what they got.

Farting can only keep you amused for so long. Soon the subject of football surfaced and the strange little noises were becoming indistinguishable from the background noise, apart from the one time that Froggy stood up and did a massive one and said, 'Melody, jealous?' At that particular point Naina thought it was best she went to the Ladies. Sandra followed, like static.

The pub catered very well for the women, with a long, mirrored vanity area and hairdryers on either side. Little soap dishes with pearl soaps, a few ashtrays for those who used the place as a rendezvous for women tactics, pedal bins, two plastic chairs so women could chat to women on the loos, and a condom machine with a sign that said, 'Don't let him forget.' Music from the pub stereo was piped through the ceiling and normally there were more women in here than outside, except on footy nights, when most women had sense and stayed at home.

Naina brushed through her long straight hair, slightly tipsy, and grateful for the relative quietness of the loo. Sandra stood beside her, applying lippy.

'Make sure you don't drink too much more, Naina, or you might end up putting Dave in it.'

Naina had paused with the brushing while Sandra spoke, but now continued, 'You mean put *you* in it,' said with poison.

'Well, I hope you are really proud of yourself, Naina. You nearly wrecked mine and Froggy's relationship.'

The brushing stopped for good this time, Naina turned round to face her. 'You wrecked your own relationship the moment you slept with Dave.'

Sandra tried to tut it off, tried to remain oblivious to such a comment, but deep down she knew: the truth did hurt sometimes. 'Tell me, what's your relationship with Dave? It seems really strange to me. What do you do? Give him a shag once a week?' She paused. 'What's your other two blokes think of that, Miss Mother Teresa? Or don't they know? You slag.'

A middle-aged woman wandered out of one of the toilet cubicles and gave them both equal looks of distaste, washed her hands and left. The noise of the pub flowed in for a few seconds until the door closed on its safety spring, leaving them both on their own.

'It seems to me, Sandra, that you haven't got Dave out of your system yet. I can assure you that you're out of his.'

The wound cut deep, and Sandra turned around and walked straight out. Naina smiled, she had guessed right, Sandra still had a thing for Dave.

Meanwhile Kate eyed Dave, she wanted to upset him while Naina was in the Ladies. His grin was beginning to annoy her. 'A new gym's opening.'

Dave's smile disappeared. 'Where?' His voice had an urgency that was highly amusing – to Kate.

'Uhm, nowhere, just wanted to see your face.' The table laughed.

'Kate, you flamingo's arse. Go and scrub some bogs.' He puffed on his fag, the annoying grin returned.

The same grin that Kate remembered from when she was first introduced to Dave through Naina. Instantly she had disliked him – far too good looking. She never trusted men who looked too good. Maybe Dave had sensed the sneer in Kate's demeanour, as that whole evening's conversation had been entirely devoted to pink: pink salmon, Pink Floyd, the mystery of the missing pink from the Battenburg factory, *Pretty in Pink* the movie, pink sherbet, ice cream, Marigolds, even big steaming lumps of ET's pink pooh. No one could help but laugh, even herself, but she still disliked him and most likely always would. And the more Naina liked him, the more Kate disliked him. He was no good to her, no good to anyone. Looks and biceps didn't buy Kate's respect. And respect, ha! He had none for women.

Naina applied a coat of chocolate-brown lipstick, and headed back into the noisy pub. Sitting down, she was quite relieved to see that Kate's pink coat was back on.

'I'll ring you, Pete. Naina, shall we go?'

Naina stood up, wrapped herself in her coat, bid farewell to all, especially Sandra, and left trying hard to prop up Kate, whose legs were limbs of jelly.

'Hold on, Naina.' Dave got up, fag in mouth, pint in hand. 'I'll come out with you.'

And the three jigsawed their way through the red sea of jerseys.

A cab was ordered, and Kate left them to it, humming a little tune to herself, holding Pete's phone number like a fifty-pound note in her fist.

A small area below the gangway to the pub entrance was nearly devoid of light, and sometimes romancing couples would use the opportunity to warm each other through, stealing the odd kiss and sharing the odd shag. The landlord was sick of finding used condoms under there, but it was better than puke, he supposed.

'Naina, you look gorgeous,' Dave said, undoing her coat, putting his hand on her bare thigh, and kissing her mouth.

She grasped his zip firmly and tugged it down. 'I haven't got long.' And knelt down, pulling his jeans down to his Nikes. She looked to his black trainers – so clean, one of the laces needed retying. She began to . . . there was a dull tapping on her head. Oh yeah, she was supposed to be doing something else. So she did.

Forty minutes later, the taxi drew up, honked, and Naina and Dave held a hug until Kate yelled out something along the lines of 'Come on, Naina, if you haven't found his willy by now, you never will', followed by a witch's cackle. And the two drunk women left.

Inside, Dave returned to the messy table with its scattered empties, fag ends flowing out of full ashtrays, empty packets of peanuts. He sparked up a fag, and ordered Matt to get him another drink. He was given the finger.

'Nice lipstick, mate, suits you,' Jingle digged.

Sandra flashed a look to Dave's face, to his lips, to the chocolate-brown lipstick now coating them like a deep varnish. Dave and Naina had been out there, in the cold waiting for a taxi for gone half an hour. Sandra's stomach shifted, jealousy flared. But she had Froggy, she should be happy; she looked at Froggy now with a dry roasted peanut up each nostril and four or five cheesy Wotsits hanging out of his mouth. She had safe, monogamous Froggy. Then she stared at Dave, possibly the biggest liar in the entire world; the one who would make women feel so special while he was on top of them; then after completion, look at them like he had done them a huge favour. But like good quality wood, no matter how much you whittle away at it, you are still left with good quality wood – he was gorgeous. He could walk into the most boring party and turn it round. A confidence that you just can't pretend to have; an aura women fell for. Sandra knew which one she would have out of Froggy or Dave, if she had the choice.

Dave wiped the lipstick from his lips with the back of his hand and smiled to himself. Sandra plotted: she would make it her mission to turn Dave against Naina.

All she would have to do would be to plant a few idle seeds of doubt in Dave's mind, then wait for the watering can of insecurity to nurture and feed the seeds until they were great blossoming flowers of treason with tendrils of hurt. Sandra smiled to herself. God, it was great to be a bitch.

'Dave.' Froggy stood up, balancing like a baby on his drunk heavy legs. 'Can you remember her name yet? The one with the so-called tattoo of your name? The one with the fiancé? The one that fancies a shit? The one that's got you tomorrow night? Remember her now? The one you're willing to drop everything for, everything.' He stepped backwards laughing, and fell smack on to the table behind him.

Yeah, he would also be dropping one more thing he hadn't thought of – *Naina*, the conniving little bitch. Sandra smiled.

There were a few strange little noises.

Chapter Eighteen

D ave stood balancing on the blue sofa chair reaching for the last of the Christmas decorations. He wanted to make the flat less Christmassy, less Noel, less festive. The only star he wanted to shine down tonight was the twinkle in Naina's eyes. And if she fancied a Silent Night she was coming to the wrong place. He was going to make her sleigh bells jingle and jangle if it was the last thing he did.

Naina was due to arrive at 7.00 p.m.; it was now 6.50 p.m. He had read up in *Woman's Own* about what he might need for the perfect Valentine evening:

1. scented red candles
2. slow love songs
3. massage oil
4. sexy underwear
5. chilled wine
6. no interruptions

Fuck all that, he thought, I've got a king-sized bed.

He wondered if the sweet old couple below still celebrated Valentine's. He hoped they did in a way. Maybe Ivy gave Stan something special on occasions like this, like removing those dentures and giving him a quality blow job. Or maybe they just sat closely together on the flowery sofa, dunking McVities Rich Tea biscuits in their Botanic Gardens bone-china cups, whilst watching *Stars in their Eyes*, with a hot-water bottle snug behind each of their crooked backs. He sort of preferred they did the latter really.

Dave tossed Rudolf in the chrome bin, walked into the cosy bedroom, and threw some clothes on: a California Zone petrol blue top, black baggies and Nikes, not forgetting his Davidoff. Back in the living room he retired to the sofa, flicking through the various channels on his wide-screen TV. The hungry fire snapped away with a couple of dampish logs, setting off a pantomime of fire-dancing shadows in the dimmed light. He switched the TV off, flicked the remote to his stereo and cast his thoughts to nowhere while he listened to 'November Rain' by Guns n' Roses, lying back on the huge sofa with his eyelids closed.

Naina paid the £4 fare to the skinny taxi driver, who counted out the four pound coins like someone who had been diddled one too many times. Then she picked up the chilled bottle of white wine wrapped in green tissue paper, and buzzed the intercom. The entrance door unlocked, and she slowly climbed the blue carpeted stairs in her black strappy sandals, her small Christian Dior vanity bag tight to her shoulder. Mum and Dad had lectured that after this week was over she would have to spend at least one night a week in, learning to cook the Indian way – Ashok would not be too impressed with the only dish she could cook so far, 'the chuck-it-all-in curry'. And if Kate was so dead against Naina sparing one day a week, then she could come and help. Kate was also dead against Naina sleeping with Dave, her warning was not dressed up, it was not subtle, it was true and Kate-like: 'Naina, don't sleep with that lying bastard, he's a user!'

And here she was, only feet away from what Dave would probably call The Dave Experience. She asked herself why? She had saved herself all these years, she was about to get married . . . She didn't have the answer. The best she could come up with was that she just wanted to break one rule before she handed herself over to Ashok. And on her wedding night with Ashok, what excuse would she use? Would she say that she used to ride her bike too hard as a child? Or, maybe she had been born with a genetic defect – no hymen, or, would she use Dave's suggestion of getting a small syringe of red ink and squirting it on the bed sheets, while Ashok was removing his turban? She didn't know, she was just living for the moment.

Dave opened the blue gloss door and greeted her with a warm kiss as she stepped inside the heated flat.

'I was just this very minute thinking about you, Naina.' They both laughed and she passed him her coat and the bottle of Chardonnay.

Naina's nerves were delicately balanced. A high-wire act, feeling excited on one side and on the other feeling disturbingly bad. And as if Dave could read her mind, he handed her a large glass of vodka and orange, whilst keeping his eyes fixed on her, confused.

Naina swallowed an enormous gulp, settling the score with her tumbling nerves. 'It's my hair that's different, I've had it highlighted.'

'I knew that; suits you,' he remarked, sitting down next to her on the sofa, satisfied that she wasn't an impostor. 'Naina, I'm not going to lie to you.' Here we go, thought Naina. 'I think about shagging you every time I see you. I don't even get to hear what you're gabbing on about half the time, I'm too busy wondering what it would feel like to . . . anyway, after tonight, you can be assured that I will listen to every word you have to—'

Naina butted in, 'Carry on talking like that and I'm off!' She meant it.

That was it, thought Dave, what's the point in being honest if you're treated like this? But he would have to be honest with himself: he'd slept with many women, many many beautiful women, but none compared. This beauty before his eyes shone in a league to which only a few dared be invited. Not just shone, she burned, like the middle of a shooting star. He watched her slender fingers slide through the brown ribbons of tint in her black shiny hair. He couldn't hold out much longer. He had about as much patience as a rude interruption and his self control's sell-by date was about half an hour before Naina had arrived. To sum up – he was gagging for her.

Naina nervously sipped her bevvy. She doubted that Dave would consider a whole game of Monopoly as foreplay, he might take that as a sign that she was having second thoughts. But he was her ideal dreamy man, you couldn't have second thoughts about him, it didn't make sense. Then she recalled Kate's remark: he's a user. Then Sandra's comment: he's only after a cheap shag. Then Leena's point: he's a womanizing bastard. And even more importantly, Dave's surmise: I just love beautiful women – sue me.

'Dave, fancy a game of Monopoly?' Naina began. 'You can be banker if you like.'

More like a wanker if I take up that suggestion, thought Dave. 'I thought you'd never ask. Hold on, I'll go and get it.' He stood up, with a smile that went all round his face, without even passing Go. 'Back in a sec.' Some evening this was going to be, he thought, as he strode off to the dining room.

He pulled out the tatty Monopoly box from the mahogany sideboard, thinking of ways to shorten the game. 'Won't be a minute,' he shouted through, as he lifted out the game board and ripped it in half, hid half of the property cards, and most of the money in the side drawer. Ha!

Dave returned with a fixed grin, dropped the box on the glass table, flopped down close on the sofa, and then lit up a fag. 'I don't mind Monopoly,' he puffed. 'It's that other game I can't stand. Now what's it called?. . . Monogamy.'

Naina leered, then laughed. His eyes sparkled and she leaned over and kissed him continuously on the lips, while Dave grappled for the ashtray to stub out his fag – he wanted his hands free – and pushed her gently back on the sofa.

'I'm gonna do you so bad, Naina,' he whispered as he rose to dim the lights.

'A bit of subtlety, Dave, would be nice.'

The open fire spewed out heat. Soft feathery

touches of warmth breathing glowing flame-light onto their already hot embrace. Each flame spawned another as the logs faded away, as two maniacs tried to rip each other's clothes off.

Naina stared at Dave's half-naked body; as the darting light caught his muscular torso, each curtain of shadow on his stomach exposed something peculiar and she dished him a look of worried concern.

She fumbled for words. 'Dave . . . what's . . .' And pointed to the large extreme bruising on his front which made him look like he had been dipped in an artist's palette: yellows, greens, blues, purples and reds blended into a sore-looking mess. Monet would not be proud.

Naina, in just her red lace bra and knickers, clambered upright, using the sofa arm for support, and scrambled bare-footed across the wooden floor to switch on the main light before returning to take a closer look at Dave's tie-dye skin, crouching down to inspect it. 'So?' she enquired worriedly, staring up to a fidgety – obviously about to lie – Dave.

'Wedding rash! I told you about it. Someone's obviously proposing right this very second. You watch it spread before your eyes.' He stood peering down at his stomach. 'Anyway, while you're down there . . .'

'No!'

'Forget about it, it's nothing.' And his voice was firm. He grabbed her warm hand, pulled her up. 'Come on, nurse Naina.' And the two 'friends' headed into the bedroom, Naina walking purposefully, and Dave like he was on hot coals.

Chapatti or Chips?

Fair play to the person who invented lingerie, contemplated Dave. And whoever invented 'red' was an artistic genius. Red lingerie was like a prism to man's desires, splitting up all his disgusting thoughts and redistributing them into his pants. And with all Dave's thoughts now in his pants, he watched Naina's firm round bottom move gracefully beneath the red-laced panties and his testosterone had a party; a loud rowdy bunch of hormones ogling and panting, urging Dave to stop staring and get a move on – before they had a brawl.

Clean sheets!

Dave scanned a neat line of CDs balancing on top of the stereo – a queue of artistes waiting patiently to be chosen for Dave's love festivities – then he remembered his manners. 'What d'you fancy?'

Well, the room seemed perfectly warm and cosy, the bed was temptation itself with huge wallowing pillows riding a king-sized blue duvet, and the lights were low and dim. It didn't really need music, but still.

Naina fingered her way through the collection, finally deciding on *Mixed Ballads*. She tried to ignore the little square red sticker labelled 'romping music', pushed in the CD, and turned to face Dave who sat on the bed, as 'I Will Always Love You' by Whitney Houston began to mush away. He smiled, not at her, but at himself and it made her wonder. How many slags had he slept with while Whitney played?

'How many women have you seduced on that bed?' Naina asked, stepping towards him.

Dave sighed. When he'd first spotted the potential bed in Habitat, a rather large weighty woman was

215

sitting on it, almost straddling it, bouncing up and down, and Dave had thought, 'Fuck me, if it can handle her then . . .' He glanced at Naina. She was smiling, but that meant nothing. Claws could be lurking behind that smile. Should he lie? Should he tell the truth? Should he have a blackout?

'Naina, there may have been quite a few women, but none of them came even close to your beauty.' He stood up, and took her tiny waist in his hands. 'How did that sound? Did I say the right thing?' And began to kiss her sealed mouth. Sorted!

He watched her slim hands with their long painted red nails yank down his Calvin Kleins as he lay back on the sturdy bed – sex was better than Nurofen, he thought, as the abdominal pains began to fade into nothingness. And their eyes harboured plenty of unkempt lust, solid feelings rooted in anticipated excitement of what was to come. Dave rolled Naina over on to her back, unclipped the red bra – one handed – and began to hear his favourite sound in the world as he gently eased down her red lacy knickers.

Their hearts pounding, frantic, unstoppable, as they kissed with fiery rhythm. Naina began to well with ecstasy, she knew she was going to remember this night for ever. And for ever was just beginning as they shared a look that swallowed up all her fears of betrayal, fears of being used, fears of the pain and regret afterwards, and she knew right there and then that, no matter what, it would all be worth it. To give herself to the man she chose and not who her parents chose. The music faded pleasantly to empty decibels, and all that mattered was the two of them, together, on his bed, as one. Dave lifted himself up, longingly looking down to her sexy, naked cinnamon body.

One handed he shuffled on a condom then gazed into her brown eyes, glazed like polished oak, swimming with a hundred thoughts. He'd waited for this moment too long, and now it was here, now at last he was about to fulfil his yearning. Her scent untapped the sweetest of visions, a mixture of Obsession, shampoo, and Sure roll-on. The chase and flirting with her, the guessing games and innuendoes, all of that was about to vanish along with her innocence, to be swapped by a hopeful, lasting memory of Naina being the best tease he had ever ever had and how he finally bagged her. But before all that lovey-dovey nonsense, he had to show her a good time.

His advantage, from where he was kneeling, was that she'd never had a man before. Nothing to compare with. Nothing to measure up to. The disadvantage from where he was kneeling was that he'd read numerous times in *Woman's Own* that a woman's first time having sex was normally 'crap' – always moaning that they didn't know what all the fuss was about. Well, he wasn't letting Naina walk out of here thinking 'crap'. When she walked out of here – if she could walk at all – she'd be thinking, 'I can't go back to being normal after *that*.'

Dave kissed Naina's stomach, caressing and smouldering. Her breathing deepened, enjoying his touch as he glided upwards towards her pert breasts and she sighed internally. His promiscuous hands journeying and exploring, expertly touching dangerous areas, throwing the 'Indian – Keep Out' signs to one side and trespassing on another man's woman.

Dave gazed into Naina's dancing eyes, gelling this moment for eternity. Her naivety, preserved for so long, was about to disappear. He kissed her powerfully on the lips, and then . . . he jumped off the bed, muttering a few unprintable swear words.

Naina sat up, watched him frantically pulling on his Calvin Kleins. His face was so taut it needed Oil of Ulay and every fucking other fucking word was a fucking swear fucking word. Naina wrapped herself up in the massive duvet, unsure and bemused by Dave's actions. It was almost as if she didn't exist any more.

'What's up, Dave?' she asked softly to his back.

He slowly turned round, looked up to the ceiling. 'Nothing!' he said, cold as ice, and his Adam's apple gulped. 'Sorry.'

'Did you . . . you know . . . cum early?'

His head snapped down. 'No I fucking didn't cum early. I can keep it up for hours.' He stood firm, legs astride, like a man. 'No problem!'

Whoops! 'Well, what is the problem then . . . is it me?' she asked, worried, annoyed. 'You shag every other woman in sight but you can't shag me, can you? What's the matter with me?' she shouted, tears loitering in the corners of her eyes.

He sat down at the foot of the bed, his back still to her. 'It's not you, Naina, you're gorgeous.' He paused, tightened his vocal chords, lowered his voice. 'I lost it, I lost my fucking erection.' And, ignoring the pun of his actions, his head went limp.

Stunned, Naina controlled herself, tried hard not to

laugh, then: 'Well, where did it go?' She did laugh now, rolling about on the bed, imagining the giggles from Kate and Leena when she told them tomorrow. Now it was she who didn't seem to know he was in the room, lost in her own world. Then she got a grip. 'Sorry, Dave, sorry, it's just that . . . sorry.'

'Shall I get you some popcorn or maybe some tortilla chips, and some dips? Then you can have a *really* good time at my expense . . . Naina.'

'Look.' She scrambled across the springy mattress as best she could. 'I'm sorry.' Her arms embraced him from behind. 'Really sorry.' And she rested her head on his shoulder. And she was.

Dave took comfort from her cuddle. This had never happened to him before. And what started off as a pebble of a thought, soon became an avalanche. What if it never went up again? Ever! A third of his pub jokes were about blokes who couldn't satisfy a woman.

'Naina.' Dave's voice sounded desperate. 'Don't tell the boys, will you? Beautiful Naina.'

So, if she and Dave were the only people left on earth, then that would be the end of the human race. Dave was a total washout, thought Naina.

She then thought of mystical things: maybe there was a new moon, or an alignment of the planets, or maybe Dave couldn't admit that when it came down to it he needed a pump – or Viagra. Now the clean sheets made sense, he never got them dirty. He was all mouth, all gob and no action. And what was all that talk about the moon nearly going out of orbit because of the humungous gravitational pull of his willy? And what about the eclipse, that was his willy as well, was it?

Dave lay back on the bed and pulled her back down next to him. 'My life is over.'

She looked over at him. 'I know,' she agreed. 'All those beautiful women, they'll just walk past you now, smile, then walk on by. It's all gone, Dave, kaput!' Naina replied mockingly. Then, vicious. 'Don't be so melodramatic, look at you, you're pathetic, "my life is over", you moron!'

He smiled, turned over to face her, she stared at the ceiling and spotted something. Dave had stuck a piece of card above the pillow end of the bed. A bit hard to focus on but the printed words fuzzed their way through: 'Naina, important. You must yelp, scream, bark, moan and shout: "I'm cumming, I'm cumming." FAKE IT!' And before she had time to fake anything, they were kissing once more, passionately, almost with a fever.

Dave lay on top of her with a rocket of a hard-on, pushed open her legs and showed her what a man he was. It was everything she had dreamed of: giving herself away to a man that she had chosen, a man that she found attractive, pushing her hips up towards him while he pushed himself deep inside her. All their earlier escapades washed away in a sweaty clasp of love. A journey of intimate pleasure, a rolling sensation of delight demoting any pleasure that she had had before to the gloomy wastes of 'just fun'. This was more than fun should be, this was heaven on a stick, this was dangerous, dirty, guiltless passion. This was living life. This was sex, that was about the size of it. Sex! And boy did she love it.

Dave relaxed back, propped up on the pillow, lit up a fag, smiled his accomplished smile. 'I've finally collected the orgasm I was after.' And he blew out his smoke.

Naina squinted her eyes at him. 'I am not a bloody Pokémon card!'

Exhausted by their exertions, she nodded off, leaving Dave staring across at the trickle of light washing through the bedroom window. If this was a thriller he would murder Naina tonight, suffocate her with the duck feather pillow, so that she couldn't tell anyone about his floppiness earlier. Somewhere in the far reaches of his mind, he recalled an article he had read in *New Scientist* entitled 'The Rise and Fall of Man'. It inferred that the failure of a man to maintain an erection meant he probably had a psychological problem. While Naina hogged the bed and duvet, Dave grasped his willy, thought of something disgusting, and wallop, up it popped. Yeah right, psychological problem my arse, and he smiled himself to sleep. He'd taken Naina to Disneyland. Sorted!

Chapter Nineteen

A *couple of days later.*

Dave sat in the newish, red, 3 series BMW courtesy car on the opposite side of the road to Naina's semi-detached house. It was a cold Monday night, 5.30 p.m. He smoked a fag, waiting, watching and hoping. On either side of the road, a relay of streetlights illuminated most of the short stretch in an orange glow. Sporadically cars would pull into their drives, mostly men would step out, walk up their small cared-for lawns carrying bags and briefcases, and enter their rejuvenating pods of whisky, Radox bath salts, TV, slippers and home-made quiche. Possibly explaining that it was fortunate they were on this planet, for if it wasn't for them and the brilliant job they did then the world would be a disaster. The wives may then say, 'Yes, dear, but you do know we're going to my mother's for the weekend, don't you?'

Dave turned off Horizon Radio, popped in a Guns n'

Roses CD – *Appetite To Destruction* – and listened to Axl blare out 'Sweet Child of Mine'. Light was emanating from Naina's bedroom through the pink curtains, the traffic flow was faltering, evening home life was brewing, and still no sign. Two smokes later, the leaf-patterned glazed front door to Naina's house opened and three witches, dressed in the Devil's hand-me-downs, drifted down the drive, over the road, and past his car. Dave could just make out: 'Marilyn Manson's playing at *The Bowl*. Can you believe it? He's going to be so close to us.' And then a low, rumbling, chanting demonic noise, as they disappeared down a side alley.

Beetles make an unmistakable noise with their exhaust, like they've got a constant cold, always clearing their throat. The chug-a-chug-chugging, hacked from behind, and the welcome view of the off-white Beetle appeared in Dave's rear-view mirror. Throwing the half-smoked fag out of the window, Dave quickly ran across the road, and greeted Kiran as he emerged from his car.

'Hello, mate, remember me?' Dave asked in hushed tones.

Kiran, holding his college books, jumped. Normally so good with words, this time he had none. He stared trance-like at Dave.

Dave stood close to him and continued, 'I've got a CCTV tape of you and your sidekicks of the other night. I'll wait in that red BMW.' He turned his head and pointed. 'If you're not there in two minutes, I'm driving straight to the pig shop with the tape. Two minutes.' Dave cut across the road, Kiran still stared, dumbfounded.

Dave sat in the car and watched Kiran dump the books in the back seat of his Beetle, and then nervously cross the road, to climb into his passenger side – this was one exam Kiran had not studied for.

'Buckle up, we're going for a ride.' The car screeched off.

Kiran was having a new experience – fearing for his life. Dave's little throw-away remark, 'It's not very nice, five against one, is it?. . . Innit. You'll soon find out,' accentuated the experience and by the time the car rolled into a half-finished new housing estate, up a muddy wet track in Campbell Heights, he was reliving a particularly nasty scene in *Casino*. The engine ticked off and Dave faced him.

'I can wreck your life. You could go to prison for what I saw on that tape. I saw you, all five of you, without those stupid balaclavas on, sitting in the van laughing. I saw you run your fingers up and down my car, and if that wasn't stupid enough, you only wore the same frigging tracksuits that you were wearing when you came into the gym earlier that day asking Steve about me. It's all on tape, believe me.'

'Are you going to take it to the police?' Kiran asked, the righteous Indian passion now gone from his voice.

'No,' and Dave stared at him, 'because of Naina.' He lit a fag.

'I don't care what you do to me, but she's my sister, and I don't want you going anywhere near her,' Kiran said flatly.

And Dave smoked, looking out on to the scene: foundations of houses lay in murky pools of water covering the concrete. Sandbags, trestles, an abandoned orange cement mixer, stacks and stacks of bricks in thick polythene. A perfect place to bury someone.

'And what does Naina want? Or does she have no say?' Dave asked.

'You don't know our way. We're not like you English. Our culture does not mix with yours!' Kiran's petrified nerves were pitching his voice high.

The windows began to steam up and Dave pressed the buttons to infuse some cold blasts into the stale heated air. It made sense to despise Kiran, but he couldn't bring himself to hate this proud young Indian, with his diehard traditions and air of uncompromising distrust. Distrust for his race. Distrust for the white man.

'Kiran, you seem to me quite capable of talking about the advantages of an Indian upbringing all night.' Dave puffed. 'But please sum it up for me, I'm interested here. Tell me, why are you better than me? Why would you not want me – this white piece of shit – mixing with your sister, Naina?' And even though Dave had tried hard to keep his voice refrained, when he got to the 'white piece of shit' the words were spat out.

There were acres of filing cabinets in Kiran's mind. All full to bursting with arguments of the pros of the Indian way. And now this 'white piece of shit' wanted him to sum it all up. A thousand turbans in his head rattled together, one million Indian Gurus all rubbed their hands in rejoice and all Indian women were allowed a day off from cooking. Kiran was about to make the speech of the century.

'We Indian—'

Dave interrupted, 'I'm bored,' then laughed. 'Sorry, go on.'

Kiran's look was that of disgust. 'We Indian people live our lives by a very wholesome set of rules. We do not drink, we do not gamble, we do not have affairs and we do not have sex outside marriage. We place our family before everything else. We look after our sisters, our mothers and fathers. We make sure that no one is an outsider and everyone pulls together as one strong unit. That's why we have no divorces, that's why we are successful, that's why we must protect our way of life and especially our women. Do you understand?' Kiran paused. 'Especially we must marry within our own religion. We must keep our religion and our roots alive.' And Kiran then mocked, 'Innit!'

Dave studied Kiran. 'Okay. Granted. But it sounds to me like you're selling me a car. Telling me of all the brilliant mod-cons, all the wonderful interior, all the fuel injection. But when I come to put my foot down on the accelerator, the fucking thing doesn't work. And it doesn't work, Kiran. You can't go round preaching to everyone that the Indian system is better than everyone else's, with shit talk like that. Unless you can answer me simply: why do women have to do as they are told? Why are women allowed no choice? Why can it be so wrong for someone to be an individual and not one of your Indian cogs? Some of it makes good sense, but, honestly, some of it is utter bullshit.' And Dave nodded sagely.

Kiran did answer simply: 'You'll never understand, you're white, innit.'

And Dave swung a three-point turn and sped off, carving new track marks in the soggy mud. Arriving shortly afterwards outside Kiran's house.

'One more thing, Kiran. Naina and me are just mates, nothing more. I don't want you to tell her about this, I don't want you stopping her seeing me or any of her friends, and I don't want you hurting her, punishing her or threatening her. If you make her life worse in any way, I'll come for you personally. And remember, I've got the tape.'

Kiran nodded. 'Can I go now?'

Dave peered across at Kiran's stubborn-looking face, grabbed him by the scruff of his neck and produced from nowhere a shining sheath knife, placing it gently against Kiran's Adam's apple. 'You fucking try anything like that again on me . . . am I making sense, Kiran? Remember, I don't take shit from shit. Now get out of this shitheap of a car that I've got to go around in because of you.'

He watched Kiran leg it across the road. He shouldn't have had to do that. He hadn't wanted to do that. But, in all fairness, he'd *had* to do that.

Pubs? No. Women? No. Mates? No. The gym? No. The pagoda? No. Alone?

He wanted alone, and Dave drove away into the darkness, listening to New Order. The last few days had opened his eyes. The Indian way. It made no sense to shrug off a woman's freedom simply because it was 'traditional', but there had been a guarded ferocity displayed by Kiran that Dave had not come across since, since, well, he'd never come across anyone so passionate about their upbringing before and it made him do something he didn't want to do. It made him reflect.

The warm car followed no particular route, just

ambling onwards until, somehow, it arrived at a place Dave had not revisited for ten years: his childhood. He walked slowly across a small playing field, his feet taking him as though they belonged to someone else. Over a man-made grassy mound, with a silver rusty short slide leading down and over the other side. He lit a fag. In the distance, some house lights leered outwards. Amongst them, the downstairs lights of his parents' house. As his footsteps quickened, his trainers seemed to shrink in size, his shoulders lowered, and he was a kid again, walking around in circles, desperate to walk off the pain lashed to him by his stepdad's cane and ruthless smile.

The tall holly tree was still there, it had aged well. Unlike the cranky old wooden fence behind it, which the younger OOzing gang used to sit on. He rested against the damp bark, and knew there was something missing from this place. And then he remembered what was missing, for it suddenly returned like a forgotten dream – his fear. The fear which used to scrape his insides bare. No kid deserved this nightmare.

He spoke to himself: 'I'm not going to do this,' but rose up, dusted down the back of his jeans and Gucci T-shirt, and set off down the small grass verge that would lead to his parents' modest house in Church Green.

The front lawn was tediously tidy. Expensive Austrian-style netting brushed the windows, and the front door was polished, painted and immaculate. Maybe they didn't live here any more. Maybe they were dead. He knocked at number 218 with his fist.

He'd left this place with nothing. Sixteen years old,

a mess: 'You're not wanted by any of us. Now fuck off and don't fucking come back, you little shit.'

But now he was back, and his stepdad answered the door.

Chapter Twenty

'Jesus, I cannot believe you slept with him.' Leena paused. 'A male prostitute.'

'Keep your voice down, Meera or your mum will hear,' Naina replied, jumping off the bed and closing Leena's bedroom door.

Downstairs, Leena's mum and elder sister Meera were preparing dinner. Great wafts of ghee, onions, garlic, ginger and chilli merged with Leena's stolen Poison; and by the sounds coming from below, Meera was a bit of a calamity in the kitchen.

'Why did you sleep with him . . . Naina? He's a pig.' She turned up the stereo – *Club Ibiza*, and flopped back down on her bedspread coated in cherubs and clouds.

Profound or pathetic? Naina opted for the latter. 'I couldn't get him out of my mind,' she whispered.

'Crap! Tell me.'

Profound. 'Okay, India is starving me of oxygen, I cannot breathe.'

Chapatti or Chips?

They both laughed. 'Oh shut up, Naina, jeez, I wonder about you.' Leena softened her giggle. 'Have you thought of what will happen on your wedding night, when Ashok realizes you're not a virgin? Have you thought about that? For God's sake, Naina, you're going to be on your own with a strange family. You hear stories of what these families do to girls that are seconds. I just hope that Dave was worth it. You could lose your whole family over this.' She looked hard at Naina. 'Honestly, Naina, where the hell are you going to hide this syringe full of red dye? In your dowry!? Another one of Dave's crap ideas. I'm disgusted at you and just wait till I see him.'

'What the hell have I done?'

His snout was a thousand bottles of whisky bigger. His teeth, ten thousand fags more yellow. And laughter lines leaked from his beady menacing eyes like cracks in badly set concrete. His foul stench was gone, but still he was rotten. They stared at one another for three long ticks of a watch.

'Just released you from inside, have they? Those screws got sick of you too, eh?' His balding head didn't turn, it twitched round to the hallway. 'Oi, Wendy, your little shit's here, coming to scrounge some money off us.' He twitched back. 'What was it this time? Burglary? Arson?'

Wendy arrived. Mum. Her face was still young but she moved like an old person as she appeared at the doorframe. Short dyed blonde hair, baggy navy tracksuit and baby pink backless slippers. She stared, her large blue eyes connecting with Dave's. 'Nice of you to show up. What is it? Money?'

231

More silent stares, then: 'This isn't fucking pay-per-view. What d'you fucking want, you little shit?' said Jack. Stepdad.

'Why did you do it?' Dave stared at Wendy. 'I'm your son, why?'

'You're not my son, never was. You're the son of that no-hoper that left me. Left me at breaking point. I did the motherly thing, I raised you up to sixteen, other mums would have thrown you out. Nothing but trouble you've been. How many times did we have to collect you from the police cells? Eh? Go on, piss off.'

'How could you let him do the things he did to me? How could you sit there? My own mother. I was just a kid.'

'Carry on like that, I'll give you some more, you little—'

Dave grabbed Jack's neck, pushed him inside, let go, and watched the wretched man tumble to the floor. 'I was so scared of you. You'd make me piss my pants, and then you'd laugh at me. Well, Jack, did you not think that little scared kid would one day grow up, and he would come back for you, hey?' And Dave lifted his fist.

'Stop it, you leave him.'

Dave turned to face Wendy. He'd often prayed for those words, cried for those words, screamed for her to just tell Jack to stop laying into him. 'You're both pathetic.' He turned and entered the living room.

As if preparing for old age, the two of them had amassed hundreds of ornaments. Pity that, as Dave used his forearm to . . . and then he stopped, and saw what he had dreaded he would. And he stood there, staring at the countless family photographs.

Treasured segments of time, for one family. Treasured segments of lives without him. As though he had never even played a part: his face, himself, was nowhere. He was orphaned from their mantelpiece and the aching thoughts he had held on to for all these years, that maybe his mum did love him after all, fluttered their wings and flew away. They'd already nailed the lid on his coffin and, now, he would do the same to them. He didn't need them. He didn't need his mother's love. In fact, he didn't need love at all.

He walked away from his demons. Got in his car. And left his childhood behind in a trail of burning rubber. Jack-a-fuck-in-ory.

Dave lay back on his sofa and reclined his mind a little. Streams of weed smoke jettisoned from his mouth and thoughts encrusted in a childlike shell began to rupture, then break. He knew, deep down, he'd been misleading himself. Hoping against hope that all those loathsome memories of his younger days were exaggerated by his fertile childhood imagination. But how can someone exaggerate loss? The loss he felt as he struggled to be part of a family that didn't want him.

Arguments as to why he had even bothered going back today now stale, he decided on a quiet night in. Just him, one massive pizza, boxing on the box and a mind-blowing session of . . . he looked into the nearly empty tin. Damn. He'd run dry of ganja. And then he sang to himself remembering it was delivery day down at The Three Kings: 'Wild thing, I'm gonna make my head spin, I'm gonna smoke the real thing, wild thing.'

His horticulturalist could always be found down at the local dive. And he picked up a wad of notes, set the burglar alarm, and sped off down the road, listening to Queen.

The Three Kings was more like a tavern than a modern pub. Low ceilings with crooked beams and a cobbled floor with wobbly tables. Behind the counter a buxom-wench barmaid called Sally was serving half-measured pints to shady-looking men selling off-loaded perfumes and half-priced denim jeans. The pub was only fifty yards away from Revival Nights nightclub, and most evenings a crushing flow of scantily clad women would percolate through, tanking themselves up for a night of stiletto stomping, and soggy smooches.

Dave parked the car up the road, and wandered down to the pub entrance.

'Hello, Dave, what are you doing down here?' growled the bald stocky doorman, in a blue blazer, shirt and dickey-bow. 'It's a bit fucking cold to be wearing a T-shirt, you poser.'

'Sockets, you're shrinking, you should get down the gym. You big fucking poof.'

Sockets play-acted a punch just past Dave's head. 'Go on, in you go, I'll let that comment slip.'

Sockets trained at Dumbbells and considered himself the biggest genetic freak of muscle since Arnold Schwarzenegger. One day he was going to shock the world, walk down the aisle, jump up on stage, rip off his T-shirt and stand on the Mr Olympia stage yelling: 'I'm the Daddy now, I'm the Daddy. Dorian Yates – Diesel – if you're listening, challenge me!'

Inside, the smog was dank and stale, with the small electric heater over the entrance door making a futile attempt to outwit the cold. The place was a bit of a paradox – it was actually rude to be polite here. 'Please' and 'thank you' – well, you may as well be talking gibberish. As Dave pushed his way through the rabble his eyes were already checking for Half Ounce Billy and his dreadlocks extensions with their multicoloured beads. Billy wished he was born black – it was as simple as that.

'Pint of Carling. And Sally, make it a *real* pint.' Dave watched her clumpy freckled forearms pick up a cleanish pint glass and trickle in the watered-down lager.

She slid the pint across the waxy surface into Dave's waiting hand. 'How are your kids, Dave?' Sally asked with her broad Irish accent and a dirty laugh.

Dave passed her a fiver, sipped the rank lager, and toasted Sally. 'They're all picking spuds along with your dozen.' Smiled, then turned to look at the words on the blackboard, over the fruit machine, in chubby red chalk writing:

Sally's special.
Rollmops and Chips
Only £5.00

Half Ounce Billy was the nicest grandson that a granny could wish for. Nearly every night he would pop in to see if she was okay. He'd check upstairs where she could no longer climb, to make sure that intruders were not busying themselves with her Lily of the Valley bath salts and Holland & Barrett hand warmers. Unbeknown to 85-year-old Bertha, her cottage was the main warehouse of weed and skunk throughout the whole of Buckinghamshire. She was the sweetest. The sweetest doped-up, skunk-weeding high-as-a-kite biddy in the whole of the UK – and she hadn't felt the throbbing pain of her arthritis for years.

'Usual?' Billy enquired, standing close to Dave at the bar.

Dave nodded and handed him the notes. Billy tucked the small polythene snappy bags in Dave's jeans back pocket and walked off.

Dave gulped down the last of his drink, and turned to Sally to bid farewell.

'Have you got a light?' A woman's voice.

Dave twisted his head round. Now hang on a minute. She was pretty; the last thing he expected to see in here. He flicked the red plastic lighter to the fag in her outstretched French-manicured hand.

'Thanks.' She blew the smoke up in the air. 'You smell sexy, what's that you're wearing?'

Fuck the boxing, fuck the pizza, I'll fuck her. 'Davidoff,' with a certain pride. 'What are you doing in this dump?'

'Looking for handsome men, and looks like I've found one. You're not married are you? Men like you are always married.'

She stood in close, about twenty-seven years old, he reckoned, dressed in a dark grey trouser suit, long straight brown hair, big brown Bambi eyes, not much make-up, but then she didn't need it. She was stunning, totally out of place here, and her slightly posh voice had a vague northern tone.

'No, but you are.'

She looked down to the gold band on her wedding-ring finger. 'Does that bother you?'

'No, it makes it more fun. What's your name?'

'Laura, and you?'

'Dave.'

'Nice to meet you, Dave.' And her hand went to his balls. She smiled and held his gaze.

Dave leaned in to her ear. 'When was the last time your husband made you meow?'

She giggled. 'I'll eat you.' And seductively licked her puckered lips.

Hardly Romeo and fucking Juliet, thought Dave. Cheap-talking filthy slag, getting turned on with shit chat-up lines like that. But she was extremely pretty – and willing.

And they left. Dave with a throbbing hard-on. They didn't make it further than the back of his car, just out of view of the Shazzie's Kebabs van.

A frantic scene of unclothing, 'We Will Rock You' in the background, and a quick look around to make sure it was safe to pork.

A small group of hungry people were beginning to get anxious that maybe a defenceless kitten was trapped in the BMW as they queued for their doners outside in the cold. The shouting of 'extra onions', 'no chillies for me, please' and 'a can of coke' could be heard in between meows and Dave thought, 'I will never shag outside a kebab van again, it makes me sooo hungry.'

After Dave had got what he wanted out of Laura, he sat back fully clothed in the front of the car, smoking a fag and twiddling with the volume on the stereo, while Laura had to finish herself off in the back seat. Because, frankly, Dave could not be arsed. He waited for Laura to get dressed. Just by her suede ankle boots lay a large Office World cardboard box filled with Dumbbells Gym colour brochures. Laura grabbed a couple, folded them up and slid them into her jacket pocket.

'Here's my numbers, Dave – mobile, work, home and e-mail. I'll wait for your call then.'

Dave, without sparing a glance at her, politely grabbed the hastily scribbled numbers. 'I'll phone you.' Watched her walk back in the direction of the pub, then drove off, opened the window and chucked out the numbers into the darkened road. The ripped paper caught the wind current, looped the loop, stalled like a dying butterfly, then swooped to a waiting puddle beside the busy V4 Watling Street dual carriageway. And the four numbers muffled, mingled, merged and blobbed until they joined the large voluminous telephone directory of discarded, lost and forgotten women's phone numbers.

Chapter Twenty-one

Although Leena lived in hope of being frisked, and she too, like Naina, had Indian parents who were mild, to upset the Indian way for a cheap thrill with a cheap man was passing yourself off as . . . cheap. Indian women were under no circumstances allowed to be cheap. Their virginity was a luxury item that no man could afford – until wedlock.

As Leena knocked hard, above the din of clanking weights, on Dave's office door, she viewed the huge arena of dangerous machinery in the main gym area. My my, to think a pig managed to organize all this.

'Come in.' Dave's voice.

Leena gently pushed open the door and peeked her head round. 'Can I have a word?' and she sat down, her short skirt edging up her skinny legs, and her tight red top daring but withholding. A mass of jet black hair. Curls bubbling to and fro.

Dave cleared away a stack of corporate membership

forms. 'So, to what do I owe this pleasure?' he asked, lighting a fag and leaning back in his executive chair in his non-executive Platinum Wear.

'I'm not going to beat around the bush, David. The thought of Naina sleeping with you makes me want to vomit!'

He laughed. 'What's it to you? Are you Naina's bed manager or something?'

Leena sneered. 'Her family will find out, you know, they always find out. Her family will drop her. In India, women are burnt for something like this, in their saris; it's a crime.' She popped in one of Dave's fags and lit up. 'You couldn't keep it zipped up, could you?'

'She's an adult, I didn't force her. And sorry if this sounds too polite, but it's none of your fucking business.' He pulled himself forward. His biting blue eyes dug deep into Leena's brown.

'It is my fucking business, when you're screwing her life up. Jeez, you're so smug . . . anyone would think you could shit gold.' She blew smoke in his face. 'Do you love her?'

'No.'

Leena blinked hard. The 'no' was automatic, razor sharp.

'She's getting engaged today. Back away from her. You're confusing her mind. If she screws it up with Ashok, she'll lose her family, her whole family, David. She'll have no one. You won't be there for her.' She paused. 'And even I know that you don't want that for her.' Leena, amazed that Dave was listening, continued, 'She was round my place last night, bawling her eyes out. And I'm sorry to say it, but she regrets sleeping with you. It's going to be really hard for her to marry Ashok, don't make it harder, and don't put negatives about the Indian way in her mind. You really don't know what you're talking about. It's something we are born into and no one can really understand, unless they're Indian.'

'Granted.' He blew smoke back into her face. 'Look, Leena, she's my mate, she comes to me, she cries to me and I give her the best advice I can. Even if it is 'white' advice. Anyway, I don't think I'm the problem here. I think you should go and talk to this other prick she drools over, this mystery piece of shit. He's what's screwing her up.'

'Jeez, what are you on? Mystery piece of shit?'

'You know? That fucker she fancies – selfish bastard.'

Leena only knew of one bloke that Naina had the belly flips for – and that selfish fucker was right in front of her eyes. God, Dave was a moron sometimes. She continued, 'Anyway, I've said my piece. I know you won't tell her I came here.' She stood up. 'By the way, you've got a lovely gym. I'm impressed.'

'Before you leave, Leena.' He leaned back in his chair, put his Nikes up on the desk. 'Next time you put your hands over me, remember you're Indian!'

Leena flicked back her memory to a dull vision of herself, totally pissed and making a mild attempt at 'fondling' Dave's muscular thighs. Perhaps there had also been a mild attempt of opening up her mouth and begging him to give her a tonguey. Perhaps? She'd been trying to forget it for months.

Leena ignored him. 'Talk about seeing it from your perspective, David. Jeez, just leave Naina alone!' And she left – stealing Dave's dinky Dictaphone en route.

You can't plan a panic, they just happen. You can justify one, like, it caught me by surprise, or, I didn't expect it to happen to me. But sometimes, even when you know exactly what is going to happen and when it's going to happen, there it is, that awful intolerable nasty bitch of an emotion – panic. And it makes you spin inside.

Naina was getting officially engaged today. No balloons, no booze, no party and no romance. Just the basic ring swap, and plenty of panic. There would be no getting down on one knee, no cuddles and kisses, no weepy eyes, no scenes of the Eiffel Tower, no love. Just two sets of parents, swimming in pride.

Yet again Naina viewed her reflection: a very Indian-looking woman looked back at her, dressed in a plum-coloured raw silk shalwar kameez, heavily laden in fine-cut beads, high-heeled plum sandals, matching nail varnish. Even without the smile, she looked beautiful. One could imagine her surrounded by servants in a palace of yesteryear, eating fine foods and cooling down her supple light brown skin with a gold-threaded fan. She wouldn't be smiling then either – no *EastEnders* back then.

On edge, Naina sat back down on her bed and pondered. They would be here soon. He would be here soon – Ashok, her future husband. A husband to whom she would hand herself over and say, 'I'm yours,' and pray that in time a love and bond would grow between them.

A few stubborn birds that hadn't flown abroad for

winter tweeted outside as Naina walked across to the window and looked out on a view of the road; a view she had watched for many years, a view she knew, a view she would soon be saying goodbye to.

She gawped at the brand-new silver Mercedes pulling up quietly on the drive, behind the parked red family Mondeo, and Ashok, dressed immaculately, opened the driver's door and stepped out in his filthy-expensive designer black suit. Naina ran to the bathroom and puked.

A collaboration of noises in the hall downstairs, the closing of the front door, the gentle nudge of Sonia to get down there, and Naina descended, masked in a smile, and entered the watching living room. All eyes on this official day were now officially on her, and she hated it.

Sumita – Naina's elder sister – gave Naina a reassuring look: It's okay, I've gone through all this. I know what you're thinking, but really, it's not so bad. Naina weakly smiled back.

Sumita, now twenty-eight, and married to Kalvinder Singh for four years, was happy now. It wasn't always that way. Her mother-in-law, a.k.a. The Battle-Axe of Southall, held Sumita in contempt for two full dark years. Mum worried for her, her daughter seemed far from happy. But everything poor Sumita did, Sumita did poorly – according to one battle-axe in Southall. She added too much salt. Always too much salt to her cooking. Her potatoes were always underdone, like granite they were. Her shalwar kameez were sewn shabbily, her saris were dragging on her chappals, her bindis were lopsided, chapatties too heavy, lentils too mushy, Punjabi too weak, English too strong, paneer too lemony, jalebis too sweet. But, her baby was perfect. He would be.

He was a boy. Naina watched Sumita's hand resting on Anil's soft black-haired head and traded a smile across the room with her young nephew. It was enough to make you broody.

Mum looked proudly on Naina, and her dad was sucking up to Ashok's dad, convincing him that he had made the right choice.

'Naina stays in every night and cooks for the entire family. Delicious meals. Incredible she is, incredible,' said Dad, dislodging Kiran's look of smugness.

Ashok stared cloth-eared through all the boasts of Naina's dad. He didn't care that Naina could cook saag, aloo gobi, dhal, Bombay potatoes. He watched her elegant hands flutter nervously with her long hair, he watched her eyes stained in an unusual glossy brown, he watched his bride-to-be. She was stunning, and he knew he would fall in love with her, whether she could cook or not.

Tea was served in best cups and saucers, with Indian sweets – laddus, burfis, gulab-jamans and jalebis. Sipping and munching, wedding talk and more wedding talk, boasts and more boasts. The time soon came for the ceremony.

Naina stood up facing Ashok, he was taller than she remembered and good looking to a T. His walnut brown eyes were warm, generous and welcoming, but Naina returned the gaze for only a split second before she looked down to his smart, shining hand-made black shoes. Ashok held Naina's soft left hand and slid on the diamond-clustered twenty-two-carat gold ring, sparkling with pride – like she should have been

– and their hands touched for the very first time. She then slid on his twenty-two-carat gold ring and a promise was sealed, after which Indian sweets were placed in each other's mouths to complete the ceremony. They were now officially engaged to be married.

The dreaded moment arrived when Naina and Ashok were allowed to be alone again, private and vulnerable as the door was closed behind them in the small tidy dining room. A few pictures of Naina, Sonia, Sumita and Kiran from school days were hung on the flower-patterned wallpaper. A picture of Guru Nanak sat on a side table next to a small model of the Taj Mahal with its own built-in lights.

'I was nervous seeing you today,' Ashok said, facing Naina on a dining-room chair.

'Me too,' Naina replied. 'It's a lovely ring, did you choose it?'

Ashok held Naina's hand, gazing down at the ring. 'My sisters helped me choose it. I'm glad you like it. I was so worried that you might not.'

Naina smiled. 'No, it's perfect.' And she let him hold her hand, with a slight sense of discomfort.

Ashok pulled his hand away, possibly sensing Naina's agitation. 'Where would you like to go on the honeymoon? Your choice, completely.'

Honeymoon! 'Surprise me. Somewhere hot would be nice. I don't really like the cold.'

Ashok's nose was strong and slightly pointed. As he scratched it, his mind spun through possible 'hot' zones for their honeymoon. A second later: 'What about Hawaii?'

Naina nodded.

'I'm really looking forward to marrying you, Naina. I think we will be a good match.'

Marriage is for insecure people. Like bad graffiti the words popped up in Naina's head, with Dave the person who sprayed it there. The last time she'd seen him, he'd said, 'I'm shagging the innocence out of you, Naina. Creating something for poor Ashok to strive for.'

Ashok continued, 'This is for you, and I chose it myself.' He handed her a small red felt box.

'Thank you. Do you want me to open it now?' Naina asked.

'Of course.'

She opened the padded box, and it shone as bright as her eyes did. A twenty-two-carat gold diamond choker fit for a queen and very *very* expensive-looking. The most expensive present anyone had ever given her. She was speechless, touched, and for want of a better word 'moved'. She lowered her eyes and smiled.

'Thank you so much, it's beautiful. I'll wear it on our wedding day,' she said. And before any other words could be spoken, they were both beckoned back to the living room.

As Ashok and his family were waved goodbye, Naina grabbed a few quiet seconds to herself to reflect. The next time she would see him would be on their wedding day and from that moment her Indian clothes would be staying on for good – so to speak – and she would remain the Indian Naina that she was born to be.

After Dad explained the new full Indian menu that she would have to learn how to cook by her wedding day, Naina restlessly joined Sonia in their bedroom. She flopped on the bed and cried. Not because Ashok had not bought matching diamond earrings to go with the choker, not because Ashok had turned into a slimy monster – far from it, he was really nice. The problem was, if she was honest with herself, that Mum and Dad had chosen the perfect partner for her. One who would most certainly take care of her, one who would make a good husband, one she would have a good life with.

Naina lay on the bed staring up at the ceiling, feeling the heavy burden of guilt that she had caused for herself by betraying her parents, by sleeping with Dave, by not quite being what Ashok was being led to believe she was. By, plain and simply, being a first-class Indian slut. Ashok deserved better.

Sonia handed Naina a powder-blue tissue, not quite understanding why her sister was crying.

'Naina, he's lovely. You're lucky.'

And Naina cried some more.

And downstairs, Mum cried as well, so proud, so proud:

'Who would think this day would come?' Mum blubbered in Punjabi to Dad.

Dad removed his special-occasion burgundy turban and placed it beside him. 'I would trek to Bombay on foot to find a good man for my daughters if I had to, eh?'

Mum smiled.

Dad continued, 'Bloody good job he only lives in Dagenham.' They both laughed.

In time Naina's tears dried. Sonia was chatting away on the computer to some manic depressive on chat-line; Mum and Dad were still discussing the day's events. Naina sat up, told herself to get a grip, removed her Indian clothes, flung on some jeans, trainers and a short lemon cardigan, wiped all her make-up off, tied her brown-streaked hair in a ponytail and from her Nokia phoned Dave.

'It's Naina, can we meet?' Her voice was flat.

'I'm free later, say, eight?'

'Now, I need to see you now.'

A pause. 'I'm with a beautiful woman. Can't this wait?'

'No, now, it's important.'

Dave agreed, and they arranged to meet just down Naina's road by the BT telephone box.

Dave looked across to Paula, her sweet smile of ten minutes ago now gone.

'Paula, I'm so sorry. Did you hear me say beautiful woman?' He smiled his Dave smile. 'I've really got to go down the gym, it's an absolute emergency. I don't know why I bother sometimes. Dave this, Dave that, they can't do a thing without me down there. I have absolutely no social life, it's a bloody crime.'

Fifteen minutes later Dave skidded up to the isolated phone box. Naina was sitting on a low brick wall, kicking her heels, looking painfully depressed.

'Do you want to see some puppies?' He leered through the window and Naina jumped. The car was unrecognizably red.

'Where's your car?' she asked, getting in, confused.

'It got stolen. A jealous traffic warden, I think. The FBI are on to it.' The car skidded off. 'Where're we going?'

'By the lake? Somewhere quiet.'

Dave seemed determined to break the courtesy car's gearbox as he shifted through the roundabouts at speeds meant only for police cars and Mad Max.

'Slow down, we'll end up in a hedge,' Naina shouted above the noise of Nirvana – 'Smells Like Teen Spirit'.

He lowered the speed and carefully drove into the large gravel car park at Willen Lake. A whole army of windsurfing boards lay propped up against the side of a wooden barn, waiting for the better weather to arrive. The enormous lake, almost ripple free, reflected a flawless silver moon, and a dozen or so lamplights illuminated the track that circled the lakeside. It was peaceful, mostly deserted, and an escape from the humdrum of busy life.

They strolled down to the mini shoreline, with the ebbing of a minuscule tide, and parked their bottoms on a damp wooden bench overlooking the mysterious sheen. Noises from the lakeside pub and eatery came intermittently with the cooling breeze that chaffed its way over the flat basin of water, and Dave hung his arm round Naina's already shivering body, cradled her head in his shoulder, and they said nothing for a few cold minutes.

'Well,' he began, 'what's up?'

Naina raised her hand up, and the stones of diamond blinked in the moonlight. 'That's what's up.' She breathed in the cold air. 'I saw him today. My . . . future husband.'

'Ashok's got taste,' Dave said, referring to the ring as he took hold of her hand and held it. 'So, you didn't listen to anything I said. You can't marry him for your parents, Naina, it's wrong.'

'It feels wrong. He seems nice, too nice. But I'm still going to marry him.'

And Naina began to cry. Her tears soaked up first Dave's left sleeve then his right until finally, he thought, he may as well be standing in the lake. He seemed like the only person in the world that she could cry properly in front of. Kate and Leena would ply her with drink and a joint and say, 'Could be a lot worse, it could be Dave you're marrying.' And that would be that. Sonia, well, she would just say, 'If it's as bad as all that, then I would suggest following the lines of my song entitled "The world's got me under its thumb, bring me a gun".' And Mum and Dad would say, 'Tears – in India, where there is little water, they'd be grateful for those.' Naina always thought that was a really crap parenty thing to say, but it made her smile nevertheless. So, Dave *was* the only one she could cry in front of properly. And boy was he getting it tonight.

A middle-aged man in a green waxy riding jacket with an overly excited white poodle sped past, eyeing the sobbing Naina with Dave's arms round her. God, the amount of times he'd walked beside these lakes and witnessed scenes just like that. He'd go home to Maddy and say, 'Another woman in MK up the duff.'

Dave's heart was beating at a slow pace and almost like a cat purring it was soothing, Naina was becoming less tearful. His silence, almost an agreeable noise, counted sometimes much more than deliveries of great speeches or worldly-wise advice. And somehow just by being there with him, at that moment, by that lake, she knew, come what may, there was something about him that was now part of her soul.

Dave wanted to tell her things that were blatantly obvious to him, although she probably wouldn't want to hear them. He wanted to be truthful. He wanted Naina to realize that one life is all we get, just the one. You must grab it with both hands, hold on to it, thankful for each and every day, and when you are eighty-odd, you can look back and say: I had a good life, I had some dreams, I achieved everything I wanted. You should not have to look back and say: my parents forced me to marry someone that I didn't really want to be with, and someone I was not truly happy with, and to think that I missed out on true love with a person who loved me as much as I loved them. He wanted to say all that, but he couldn't. It was a bit of a mouthful and anyway, who was he to give advice on love and marriage?

'Naina. He that pulls his water from the well, quenches his thirst.' He stared at Naina who tried not to smile. Dave was being deep. He continued, 'And he that asks another to fetch his water, will drink the water warm.' The effort to think looked like it was exhausting him. 'Well, does any of that make any sense?'

'Erm. It's getting cold, Dave. And, no, it doesn't make sense.'

'What I mean is this: sometimes you've got to make your own decision. Only you can do that. Only you can fetch your own water from the . . . oh, it doesn't matter. I made it up anyway.' And for once in Dave's life he looked embarrassed. It didn't suit him at all.

Naina tried to relieve Dave's scarlet fever. 'It's sweet, Dave. Intense, but sweet.' And she gave him a warm, sweet intense hug.

A few more minutes passed, and he tried again. A different approach this time.

'Naina, did I ever tell you about the time when it was non-school uniform day and I came dressed as the headmaster's wife in a yellow summer dress, Doc Marten's and a pink wig, with a big sign on my back saying: "I porked the headmaster's wife"?' She giggled. He always knew how to make her laugh. 'And when he told me to put my hand out for his cane, I said: "Sir, I didn't think you were allowed to dish out capital punishment to girls."'

Naina laughed, and with a playful pull, helped him to his Nikes. 'Come on, I'm starving.' They slowly headed back to the BMW.

'I've been meaning to ask you something,' Naina began.

Dave butted in, 'Naina, I'm not in the mood and I don't want to talk about it.'

'You never want to talk about it, though. If things were reversed, you'd be nagging me, saying, "It's good to get it out in the open." So come on.'

The car sped off, and Naina carried on, above the engine roar, above the loud stereo, above the stubbornness. 'You seemed like you had a lot more that you wanted to tell me the other day, but you shut up. If you really don't want to talk, then I'll be quiet. Dave?'

The car pulled over, the engine stopped, and Dave peered to the red Little Chef sign. 'It's no big deal, loads of kids get beaten up. Anyway, Little Chef, all right?'

'Do you ever see your real dad? And no, Little Chef is not okay.'

'No, he left for another woman. Wrote to me for a while, you know, Christmas and birthday cards. Moved up north. When I was nine, I wrote to him, begged him to take me back, told him about Jack, my stepdad, and he wrote back and said there was nothing he could do.' He paused. 'Said he'd got a kid and a wife and she didn't know about me. That was the end of the Christmas cards. Never heard from him again.' He stared out of the window. 'What's wrong with Little Chef? They do some wonderful pancakes and syrup.'

'I'll tell you why Little Chef is not okay. Look!'

Dave stared at the half-built Little Chef. No windows. No roof. No door. Just a very big lit-up sign.

'Oh,' he said.

'Oh! But if you ever want to talk about it again . . .'

'Yeah, I know.' And he leaned over and kissed her on the cheek.

They ended up eating in a swish Italian restaurant, where the manager looked down at Naina's 501 jeans distastefully as if they were inappropriate for his classy joint, until Dave flashed his ladder of credit cards, when all of a sudden jeans were *in*, and a glass of wine was offered on the house.

It was a nice end to Naina's engagement. The celebration shag went down rather well too.

Chapter Twenty-two

Pete worshipped the letter box. He preferred to think that postmen didn't really exist and that the parcels and letters he received arrived by magic. He liked to believe that his letter box was like a time warp to another dimension. A pretty strange bloke maybe, but he was one of Dave's mates. Sometimes, when he had to sign for his deliveries, he would say to the postman, 'Have trouble sending my parcel through the vortex, did you?' And the postman would think: 'Nutter at number thirty-eight.' It was almost like Christmas every single day. Pete was obsessed with ordering things off the Internet. CDs, books, clothes, presents, food, booze, everything.

Pete thought he looked like a younger Kevin Costner. He didn't – well not much, maybe. He said if you paused the film *Field of Dreams*, at the part when Kevin sees his father playing baseball, and if you squinted your eyes, then he looked just like him. He still didn't – well not much, maybe. His brown hair had been through many stages: shaved, spiky, floppy, sloppy, and now it was like Kevin Costner's in the film *The Bodyguard*. That morning, as he picked out a tie to wear, the postman knocked – the postman never knocked twice – and Pete's light blue eyes, the colour of early morning dawn, did a back flip. Pressie time.

Three parcels, two letters. He opened the tempting pink envelope first, and read the letter out loud to himself. 'Pete, This is a very difficult letter to write. So I will keep it short. Dave has told me in confidence that he has slept with Sandra when she was pissed, in Froggy's bed of all places. I find this disgusting, and I find it hard to sit at the table watching Dave being all buddy to poor Froggy, who hasn't got a clue. I think it would break Froggy's heart if he found out, but I think you deserve to know what a bastard friend he is. Dave isn't quite what he makes out he is and only looks out for No. 1. From Naina.'

And Pete finally swallowed the mouthful of toast. It was 8.35 a.m. Far too early to think straight. What a weird way to start the day. He knew what thoughts should be exercising their right to use his head-space, like: 'That's bang out of order that is, bang out of order.' But even without the caffeine particle accelerator in action, he knew he should have expected as much from Dave really. Dave had even said once many years ago, 'Wouldn't it be great if we all had kids and they went to the same school?' and then he'd given his Dave smile and said, 'Funny thing is though, they'd all look like me.' And he'd laughed.

Pete opened the rest of his post, wondering whether to tell Dave about the letter or not.

Wondering over, he picked up the phone. 'OOzing. Dave, it's Pete.'

'What time is it? OOzing.'

'Nearly nine. You'll never guess what, mate? My baseball top came through.'

'Pete, fuck off, it's the middle of the fucking night, mate.'

'Did you shag Sandra?' Pete laughed – hilarious.

Even through the phone line Pete could tell Dave was now a hundred per cent awake. 'Who told you?'

Pete went on to explain about the letter, and read it out – three times.

'Naina wouldn't do that, not Naina, no way,' Dave said, annoyed.

'She has, mate, it's right in front of me now.'

As Dave replaced the phone, a headache thumped like a herd of buffaloes across his frowning forehead. Pete – the true mate – refused to lecture, refused to judge. His only real piece of advice was the advice that hurt the most: 'Drop Naina!'

Life always has its little true-life Cluedo conundrums. Clues steering you in the direction of the culprit. Dave lit a fag, desperate to comprehend something that didn't comprehend. For fuck sakes, he was with Naina only last night, enjoying an Italian meal, comforting her from her tears. How could she sit there knowing this letter was in the post? Did she think Pete wouldn't tell? Why? No, actually it was much more than why. It was how. How could anyone betray someone this way?

Dave lifted his heavy legs out of bed, and slumped

with his hands on his head, elbows on knees and waited for inspiration to come. Naina just wouldn't do it, it was beyond her, it didn't qualify as being in her character. But it had to be her – Sandra, Matt and Naina were the only three who knew. There was no way Sandra was going to tell, and Matt didn't even know it was in Froggy's bed, so, it had to be Naina.

A quick vigorous shower, then Dave picked up the phone.

'Saviour Life Insurance, how can I help?' spoke a chirpy, polite woman.

'Can I have extension 6745, please?'

'I'll put you through.'

'Hello, extension 6745, how can I help you?' A male voice.

'Can I speak to Naina please?'

'You want to speak to Naina?'

'Yeah, is she there?'

'You want to know if Naina's here?'

Dave clenched his fist. 'Can you get me Naina, please?'

'You want me to go and get Naina?'

'Are you a retard?'

'You want to know—'

Dave butted in, 'Please, look, I'm really trying here. Please get me Naina before I go fucking mental.'

'There . . . is . . . no . . . need for that obscene language. I will go and get Naina.' And he went away wiggling his tiny bottom, short steps, one hand out to one side, looking for Naina through the hoards of filing cabinets, with goose bumps the size of geese crawling over his body – oh Lordy, how he loved winding up that arrogant man.

'Ah, sweetie, I thought I might find you here. Ooh, let me see.' And Graham huddled up to the desk and looked to where the office bitches were office bitching over pictures in some glossy magazine of Tinseltown stars at some charity gala. 'Collagen!!' And Graham was in his element.

Ten minutes later, leaving not one of the stars without at least one personal criticism, Graham waved his hands in the air, bouncing up and down on his swivel chair. The five bitches stared.

'Ohh ohh, Naina, sweetie, I forgot to tell you. The beast is on the phone,' he remarked. 'I must warn you though, sweetie, he seems in a bit of a tizzle . . . he spoke to me like a savage.' And he shivered with delight.

Naina gave a strained look of ignorance to the four bitches with their raised eyebrows. 'He's just a friend.' And she left them to it.

And the 'to it' – gossiping – was about the only thing that kept Naina sane in this place. Dad had said, 'Study hard, and you'll get a well-paid job.' So Naina studied, got her 'well-paid job' and realized that good pay didn't go hand-in-hand with enjoyment. The thrill of waiting for people to die lost its edge after a while. Widowers and widows hoping to get their insurance pay-out, before they too snuffed it, were not the happiest of folks to deal with. But it was a well-paid job and she was a group manager, and she did make her parents proud. More proud than if she'd taken up the vocation she really wanted when she left school.

'You want to be a what?' Dad had asked.

'Beautician.'

'So when we marry you off, what do we tell them? You put make-up on other people. That's not a job.' He threw her *Cosmopolitan* back on the table. 'Bulwinder's daughter was a chemist and she married a doctor. Surmeet's daughter is a lawyer and is marrying a barrister. And my daughter wants to be a make-up artist and she will marry a dustman.' A week later, circled in the *Citizen* local rag by Dad: 'Tax Officer Higher Grade' and 'Insurance Claims Manager'. The choice was hers.

And she hated the place. Couldn't wait to see the back of it. Couldn't wait to stomp right in to red-faced Cartwright's office and tell him to stop calling her My Delhi Angel Delight, and tell him he could stick his job where the sun never shone – right up his office.

Maybe the scorn for the job stemmed from the nullification of ambition. Maybe it's hard to get excited or enthused by something when deep down you know your arranged marriage will put a stop to everything. Your arranged marriage will take you to a new town and a new life. What life? Bringing up kids, cooking and cleaning. Playing all goody-two-shoes and praying you don't step out of line with the all-important mother-in-law and extended family. Hoping deep down that somehow you've been blessed with persuasive ovaries that can sweet-talk the sperms into being male, so that you give birth to a son and not a daughter. And when you give birth to that boy, once all the relatives have been informed and the laddus have been dished out, you can breathe a deep sigh: you have fulfilled your first obligation. But cripes, what if you give birth to a girl? One word:

disappointment. Actually four other words: try harder next time. And there will always be a next time. Six disappointments later, you'll still be ordered to give birth to that boy. Cripes.

Naina wandered back to her tidy desk to find that Dave had hung up. She debated: gym? Home? Or, she looked at the time – 9.23 a.m., bed!

'Dave, it's Naina . . .'

'I need to see you.'

He sounded odd, almost pissed off. 'What's the matter?'

'Can you do a sicky?' he asked, softening his voice. 'I can pick you up in ten minutes outside. I really need to see you, it's important.'

Naina suddenly had a migraine. Those awful office cheese sandwiches.

Dave had been this way once before, she thought – almost frantic, acting strange: He'd pulled her into his car, driven at full speed and turned down a deserted road, sweating in the summer heat: 'Versace is dead.' She had nodded her head. 'Dave, he died years ago.'

Naina threw on her winter coat and headed out to the red BMW in her black trousers and black platform leather boots. It was beginning to rain.

The speckles of rain hit the waxy red paint finish and rolled down the bonnet. Naina caught sight of Dave's icy expression as she dipped into the car and knew this was not about another fashion guru dying.

'Why did you send Pete the letter?' he asked, facing Naina. She looked beautiful.

'What letter?' she replied, confused. 'What are you going on about?'

'Come on, Naina, what did I do to you to make you

do this to me?' His voice was calm.

'I don't know what you're talking about, Dave. What letter?'

Dave looked outwards. 'The letter where you told Pete that I slept with Sandra. Do you remember it now? Or do you send him so many fucking letters that you don't even know which one I'm talking about?'

Naina directed her gaze to where Dave was staring, silent, unmoving, confused and nervous. 'Why are you doing this to me, Dave? You got your shag out of me and now you want to mess with my mind like you mess with all the other women. Remember, I know you, Dave, I know how your mind works.' And Naina changed views and peered out of the side window – she didn't want to see his face any more.

'And I thought I knew you, but I don't, and quite frankly I don't want to.' Dave fumbled for a fag, popped it in his mouth, but didn't light it. 'I told you all that in confidence. I trusted you. I told you stuff I wouldn't tell anyone.'

Naina twisted her head round so sharply it made a clicking noise, eye contact was established. 'You'd obviously made your mind up before you came here, so you're not such a good mate yourself. You're not even willing to listen to what I have to say.' She thought of knives and sharp tools and things that might hurt, then thought she'd better leave. 'I'm going.' And, picking up her black canvas bag, she opened the door and stepped to get out. 'Is that all you wanted out of me? A shag to fuel your ego. And now you come up with a stupid pathetic way of dumping me. Well, you can fuck yourself.' And the door slammed shut, nearly knocking the man-sized tissue box off the dashboard.

He watched her scurry across the car park. And where once their friendship weighed as much as a twenty-storey building, now it was about as heavy as the shadow that lay on his mind. It was over – he would never be able to forgive her for this.

Dave switched on the engine and turned on Horizon Radio.

'There will be major hold-ups on the M1.'

'Who gives a shit?' And he drove off.

Chapter Twenty-three

'The dogs in the streets of India wouldn't eat this!' Naina's dad was referring to the mushy pool of papier mâché which was supposed to be fluffy basmati rice. 'Ashok's family will send you packing saying "Indian girl cannot cook rice." No daughter of mine is going to show me up.'

'I have shown her how to do it hundreds of times, she doesn't pay attention.' Mum despaired.

Naina and her family sat around the small, cloth-covered dining-room table, playing host to one massive patterned china bowl of something unidentifiable. Naina was shaking with embarrassment when she brought it out, and tried to disguise the disaster by adding two handfuls of ripped-up coriander, a few raisins and some chopped almonds. The words 'Da na' possibly didn't help matters much.

Kiran grinned. 'I'm not eating this . . .' He looked

to Naina, then pushed away his plate and then pushed his luck. 'I'm not eating this shi—'

Dad clipped him round the ear, knocking his New York cap off his head, and Sonia cracked up laughing.

Dad continued, 'You're going to have to stay in cooking every night from now on. It's for your own good,' he said, fondling the soggy rice with a dessert spoon.

Mum helped matters. 'Look what happened to Sumita with her mother-in-law. Your dad's right.' She looked to Dad. 'My mother taught me to cook at ten, and I did it with enthusiasm; these kids have no interest. We're too soft on them, they have it too easy, don't they?'

Naina rolled her eyes, here we go.

'When I was your age,' Dad began, 'I had no shoes. I had to walk through the village every day in the burning hot sun. Flies everywhere. Big ones, as big as a bird. I would have to fetch a bath full of water on my head, with flint-stones on the ground. But I never rested, I never spilt a drop. Water was like pure gold.'

'Dad,' Sonia spoke through a mouthful of chapatti, 'can I make a quick joke?'

'Be quick, Sonia. I have much explaining to do about my village.'

'Okay,' she swallowed. 'If you walked with a bath on your head, why didn't you just turn on the taps instead?' Kiran, Sonia and Naina spewed out laughing with Mum not far behind.

The laughter soon simmered and the real speech from the head of the household began.

'What do you kids know? With your mobile phones, Internet, TV, video, luxury items.' He shouted this bit: 'IMPERIAL LEATHER SOAP. We came from India with just five pounds. We had nothing. We left our family behind, all for you kids, and this is how you repay us; backchatting us and rice that dogs won't eat . . .'

The OOzing gang sat at the cluttered pub table. Borderline pissed, but through passport control and into quarantine with their piss-taking.

'Jingle, you vegetable. You cannot tell how intelligent someone is from their fucking postcode, you dick,' Dave shouted above the music.

'Well, Dermot reckons when the MK6 lot were born they couldn't even read or write. He says they're all thickos down that end.'

'Jingle. Someone help this moron. It's not the sodding postcode that makes you thick.' Dave gulped his Stella, dragged on his fag, and slouched back.

The stressed bartenders gave a knowing look to each other – keep an eye on the six rowdy blokes by the fire exit.

Matt looked to Pete who looked to Froggy who looked to Andy who looked to Jingle who looked to Dave who looked . . . quiet.

'All right, mate?' Froggy asked Dave. 'What's up? You can tell us, we're your buddies.'

'It's not you lot, it's the other species, women. I've had enough of 'em.' He gulped down half a pint. 'They have only two modes: egg time, which is bedtime, and towel time, which is growl time.' Dave nearly fell off the stool laughing. 'These women, always going on about how hard it is when it's growl time. Well, put a fucking sticker on your head then, we'll keep away.' Then he added, 'Gladly.' They all laughed. 'Back-stabbing bitches, that's what they are.' Dave turned his head round and smiled to the three women sitting directly behind him. Low and behold, they were listening in.

Pete studied his womanizing buddy. It wasn't like him to be upset over a woman. He wondered if his relationship with Naina went a little bit deeper than Dave was letting on. Pete almost felt guilty for being the harbinger of bad news with the letter.

'La la la do do do doobie do, la la la do do.' Dave viewed the caller display and answered his mobile – it was the gym.

'All right, Steve . . . Who? . . . Say again . . . No, I don't know her . . . No, I don't know her, are you deaf? . . . Just tell her to piss off . . . Well, just tell her not to call, I don't know her, okay? . . . I'll lock up tomorrow night . . . Yeah, cheers.' He put the mobile down, swigging his drink as his mates looked on.

'Oi, Dave,' Jingle shouted, rummaging in his fluorescent council worker jacket. 'How d'you get your phone to make that tune?'

Dave stared. 'Pass it over.'

Jingle handed Dave his mobile, a big beaming smile on his face, he loved that tune. Dave programmed the tune in and passed it back.

'Cheers, mate, you're tops. Give us a call and let's hear it.'

'La la la do do doobie do, la la la do do.' 'Hello, who's this?' Jingle asked.

'It's Dave. Is Jingle there?'

They all burst out laughing.

*

Naina cried alone in her bedroom. Vanessa Mae's *Storm* plucked the air softly in the background, and an incense stick smoked. It was an 'un' day. Unfair, unappreciated and unhappy.

Lust, she couldn't have any. Passion, none of that either. What about romance? Do me a favour. And love? Even in whispered tones, what about that? In whispered tones 'No', then louder 'NO', then louder still until it's so deafening you can't even make it out: 'NO; you must accept your parents' choice of a husband.' And what about if you don't fall in love with 'your parents' choice of husband'. What about if you can't stand the sight of him? What about if his annoying habits are so annoying that it makes you dizzy and your skin crawls . . . off. What about if he's a creep who dribbles at the sight of your body and then climbs on top of you every night and then dribbles over you. What d'you say? I'm doing it to please my parents. What about that?

Naina wiped her eyes. She wished she'd never met Dave. Why couldn't he have been born with ginger hair? The attraction towards him, this bloody 'urge', should have worn off by now. It should not have become stronger. Naina lay back down on the bed as comparisons of Ashok and Dave began to invade and argue inside her head.

Ashok was homely, nice, delightful, good looking, possibly caring and sensitive, maybe strong and emotional, rich, of good stock; he might even be fun to live with. Maybe not the nightmare husband after all. Importantly, he was her parents' choice; so there would be no comeback. As for their future: kids. With two Indian parents, there'd be no confusion there.

Plus a huge heap of relatives for the kids to grow up with and a childhood much like her own. And if she were honest, it had been a strict, fair, but fabulously brilliant one with memories that filled her with joy: chasing Sumita round the garden with Dad's axe, and Sonia, watching her grow into Death. Even Kiran, the strong one of the kids, who used to crack her up with his dreams of being the English Sikh from Bucks who would defeat the world in boxing while leading England to World Cup victory in football, at the same time battling Pakistan and thrashing them at cricket. While all that was going on, Kiran would also be protecting his family, buying up real estate and selling it off for profit. In the evenings he would study, get forty-three degrees, beat Dad at chess, beat Mum at knitting, beat Naina at everything and even become the first Sikh man on the moon. All before he was ten years old. Memories so real that for a second Naina forgot that she was supposed to be comparing. Oh yeah. Pig boy.

What did Dave have to offer? God, he had it all. He was a womanizer, a liar, a loudmouth, a thug, with no future, a murky past; a stranger to love and a villain to marriage. He was the worst of all possible worst-case-scenario boyfriends. Yet still, with all that stuff floating in Naina's skull, he was, and this was hard to say, her favourite person of them all. He made her laugh, helped her when she cried, he struggled to be friendly even when she was not. He had morals even though they were well hidden sometimes. He had looks, and boy did he have those. He had made love to her and made her feel like a real woman at last. He had no shame, said what he thought, thought what he said, and if anyone had a problem with that, then 'fuckem'. But her family would be gone should a man such as Dave ever cross that barrier and fall prominently head over heels for Naina. Like a shrinking violet, they would fade away if she ever chose to go with a man such as Dave. She would lose it all. And it was a lot to lose.

Like being on a springboard with nowhere to spring to, Naina found herself consumed with emotional thoughts of Dave. He'd caused heartache in so many. Wandered into their lives, revved up their emotions and then just when they thought this was it, this was their man, he dumped them, forgot about them, and set his sights on whoever's next. Naina didn't want to be next, she wanted to be now, she wanted to be tomorrow, and she wanted to keep him.

A wisp, a vague wisp of hope that Dave would be her knight in shining armour and rescue her from this impending wedding had been blown out of the window today. He hated her.

Sandra sat with her feet up on the orange sofa. She had the company of her huge smile to watch the TV. Not that she could really concentrate, I mean how could TV compare to real-life drama? She promised herself one more look at the photocopy of the letter she had sent Pete, before she would burn it. Amusing to her was how easy Naina's signature had been to copy: so basic, so inartistic, not like her own with her flowing lines of curved architecture. And the words, they had just come to her, brilliant, faultless. The best part was that Naina's childish signature was copied from an apology to her and Froggy. It was classic.

She flicked through the channels, messed around with the volume control. Froggy wouldn't be home for at least another hour or so. She wondered how things were going down at the Squirrel – whether Froggy was pissed yet, wondering whether Dave had fallen out with Naina yet.

Headlights from passing cars swam on the cream curtains, then faded away like an untimely lighthouse not quite making up its mind whether to warn the ships of rocks or not. Sandra was sure of a few things though:

1. Pete would definitely not tell Froggy.
2. Pete would definitely tell Dave.
3. Dave would not suspect her for one minute.
4. Naina would deny it.

The plan was infallible. Dave and Naina's friendship would be broken like a weak thread of spider's web, and the thought made the taste of Sandra's chocolate digestive biscuit so much sweeter.

Chapter Twenty-four

Margaret the traffic warden moved with the fluidity and momentum of a battleship destroyer. But she could stop on the turn of a hat, or the sound of a handbrake, or the silent winking of hazard lights. She could even smell tyre rubber on yellow paint from fifty yards away.

Dave sat on the low white-bricked wall, on the opposite side of the road to his red BMW parked blatantly on a double yellow, smoking a fag. He watched Margaret idle up and smiled to himself. He wanted to argue with someone. It was Saturday lunchtime with a cold temperature but a sunny sky. Most shoppers had the sense to use the huge free multi-storey car park just round the back of Waitrose. Most shoppers did not get a parking ticket. And most shoppers did not play games with traffic wardens.

Margaret stopped by the BMW, peered in the

window, gave a quick look around, then carried on her slumbering walk.

'Oi! Margaret,' Dave shouted, chucking down his fag and walking across the road. 'Oi, Maggie.'

Margaret turned round. 'Oh, it's you. What a privilege.'

Dave pointed to the BMW. 'That's parked on a double yellow, are you blind? Come on, let's see you ticket it.'

Margaret backed up to the BMW. 'It's probably someone who's just quickly popped into the chemist. I'll give them ten minutes. We do give leeway, you know.'

Dave shook his head. 'And if that was my black BMW parked there, would you give me ten minutes? Leeway, my arse.'

Margaret smiled, the big whites of her eyes like plates. 'No! You've had your fair share of leeway over the years.'

Dave couldn't take it. 'And you've had your fair share of food, but that doesn't stop you eating for the entire town, does it?' He demobilized the BMW, got in, gave her the finger and skidded off, smiling.

Margaret fumed as she watched the disrespectful man power off. She would have to warn the others: he's now driving a red BMW.

When Dave first opened the gym, he would park his car in a side road, and jog up to the gym entrance to meet the waiting customers. So fit. Nowadays, he'd normally arrive kicking up gravel with his back tyres and fall out of the car, smoking a fag, and nursing a hangover from the night before.

Steve with his pumped-up biceps was inside,

polishing the green plants at the doorway in a concoction of half milk and half water. Dave had read in *Woman's Own* of the fabulous cleaning tip and it worked a treat. They shone like an Amazon rain forest. Steve didn't even notice Dave walk in; he was far too busy admiring his reflection in the mirror on the far wall.

'All right, Steve?'

He jumped. 'Oh, all right, mate. Naina's waiting for you. She's been here for about half an hour.' And Steve tensed his arm. 'What do you think, Dave?'

Dave hadn't seen Naina since Wednesday – since they'd argued. 'Yeah, your arms are great.' And he walked through. Steve followed.

'That woman phoned again, she just can't take no for an answer.' Steve paused. 'I think you should ring her, she sounds—'

Dave interrupted, 'Tell her I've gone abroad.' His eyes then met Naina's as she sat on the leather sofa, just round the corner to the entrance.

Naina sprang up. A light, short, green fleece top with a little zipper by the neck, black pedal pushers, black Ellesse trainers, and her hair tied back in a ponytail. No socks. She looked nervous.

'Can we talk, Dave?' she asked, trying to read his eyes.

'No problem.' He looked at Steve. 'I'll be in the office.' And he opened the door for her and followed inside, kicking it closed behind him with his Nike.

A Euphoria CD was driving the gym speakers insane, but the office walls insulated most of the noise except for the heavy base which vibrated through just about anything. The two sat opposite each other over the desk and Dave lit up a fag.

In a gym environment Naina felt like a fish out of water. But she couldn't have Dave think that she was a Judas. Maybe the few days' respite had calmed things down a little, and they could discuss this like adults. By the lake, he had shown such understanding, cheered her up, comforted her. He was a true friend and she didn't want to lose him over some misunderstanding.

'Dave, I honestly didn't write the letter. You've got to believe me.' She faced a stubborn, non-believing, confrontational face. 'Why would I?' Naina's voice did not sound like the one she had practised over and over in her mind.

'Why would you? Now, that's a question. I don't know, I'm just gutted that you did.'

'Someone is obviously playing games and you're falling for it.' She stared through the curtain of smoke. 'Who have you told about . . . you know?'

'What? Me fucking Sandra?' Dave replied sarcastically. 'Well, you're the only one who knows I had her in Froggy's bed.' He paused. 'Why did you do it? I thought you were my mate. But you sneakily stabbed me in the back.'

It was the wrong time to quote Lee Harvey Oswald – 'I'm a patsy' – but she didn't like the tone in Dave's voice: accusing, belittling, unfriendly. 'Mates, I'll tell you about mates. You shagged your best mate's girlfriend, that's true friendship, Dave.' Her features moulded, sharpened. 'So don't tell me about friendship.' Her lips were dry ice, her eyes like hot iron. She could explode any minute. And the last bit she shouted: 'YOU'RE JUST ONE BIG NASTY LIAR!'

There was no time for a casual puff of his fag, no time to look cool and in control. He pulled forward on his hands to come within a foot of Naina's face. 'Liar? Your whole sad marriage is going to be one big fucking lie. And it's Ashok I feel sorry for, ending up with a slag of a wife! What would he make of you fucking a white man?'

Naina's eyes lost their gleam, they looked like hollow bruises, hateful bruises. She spoke calmly and coldly and stared him in the eyes. 'You may have looks and you may have money, but you are one hurtful person.' She stood up, telling herself not to cry in front of him. 'I hope I never see you again.' Pulled open the door and slammed it shut behind her.

In the gym, the stereo was conveniently playing Moby – 'Why Does My Heart Feel So Bad?' Dave killed the fag with an angry stab in the ashtray, looked to the ceiling and muttered, 'Yeah right, like I care.' But inside he was wrecked. He wished he could retract those last words he'd said to Naina. The hurt he'd seen in her eyes, the expression on her face: what a bastard thing to say. He could chase her, but then what? Once you had punctured the friendship, it would always deflate and never be the same again. And his repair kit, 'Sorry', might not work this time.

Later.

Sandra opened the front door. It was 8.15 p.m.

'Hello, Dave.' She stood aside and let him pass.

'Hi, Froggy about?'

'Just missed him. He'll be back in about half an hour. Do you want a coffee?'

'Cheers.' And he sat down on the orange sofa.

Stars in their Eyes was on the box. Dave looked at the screen waiting for the coffee. He didn't even know Whoopi Goldberg had had a hit record. Sandra returned after a minute and handed him a cold can of lager.

'Not on a date, Dave? It's Saturday night.'

'Nah, not in the mood tonight.' He cracked the Carlsberg, and gulped down a hefty mouthful.

Matthew Kelly put his arm round Whoopi: 'How do you feel? That was the best Diana Ross we've had on this show.' And suddenly the 'Chain Reaction' song made sense to Dave.

Sandra ran her fingers through her shoulder-length blonde hair and sat opposite Dave wearing a pair of loose grey tracksuit bottoms and a tight black T-shirt with 'Babe' written across the front in small fake diamonds. 'So what's up with you, Dave? Froggy said you've been a bit down.'

He lit a fag. Sandra leapfrogged over to the side table and returned, plonking down the ashtray, then sat where she was.

Dave ignored her comment. 'While we're on our own, you'd best know that Matt and Pete know. But don't worry, they won't say nothing,' he rattled off, turning the fag in his fingers.

'What do you mean, Matt and Pete know? You told them?' Sandra asked, surprised. She knew Pete knew, but Matt?

'Don't worry, I've sorted it,' Dave responded loosely, dragging his words, mentally urging her not to throw a wobbly.

'But why did you tell them? You told Naina, now

you tell them. What's wrong with you, Dave? Do you want to get found out?' She shifted uncomfortably in her seat, rubbing her ankles as if they were cold. 'You've such a big mouth, Dave!'

'It wasn't me. Matt guessed from what Naina said when she was pissed that night, and Pete,' he stumbled, 'well, Pete found out from Naina, direct.'

Sandra tried to hide her triumphant smile, a pleasing sensation was working its way through her entire body. 'What a bitch! Why'd she do that? She's always hated me, but to do that to you, *what a bitch*.'

Dave finished the lager and popped in the can tab so it tinkled at the bottom. 'I don't know why she did it.'

'Did you have a go at her? I hope you did.'

'We're not speaking. Don't fret though, Pete and Matt won't say a word.'

Sandra rose, walked out to her Shaker kitchen, dragging her shapeless Totes on the cream carpet, and returned with a new bottle of Smirnoff, two crystal-cut glass tumblers and a carton of fresh orange. She poured out two large drinks, her hands trembling, passed Dave a tumbler and sat next to him on the sofa.

Froggy was a good companion, a fairly good lover, and even quite good looking. That's the point – Froggy was just 'good', but he wasn't Dave. Dave was dangerous, exciting, full of life, unpredictable. The problem with Dave was that he hadn't met someone who could keep up, someone who excited him, someone who kept him wanting more – someone who could keep him in line. She was just like him, willing to fuck with everyone else's feelings. It shouldn't be too hard. A bit of sympathy, a bit of alcohol and Dave being like he was would be in her and Froggy's bed before long.

Then she pushed the button for sympathy, opened the ducts, and let the tears flow like the River Ouse. 'Froggy's going to find out, I love him so much.'

Oh *great*, thought Dave. Perfect. 'Sandra, pull yourself together, he'll be back in a minute. Then he *will* know.'

Sandra poured her cold spongy heart out. Streams of salty fake tears ran down her face and fell to her spotless grey bottoms. Inside, she was laughing. Even admiring how well her performance was going. She did a few gasps for effect, as though she had trouble taking breaths, breathed deeply, and clasped Dave's reluctant hand. Rocking backwards and forwards as if she were in an invisible rocking chair, hooting with laughter inside, just hooting.

Dave placed his arm round her shoulders. 'Sandra, sort yourself out, for fuck sake.' He hated picking up the pieces of his past women.

She removed her hands from her blotchy red face. 'Froggy is everything I've got, I can't lose him, really I can't.' Her face was blurred with make-up. 'I hate Naina, she'd better keep out of my way.' Sandra sniffed. 'Sorry I shouldn't say that about your friend. I really honestly thought she'd be the one that you'd fall in love with. I really did.'

Dave laughed. Love? 'No, we were just mates, nothing more.' He removed his arm from her shoulder and lit up.

'I know me and Naina don't get on, but you two, I just thought that . . .' Sandra appeared to be struggling. 'You look great together.' Internally she was puking. 'Sometimes I really do regret sleeping with you, Dave, especially you being all buddy to Froggy.' Sniff. 'He's so trusting. I lie awake sometimes and I think.' Sniff. 'What have I done? And poor Froggy hasn't got a clue. It's almost like we're taking him for a ride.' Sniff. 'Doesn't it bug you sometimes?' Her voice was threaded with a quiver – she could break down again any minute.

Dave stubbed out the fag, twisting it in the orange and cream pottery ashtray. 'I should get going, Froggy's obviously running late.' He stood. 'Thanks for the drink, tell him I called.' And didn't wait for a reply, calmly closing the front door behind him. Calmly, ha! He wanted to smash it off its hinges.

And he calmly drove to Pete's house.

'OOzing, mate, what are you doing here?' Pete asked, letting Dave through. 'Kate's here.'

'OOzing. I know.' Dave pointed at the furry pink polar bear coat hanging in the hall. 'VILE, hey?' And they both laughed.

Inside, Kate mirrored Dave's look of 'yuck' as they stared at each other for a second. She was supposed to be having a night in with her new boyfriend. Pete had promised her he wouldn't drink tonight; she had promised him a night to remember. Now pig was here, Mr I-want-to-be-the-centre-of-attraction, home-wrecker boy, testosterone twit.

'Can't stay, I've just come to collect the letter from Naina.' And he was gone.

Under his breath, Dave read the letter out loud to himself, beneath the dim in-car light. The words were cold, clumped together, and even though typed they were M e S s y. Bold when **they** shouldn't have **been**. CAPital LeTters IN the WrOng PLAces. An.d n.o f.u.l.l. stop.......s.

He'd received many e-mails from Naina. Ts were crossed, Is were dotted, little borders even decorated the outside. Naina did everything with panache, style, feeling and patience. This was the work of someone who was very sloppy indeed. Someone who spoke before they thought, touched before they looked, swallowed before they chewed, and that someone was his best mate's girlfriend. Sandra. One hundred per cent Sandra. She'd almost quoted him the letter back at her house, using the same phraseology, 'All buddy to Froggy' and 'Froggy hasn't got a clue'. He wondered why though. Why would she write this letter?

Outside the car, traffic whizzed past. People to meet, places to go, things to do, ovens to clean. Hectic. Inside, just him and this letter and thoughts of what it had done. He wished he could turn back the clock and undo the things he'd done, take back the words he'd said. Now, he'd lost his friend. Lost his friend for not even listening to himself. He knew Naina couldn't have written that letter, he knew inside, yet he branded her with his foul mouth and unhooked her anchor and told her to sail off – well, fuck off really.

He'd treated her like a criminal. The pit of Dave's stomach was molten, enflamed, wretched. He remembered Naina's beautiful face denying his accusations, trying to justify something that she need not have – that she was a true mate. By the lake, only the other day, Naina had kissed him and said, 'Even with all your faults, you're one in a million. And when I get married and move to Dagenham, you'll be the one I miss the most.' And Dave had said, 'But we can still see each other,' and Naina had replied, 'No, we'll never be able to see each other.' Yeah, he'd treated her like a criminal. He'd treated her like a common thief. But there was only one thief, Sandra, she had stolen away his friendship with Naina.

He switched on the car stereo and wondered about human beings for a while. What did Sandra do? Wait until Froggy was asleep and then by candlelight, with one finger, slam out the slanderous Sanderous letter on her beige and brown kiddies' plastic typewriter. And then seal it with her witchy venomous spittle. Sandra the forger.

He fiddled with his rose-gold earring, thinking back to the classic mistake he had made at school when forging a sick note. The end went something like this: *My beloved son David, so talented in many ways, including the bed department, cannot attend your boring lessons, because he's nursing a sprained wrist, from* **wanking** *over your wife*. The caning he'd received was worth it. And the ten-pound bet he'd won was worth it. He never thought he would be at the receiving end of a forged letter himself.

Half an hour later, he switched on the computer and logged on to the Internet.

And began to type Naina an e-mail.

Send To: sleepezzee@spiral.com
From: stranded@lexco.com

SEX-PINT-FOOTBALL-SHAMED

Now that you're not here
I want to bend your ear

I am a big disgrace
So slap me round the face

I hope the slap will make it better
I know you didn't write the letter

I want to send a kisssssss
She's at the end of this

It took me hours to write this rhyme
Pleasepleaseplease a minute of your time

So sorry beauty enriched Naina, may I say,
I love what you're wearing, gold pales in comparison.

I'm Utterly Butterly disgraced at myself.
Weevil Dave XXX

He pressed Send and watched the little envelope curl up, shrink and head towards Naina's house – via Bill Gates's bank account. Logged off, turned off the computer, and thought: Danny Zuko would not have had to resort to bad poetry for Sandy.

Three fags later, without smoking one, he reluctantly had to admit to himself the terrible truth. He was going to lose everyone. Naina was gone, a crappy e-mail wouldn't solve that one. Froggy was a time bomb – any second now Sandra would light the fuse. And his family, well, he needed to be drunk even to think about them. Dave had to admit it, perhaps they were better off without him.

Chapter Twenty-five

The yellow flag scoffed at the wind. It would take more than a daring breeze to befuddle its image. Held firm and lofty by a twenty-foot flagpole, the Sikh flag – Nishan Sahib – peered down upon its temple. Dad stared upwards, as he normally did, to the saffron material printed with the Sikh symbol: a large near circle like a waxing moon, dissected by two curved swords on either side of a straight sword.

'Pay your respect. And you, Sonia, go on,' Dad ordered, pointing up.

Naina, Kiran and Sonia glanced up. Respect!

Inside the enormous Gurdwara, through the Guru's door, heads were covered and shoes discarded. Women on the left and men on the right, all sat cross-legged like a hundred kisses on the white-sheet-covered floor. All facing ahead listening to the Granthi with his chavar, paying homage with their patience, as he read aloud from the *Granth Sahib* (a book filled with hymns, written by the Sikh gurus). The sugary perfume of roses and kitchen smells mingled with the delicate hum of feet.

Time stops in here and you don't dare laugh. Naina didn't understand half of what was being read out and the numbing of her behind through the hard floor was lightened only by the knowledge of the food soon to be served up – in plastic buckets.

She always used these monthly visits to take stock of her life. In here, her Indianness was brought home to her. It felt secure to be part of a community where looking out for each other took precedence over most things. In this one room, at least four generations of Sikh heritage were laid out on one huge floor, in a foreign land. It could make you proud. It did make you proud. It was like a mirror, forcing you to look at yourself. And what stared back from the mirror to Naina was a 'coconut': brown on the outside, white on the inside. And she didn't want to be a coconut. Mum and Dad had faced storms when they came to this country. They didn't buckle up in the jumbo jet, stare at each other and remark, 'We'll just drop our roots when we get there, when we get to the white land.' They didn't turn at the first road block when English people stared at them and little white kiddies looked to their parents and said, 'Why is that man a funny colour? Why does he wear that silly hat on his head?' as their parents crossed the road as if the colour were contagious. They didn't stare at the TV screen when the Brixton riots were out of control and say, 'Maybe they are right and we shouldn't be here.' And they never once, not even in a hint, promised it would be easy.

Naina felt proud sitting here amongst this tight-knit community. Mum with her head covered in bright orange, Dad with his best friend on his head, Kiran with a handkerchief, and Sonia . . . Naina stole a further glance Sonia's way: her head was covered in pink, with two wire strands leading down to her . . . Sony Walkman. Yes, so proud. She nudged her, and Sonia pulled the earphones away, guiltily.

The three raagis played away on their instruments, accompanying the hymns, whilst a scattering of women's voices throughout the hall sang with confident and surprisingly tuneful speedy harmonies. Pictures of Gurus lined the white walls and tinsel decorations spruced up an already cheery hall.

Naina soared back in her mind to a time when she was not quite a coconut. A time when she never questioned her parents' beliefs.

It had been home-economics class. Her long plaited hair tied behind her, her skirt just above her ankles, her sleeves rolled up her skinny elbows and her ears slightly sore from her latest body piercing – a third set of earrings. The dish of the day was chilli con carne. And the bitch of the day was Denise.

'Your mince is a weird colour,' grimaced Denise, squirming in her blue and white striped apron.

'Yeah, I know. It's lamb mince.'

More squirming. 'You can't cook chilli with lamb.' Denise pointed to the printed ingredients. 'Look, beef, it clearly states beef.'

'Our religion does not permit us to eat beef, the cow is sacred. So I brought in lamb instead. Okay?'

Denise raised her voice. 'You lot are well weird. How can a cow be sacred?' And she encouraged the class to laugh. A few sniggered. 'And you all smell funny.' More sniggers.

'Ignorance becomes you, Denise.' And Naina slapped an un-sacred cow hard round the face, sending her towards her pen. And it felt good, sticking up for her way. Not once was she ashamed of her religion and not once did she want to be like the white girls. She was proud of who she was. Her roots, her family, her skin, her smell – just as proud then as today.

God, she loved being Indian sometimes.

You could play a tune on the empty hungry bellies by the time the vegetarian dishes were shared out. And everyone tucked into the free food – langar – as they sat in rows, munching and chatting, catching up on gossip and spreading urgent news: 'Cheap seats on return journeys to India, saw it on text, only 650 ponds.' 'I'm vonting to sound cheerful, but I fear Narinder studies too little, and if I become too harsh he doesn't study at all, vot shall I do?' And the information highway would gather speed, so by the time the final deep-fried samosa hit the bottom of the last stomach wall, the gossip has been twisted and the information distorted. Tickets to India now cost only 350 'ponds', and Narinder fell asleep in his exams and was kicked out by his tutor. The Indian Internet.

Naina weighed out some thoughts as the empty, smudged plastic plates were taken away. It was one of those moments. A decisive time. Dave was out there in his world, she was here with her world. And these two worlds surely could not be mixed. Dave would have to go, along with his apologies, and she would have to do what was right. Her parents had not come all this distance to have their family diluted down by the English way. Yes, Dave *would* have to go. And his alluring blue eyes, gorgeous looks, muscly body, sense of humour, undeniable sexiness, foul mouth, it would *all* have to go . . . And good riddance, thought Naina, as she wiped her eyes with the temple tissue.

Chapter Twenty-six

Once every month Dave would trot downstairs and knock on the door of the flat below. At first Dave's choice of words were a little 'down-heartening', but, in time, the mere fact that he came down showed something. They didn't know what, but it showed something.

He knocked on the blue door, Ivy answered.

'Just checking that you're still alive, just being a good neighbour,' Dave said, with his concerned, caring look.

'Thank you, David, I'll see you next month.' And she smiled and closed the door.

Dave drove at his hungry pace, which normally meant just ignoring the highway code. Meat Loaf – *Bat Out of Hell* – blasted out of all four speakers, and the challenge to get to McDonald's without changing gear was on. By some miracle, he arrived safely at Westcroft drive-through and stopped at the intercom with its faded silver box, which wore a few dents from angry people who had been told, 'Fillet of fish will take ten minutes.'

'Can I take your order, please?' asked a boy who sounded ten.

'Big Mac, please.'

'Any fries with that, sir?'

'Just a Big Mac.'

'What about a drink, sir? Coke?'

'Just a Big Mac.'

'Is that the Big Mac deal with fries and drink, or just—'

'Just a Big Mac!'

'No dips? Apple pies? Fanta?'

'JUST A FUCKING BIG MAC, ARE YOU DEAF?'

Five minutes later Dave parked the car in Safeway car park and scoffed down the 'Big Mac'. Then he pulled up his Gucci T-shirt and looked down to make sure that his stomach muscles were still a sharp six-pack. Phew! He smiled his Dave smile. The weather was clear and crisp: blue sky, mild chill, lots of sun.

He turned the key in the ignition and headed off to Naina's house. He hadn't heard from her or seen her since she had come to the gym on the previous Saturday. It was now Tuesday. She'd ignored his e-mails and phone messages and now her employer had informed him that she had taken most of the week off work. He was desperate to see her.

But he wouldn't be able to just walk up and knock. Throwing stones at the window was not an option either. So, he would have to wait in the car, nearly out of sight, and pray that sometime during the day she would leave the house. He had his phone, music, heat, fags, Lucozade, Red Bull, Orbit chewing gum and the last three issues of *Woman's Own*. Oh yeah, and there was a huge ash tree about ten yards up the road – just in case. It was 1.00 p.m.

He reclined the seat, rested his head back for a few minutes and woke up at 4.30 p.m. to the knocking on his driver's window. He removed the soggy unlit fag out of his mouth as his eyes tried to focus on the encroaching darkness outside and then he jumped. What the fuck! He opened the electric window. Jesus Christ!

'Hello,' said one of three, the other two just stared. 'I'm Death, that's Damnation and that is Destruction.' Sonia pointed to her two gothic friends.

Dave shivered. This was not a dream. He was still on earth. But right before his eyes were three witches from hell, all dressed in black oversized woollen jumpers, black skirts with sewn-on tassels of black leather, black fishnet tights with r.i.p.s., Doc Marten's, huge silver crucifixes, silver skull rings, black eyeliner, black eye-shadow, black lipstick, even black tongues. Multicoloured ribbons were entwined in their black hair. They were very frightening.

Dave lit a new fag. 'Hello, Death, what can I do for you?'

Sonia leaned in, her wide eyes scanning the inside of the car. 'Are you a pervert?' The two friends behind her just stared.

'No, I'm a doctor; you three are very ill.'

Two of them began to chant demonic noises.

Sonia continued, 'I've seen you before, *Doctor*. You sit there and watch my materialistic sister get undressed up there, don't you?' She pointed a black fingernail to Naina's window. 'Do you masturbate here, while she undresses? Is that why you've got the man-sized tissues?'

The demonic chant became faster and louder, it was obviously well practised as neither of the other two witches missed a beat.

Dave burst out laughing. 'Hang on, Death.' He then looked at the other two, 'Can you stop that, please?'

Both held their crucifixes up at him and hissed, and then stopped and began to stare again.

'You send her filthy e-mails, don't you? You're Dave, aren't you? I can see why my sister went for you. That's my sister all over, she just goes for the exterior. You and her have had sex, haven't you? I read it in her diary, I know everything.' Sonia paused. 'Where's the black BMW? We liked the black one.'

'Look, I'm not going to pretend I'm not scared, and I think it's really good that you've got your own little club, but what are you meant to be? It's Sonia, isn't it?'

'It's Death!' Sonia scolded. 'I am Beelzebub's love child.' She smiled proudly.

Dave sniggered. It was amazing: underneath all that black make-up, she was really pretty, nearly the image of Naina. But thankfully worlds apart. What went wrong in her upbringing? Naina was so feminine, so sexy, so lovely. And this thing called Death, with her two Grim Reapers, well, words failed him.

'Death,' Dave forced a smile, 'is Naina about?'

'Might be, why?'

'Could you get her for me? I'll make it worth your while.' He chucked his fag past Sonia and it landed by Destruction's DMs. She stamped on it.

'How much?'

'Thirty quid. You bring her out here, discreetly, and the money is yours.'

Sonia glared at her two friends, who nodded a demonic approval. 'Fifty pounds and I'll tell her that you're really upset, and it took you five hours to write that stupid poem. It was crap. Not broody enough, not lovey-dovey enough. If you really knew Naina, you would have known that.' And she walked off, leaving her two friends just staring.

Dave lit another fag and smiled at the two staring witches. 'So, what graveyard do you go home to?' He tried to outstare them. It was no use. They wouldn't even blink, and he found himself humming a tuneless tune to himself and gazing down at his Nikes.

It was nearly dark and the staring of the two witches was beginning to become unnerving. Naina finally came out with Sonia. Her face was tight, fixed, and definitely not welcoming. It was going to take more than fifty quid to sort this out.

She opened the passenger door, and sat down. If the atmosphere outside the car was moody, then this was no better. Sonia whipped out her hand and countless silver bangles jingled to her wrist.

'Sixty pounds, you said.'

Dave removed three crisp twenties from his wallet and placed them in Sonia's claw. 'Don't spend it on drugs.' And that was the only time all three witches smiled. As they walked off, Dave was sure he heard 'Sucker!' And with a burst of demonic giggles, they disappeared in the darkness down a side alley.

He faced Naina. Even when clearly angry, her features were still pretty. The small curve of her nose, the long eyelashes flickering, the soft angles of her cheekbones, the elegant chin and those lips, full, pouting, kissable – she was beautiful.

'So, how have you been?' Dave asked, choosing his words carefully.

'Let's hear it.' Her face looked forward, straight ahead.

'I'm sorry for what I said. It was low, it was inexcusable.'

'Is that to make you feel better? Or is it because you're truly sorry?' Naina still stared ahead.

'I'm truly sorry.'

'Right, can I go now? Apology accepted.' Her voice was cold.

'Are we mates again then?' The words came out stuck together like burnt food on a frying pan. Almost one quick word.

'Never!' She turned to him. 'I hate you, Dave. I accept your apology, but I hate you. Can I go now, please?'

Whatever Dave thought was going to happen, it was not this. She actually meant it. There was no fear in her voice that she was saying the wrong thing, no concern that she would later regret saying it. It was pure, simple, it was honest and when she pierced his blue eyes with hers, he knew: he knew that it was definitely over. He had lost her for real this time. And it left a horrible empty sensation.

'Dave, you were my best friend, my best mate, and now you're nothing in my life. Nothing at all.' And Naina stared for two or three seconds, then walked back inside her house. She was gone.

Dave was now the not-so-proud owner of a

fractured heart. Oh, the advice he dished out to his mates when their hearts had become weak over a woman, how hollow that sounded now: women, there's no point getting upset over them, no point getting all gooey over them, no point giving up drinking for them, no point giving in to them. Go and get yourself another one, she was a slapper anyway, we all thought so.

Dave made his way back to Stone Valley with a head full of home-truths. Cars had to wait behind him in the rush to get home because, quite frankly, he felt like driving at 15 m.p.h. And if it meant that the drivers were late home and had to explain to their wives why they were late, then they shouldn't have married the moaning bitch in the first place. That's how he felt. Stuff them all.

Or maybe 'Fuck them all', as he reached for his 'Handy Honeys' book. He passed quickly over Naina's pages, didn't even want to look at what was written there. He felt like a 'T' tonight. Tracy, Tina, Tonia, Tanya or even Tagliatelle – the Italian one.

'Tracy, it's Dave, are you free tonight? Sorry about last time.'

Tracy was not free.

'Tina, are you free tonight? It's Dave. I'm really sorry about last time.'

Tina was not free.

Or there was always Tammy. He'd seen her only two nights ago, a bit too close for his liking, but what the heck.

'Tamzin, my little beauty, are you free tonight? It's Dave . . . Great . . . My place . . . Half an hour . . . Super, see you then.'

*

An hour and a half later.

'Tamzin, can you go now, please, I'm feeling really rough,' Dave whimpered.

Tamzin left Dave in bed, dimmed the lights, then crept out, slightly unsure whether this man was really 'too good to be true' any more.

As soon as 'Tamzin my little beauty' was gone, he leapt out of bed, walked to the kitchen and poured himself a Stella in a refrigerated pint glass. He loafed back on the sofa with his lager, watched the fire dying, and thoughts of Naina boomeranged back. Having sex with Tammy had done nothing to wipe Naina from his mind as he had thought it might. And he was sure a barrel-load of the beer wouldn't either. He'd really screwed up this time. The image of Naina smiling could not be found in his head; instead all he could see of her was the last look she gave him, before she went back indoors – the look of *hate*. Suddenly the Stella tasted off and he threw the pint glass across the room. It span in the air, sending the liquid spraying like juicy sparks on a Catherine wheel, until the glass hit the far blue wall and shattered on to the floorboards below.

Dave leaned over, picked up the cordless phone, and dialled Froggy. Sandra answered.

'Hi, Sandra, it's Dave, how are you?'

'Hi, Dave, good. You?'

'I don't know if I read the signals right on Saturday night, but, if you want sex, then I'm up for it.'

A pause, then Froggy's distant voice asking who it was as Sandra almost whispered, 'I'm definitely interested. When?'

'Take the day off work tomorrow, I'll be round about one. Can you put Frog on?'

'Okay, Dave, one tomorrow. I'll just get him.'

'OOzing.'

'OOzing.'

They spoke for about ten minutes about nothing in particular. Dave placed the phone down on the arm of the sofa, lit up a fag, lifted his legs up, parked his Nikes on the glass table, and smiled his Dave smile. Fuck the lot of you!

Chapter Twenty-seven

Dave was down the gym early on Wednesday morning on his third set of barbell curls. Eight reps later, puffing, he released the knurled EZ barbell, dropping it onto the black rubber matting. The best set he had had in weeks. His arms were pumped with blood, his white Baggy Boyz T-shirt was drenched, his hair wet, and he felt a whole lot better. In fact, the whole gym was sometimes used as a large Hoover to suck up people's frustrations. Like the bloke who didn't get that pay rise, or the bloke who found out his wife was sleeping around, even the bloke who got beaten in an arm-wrestling competition by a woman. Or, in Dave's case, the bloke who had just lost his best mate. He picked up a small white towel, wiped his face, and headed towards the showers.

Steve was at Reception sorting out the staff schedules. He just loved the place, it was where he would spend his honeymoon if he got married. A dream come true to work in a gym and get paid for it. He could sit there all day talking to the members, boosting their egos, improving the gym morale, accepting their compliments about his arm-size, his small waist, his chunky thighs, but he did need to work on those pigeon calves. And then there were the other members of staff, the ones who he tried to enthuse with the same energy as himself. The ones whom he was constantly warning for not tackling the job *professionally*.

Another tacky sign in the men's shower room: 'There's one part you can't make bigger – live with it' – Dave's idea. He switched on the shower, more like a fire hydrant, and washed himself down with the complimentary shower-gel. As the hot water powered, his mind trickled and the steam rose like great blankets of cloud off the reddish-brown safety-tiled shower floor. Sandra obviously wanted Dave enough to push Naina out of his life, and she obviously wanted him enough to risk wrecking things with Froggy, for both of them. He wondered if Sandra loved Froggy at all. He turned off the shower and stepped out on to the wooden duckboard just as the white curtain of the shower next door pulled across and a man stepped out. He had on a black swimming hat and swimming goggles (presumably to stop soap suds hitting his eyes). Dave looked at him and regretted it as the man smiled. On both of his nipples were . . . nipple rings? And Dave had to stop himself from looking down, just in case.

Fifteen minutes later, Dave was driving along in his car, heading towards Froggy's house in Kents Hill

Nisha Minhas

Park, a quieter end of town, listening to Talking Heads – *Psycho Killer* – and after a mile or so he turned into a Shell garage and wandered into the shop.

Naina tipped in the tablespoon of turmeric. The sliced fried onions, chopped garlic and ginger changed to golden yellow as the wooden spoon gently stirred. She dipped her head inwards and wafted the fantastic aroma with her upturned palm, bringing the choking steam to her nose. A small red cassette player sat on the kitchen window which overlooked the large back garden. The piano intro of 'November Rain' by Guns n' Roses began, and Naina quickly stepped over to the cassette player and flipped the tape over to 'The Chauffeur' by Duran Duran. She hopped back, continued stirring and added in cumin, salt, chilli powder and coriander powder. She was getting the hang of all this cooking malarkey, it wasn't so hard, Mum had taught her well.

Sonia, dressed in her civvy clothes: bottle-green and burgundy school uniform, barged in. 'Where's Mum?' Sonia was home for school lunch.

'Gone to Ranjit's house, catching up on gossip.'

Sonia rolled up the wooden bread bin, pulled out the square-cut Kingsmill loaf and began to butter two slices. She then layered thin circular segments of cucumber, added a chunk of honey roast ham, jammed the slices together, ripped them down the centre, stuffed one half in her chops, and began to speak with her mouth full.

'Naina, what are you trying to cook?' she asked with sympathy.

300

Naina stuck out her tongue. 'Aloo gobi for tonight.'

'If you give me a tenner, I'll give you some juicy gossip: deal?' Sonia began on the other half of her sandwich.

Naina swung her head round. 'You got sixty pounds yesterday. Just tell me the gossip.'

Munch munch munch. 'I heard Kiran the other night on the phone, speaking a little bit too loud.' Sonia smiled. A small piece of cucumber was lodged between her middle two teeth. 'He said Dave was blackmailing him. He made him sit in the BMW with a knife to his throat and he threatened Kiran with a tape.' She waited for a reaction from Naina, then carried on, 'Listen to this, Naina, Kiran could go to prison with what Dave has got on that tape. Wicked, isn't it? I don't mind this Dave bloke. Imagine it, Naina, we get to visit Kiran in Woodhill prison, wicked.' Sonia giggled. 'And the really funny part, Naina, is . . .'

Naina looked at Sonia, her eyebrows raised, like what is so funny?

Sonia giggled again. 'You're burning the dinner. Mum's going to kill you.'

The large stainless steel saucepan was almost thrown off the heat. Smoke alarms were threatening to sound.

'Are you sure you heard right, Sonia?' Naina asked, nerve-struck and shaky, immediately concerned. 'A knife? He had a knife to Kiran's throat?'

Sonia was dead sure, she was Death after all, Sonia knows all. And Naina headed for the phone, dialled Dave's mobile number and hung up on the answerphone. Whatever he was playing at this time was beyond her imagination but, knowing Dave, it was beyond everyone's imagination.

Sonia's 'deep' voice emerged. 'He that lives by the sword, then he shall die by the sword.' And she left with the sound of Naina's voice hurtling up behind her.

'This is really serious, Sonia.'

Naina sat down on the red flower-patterned sofa in the living room. Knives? Just the word itself was enough to bring a bloody battle in her mind. And she boiled. Kiran and Dave? On the wall above the sofa chair hung a large colour photograph, the size of a pillowcase. It showed a sprightly smiling Kiran aged twelve standing with his arms around Sumita and Naina. Sonia stood below his trouser belt. Naina remembered that day. Sun, no breeze, Mum's home-made warm lassi and a wooden fruit crate. Kiran stood on the crate, ordering Dad to wait until he was ready for the photograph. There was no way he was having his two older sisters look taller than he. For he was a man, and he was their protector. And now he, the older Kiran, was being threatened by a plain and simple . . . thug. Naina knew beneath Dave's charming exterior lay something that promised violence. Stories bounced thick and fast from his mates – who were no better than he was – of Dave's heroic confrontations, of his past brushes within the law, and outside the law. All the stories bore out one thing though: Dave hated bullies, despised them, he hated people who picked on those who were weaker than themselves. And now he was picking on Kiran and she couldn't figure out why. Maybe she didn't know who Dave was at all.

Chapatti or Chips?

*

Dave knocked on Froggy's and Sandra's front door. A solid confident knock with a solid brass knocker. Sandra instantly opened the door and smiled – he was here and he looked gorgeous.

'You look lovely,' Dave remarked on Sandra's short red mesh dress, almost see-through, actually it was see-through: her red G-string and bra were clearly visible underneath. Her shoulder-length blonde hair appeared to have been conditioned every day for a month and her make-up was perfect; not too much, not too little, just as Dave liked it. In fact if Dave were to use a single sentence to sum her up, it would have been 'Made lots of effort.' She did look beautiful and her red high-heeled sandals finished her off wonderfully. Froggy would have been proud as punch.

Dave walked in, closed the door behind him and kissed her on the lips. The smell of Opium gently massaged his mind and the closeness of her stunning body sent wild thoughts adancing. He pulled away, took her hand and entered the living room.

She had wanted this for so long. Thought about this moment so many times. She knew how to play him, this was her second chance, and this time she would keep him and change his ways.

'Drink?' Sandra asked, in between kisses.

Dave reached for his back pocket, pulled out the box of ribbed condoms and tossed them on to the table. He then removed his grey Armani T-shirt. Sandra's eyes glowed as her warm hands played with his black leather belt, teasing, flirting, tantalizing. Slowly she began to undo the buckle and crouched down.

Nisha Minhas

Dave stepped back. 'Let me see you strip off, I want you to tease me.'

Froggy pulled up outside in his BT van. Sandra's white Nova was still in the drive. Odd. She should have been at work. Dave's red BMW was parked wonkily behind it. Even odder. Froggy parked the BT van behind the BMW and sat there smoking. He looked at his mobile, at the display: no calls had been missed. It wasn't his birthday, this was no surprise party. Dark thoughts seemed to work their way up and down his ribcage, scraping the surface, digging out his fears. No, Sandra and Dave, it was not feasible. No way.

Froggy had never before had the weird feeling he was feeling right then: sneaking up on his own house. He felt the creaking of his knees as he crept along like an old man with a crooked spine, his head kept low, below the window sill, before, like a periscope, it began to rise. Through a triangular gap in the corner of the netting, a shaft of light shone straight into the living room – the gateway to Froggy's own private hell. Sandra was almost naked, wearing only a red satin bra, and then she removed the bra and waved it above her head, throwing it behind her. Dave's bare back was to the window as Sandra came towards him, smiling, wrapping her arms round him with a warmth, a look that Froggy had never before had the privilege to see: she was glowing.

Sickness tore through his insides, invading, unwelcome, and ghastly. He could not bear this any more, he had to get out of here. And inside the van, he perched on the edge of insanity, ready to ram the BT

304

vehicle right into the smug red obnoxious BMW. And then he felt a cold chill, like a wind on top of a mountain, sweeping all thoughts aside. He glanced at his house, put the key in the ignition and calmly reversed the van. A mile down the road he took refuge outside a lorry park in the industrial area. Wound down the window, looked out to the monster HGV lorries, and cried his heart out. He really loved Sandra. And Dave – he really loved him too.

Dave pulled back from Sandra's embrace, picked up his T-shirt from the floor, and stared at her coldly. 'Sandra, you bitch, put your clothes back on.'

Numbness stifled Sandra's fire of passion. 'Pardon? Dave?'

He pulled his T-shirt over his head. 'You wrote that fucking letter, you bitch. And you sat here the other night, crying your crocodile tears over your love for my best mate, you're sick. If you really loved Froggy, there is no way, *no way* that you'd be doing this.' He paused. 'You just don't turn me on, Sandra.'

There were tears in Sandra's eyes. 'What letter? What letter? Dave?'

'You tried to drive a wedge between me and Naina. What is it? Jealousy? Jealous of her looks, are you? Her body? Maybe you're jealous of everything she is and everything you're not.' He paused. 'Naina's out of your league, Sandra, always has been. Even with all your tricks, you don't compare to even half the beauty Naina has.'

Sandra pulled on her dress, twisting the fabric in a rush to cover flesh that Dave now saw as repugnant, her brain filled with raw thoughts of envy and hate for

that horrible word 'Naina'. She'd been played like a
fool right here in her own house. And right now if she
had a gun, both Dave and Naina would be shot
straight through the heart. She leered up at Dave, her
hair slightly ruffled and a smile that reeked of evil; she
had a trump card and was about to play it. 'When
Froggy comes home tonight, I'm going to tell him
about me and you.' The words were delivered like a
fast ace.

'You're bluffing, Sandra. You tell him, you lose
him.'

'No, Dave, he loves me: he'll forgive me, but he
won't forgive you.' And if this were a Disney film,
Cruella De Vil would have laughed like a hyena.

Dave picked up his keys and mobile. 'You'll lose
him.' And he walked out.

Chapter Twenty-eight

It had been snowing again, but this time it was indoors. A huge *huge* strengthened-glass screen protected the onlookers from the skiers and snowboarders as they careered down the thick snow, dressed in their fashionable skiing wear, obligatory bobble hats, scarves and various-coloured eye masks. Switzerland abroad. One guy in particular was immensely annoying; weaving in and out of tumbling beginners, leaving great wakes of snow in their fallen faces, humming down the slope like it was his. 'Tosser,' thought Dave, wondering why no one had tripped him up.

Dave sat in the ski-slope coffee shop, dressed in a Valentino tight black T-shirt, dark grey combat trousers, dark grey Nikes and Davidoff. Intercom messages were interrupting the instrumental music at regular intervals. 'Code 1', 'Code 7', 'First aid on slope, man hit head on glass.' Only 10.30 a.m. and he was surrounded by the nattering and yapping and laughing of people all around him. Dave slouched there, half asleep, drinking a Kenco coffee from a plastic beige beaker, wondering why Naina wanted to see him. She was already fifteen minutes late. The midnight phone call a few hours ago on his answerphone was weird. No explanation, no feeling in her voice, almost robotic: 'Meet me at the SnoZone coffee shop at 10.15, tomorrow morning.'

The show-off on the ski-slope slipped, and snowballed to the bottom. At last! Dave laughed out loud, looked around to see that no one else was laughing, then got back to his coffee. Miserable sods.

'Whose misfortune are you laughing at this time?' Naina digged. 'Can't just let people get on with things, can you?' She sat down on the red plastic chair, with her back to the slope.

'Coffee? Or manners?' He lit up.

She looked into his blue eyes. 'Why did you put a knife to Kiran's throat?' Her icy voice had a humbling effect on Dave's smile, and it skidded off his face.

He tried to mask his surprise. 'Look, Naina,' he whispered, 'I just wanted to shit him up.'

Naina stood up, fuming. 'Why? What the fuck is wrong with you, Dave? He's my brother; you don't just go around shitting people up. What are you?'

'Naina, calm down, sit down. Look, all I did was rub a blade at his throat, I was never going to actually cut him. Come on, what sort of bloke do you think I am? Naina?'

She grabbed his arm. 'He's my brother, Dave. You . . . you . . . why?' She glared. 'I think we should go outside, before I lose it totally.'

Outside, they walked fifty yards or so in silence and came to the Fishermead bridge that hung over the H6 Childs Way dual carriageway.

Naina began to shout. 'You're on a different planet, Dave; I swear, getting a kick out of that, you must be sick! Why? Was it because you thought I wrote that letter and wanted some sort of revenge? Because that's how you work, isn't it? Someone crosses you and you get them.' She watched a huge looming lorry just about sneak under the bridge. 'What is it? Your stepdad kicked you around a bit, so fuck everyone else, trample over everyone. I wish I had never met you.' She walked off, calling back to him from the distance. 'You're a loser.'

Propelled more by the shock than anything else, Dave caught Naina up beside the huge car park that stood before the skiing complex.

'Whatever you think of me, I did it to protect you and nothing more. No one puts a fucking knife to my throat, no matter whose brother he is.' His voice was harsh, as though it was painful for him to get the words out of his mouth. 'I think the world of you, Naina; I never believed you'd go this low.' And walked off.

Pay and display in MK was well worth the money, thought a few onlookers. This was a show that was never mentioned in MK shopping centre brochures. A penny a minute and you get a lovers' tiff for free.

Naina stood, unaware of the surrounding scrutiny. She expected to hear the vroom-vrooming of his car, then maybe a lunging skid, and possibly even a hail of abuse to the nosy watchers. Instead, his head just disappeared from sight, into his car, which remained parked where it was.

'Are you okay, dear?' A middle-aged woman, with a husband who clearly wanted to stay out of it.

Naina nodded yes, gave a feeble smile and dithered over to Dave's car. Through the car window, she urged him to look at her, but instead he sat there smoking, eyes pinned ahead, face like a brickwall. She clutched at the door to the BMW and opened it. 'What did you mean by put a knife to your throat? My brother, Dave?'

He peered across. 'Like you didn't know, Naina.' And she tore her eyes away from him. She didn't. And straightaway Dave knew she didn't. 'He didn't fucking tell you, did he? What crap did he feed you?'

Naina stood there, framed with confusion.

He continued, his voice cutting and severe, 'Get in. I'll tell you all about your lovable brother. I'll tell you all about how he didn't want this white piece of shit's hands all over you and how he was only being pulled by India's puppet strings. India, my fucking arse.'

Naina sat in, closed the door gently, refusing to look at Dave. She stared at the cinema-size screen stuck to the outside of the Xscape skiing complex. Flashing images of sports' advertising were selling nothing to Naina, as she watched with total indifference; her mind on a thousand other images.

A small vacuum of silence, then. 'I'm sorry for what I said on the bridge about your stepdad, it was out of order. I only said it to hurt you, I didn't mean it.' She glanced over. 'I'm sorry.'

'S'okay.' He dragged on his fag. 'Anyway, apologies bore me.'

He looked to Naina, staring at the 'No smoking' sign on the glove compartment. When he had first laid eyes on her, back in Florelli's, he'd assumed. Assumed within two weeks she'd be in his bed. Assumed by week three he'd have dumped her. Assumed by week four he'd not even remember her name. Never had he assumed they would be arguing like a couple, one year later, over a poxy bridge in MK.

He leaned over and gave her a cuddle. 'Just forget it. Come on, let's go somewhere quiet.' And they drove to Campbell Park, home to MK cricket in the summer and MK sheep in the winter. Sometimes both, when the team was short of a shortstop. They peered out to the cricket green, tucked up in the warmth of the car. A few lively kites were being controlled by unlively controllers on the top of the hill that stared down at the pavilion below; and in the belly of the cricket pitch a discarded lawnmower sat like a mechanical umpire left to rust.

Dave faced her. 'Naina, look, I think your brother takes India too seriously.'

'Stop beating around the bush and just tell me. I know he's a prat, just tell me!'

So he did.

And like a ball bearing in dry sand, the truth had trouble sinking in. But sink in, it did, landing with a huge thud in the pit of her stomach. She felt quite ill. Dave had kept all this quiet. The knife, the car, the video, the innits, the punches. He had protected her and it proved he really did care for her; and it made her feel special. It made her feel much more than just a friend. And she liked that feeling very much.

'I can't believe Kiran follows me,' Naina said disgusted.

'Well, you'd better be careful with this other bloke,

you know, the shit? He probably knows all about him as well. You shouldn't be so damn loose, Naina. I told you about being loose. Men hate loose women.'

She laughed. 'Dave, if there were no loose women, you'd be getting none.'

He dropped her off at the bottom of her road, gave her a quick kiss and cuddle, and they arranged to meet later at his flat at 7.00 p.m.

During the short walk up Wildacre Road, Naina inwardly chuckled to herself. How could Dave still not have sussed that the 'Shit' was him. And she opened the front door and was nearly floored by the smell of saag. Yuck!

Never be early. Rules are rules. One minute past seven, Naina buzzed the intercom. Climbed the carpeted stairs and entered Dave's flat.

'You look gorgeous!' he stated, holding her long coat and taking a good two steps back to admire the view.

She admitted, she did. And so she sodding well should do. It had taken her three hours to spruce up: a short strapless black dress, daringly stopping just below the middle of her bare-toned thighs, which fed to her high-heeled, strappy sequinned sandals. Her long black hair, streaked with chestnut tones, had been tortured into shape with everything known to Boots. Only a smidgen of make-up that had taken a smidgen of two hours to apply, and a dusting of Obsession in all the right places. Knockout.

He could have made a bit of effort though, she thought, checking out his designer white T-shirt and denim jeans. Naina smiled, all bashful, but her plan was anything but bashful, she was going to make Dave gag tonight. He could look, but he couldn't touch. And maybe it was ambitious of her, but she would not let him touch any of her body again until he had declared total love for her. Watch him squirm!

She sat down quite close to him on the sofa, crossing her thighs, and sipped her wine. 'Kate's out with Pete again. Never get to see her these days.'

'Two sickos.'

'God, you're so negative. Are you never going to get married? Don't you ever want to get close to someone? Other than your OOzing mates.'

'Heavy.' He lit a joint.

'I know what your problem is, I can see right through you.'

He stubbed out the wakky tobakky and turned to face her. 'It's all right, I'll give you my own psychological profile.' He paused. 'I am torn up about my past. My parents didn't love me, nobody loved me, *poor* Dave. So, I just can't trust anyone. If I get close to a woman, she'll let me down, just like my family did all those years ago.' He chuckled. 'So I have a defence mechanism, I shut all feeling out, I dump the women after three dates, just in case I begin to have feelings for them. I can't let that happen, because of my awful *awful* past. I am a desperate case.' And he slumped his head down. He looked up. 'Am I right?'

Naina nodded 'yes'.

He smiled. 'I'll tell you the reason I am like I am. It's quite simple . . .'

'La la la do do doobie, la la'. He checked the caller display and answered, it was the gym. 'Hello . . . She phoned again? . . . How many times? . . . Twenty fucking-nine? . . . Just tell her to piss off . . . No, really . . . Yes, say the words *piss off* . . . Okay, cheers, Steve, bye.'

Dave placed the mobile down on the glass table. His face seemed as if it warranted a pint or two.

'What's that about?' she asked. 'What trouble are you in now?'

'Some woman keeps ringing the gym, leaving her number. She called fourteen times yesterday and twenty-nine today. But the night's still young.' He paused. 'Laura.' He worked the word in his mouth like a chewy bit of gristle. 'I shagged her outside a kebab van, and now she won't leave it alone. She's doing my head in.' He re-lit the joint and inhaled a deep surge of smoke into his lungs. 'I don't even know where she got my number from, 'cos I certainly didn't give it to the . . . bitch.'

'Why don't you just ring her?' Naina asked, trying to prise the spliff from his fingers.

'Because she's not worth the twenty-pence phone call.'

Naina stood up, wiggling her bottom all the way out to the bathroom.

Dave turned and watched, smiling his sorted smile as he gazed at her departing perfect form. It was blatantly obvious she wanted sex tonight, dressed that way. God, women were so see-through. He popped to the kitchen and returned with yet another bottle of wine, unscrewed the cork – with the bottle between his legs – and poured out two more large portions. This was an interesting point: how long could a man tease a woman – who was obviously crying out for a bit of bedtime romance – before she began to look desperate for sex?

Her heels thudded behind him on the pine floorboards, and he made an effort to wipe the smile off his face. On the living-room wall by the stereo hung a new large framed picture. Naina walked up to it: it was a strange blur of fuzz. On closer inspection she could make out extremely small writing. At the top it was titled 'Bard in a Frame'. A small metal-trimmed magnifying glass hung off a brass hook beside it.

She studied it. 'What's this?'

Dave turned his head and knelt up on the sofa to inspect. 'It's the entire works of Shakespeare zoomed down. *King Lear*, *Romeo and Juliet*, *Hamlet*, you know, all of it.' He flopped back down. 'I bet when he wrote all that stuff centuries ago, he never thought that his words would be used to cover a lager stain on the wall.'

The intellectual side of Dave was what most attracted Naina, and she rejoined him on the sofa.

'So, you were about to tell me . . .'

'What? Why I don't commit to women?' She nodded. 'I thought that was obvious. How do I say this without sounding like a complete bastard?'

'It never normally stops you. Just tell me.'

He smiled. 'Women,' he smiled even more, 'beautiful women turn me on. I can't get enough. That's about it really.'

'Fine, okay, handsome men turn me on as well. Doesn't mean I would go and get one just to dump him three dates later. So what's the story there?'

'Look, I can't afford to fall for a woman, my life would change and I love it as it is. It's as simple as that – you know what women are like. It frightens me, we'll end up sitting in together on a Sunday night watching *Heartbeat*. They're evil like that.'

'*Heartbeat*'s not bad though. It's never been quite the same since Nick Berry left, but Greengrass . . .'

He smothered her with a cushion.

The bottle soon emptied. Naina's dress was rising, sexual innuendoes were creeping their way into the banter. But the son of a gun just wasn't taking the plunge. Why? And now he wanted to talk seriously, about families of all things.

'So, tell me,' he started, 'all things considered. Would you say that your parents loved each other? Seeing as they had an arranged marriage.'

Blimey. Naina shunted her dress down. How the hell could she turn this one into a sexual innuendo? 'Erm, yeah, they seem happy. I mean, I don't see them kissing or anything, but then again Indians don't kiss in public, it would be like having,' she stared deep into his eyes, 'it's almost like having sex, *Dave*, sex. Yeah, just like sex sex sex in public.' She gulped down some wine, wondering why Dave just wasn't interested in her any more.

'So you think they love each other. So, there's nothing saying you can't fall in love with Ashok.' He blew out a smoke ring and pinged it with his finger. 'Don't get me wrong, though, I still think it's unacceptable for your parents to choose your husband.'

'Fuck Ashok. Christ, Dave, you're so heavy; lighten up, will you? Anyone would think you haven't had a shag in three days the way you're going on,' remarked a frustrated, drunken Naina.

Naina's mobile rang. 'Hello . . . Oh, it's you . . .

What? Checking up on me are you? . . . Yes, I am round Kate's as a matter of fact . . . Yes, I am staying the night . . . I'll go and get her for you . . . No, Kiran, you wanted to speak to Kate so I will go and get her for you. (KATE, my brother's on the phone for you, he's checking up on me, he thinks I'm with a man.) . . . You don't want to speak to her now? Don't want to look stupid? . . . Well then, you little Indian rodent, stop checking up on me. Now go back to your nursery books.' She hung up and turned to a smiling Dave; he'd just become enlightened: Naina was a natural liar.

She sat back down, real close to him. 'He thinks I'm with a man, having sex. HA! . . . The chance would be a fine thing,' she said, cutting and bitter, and swallowed the remainder of the wine.

'Right. Fancy watching the football on Sky? Kick-off's soon,' he said, reaching across her thighs for the remote. 'And then,' here's the stinger, he thought, 'then we can watch,' and he zeroed in on her brown eyes, '*Robot Wars*.' He refrained from laughing.

'If you need me, pig,' Naina wobbled up, 'I'll be in your bed.' And she stomped out.

How long could a man tease a woman before she began to look desperate for sex? He glanced at the clock. About fifty-five minutes. Sorted! He walked out to the bedroom smiling his Dave smile, his top flung to the floor.

He ripped away the duvet. Naked, ready and waiting. Perfect!!

With a torrid hangover Naina awoke to the squabbling birds bitching about the cost of roof insulation. Dave slept soundly until her bouncing up and down on the mattress bruised his coma, and punched his eyelids open.

'Oh, you're awake!' Naina marvelled. 'Would you like to make me a coffee?'

His eyes squinted at the time – only 7.00 a.m. 'With or without battery acid?' He rolled back over, mumbling something into the pillow about putting someone's head in an oven, then sniggered into a snore.

Withering thoughts of last night bumped around in Naina's head, jostling for space: Dave's speech, his self-assessed psychological profile, was too neat, too perfect, too planned? Only a sucker would have been sucked in by that – or a drunken person. You can't just wipe off your whole family and put it down to 'bad experience', without some mental backlash.

Naina watched the hungry clock eat up the minutes one by one until it had devoured a whole hour, leaving her in a predicament: who needed her the most – work or the warm and cosy bed? Maybe she should sleep on it. Three hours later she awoke to a decision.

'Sod work, it's Friday,' insisted Dave, pulling her back into bed. 'You've got to play hard-to-get with your boss sometimes.'

Naina removed his wandering hands. 'Excellent idea, play hard-to-get.' She whipped the duvet back and jumped out of bed in his red Gucci T-shirt then drifted out to the enormous kitchen, waited for the Flavia coffee machine to wake up and scooted back to bed with two mugs, two Penguins, his post and his early morning paper – the *Independent*.

And for a fleeting moment, it felt like being a couple. Waking up next to the man that she had chosen for herself. Basking in the shine of togetherness. Even suffering the hangover together. The Penguin tasted pretty damn good too. But, like a waxwork mannequin, it was all an illusion, and after she left he would pick up the phone, and another woman would be in the bed before it had even got cold. That was no illusion. That *was* Dave.

'Fancy a shag, Naina?' Yeah, that was Dave.

'No!' She still couldn't believe that she had given in to him last night. Tell a lie, she still couldn't believe that she had virtually thrown herself at him. 'I didn't take a day off work just to see to your needs. Go and pick up someone else!' Naina cast him an indignant glance.

Dave lit up a fag, stuffed another pillow behind him and watched her get dressed. Watching women get dressed was boring, like re-wrapping a Christmas present. 'Naina, forgive me if this sounds slightly rude, but maybe a good shag would—'

Naina broke into Dave's crudity, 'It's all sex with you, isn't it?'

'Yeah.' He smiled. 'It's hardly my fault that my amygdala is damaged, is it?'

'Dave, stop reading *New Scientist*.' She stood in front of the inside wardrobe mirror, applying her lippy. 'What makes me different to your other three million?' And she muttered under her breath, 'Slags.'

'Who said you were any different to my other *slags*?'

She turned round to face him. 'But I am, aren't I? Different. I mean, lucky me has been fortunate

319

enough to be called back . . . to your bed, more than three times. So why haven't I been dumped?'

Dave broke her gaze. 'I'm in a quandary here. If I dump you, I lose our friendship, so, I suffer in silence.' He strained not to laugh. 'Call me a mug, call me whatever you want.' And then he did laugh.

She raised her eyebrows. 'And you suffer in silence about your parents as well, don't you?' Naina sat down next to him. 'I really do think you should talk about it. It's too late to say I'll look at you differently, because I already do.' She tried not to be all mushy pea about it, but she couldn't help it, and took his hand. 'And I'm not going to give you sympathy, you know you can trust me.'

And there was nothing spiteful or revengeful in how he told his tale. It was almost as though his memories belonged to someone else. Almost as if he were telling it in the third person. And as he gently spoke about his unhappy past, Naina looked at Dave not as a man who had been screwed up by his childhood, but as a man who had risen above it, and for that, she admired him more.

'I think you should go and see your mum again,' Naina suggested. 'Give her a chance to explain things.'

'No,' he said, pulling on his jeans.

'I think you should, Dave.'

'I'll think about it.' He paused. 'But I'll be fucked if I go crawling on my knees to her.' He leaned over to Naina on the bed and kissed her on the cheek. 'I was wrong, you're a better slag than the others.'

She laughed, and she too was wrong. Dave's past had nothing to do with his lack of commitment; he just loved beautiful women and having a good time. Well, she wasn't sure about being the beautiful woman bit, but she sure as hell wanted him to have a good time.

'Dave, as I'm the slag who shines the most, the lucky slag –' she unzipped his jeans as she kissed him passionately on the lips '– I'll let you . . . wait right there.'

Dave waited . . . and waited . . . and . . . 'Naina!? I'm dying here.'

'Sorry, Dave,' a voice shouted back from inside the living room. '*Robot Wars* is on TV.'

Chapter Twenty-nine

Thirteen people sitting around three pushed-together tables in the Squirrel. Some say that the number thirteen is unlucky because the people at the table for Jesus's Last Supper numbered thirteen.

And it was Friday. The pub door kept swinging open to admit more drinkers, but nobody seemed to leave. It was like bacteria multiplying on a Petri dish. There was no worry of a fire starting because there probably wouldn't be enough air to fuel it; just thick smoggy smoke circling the room, giving the appearance that everything was out of focus.

But bitch stares never came out of focus. Like lasers of pure energy they targeted a beam of hatred and channelled it towards their victim. The untapped energy potential of 'bitch stares' in this one pub alone that night, could power the Isle of Wight.

There was an atmosphere, sort of clammy.

Borderline unfriendly, an orgy of unrest. As if someone had poisoned the drink. A fag relay was constant.
As soon as someone put out a fag, another would
light. Music blared, pint-pumps pulled, glasses fizzed,
and lighters clicked.

Dave nudged Naina, trying to get her to stop
staring at Sandra. 'You're a bit quiet, Frog, what's up?
I thought it was good to talk.' He laughed at his own
joke.

'A bit knackered, that's all,' Froggy answered. 'But
I'm sure my good buddy Dave will liven me up a bit,
hey?'

The effort to restrain himself from lunging over and
popping Dave with a pint glass was overwhelming,
but Froggy had painfully lasted this long without
saying anything to either Dave or Sandra, and he
wasn't going to spoil it now. And just as Dave loved
playing emotional games, so, too, did Froggy – they
were best mates after all, both as sick as each other.
The image of Dave sleeping with Sandra was etched,
crystal clear, in his mind. He even knew what lines
Dave would more than likely have used to get her to
drop her knickers – Dave's favourite sound in the
world. When Froggy had arrived home that night,
that awful night, Sandra was dressed in her work
clothes, just like any other day, moaning about how
hard she had to work at HSBC Bank, and he
wondered how many other 'hard working' days
there'd been when the two of them had been at it like
rabbits in his house.

A small argument broke out between Pete and Kate.
Jingle, Melody, Andy and Froggy tried to calm things
down.

'You think that's funny, Pete . . .' said Kate.

That's all Dave got to hear, as he watched Naina lean across the table to Sandra and whisper in her ear. He noticed Naina's short, clinging silver-grey dress rise up her beautiful pins. That, he thought, *that*, is perfect rump.

Naina spoke carefully and clearly in Sandra's ear, 'Dave said that you were really flabby under that tart red dress. Must get you down.' Then she sat back down, crossed her slim toned legs and smiled over to the tightly knotted face of Sandra.

'Look, Kate,' began Pete, sort of talking to the table more than to her, 'all I said was, it was a good job that your fur coat wasn't real fur.' He smiled around the table like he was the comedian. 'Because.' Another smile. 'Then all the pink poodles would be extinct.'

Dave was the only one who laughed.

Kate pointed to Dave. 'It's him that started taking the piss out of my pink coat, and now like a little mug, you follow.' She shifted her view to Dave. 'Ain't that right, little boy?'

The whole table cracked up at Dave's expense. Over time, with Dave's constant wisecracks at other people's misfortune, it had got to the point when he only had to say a word slightly wrong and everyone would be in fake stitches. A referral to the size of his manhood, and the laughter didn't need to be faked.

Sandra recovered from Naina's low-blow like any true bitch would, took a sip of her Bacardi and Coke, waited for the table to quieten down, pursed her lips, and then she broke down crying, gulping for breath, big whopping false tears splashing on the wooden table, and all twelve people broke their flow of chitter-chatter and zeroed in on their distressed-looking friend – whatever was the matter?

Froggy placed his arm round her shoulder. 'What's wrong, Sandra?' he asked instinctively, forgetting his feeling of betrayal for the moment.

Everyone wanted to know, especially Naina.

Through thick gurgling blubbering sobs, Sandra reared her head, red-eyed and spiteful. 'Naina just said that I was fat and ugly and that no man would ever fancy me. She said I was boring and that I was totally selfish and I . . . I . . . I can't say the rest.' And her head thundered into Froggy's chest. The table looked at Naina – she said that?

Dave sniggered, this was going to be a fun evening. Kate and Leena beamed. Naina's jaw dropped. A thousand eyes were staring at her for an explanation and all she could think of to say was . . .

'Well, she is. She's a first-rate bitch,' stated Naina and gulped down her Stella.

Sandra squealed like a pig. The pub was being entertained.

'What d'you say that for, Naina?' Froggy demanded angrily.

Dave didn't take too kindly to Froggy's tone to Naina. 'Come on, mate, face it, they hate each other. Sandra shouldn't dig it out if she can't take it.'

Froggy nearly exploded. 'And you'd know all about Sandra *taking* it, wouldn't you, Dave?'

Matt looked to Diane – Froggy knows.

Pete looked to Kate – Froggy knows.

Andy looked to Phillipa – Dave had better not have slept with you as well, Pippa.

Leena whispered to Naina, 'What's he mean, "taking it"?'

Sandra cried some more – if in doubt always cry some more.

Froggy looked to Dave – **I know. You bastard.**

Dave's smile didn't want to be a part of his face any more – it disappeared, as realization dawned. Realization that Sandra had broken the first rule of adultery – never tell your partner, no matter what. Now that Froggy knew, the best thing to do was to blame someone else. Dave didn't want to appear the bad guy here. He had lent Froggy his BMW once, so Froggy lent his girlfriend once, what's the big deal? And then he felt a strange feeling, almost a twitch but more like a tingle: could it possiby be his conscience which had only ever played a cameo role in his life so far? For once in your life, take the blame, take responsibility. Nearly twenty years of friendship was being discussed across the table: no words, no actions, just a private duel between their eyes.

Jingle, oblivious to everything, stood up and ushered Melody to her feet with a gesture of his hand. 'Everybody, we've got an announcement.' A few heads turned, Dave and Froggy were not in those few. 'Although me and Mel have only known each other a few weeks – and wonderful weeks they've been – We are getting married and you are all invited, my buddies.' Melody spread her white-teeth smile.

Various half-hearted congratulations were uttered until the voice of Froggy bruised the moment.

'Was she a good shag then, mate?' Froggy was standard Psycho. 'You like shagging your best mate's girlfriend, do you, mate?' Now advanced Psycho. A few drinkers on other tables forgot their deep discussions, this was more interesting than the new range of Royal Mail postage stamps. 'Was my bed comfortable enough for you, mate?'

Dave's mobile had been ringing and nosy Naina had taken the call; now she passed it to him. 'I think you'd better take this, Dave.'

Dave carried on looking at his mate. 'Tell them I'll phone back.'

Naina shouted, 'I think you'd better *take* this call, Dave.'

Dave glanced at Naina – so sweet, she was trying to help him out of this – and he gave a knowing nod.

Naina thumped the phone in his hand. 'Take the call, Dave, it's Steve, he said it's urgent. Life and death.'

Dave took the call. 'Steve? . . . I'm a bit busy . . . Say again . . . You are really winding me up? . . . Really? . . . No, no way . . . Fucking hell . . . For Christ sake . . .' Dave hung up and the table marvelled at his now very sterile face. He lit up a fag, swallowed a mouthful of lager, looked to the crowd and said, 'That's it, I'm fucked, my life's over.'

The table was like a big pond, with larger and larger stones being chucked in, making bigger and bigger ripples. What now?

Dave peered at the eyes like spectators in a zoo. But Dave was no animal, he was no trapped bird or monkey or snake, no Dave was . . . 'I'm going to be a father. The bitch is fucking pregnant. Can you believe it?' Dave was going to be a dad.

Suddenly the ripples in the pond settled, like a sheet of mercury, flat and constant, then shortly afterwards they began to appear again, larger and larger, until a huge tidal wave of laughter came from everyone's mouth – everyone's that is except Naina's, Sandra's and Dave's – Froggy laughed the loudest.

'Congratulations, Daddy Dave. Con-fucking-gratulations, you arse-wipe.' Froggy paused. 'Who's the unlucky slapper? Or don't you know that information yet? Serves you right.' And he finished Sandra's drink, then his own. 'Serves you right!! *You wanker!!*'

Dave looked at Froggy. 'This is all Sandra's fault. If she wasn't so flabby and wasn't such a crap shag, I wouldn't have gone looking elsewhere. And it would be her and you, mate, bringing up my child.' He took a gulp of Naina's drink.

As though Froggy had been held back until now by steel ropes, they suddenly perforated, stretched, then snapped, as he threw himself over the table towards Dave, kicking his legs like he was swimming, knocking filled ashtrays, drinks, bottles, phones, and purses. 'You bastard, I'm going to kill you.' And he grabbed Dave's brilliant white Armani shirt, sending them both flying to the floor. 'I'm going to kill you!'

Melody shit her pants. Matt, Andy, Naina, Jingle, Kate, Pete all dived in to pull them apart, Naina managing to kick Sandra on the way in. It was a brawl of mammoth proportions. The bar bell rang, calling for security. Drunken eyes watched it all in slow motion, newcomers to the pub would not be going back there again and even the bartenders were yelling out 'Fight fight fight.' Messy was an understatement.

Finally, like two horned bulls, the two fighting morons were pulled apart, slung down onto two chairs, and bound back by what seemed like a dozen helping-hand restraints. It was over! And then Matt began his famous 'Friendship speech'.

Fear and violence are supposed to send women's pheromones racing. Dave sat there, nose bloodied, scouting around for any beautiful women who might have been turned-on by his display of macho. But all he met with was stares of disgust from everyone.

Froggy sat there, a trickle of blood oozing down his lip. With a shaking hand he wiped the blood and Sandra handed him a tissue. He looked at her – how could you? And then spoke, 'I haven't even begun with you, you slag.' And threw the red tissue on the wet table.

Diane placed a consoling arm round Sandra, as real tears this time rolled down her flushed cheeks, and in between the sobs 'I'm sorry' could be heard.

Froggy revved up again. 'I saw you with her, you bastard! You were so busy gawping at my girlfriend, you didn't even notice me.'

Dave lit a fag; the table waited. 'Well, if I'd known there was a perverted spectator, I would have put on a show for you.' The table winced. 'Face it, you couldn't keep her. All it took was a few dirty words and I was in your bed with your precious Sandra. It was like shagging Metal Mickey, mate, as cold as a fucking robot, she . . .'

'Shut it, Dave,' ordered Andy. 'It's not a joke.' But it was too late.

Froggy flew through the air again, leaping like a toad but Dave angled his body so that he flew straight past and watched his best mate fall in a bundle on the floor.

'Out, all of you, the whole lot of you, I'm sick of you lot, get out. You're all barred!!' The landlord – Elvis – stood red-faced, pointing to the door. 'OUT! All of you.'

Jingle piped up, 'OR WHAT?'

'Get out or I'm phoning the police. OUT!'

Police car sirens quickly punctured a very frail atmosphere in the pub car park, as the shadows of thirteen people dispersed quickly away from the scene. No one was going to forget this night in a hurry. Least of all Dave.

Leena, Kate, Pete and Naina parted from the weary-looking father-to-be. But as Dave shuffled his feet just outside Pete's black 4×4 Range Rover plastered in Horizon Radio stickers, Naina glanced back and told Pete to let her out. Dave needed her now just like she had needed him when he comforted her about her engagement to Ashok, by the lake that time . . . he had been a true friend to her then.

Chapter Thirty

'If it's a boy, you can dress him in cute little Nikes. I'm sure Armani will do cute little baby clothes.' Naina handed Dave a coffee. 'And you could push him around this big wide floor in a little black BMW pram, ahh cute.' She sat next to him on the blue sofa.

He sipped the Colombian coffee. 'Thanks, Naina, you're a great help.'

Dave had read in *Woman's Own* that a woman could be pregnant for a whole nine months. Sometimes women only had babies to trap their man and some women could have quintuplets.

'Naina, tell me this. When my little one grows up, and he or she, probably knowing my luck it will be twins, asks me where they were conceived and I tell them in a car behind the back of a kebab van, what will they think?' He paused and chucked the ice pack on the floor. 'Fuck it, when they go to school, you know what kids are like, they'll get picked on. Some little shit that was conceived in a real bed will say, "Ha it's the takeaway kids."'

Naina cracked up, but underneath it, she was concerned. She didn't think Dave was taking this well at all. He wasn't.

It was already getting late; Naina had accepted that she would be staying the night – baby-sitting a distressed Dave. Melancholy music played – The Cure – and Dave's constant checking out of the window was playing on Naina's nerves.

'Dave, sit down, will you. The baby won't be arriving just yet,' she said, starting off a brand-new box of chocolates she'd found tucked away in a kitchen cupboard. 'What about Donna for a girl and Pitta for a boy. Or, if you want something exotic, sort of yuppie, Shashlik.' Naina's eyes pried for a smile from Dave.

Dave 3 2 1 exploded. His head swivelled round the room looking for objects, his heart pounded like a marching band, and he looked sort of mental, as he ran round the room in a snake-like movement, almost as if Naina wasn't even there. It was quite amusing to watch, a bit unnerving, but amusing nevertheless. Nothing came from his mouth, but it was fixed with a strained expression like he had just torn a ligament and finally after a few more laps he spotted what he wanted to kick, made a short run-up and kicked the naked bong as hard as he could with his Nikes, sending it flying across the room. Sorted!

Naina stood watching the limping Dave, who now hobbled round the flat as if he had caught his foot in a snare. She came up to him and put her arms round his neck. 'It will be all right.'

He looked at her. 'Will it?'

'Yes, Dave, everything will be okay, I promise.' And she hugged him harder.

Naina saw the irony of the situation. Here Dave was facing possibly the most responsible situation in his entire life, and he was acting like a child.

'I think you should ring her, Dave; she's been trying you for days.'

'Sod it, I'm going to Tenerife.'

'Dave!'

He hung his head in shame, then, 'I made her meow.'

'You did what?'

Dave returned to his memory of Laura: 'I put a condom on – large – and I asked her if she had had a bath. Then I made her meow. Then I got bored, removed the condom, *which had not split*, got dressed, chucked the condom out of the window, and while I waited for her in the front of the car, she finished herself off on the back seat – the dirty cow.'

Baths, meows, finished herself off, what was she? 'Had she had a bath?'

'Imperial Leather. I think.'

'Oh.' She gobbled a hazelnut whirl and a strawberry cream. 'So, are you going to phone her? I really think you should.'

Dave breathed great plumes of smoke into his lungs, trying hard to sort through his muddled mind, listening to 'The Caterpillar' by The Cure, watching Naina struggle to eat a whole layer of chocolates. Laura, if he remembered rightly, and he was sure he did, was married, insecure, just wanting a good time. Surely even she would have taken a precaution, the pill or a cap, or maybe she had been spayed. Something didn't seem right.

'She's married,' Dave mentioned, like it wasn't important.

Naina thumped him. 'You idiot, why didn't you say? It could be the husband's. You're going to have to phone her.'

Fifteen minutes later, Dave and Naina were standing inside the empty gym, at Reception. A scrawled line of messages lay on a spiral notepad by the fresh-fruit squeezing machine and Dave trawled his eyes down the list until Laura's number was spotted.

'It's here, it's a mobile. Can you ring her for me? Beautiful Naina, please.' He shoved the notepad into Naina's unwelcoming hand, putting on his puppy dog begging face.

Their voices echoed through the partially lit building. Strange oblong shadows from the big Nautilus machines smeared the red carpet, resting from the pounding they had received during the day. The place was like a crypt, harbouring spirits of blood, sweat and tears. Naina imagined the pumped-up ghosts of the after-world doing their Casper curls and poltergeist lunges, training away the moonlight hours to music by Madness. And talking of Madness, Naina agreed to make the call.

It was 2.10 a.m. 'Dave, can you stand over there please, you're breathing down my neck. Just give me some space!'

And Dave stood by the huge red weighing scales, his face glowing green from the luminous lights on the dial. He listened like a good father would.

'Hello, Laura?'

'Yes, who's this? It's a bit late.'

'I'm Dave's wife.' Dave's face turned even greener.

'Wife? I didn't know he was married. Why are you calling?'

Naina bit her lip – because I've got a pansy of a bloke who won't do it himself – 'No, Laura, why are *you* calling, bothering Dave?'

A pause, the sound of talking in the background. 'Why am I calling? Because I'm pregnant with your husband's child, that's why I'm calling. I bet you didn't even know he slept around.'

'Sorry, Laura, you see . . . me and Dave have been trying for a child for four years. We had some tests, and without putting too fine a point on it – he fires blanks.' Naina looked to a crumbling Dave. 'How do you explain that?'

More talking in the background. 'He said you're a whore. He said he didn't love you, you bitch. He said I was the best lay he'd ever had.'

Naina was becoming annoyed. 'So I want to know how you happen to be pregnant. It must be your husband's, it can't—'

Laura interrupted with laughter, then settled down; then, 'I'm not even married, you whore. And, I'm carrying his child that you couldn't give him. So your little doctor made a mistake, because I'm definitely pregnant with that bastard's child. And I want to see him, I want to see him.' A pause. 'Tell that creep, I'll be at his shoddy gym, at ten. He'd better be there.' The phone went dead; Dave's head came back up from under the counter.

And Naina sighed. 'What the hell is she? She's a

horrible person. I wonder what you pick up sometimes.' She watched him.

'Firing blanks, Naina, pher, your imagination, Naina, where did you come up with an absurd line like that? As if I could fire blanks, Naina, really, I wonder about you sometimes, you and your farfetched lies, can't believe you sometimes, firing blanks, what, me? Are you mad? Look at me, I'm healthy, I could make a dozen beautiful women pregnant in one shot. Firing blanks? I have to laugh at you sometimes I really . . .'

'DAVE!!!!!!!!!!'

'Really, Naina.'

'She's coming here at ten tomorrow, actually today. In eight hours.'

Dave was worried. 'What did she say?'

Naina smiled. 'I'll tell you on the way back to your flat, I've got a plan . . . a good Naina plan.'

Chapter Thirty-one

Very few of us will ever get to become the oldest person in the world. But every single one of us *once* was the youngest person in the world. And every now and again some of us, i.e. Dave, will act like they are the youngest person in the world.

Naina lay asleep in Dave's comfy bed, snuggled in a thick 13.5 tog blue duvet. The tip of her head was just poking out of the top, leaving her body tucked up inside like a toasted sandwich. Wonderful smells of Lenor summer breeze with a touch of Davidoff and Obsession scratched the surface of the warm air in the darkened room; only a hint of light from the luminous glow of the bedside clock broke through the veil, and an odd irritating noise in the background broke Naina's sleep. She squinted through the darkness to Dave's silhouette on the bed, his hands pulling and snapping at . . . a condom. What was he doing?

Naina sat up in bed, a yawn was kept on hold. 'Dave, I'm trying to sleep.'

'How can you sleep at a time like this? My life's in ruins and all you think about is your precious sleep,' he said annoyed, throwing the condom to the floor. He walked to the window. 'Anyway,' he shunted the thick cream curtains to one side, letting through the grey mist of a cold Saturday morning in February. 'It's nearly nine.'

Naina thought about uttering a quick retaliation to Dave's early morning bedsore rudeness, but, under the circumstances, she decided to ignore him, then . . . sod it. Baby or no baby, you shouldn't have to wake up to Mr Angry. 'I'm off home. Thanks for the sex that you didn't give me, Dave, because you weren't in the mood. What did you say? "Sorry, but one baby is enough, I'm not risking it ever again."'

Dave came back to bed, wrapping himself in with Naina and her warmth. 'Sorry, but all I could think about last night was smelly stinking babies' nappies and puke all over my Armani tops and sticking jumbo Alka Seltzer tablets in their feeding bottles.'

'Sterilizing tablets, Dave,' she corrected, enjoying the extra heat that his body gave. 'Five more minutes, then I'll get up. Five minutes in silence . . . please.'

There was a template to Dave's standard woman, as far as Naina could make out. She knew that this Laura was bound to be extremely pretty. Slim, long legs, with at least one feature that was 'outstanding'. Maybe her smile, her hair or eyes or even her skin tone. Then a bolt of jealous lightning struck her. What if this Laura, this horrible person, really was harbouring one of – how did Dave put it? – oh yeah, harbouring one of his 'crop', what then? Blokes were funny lizards. After he'd seen the cute baby with its cheeky chubby legs and powder-soft skin, he might change – suddenly he might want this horrible Laura. Dave's breathing was deeper now, sliding into sleep. It was 9.30; five more minutes. Naina stretched out her painted red toes, her first step to getting up. She asked herself: why did she care if Dave fell for horrible Laura? She'd be married to Ashok. And she and Dave would be parted as was only inevitable. Parted, she hated the very sound of that word. A quick hard nudge in Dave's shoulder.

'Oi, this Laura, what did you like about her?'

Dave moaned the wake-up moan. 'Who? Dustbin pussy?'

Naina nodded.

'Her looks. The only thing I can think of that got me into this mess is that my willy was in the wrong neighbourhood that night.' He rubbed his hand up Naina's thigh. 'If I wore two condoms, I'd risk a quickie if you want.'

Naina flung back the duvet and jumped out of bed, dressed in only a yellow Armani T-shirt. 'There must be something other than looks that you liked about her, Dave. I can't believe you're so shallow that only looks count.'

For such a physical-looking man, Dave made getting out of bed look like a strangely strenuous exertion. 'I don't know her. You know how my mind works. I see a beautiful woman, I smell sex, end of story. Who cares if she's boring, thick, dopey, or even a fucking scientist, I shag her.' He pulled on some black boxer-shorts, dragged the duvet on to the pine floorboards and began to do some crunches.

Naina watched his flat stomach contract, then flatten out, his thighs bent, a deep groove separating his thigh and hamstring like a neatly defined shadow. He watched her walk to the door, then without warning threw his calves forward, sprang himself up and grabbed Naina in the hall. 'Thanks, Naina, I couldn't have coped without you.' And he kissed her gently on the lips.

Laura stood at the gym Reception counter, admiring Steve's biceps. Six-inch stilettos pressed firmly into the rubber matting, shifting her weight forward so she almost draped herself over the marbled surface. Her bust tested the sturdiness of the delicate buttons on her tight pink shirt, threatening to burst them off if she dared to breathe more than a casual breath, and the black pencil skirt begged for a second glance from even the most married of men.

Her brown Bambi eyes watched Steve professionally jostle over all the Ultra Fuel refrigerated drinks, keeping the fridge's glass door flush and topped up. She'd been there since 9.00, and even Steve, who normally could talk for hours, was getting bored by a string of comments that always seemed to start with, 'I am very good at . . .' The next statement nearly cramped his bombshell biceps.

'You know Dave's leaving his wife for me.'

What lies had Dave been telling this one, thought Steve. 'Oh really? That's nice.' And he turned the music up – loud.

In he walked. Armani sunglasses, tight black Armani T-shirt, black baggies, black Nikes, and Davidoff. Dressed for a funeral. The shiner leaked out of the side of his glass frame, kicking out the 'Cool kinda guy' image to 'Man with black eye'. And in an artistic sense, the black eye kinda suited him.

Laura's heart did pirouettes, danced the dance of love. He was here, he came. But as she light-footed towards him, aiming to plant a warming kiss on his gorgeous face, Dave's head instinctively swerved to the side, dislodging a view that dented Laura's high spirits. There standing behind Laura's man, was a stunningly beautiful woman.

Composure is a funny thing: when recovering visually from the unexpected, some take weeks, some hours, but Laura had it on tap. Bang! She was composed.

She fluttered her long curly eyelashes. 'So that's the woman you've been cheating on. Scraped the bottom of the barrel with her, didn't you?'

There must have been a bitch tuning fork in Dave's head, for he instantly knew that Naina was about to knife out a comment like vinegar on an open wound. His hand went to Naina's arm, restraining her, while his eyes remained fixed on Laura's stomach. 'Look, freak, I don't know how many thousands of men have parked up inside your crusty wench hole, and I don't really care, but don't make it so obvious that you're jealous of my wife's looks, because you're not even close,' and the words were thrust in her face.

Laura picked off some invisible fluff on her skirt, uncaring, obviously in denial that Dave really meant those harsh words. Then, with a witchy grin, she rammed home a desperate comment: 'You must have been in a deprived state of mind when you picked that,' and her head tilted Naina's way. 'I mean, excuse me if I'm being obvious here, but she's foreign, she's a fucking paki!' She planted her hands on her hips.

Dave turned to Naina, 'Don't even bother,' then back to freak, 'Let's get this over with. We'll go in the office, all three of us.' Then Dave turned to Steve, 'And yes, Steve, your arms have grown.'

Steve acknowledged the compliment with a 'cheers mate' nod, then beckoned Dave behind Reception and pointed to the notepad, where scribbled down were three phone messages from Froggy:

Message 1 *Dave, I am going to kill you.*
Message 2 *Dave, I'm going to burn your gym down.*
Message 3 Et tu brute. *You dead wanker.*

'Charming.' He looked to Steve. 'Here's a bit of advice, mate, don't shag your best mate's woman. They never let you live it down.' And he walked to the office and pulled out a chair for Naina, leaving freak standing.

'So, when's the baby due?' Dave questioned.

'*Our* baby is due in October,' she answered directly; then, 'Must she be here with us?'

Quickly, 'Yes,' and he leaned back in his executive leather chair, 'she must. What do you want from me?'

'I want you to come to the scans with me. I want you to be part of this pregnancy, and when our baby is born I want us to be a family, a proper family.'

'Okey-dokey, shall I pretend I love you as well?' Dave smiled and whipped off his shades, revealing the purple aura of Froggy's fist.

Laura stared; her man was hurt. 'Oh my God. Who did that to you?' She almost ran to his side, and tried to place her hand on his bruise; Dave flinched away. Then she turned to Naina, her eyes sharpened, her lips thinned. 'Did you hurt him? Did you hurt my Dave?' Naina looked on in disbelief as Laura continued, 'Did you punish him for seeing me? How could you?'

Dave had dreaded the day that a lunatic would enter his life.

Naina formulated a quick list of what was wrong with this woman: everything. She was neurotic, scheming, unstable, promiscuous, uncouth, and hell-bent on trying to infer that she and Dave were something of an item. But she was also pretty with a winner of a body. Maybe Dave was right and it was only her looks that had instigated that fateful shag.

'So has the doctor confirmed that you are pregnant?' Dave asked.

Laura rubbed her stomach. 'Oh yes, we're definitely having a baby.' She turned to Naina. 'I could give him what you couldn't.'

'Fuck all that – who could give who what – this isn't *Wheel of* fucking *Fortune*, this is a baby not a prize. So, Laura I want you to prove it's mine.' He paused while the words seeped their way into Laura's strange mind. 'All slappers have to prove who the father is, because, let's face it, you're not exactly a one-man type of woman, more like a one town. You've probably had more traffic flowing through your—'

Naina interrupted, 'Dave!' He stopped. Damn, there was so much more he wanted to say.

Laura composed herself. 'When our baby is born, of course I will prove it, we'll do the test.' And she put her hand on his shoulder.

Dave got up and crossed to the other side of the small office. 'Will you stop touching me, you're giving me the creeps.' He stood behind Naina and brushed some loose strands of hair from her face. 'Mmm, your hair smells lovely, wifee, mmm, *so clean*.'

Laura's composure disintegrated. 'I didn't ask to be pregnant, I didn't ask for your child. You can't pretend I didn't mean anything to you. You don't mean those nasty things you said.' And Laura fell into Dave's swivel chair and began to cry.

Naina pulled out the pregnancy test from her handbag and handed it to Laura. 'You and me are going into the toilets to do this test now, and if the test is positive, then Dave will take responsibility.' Naina looked to Dave. 'Won't you?'

Getting Laura off the chair was like trying to get a piece of chewing gum off the carpet. Until finally, having squeezed out every last tear, she jumped up.

'Come on, let's do this test,' Laura said, wiping her eyes and following Naina out of the office.

As the door clicked shut, Dave paced the room.

Whether you are a keen expectant father or not, a minute waiting for the result of a pregnancy test still seems to take an hour whatever. The door finally opened and Dave faced the opposite wall with its glossy poster – The Anatomy of a Man.

'Just tell me, is it a boy or is it a girl?' Dave asked without a thought.

'Actually, mate, it's strawberry, we've run out of protein,' Steve remarked, laughing at Dave's pitiful behaviour.

Dave turned. 'Get out!'

Eventually Naina barged through, smiling, and his

heart began to beat again. 'It's negative, Dave, she's not pregnant.'

Laura followed Naina in, smirked, sat down and crossed her legs. 'You treated me like shit, you did, like I was nothing. I wanted you to suffer, just like I did, waiting for that call you promised.' She stole one of Dave's fags and lit up. 'You men are all the same. You just use us and go back to your wives.' She blew out a stream of smoke through the side of her mouth. 'I actually liked you, I left you hundreds of calls, but the only one you bothered to return, funnily enough, was about the baby.'

Dave viewed her like she was a maggot in an apple, disgusted. 'You're just a fucked-up bitch. You threw yourself at me, I didn't force you to do anything. And as for liking me, you don't even know me.' He reached into his pocket. 'Here, for services rendered.' And tossed her a fiver. 'Now we're square. Now fuck off! And keep the change.' Laura stood up, sneered at the note, and marched out.

Blokes call it 'woman's intuition', women call it 'blazingly obvious'. And it had been to Naina: Laura was never pregnant – things didn't sit right. Maybe it was her odd manner on the phone last night. Maybe it was the husband who didn't exist, or the wedding ring worn only to bag Dave's attention, almost pre-planned. Maybe this Laura had known exactly what she was up to from the moment Dave stepped in the pub that night. Or maybe it was just that she finished herself off in the back of his car – probably. But on this account, Naina agreed with Dave's use of the Queen Mother's English – Laura *was* a fucked-up bitch.

Dave smiled at Naina. 'It scares me sometimes, how well I handle things. Most blokes would have crumbled, hey?' And he stubbed out Laura's half-finished fag and lit himself another.

'If you had your way, you'd be in Tenerife by now.'

'It was a joke; you should loosen up, Naina.'

'Yeah, right.'

As Dave spun round on his chair, the centrifugal force pushed out a comment: 'Anyway, if I was to have a child, it would be with you.' And he carried on spinning.

Don't I get a choice in the matter, thought Naina.

More spinning. 'That's it, I've escaped another pregnancy. I'm going to have to learn to disappoint women. Next time I see a beautiful woman I won't think SEX, I will think nappies. Next time I see a beautiful woman and she bends down right in front of me, with her fantastic bum just catching the light perfectly, just inches away, and then she stands up, smiles at me, asks to sit down next to me and subtly strokes my lap, I will say, "Clean up your act, darling, this bod's not for fondling."' Dave still spun. 'It will be easy. It's time for me to stop.' And with that comment, he did, and fell off the chair.

Naina walked up to him and looked down as he struggled to get to his dizzy feet, her stilettos by his head. 'You're pathetic you are, Dave.'

Chapter Thirty-two

Dave knelt before the entrance to his old house. Blue Spark circled his outstretched hand, trying to cram in ten years' worth of fuss. His blue and grey cat, faithful and trusting, had remembered him, and stared with brazen orange eyes: 'Where the hell have you been, traitor?' The raucous noise of a Hoover sounded from inside, close to the front door. Blue Spark doubled in size, spruced up his silvery fur, then legged it down the pathway: 'She's all yours, mate.'

Dave knocked hard on the aluminium flap and the door opened almost immediately.

'What d'you want?' Wendy – Mum – asked, astounded.

Dave eyed her sour, haunted face. The other night, the makings of once pretty features had still flickered but now, in the direct sun, everything but her wide blue eyes seemed worn by the blunt winds of time. God, daylight did pay back with interest.

'About time we had a chat, don't you think . . .
Wendy?' And he pushed past her and walked into the
living room.

'Jack will be back any minute, if he catches you . . .'
Wendy stood hovering in the doorway, dressed
smartly, her white blouse and black skirt showing off
her petite figure.

Dave sat down on the floral sofa chair, pointing for
her to sit down opposite. 'Fuck Jack!' He lit up, pulled
forward and reached for the black and gold-rimmed
ashtray, polished inside and out. 'I want to know why
my own mother stood there and did nothing while
Jack beat the shit out of me.' And he drew on his fag,
watching the unflinching face of his mum.

'You want honesty.' She glared. 'Look at you sitting
there all high and almighty, nothing but trouble you
were. Even now, look at you with that black eye,
always fighting.' Wendy stepped into her living room.
'I tried to love you, Jack tried to love you. But you
wouldn't have it, oh no, always breaking the law,
always getting yourself in trouble. The times we had
to collect you from the police cell, the times we were
made to look like parents that had no authority over
their little shit of a kid. We had to control you
somehow.' Wendy plucked out a box of Silk Cut from
her handbag. 'Your sisters were fine, no trouble at
all.' Her trembling bony hand lit a fag, and her thin
lips, coated in stark red, tightened as she drew in
tobacco smoke.

'And did you not wonder why your shit of a kid
was always in trouble? Even the fucking police felt
sorry for me.' Dave glanced at the window ledge.
'Yeah, my sisters couldn't do a thing wrong, could

they? I was the outsider in this family.' And the family portrait with Jack, Wendy and his two half-sisters stared back, smiling. 'Jack's kids were angels.' And he turned his head back to face her. 'Me, I was the kid of a no-hoper that packed his bags and left poor Wendy on her own. *Poor* Wendy . . . now fucking tell me the truth!'

She sat, ran her fingers to her dyed blonde hair, the fag smoke circling above. 'You're just like him. Your father.' She stared up at him. 'Even sitting there, I can't bear to look at you. He wrecked my life. Women would run after him, he'd sleep with this one and that one, and when I fell in love with him . . . I trapped him with you. I got pregnant on purpose. That was the only way I could have him to myself.' The corners of her mouth rose, a vague recollection of success. 'It worked, he married me. We were so happy, David, once.' Wendy sighed. 'Anyway, he left me for another woman. I loved him so much and to this day I still love him. No one can match up to him. Jack's second best to him and always will be. No one wants second best.' She began to sob big flaky tears. 'You are him, don't you see? You are what he left behind. Each day, each pathetic whine from your voice, I would see him. I just wanted you gone. Some days, when you ran away, I would hope you never came back. But you did, always you came back. Once when you were about seven, you gave me this card you'd made at school, and you smiled at me. I ripped it up in front of you, I hated you so much that day. And you didn't cry, you refused to cry, so Jack came home and I made up some story about you . . .' Wendy looked up into Dave's stern gaze. 'I wanted him to hurt you. I wanted him to make

you feel so bad, like I did when your father left me.
And I am cruel and I know it. But he left me and that's
that.' And her tears fell again.

Nothing bites harder than the teeth of truth. And
any deep excuses thought up by a young kid as to why
his mum was so hateful were dispelled for ever.

Dave searched for pity but found only emptiness.
'Was there not even a little bit of yourself in me that
you saw? I wasn't just his kid, I was yours as well,
Wendy. You were my mother. The amount of times I
wanted your love, but you refused to hug me, you
refused to kiss me and you refused to fucking touch
me. I had so many things I wanted from you, but I
never got one. I was only a kid, not your punchbag. I
was forever trying to please you. You know, some
days at school, I would dread coming home,
wondering what mood you'd be in.' And his voice
rose, 'I had to creep round you, I had to virtually beg
to get you to smile. And the only reason you have for
the way you behaved is that I am just like my father.'
Dave stood. 'Not fucking good enough. You don't
beat kids, you don't bully someone just for being part
of something you can't have any more. You're just a
selfish old cow. I can see why my father left you. I
don't think you ever loved him, you're too cold, you
don't know how to love. You even turned my own
sisters against me.' He moved to the door, wanting to
say something far reaching and deep, wanting to
express how let down he really felt, but all that came
out was: 'I am so ashamed of you.'

And he left.

Walking away from the house, he stole a few
seconds to view the wasteground where he used to

play and hide. The mysterious dense wood where, as kids, civilization stopped and adventure began. A muddy footpath led to the smoking industrial factories where Jack used to work, another path led to the local shops. Dave lit a fag and wandered down to the small playing field that led to the old holly tree. And yep, sure enough, kids were scaling high into the thorny branches, risking cuts and falling from the dizzy heights. Yeah, it hadn't taken long for a new generation of kids to realize that risk to life and limb from scouring to the top branches was worth it, because you could peer into every bedroom window that side of the neighbourhood. And he smiled. In a way he wouldn't change his upbringing even if he could; all the fears and all the tears. It had made him what he was.

As he pulled forward in the car, the house in the rear-view mirror faded with the distance. All those years spent wondering why; why his mum hated him so. All those thoughts of maybe it's this, or maybe it's that. When all the time it was maybe nothing. His mum was a twisted, cold-hearted, vicious woman. And maybe it was time to forget his family once and for all. He put his foot down and surged ahead, leaving his past to rot.

Dave carried Naina's shopping bags. It was pay day.

'No one asked you to come; what did you expect?' Naina said, heading for the bear shop. 'Come on, we don't all just order every available Armani T-shirt over the phone and let some lackey deliver it to our doors.' Her footsteps quickened at the sight of a sad-looking white bear in the window. 'He's lovely, isn't he?'

'That's it; I've had enough, you're taking the piss.'

Naina entered the shop, leaving Dave propped up against the window. Next time he asked Naina if she wanted to go for a bite to eat, he would make sure the bite to eat was at least thirty miles away from central Milton Keynes shopping centre.

Finally Naina returned from the shop holding a cardboard box, with holes pierced in the top: breathing holes so the stuffed bear did not die of suffocation. Dave hoped that the bear was flammable.

After eating in Fatty Arbuckles, they toddled across the crowded car park. Small, big, and noisy white market vans, shunted into position, were reversing expertly to their loading bays. Blue, red and white striped plastic canopy covers were folded and rolled with precision; and anyone in the way – was in the way.

'Kutti,' a voice rang clear of the rest, 'kutti kutti kutti.'

Naina swung her head round to locate the caller. Standing on a lorry lift, with a rail full of clothing, an Indian man stood with two others. Three beards, two turbans, and one massive cheesy grin. Dave, who always seemed troubled by the thought he might be missing out on something, turned his head to where Naina was staring.

'What did he say to you?' he asked, noting the friction between Naina and the Indian guys.

'Nothing, don't worry about it.' She pulled him by his hand. 'Come on.'

Even on an ordinary day – whatever that means – explaining to Dave that she had just been insulted, wouldn't have been the wisest of moves. And today, when Dave's mind seemed to be in orbit somewhere else, when even the slightest things like a three-hour shopping spree seemed to upset him, she knew it made sense to tell him what 'kutti' meant only at a safe distance.

'They called you a dog!?' Dave shouted, looking back at the half-mile distance he would need to run to attack the three Indian men. 'Why the hell didn't you tell me?'

'This. This is why, look at you.'

'Dog?' Dave questioned again, opening the car door.

Two passers-by noted that Naina was, indeed, not a dog, and Naina's explanation of why she was called a dog was simple: she had been seen with a white man. She was shaming the Indian way, bringing it into disrepute – in their eyes. She was watering down their values with western ideas – in their eyes. It only takes one bad grape to wreck a whole wine cellar – in Unwin's eyes.

Dave sped towards Naina's house in Shenley Wood. Her cooking curfew time was approaching as rapidly as his temper seemed to be bunching up. He cranked up the handbrake, lit a fag, and turned down the car CD player.

'So what's on the menu tonight?' he asked.

'Lucky me is cooking channa massalla – chickpeas. And I am going to produce chapatties so round they will roll off the table.'

He laughed.

'Anyway, what's eating you up? Seeing as we're discussing food,' she questioned, facing him.

He drummed his fingers on the dashboard, looked

as though he was about to ignore the question and say something kacky like 'Mmm burnt chickpeas', then answered, 'I did what you said, I went to see Wendy today.'

Naina wanted to kick him. She'd been with him most of the day, and now, when it was time to cook chapatties, he decided to tell her. Men! 'What happened?'

He explained.

Naina noticed that the iciness Dave used to display when discussing 'parents' had now thawed. Before, whenever she'd brought up the subject, it seemed she was tip-toeing across the California earthquake fault line with 'the big one' due any second. Now, there seemed to be no risk of an impending disaster. He seemed *different* – for the better.

Naina smiled. 'So, she said your dad was a womanizer. Just hope you don't take after him.'

Dave glanced sideways and ignored her.

Naina continued, 'Well, your dad managed to settle down in the end and put all his womanizing ways behind him. It just takes the right woman, I suppose.' She waited for him to look back at her. 'You never know, the same will probably happen to you one day . . . Mr I-won't-commit. The right woman will come along and you'll be all marshmallow to her.'

Dave was playing with the window controls. Up, down, up, down. 'That's enough about me, let's talk about you. This shit of yours. How are you getting on with him? Making any progress yet?'

Naina gave a small smile. 'Well . . . I slept with him and I . . .'

'Hang on a second, Naina. You slept with him?'

She nodded. 'When did this happen?'

'Quite a few times.'

'What, in between sleeping with me?'

'Yeah. Sue me. I just love hunky men.'

Dave lit a fag and nearly burnt his face off with the lighter. 'Well, what's he look like?'

Naina deliberated, dreaming, taking her time. 'Ahh, he's got these lovely blue eyes, and his smile, ahh, he crushes me with his smile. And his body, ahhhhh, you don't want to hear about his body. Me, Kate and Leena discuss that all night long. He's just everything he is, looks, body, brilliant in bed.' Naina sighed.

'So let me get this straight. It's very important that you answer me honestly, Naina. Very very important.'

'Go ahead.'

'Obviously I'm the best in bed out of the two, but how close is he to me?'

Naina picked up her handbag, leaned over to the back seat and grabbed her shopping bags, opened the door, pecked him on the cheek. 'Jealousy is a bad thing, Dave. I'll see you whenever, chickpeas are calling.' And she walked down Wildacre Road smiling.

'Sounds like a complete arsehole,' Dave said out loud to himself.

Chapter Thirty-three

Mirrors are the eyes to yourself. Honest. Whether you believe them or not depends. Depends on whether you want to believe them or not. Naina faced the long mirror in her bedroom. Unbelieving and unwilling to accept that the Indian wedding sari she now wore, did, in fact, suit her; it was made for her. And Naina's Indian skin, an inherent gift from her parents, amongst the splendour and richness of the colourful fabric, at once invoked authenticity – she was now a genuine Indian girl – and the mirror couldn't lie about that.

Sonia watched, possibly thinking, 'My turn next. Bye bye, Marilyn,' and after Sonia, Dad could officially declare, 'My three daughters are married – it's a hat-trick,' his favourite word 'hat-trick', born from his favourite game – cricket.

Naina's thoughts were mixed. To an Indian man – to the Indian groom – the sari holds not only beauty and timeless grace, but a statement, even a signature, that the woman behind the red and gold splendour is a virgin. His virgin. And when it came to the wedding night, after unravelling the sari, he and he alone would be the only man ever to have touched her brown skin. From that moment on, his new wife would stay devoted to him until the light of life flickered out.

Naina twisted her head over her shoulder, wondering if her bum looked big – half hoping it did. But, that's the beauty of the sari: it hides even the largest bum. Not that Naina had anything to worry about. Not about bums anyway. She thought back to Ashok, how he looked: so smart, so confident. And when he placed the ring on her finger, so gentle; and it fit perfectly, unlike the way Naina was feeling inside. When he touched her – maybe just a small invasion of her space, but it felt more like a full-blown attack – it didn't feel even slightly special or right. But when Dave had held her hand and touched her, there was no voice in her head saying, 'I wish you would stop,' like there was with Ashok, more like 'Carry on, show me what you're good at.' But Dave was a pig and Ashok most certainly was not; it didn't make sense how a pig could make you feel so vibrant and alive.

And on their wedding day, Ashok would turn up – he wouldn't be in Tenerife. It got her thinking about Dave and how he'd probably act: he'd make her hunt for the ring in some cake or something, he'd tell the vicar that he'd porked his wife just before the ceremony. On the way into the Register Office he'd slip his phone number to the bride from the previous wedding on her way out, and when Naina got to throw the flowers, inside the bunch would be a note from Dave – 'Marriage is for insecure people.' He'd turn up in a Versace suit with the sleeves removed to show off his biceps, and wearing those Nikes, and all the way through the wedding ceremony there would be the constant chant of 'OOzing'. But what was the point in even thinking about Dave? Naina was marrying Ashok. She would become his wife, partner and lover.

Perfectly woven Indian sari material meant that you had to move with perfectly woven grace. Naina plonked herself down on the bed, about as graceful as a man; this whole wedding palaver was getting her down. She didn't want Ashok, she wanted Dave. She wanted to wake up beside him day in and day out. She wanted to go shopping with him in a supermarket and choose vegetables together. She wanted to flick through brochures of holidays abroad with him and let him give her the window seat – on Concorde. She wanted him to love her, just like she loved him. And God, did she love him. The damn pig was in her thoughts all the bloody time.

Sonia sat, dressed in black, with her face up close to the VDU, her one comment to Naina on her red sari was 'doolb' and then after Naina had changed back into her Civvy clothes, 'Anian, trat ouy! Anian, trat ouy!'

Naina zipped up her long black suede boots and scowled at Sonia. 'Will you stop speaking backwards, you cow, and speak like normal people.'

'Yhcuot! yhcuot, Anian,' Sonia replied. 'Naina, you insult the Devil by jesting his language. Anyway, I've got an liam-e from lover boy for you.'

'A what?' Naina asked, combing her hair, losing her patience.

'An e-mail. I've vetted it for you; you've got to tell him to stop being rude.' Sonia held the printout in the air. 'That will be ten pounds.'

A tickle reduced the amount to zero, and Naina sat on her bed reading the liam-e.

> Send To: sleepezzee@spiral.com
> From: stranded@lexco.com
>
> SEX-PINT-FOOTBALL-APHRODITE
>
> Death, please pass this on to the living.
> Death, don't be so fucking nosy.
>
> Naina, tried your mobile – no luck.
>
> Do you know where my car is?
>
> Dave x

Naina smiled to herself until . . . Thump thump thump. Next door, in Kiran's room, his music blared out.

Sonia stared up from the screen, looked at Naina. 'He's a tragedy, isn't he?'

Naina agreed. She got up and then barged down the hall through to Kiran's messy bedroom, without knocking. She walked to the thundering stereo, flicked it off and waited for the ear infection to clear.

'Get out, Naina!' Kiran grumbled, lying on his bed reading his *Mojo* magazine.

'I want a word with you.' Naina stood over him. 'Dave told me everything, including the knife.' She bashed his magazine out of his hand across the room. 'Who the hell do you think you are, Kiran? India's Hell's Angels?' She glanced to the scattering of Bollywood superstars smiling back from the bedroom walls. And then to the shrine of his favourite band: Asian Dub Foundation. And then to the magazine half poking out from under his bed: *Asian Babes*. And finally back to Kiran lying on top of his *A Team* duvet.

He sat up. 'I saw you with him, kissing. You slag. Mum and Dad should know about this really. I'm only not telling them because I don't want to hurt them.' He grinned. 'Then again, perhaps they deserve to know. You and that white fuck.'

Naina boiled. 'Maybe I should tell them about the tape as well, show them it. Maybe I should take it to the police station.'

'You wouldn't dare. My own sister a grass.'

'Remember, I've got the tape, Kiran.' And she began to walk out, careful to crunch on as many loose CDs as her heels would allow, and lithely moved to one side as a video case rebounded off the opposite wall, just missing her head. She glanced down to the case – *Chori Chori Chupke Chupke* – Kiran's favourite Bollywood film, stamped on it, walked out to the word 'Bitch' sounding in her ears, and returned to her room. 'He is a major tragedy.'

Sonia looked up again. 'Major!'

Thump thump thump.

Naina switched on her mobile, phoned Dave. 'It's Naina.'

'I'm glad you called, Naina. I was thinking, in the

Bible it says an eye for an eye and a tooth for a tooth, I think; anyway, I shagged Froggy's woman, so, let's say I pick up a woman tonight and let Froggy shag her, will we be evens?'

'Dave, I'm putting the phone down.'

'No no no, wait, how are you? My gorgeous, I was just this second thinking about you.'

'Fine, anyway, I got your e-mail. Did you find your car?'

He laughed. 'Yeah, sorry about that, it was round Andy's.'

'Well, how the hell did you get from Andy's to . . . ? Oh never mind. Are you still on for Pizza Hut tomorrow?'

'Yeah, I'll meet you there, at twelve. By the way, you smell lovely.'

'Thanks and your creeping doesn't work with me.' And she hung up.

Dave switched the phone off, and sped on up the road, listening to 'November Rain' – by Guns n' Roses. He wondered if Danny Zuko would have liked Guns n' Roses; most likely. A flashing blue light appeared in his rear mirror and he pulled over, waiting for the Bobby to come to the window.

He wound down the electric window, lit a fag. 'And to what do I owe this pleasure?' he asked PC Humphreys.

The tubby PC, fluorescent and bold, looked up and down the gleaming red BMW. 'Is this your car, sir?'

'Pardon, can you speak up?' He puffed out his fag.

Humphreys leaned in. 'Don't be a smart arse, sir, is this your car?' Noises on the police radio could be heard.

'What, this shit-heap? You'll find if you check on your little computer that it's owned by Brigleys and Briars Insurance. Sir.'

Humphreys walked round the back of the vehicle, slowly, and then back round the front, slowly, then back to the window. 'Did you write 'bastard' on the back, sir?'

Dave jumped out of the car. He came to where the PC was now pointing with his pen and smiling. He innocently looked at the policeman. 'Did you just write that, PC Humpty?' Dave smiled, Laura had spelt bastard with two Ss.

On the radio Humphreys talked, 'We've got a loose one here, I shouldn't be too long.' Then back to Dave. 'No, if I was going to write it, sir, I would have written ARROGANT BASTARD instead . . . sir. Now your documents, please.'

Twenty minutes later Dave was free to go. He watched the brand-new Thames Valley Vauxhall Astra police car zoom off with its light flashing, and then he reached into his glove compartment. 'Reducing crime, disorder and fear, my arse,' he said, slammed down the bag of hash on the dashboard, and smiled his Dave smile.

The smile was short-lived, as his car pulled up outside Froggy's house. A scattering of lights down the road, plenty of parked cars, home-sweet-home for so many people. He wasn't looking forward to this one iota.

This time the knock was dull, tentative, almost wimpish; and a surprised-looking, haggard Sandra came to the door. 'What d'you want . . . Dave?'

Through the dimness of his shades he could tell

she'd been crying. 'S'Froggy about, please?'

Sandra retreated back inside, leaving the cold air to blow through the open front door. This was the first time Dave could remember being left outside on the mat. A loud thumping came down the stairs and Froggy, dressed in white boxers, white T-shirt, and shades, tweaked his hair in the hallway mirror then turned to Dave at the entrance. 'You can fuck off, mate; nice glasses.'

Dave peered at Froggy's boxers. 'Classless pants, mate.'

Froggy removed his shades.

Dave removed his.

Their eyes studied each other, examining their handiwork, and then Froggy broke the silence. 'Why did you do it? Was she just another shag?'

And the answer was not an easy one. 'I'm sorry, you're my best mate and I shit on you. I'll be honest with you.' Froggy clenched his teeth. 'I wasn't pissed, it was only the once, when you two had just started seeing each other. You said yourself that she was a cheap piece of fanny, so I never saw you two, you know, getting together. I'm being honest here, mate. If I ever thought that she meant anything to you, I wouldn't have done it.' Dave reached for a fag in his empty pocket. 'Look, Frog, I never thought that you'd end up falling in love with her.' And Dave swallowed his pride – it wasn't much of a mouthful. 'Look, Frog, I'll do anything to make it up to you. I'm sorry.'

Across the road, a small front gate was banging to and fro with the gusty weather, like the cross voice of the wind itself. Froggy pushed past Dave, crossed the

road and pulled the gate to the latch, then came back
and joined Dave outside on the front porch.

'It doesn't matter now. Sandra and me are finished.'
And Froggy looked to the top of the house, as if he
were checking the guttering. 'Do you know how it
feels to be taken for a ride by your best mate?' He
didn't wait for an answer. 'You and I used to say, fuck
everyone else, fuck 'em all, but we never fuck each
other. Remember that? You fucked me, you and your
shagging. Do you know how pathetic you look? Every
night, I shagged this one or I wrecked this one's life . . .
Dave.' Froggy came in real close, his eyes like torches.
'You are a nothing. We could all do what you do – all
the lies – everyone can do it, but we don't, we've got
a little bit more up here.' He tapped his head, Dave
watched motionless. 'How would you like it? One day
you think you're settling down with a woman that
you really love.' Froggy was back looking at the
guttering. 'And I really loved her, Dave. How would
you like it if I, me, your best mate was shagging her
behind your back in your flat?' Froggy's voice was
now a low growl. 'I know you, it would mess your
mind up so bad, you wouldn't be able to handle it.
Dave the man, the one that wrecks everyone else's life
finally has his life wrecked.' And Froggy finally
paused. 'Honestly, mate, I feel like ripping your face
off . . . we've known each other since we were six.'
The gate started banging again, Froggy looked in
despair.

There was a hurt in Froggy's eyes, a distant look,
almost of hopelessness, and Dave knew it was his
fault, and only his fault. He hated himself for what he
had done to Froggy. It was unforgivable.

Dave stared at his lost friend. 'You mean a lot to me, you're a better man than I am. I stabbed you in the back. For what it's worth, I'm sorry.' And he crossed the road to close the gate, then got back into his car, knowing his friendship was dead: he had lost Froggy for the sake of one crap shag.

On the way home, the CD played 'All by Myself' by Carman.

Chapter Thirty-four

Spread out on Dave's polished mahogany dining-room table was the entire contents of some woman's handbag. There had to be a clue in there somewhere of who the slapper in his bed was. The night before was just a grainy picture with only fleeting images of heavy drinking, plenty of dancing, but still no recollection of her identity.

A severe headache had seized up just over his left eye, and with a face that looked like it had quit, he examined the bag's quota of useless women's carry-around: tissues, lipsticks, powders – in fact most of Boots. Receipts, keys, small pair of leather gloves, blue fluffy purse with stuck on eyes, a mobile, address book and a pair of stowaway knickers. Carefully he placed all the items back, except the silver address book and purse, and in order for the bag to appear untouched, he violently shook it up a dozen or so times.

Dirty cow: two condoms in the purse. And her name, like an organized person, he found on the inside flap of her address book – Josie Martins. He smiled his Dave smile, and placed the address book and purse back, wondering why the bag was now filled with a sort of beige talcum powder. He thought maybe it was like one of those security devices they put with money cases and the red dye shoots out. Women, sneaky cows.

Horizon Radio played softly in the kitchen. He clunked the button down on the kettle, pulled out a stale loaf of white bread, gave it a quick sniff, grimaced, then Utterly Butterlyed two end crusts. Slicing up a juicy beef tomato, he hummed to himself; pushed down the pedal on the chrome bin, picked out the off-bacon and slid across to the sink where he washed off all the fag ash and yoghurty stuff. He dried the six slices of bacon (he was feeling generous) with a red tea towel and whacked them under a hot grill until they sizzled. Even off-bacon smelt okay cooking, but there was no way he was having any.

Josie sauntered in casually dressed in Dave's white Valentino T-shirt. 'Mmm, something smells nice.' She came up to him and kissed him. 'Hope you don't mind, but I helped myself to one of your T-shirts.'

Dave peered down at the slim, blonde, busty beauty. Wow. 'No problem, Josie.'

She jumped up onto the counter letting her bare skinny legs swing. He hated it when women made themselves at home, it was though she was hinting to move in. Next it would be their engagement and then where would it end? Maternity ward that's where. And he wasn't fooled by the old hair trick either.

Sneakily combing through her hair and then pretending that she had woken up like that. Pher! He was going off her already. She watched him cut through the crust.

'Do you always cook with no clothes on?' she asked.

'Yeah, except when I do kiddies' parties.' He passed the sandwich, and garnish – an extra piece of bacon he couldn't fit in the bread. 'Eat up, it will get cold, Josie.'

He was totally and utterly adorable. Not only was he so passionate last night, but he cooked her a breakfast as well. That's the sort of thing ugly men do, to make up for their . . . ugliness. But Dave – he was breathtaking, and those blue eyes, so clear and dangerous. And he was very wealthy. But it didn't stop there, oh no. His firm, chiselled, rugged body was enough by itself to wet the driest knickers. And one more thing, and this thing topped it all: his honesty, his unabashed confession that he had only slept with two women in his life, because he was so shy. He was too good to be true.

Josie swallowed a delicate mouthful. 'Are you not eating any, Dave?' And she put her hand to her mouth with a little chortle, 'I thought after last night you would be starving.' Her eyes roamed down his bare body.

'I don't eat pork,' replied the shy, naked, off-bacon sarnie maker, who had been yelling at the top of his voice last night, 'I'm jamming it hard, baby.'

'Oh,' confused, 'but why have you got bacon in your fridge?'

'Grandma. She's eighty-nine, she stays with me

sometimes, bless her, she loves her bacon.' Dave conjured up a look of hurt and stared at the window. 'Not long now. Every time she stays, I think, Granny, or Miffy, that's what I call her, Miffy, is this our last time together?' He told himself to stop right there. Soon he would be making up stories about Miffy and her wheelchair and the brakes that failed just near the edge of Dunstable Downs. Stop it!

Josie placed the empty dish down, flopped off the counter edge and came over to give her sensitive man a big hug. 'Oh! I take it you want to go back to bed.' Dave's hardness, she hoped, was not brought on by granny talk.

It was 11.17; he couldn't stand Naina up. 'Look, I would love to, but I've really got to go to work. Leave your number and I'll call you.' Dave gave his 'sorry face'.

Josie went, the headache stayed, the car was gone and Dave was late. Yet again the whereabouts of Dave's car was unknown, lodged somewhere in last night's drinking. As so often was the case, he was forced to call a cab.

'Pizza Hut in central, please,' Dave asked the small taxi driver, and was tempted to say, 'I suppose it's a blessing being only four-foot tall when you drive these *mini* cabs,' but couldn't be bothered to speak. And watched the roads dither past as the cab driver made efforts to be sociable.

'What gym do you train at? I would train myself but I haven't got the time, you know, all these long hours. I used to do it once, years ago, I was big, very big. I've got a mate that's much bigger than you, he doesn't even train. Much much bigger than you he is, twenty stone and no fat at all.' The cabby looked behind him, then back to the road. 'Training: you must train about five times a week; steroids – I bet you use those. I knew a man that used—'

Dave interrupted, 'Excuse me, what's your name again?'

'It's Mike, and you?'

'Mike, a bit rude of me I know, but could you just shut the fuck up. I don't really care about you and your mates.'

The cabby spoke no more until the end of the journey, when he sulkily asked for £4.50.

Pizza Hut sat plum opposite a pyramid-shaped cinema and pub complex called The Point. Below it, underground, was a bingo centre where the lilac-hair-tinted women would hang out. Jingle would say, 'The only reason that the bingo centre is underground is to give the biddies a mock run, before they're finally sealed away in a cheap MDF coffin.' It sometimes raised a laugh.

In shades, in a tight purple Armani T-shirt, black jeans, black Nikes and Davidoff, Dave entered the already busy restaurant, found Naina's booth, kissed her on the cheek and sat on the long cushioned seat opposite. She looked ravishing.

Armani shades off, fag lit. 'Sorry I'm late, hectic morning. You okay?'

Naina paused, he hadn't spotted the new outfit – an expensive two-piece Ralph Lauren dark aubergine suit, too good for insurance, too good for Pizza Hut. 'I'm fine and—'

A tall clumsy-looking waitress arrived, interrupting them. 'Can I—'

Dave butted in, 'Biggest pizza you do, please. Everything on it, make sure the bacon is fresh, salad bowl, garlic bread and a large Coke for me, thanks.' He peered at Naina who was not too sure whether Dave's order was for him alone or for both of them.

'Erm, small Coke, please, and Dave, was that all for you?'

The waitress capped a laugh as Dave replied, 'You can share with me, Naina, if you want.' Naina nodded yes and Dave turned to the waitress. 'Whip off the beef, will you? Cheers.' And she trotted off.

Dave carried on as if he were already in the middle of a discussion. 'Honestly, Naina, since the pregnancy fright the other night, I haven't slept with one woman, I'm too scared. Call me gutless if you want, but I don't think I could go through all that again. I'm quite happy just sitting at home, on my own, reading my back issues of *New Scientist*.' He dragged on his fag. There were titters coming from the cubicle behind, he lowered his voice. 'But I'll make an exception for you though, as you're my friend; you wouldn't pull a stunt like that.' He stared at Naina meaningfully.

What was he like? Naina wafted away the smoke. 'Dave, you're telling me you haven't slept with one woman since Laura? We're talking three days here.'

More tittering next door.

Dave acknowledged Naina's scepticism. 'I'm fucking telling the truth here,' he said, slightly hurt.

'Why are you getting all worked up then, Dave?' The drinks were served, icy cold Pepsi. 'And for the record, Dave, I know when you're lying.' She sipped the cola through a pink straw. 'You're always lying.'

More tittering next door, Dave stood up and

Nisha Minhas

looked down to the party of four. 'Come on, join us, it sounds even funnier over this side.' And soon the tittering stopped. He sat back down, took one massive gulp of his Pepsi and stared into Naina's eyes. 'Velvet, your eyes are like velvet. So beautiful, Naina, and the suit compliments your,' he glanced under the table, then back up again, 'it compliments your handbag really well.'

Naina laughed.

Across from their cubbyhole was the salad bar. Experienced Pizza Hut regulars had garnered the knack of piling so much food on to the little dinky plate provided, that their shoulders were hunched with the weight. Dare anyone call them greedy and with a mouthful of corn on the cob, they would direct your eyes to the sign: 'As much as you can fit on one plate.' Pizza Hut were losing millions a year with that sticky orange sauce of theirs, capable of gluing small boiled spuds and eggs to the edge of the plate.

'Can't believe that greedy bastard, Naina; see how much he's piled on that plate. What a disgusting pig!' Dave said, stuffing an enormous portion of pizza in his gob.

Naina with her knife and fork began to cut daintily through the hot cheesy dough. 'Yes, Dave, a pig.'

She watched the ballet of bubbles, fizzing and popping in her thin tall glass. Half the pizza was demolished, while she was still on her first slice and she asked, 'Dave, do you think—'

He interrupted. 'Naina, no, don't marry him. You can't marry him.' His voice was defiant, almost military, an order of sorts.

And the apparent ease with which he had read her

mind, in a certain way was comforting. She was about to reply, when he continued, in a hushed but confident voice, 'I don't want you to marry him. I want you to be happy, Naina. You can't gamble with something as important as this.'

Naina sucked on her chewed-up straw, and he knew she was becoming ruffled; maybe he was trespassing again, so he changed the subject; Naina's eyes were grateful.

'I tried to apologize to Froggy yesterday. I wish I had listened to you, Pete and Matt. You all told me to tell him the truth before he found out. Might have made a difference, who knows?'

And the details of the apology, along with a few trigger questions by Naina as to how rough Sandra had looked, were spoken about as the pizza neared the end of its life. Naina could see that Dave was truly remorseful, and she felt a small crushing blow to her heart once more; was this the man that she *really* wanted? And her honesty taunted her 'Yes', he was. But the 'Yes' came with a few 'Ifs': *If* only he wouldn't lie. *If* only he could keep with one woman. *If* only he loved her. If only. Even now, while he sat there, his eyes were gathering information on prospective women. She'd already caught him smiling at two, seen him tip his head back so he could admire a woman's bum and then smile to himself. He even offered to help a stunning brunette fill her salad bowl, while her boyfriend watched on. But still Naina wanted him. And what about Ashok? He was more than likely Mr Perfect for someone else, but not for her.

And it was here, in Pizza Hut, while Dave pulled up his top to check that his six-pack was still visible, that an inkling of a thought, almost a blemish of an idea, rose to the surface of her head like the bubbles in her cola, inviting a possible question: what if he could change? The bubbles popped. What if she could change him?

'Naina, what colour knickers are you wearing?' he asked, interrupting her thought flow.

'Big off-white granny knickers, with all the elastic frayed.' She paused. 'Try and get a kick out of that.' And he laughed.

What if she could change him; she could only try. She had five months. You can build a lot in five months. She looked at Dave. But this wasn't about building. This was about destruction pure and simple. This was about knocking down the walls he'd erected over the years and hoping that after the rubble had all been cleared away, standing there would be a man who well and truly loved her as she thought – possibly – he might. And if he did declare his love, admitted it, then the hardest decision of her life would be thrust upon her like a ticking bomb. Was she prepared to lose her family over this one man? And she knew the answer. Just as Dave had explained how his own mother had sat with second best, sat with Jack for almost twenty years, Naina couldn't bear the thought of sitting with Ashok, for he too would be second best to Dave. She could never love Ashok. Would never love Ashok. Lightning don't strike twice!

If, by two weeks before the wedding, Dave's love for her was as strong as hers for him, then she would call off the wedding and lose her family. And only, only, only, only, if Dave could achieve the three 'Ifs'. Hard as it was to accept, Dave was her perfect man, but there was no way she was willing to share him with any other woman.

Somehow, just the whimsical thought of her 'three ifs plan' solidified the facts: she would be marrying Ashok. Dave would never change.

Time was short, Naina stood up. 'I'm late, I've got to go. Thanks for sharing a slice of your pizza.'

He looked up. 'Before you go, Naina, take a peek at that blonde woman in a blue sweatshirt, over there, don't make it too obvious.'

Naina casually glanced over, then back again. 'So? And, what am I meant to be looking for?'

He smiled the knowing smile. 'Can't you tell? . . . She's ovulating.' And Naina, nodded her head, tried not to give an encouraging smile, kissed him and walked out, laughing ruefully to herself.

Dave paid, wandered up the aisle towards the toilets, then heard . . .

'Innit, ees nu-ting man nu-ting. Eeze now eeze now, innit. Big up. Me finks me burrows me mum's car innit?' The voice was decidedly familiar. Dave turned to see two baseball-capped youthful-looking Indian men, tucking into a large pizza. One had a gold tooth. The boys were back in town.

Within earshot, Dave retired to a spare booth and held a menu high in front of him.

'Three hundred Delhi folks starred in that *Gandhi* film right. And they paid them nu-ting, nu-ting. And this geezer, Ben Kingsley right, pay him wot, three million quid, right. But get this, Kaz.'

'Tell me, man.'

'Ben Kingsley right, ees a fuckin white man, innit?'

Kaz chuckled.

375

Nisha Minhas

Nass continued, 'And as far as mee knows right, Gandhi was bloody Indian, innit.'

Dave, speechless with their intelligence, slid in next to Nass, stole a slice of Kaz's pizza, stuffed it in his mouth and sat there while the two worked their brains real hard trying to *get real* with the man that had just done a *jiggy* with their pizza.

Gold-toothed Nass spoke first, 'Ooh de fink ee is, Kazzy?'

'What d'you want, Dave? Didn't you learn your lesson? Keep away from Indian people, or we'll fucking put you in hospital. Innit.' Threatened Kaz.

Dave gulped down Kaz's lager and belched. 'Keep away from Naina, keep away from me and keep away from my gym.' He finished the lager. 'And sort out your friggin accents.' And walked off leaving them both in a pool of 'innits'.

Twenty minutes later, Dave wandered up and down the high street, not soul-searching but car-searching. Margaret the traffic warden would have to be about – she was always about. And it wouldn't take too much wit to find her.

'Oi, Maggie,' shouted Dave across the road, 'over here.'

She looked to the voice – oh, it was that horrible man again, what now? She ignored him and carried on writing out the ticket.

'OI, MAGGIE!' It was in her ear this time, and she jumped. 'You're looking extremely well . . . fed. You must be up for promotion, I admire you.'

Margaret left the pen in the middle of a car registration, and viewed this horrible man through her thick-rimmed spectacles. 'What is it that you

376

want? And if you're complaining about your car, it's been there all morning, and by the looks of things it's being towed right now.' Her eyes looked down the road, her big round cheeks took a few moments to catch up, and she smiled a gapped teeth smile. 'Expensive business leaving your car like that, you never learn.'

Dave saw in the distance a red BMW being hooked on to a lorry, and ran towards it yelling, 'Leave my sodding car alone.'

Luckily, he was wearing his Nikes.

Chapter Thirty-five

When Mark Tully wrote about going to India, his publishers were unaware that the cheeky git might have only popped on a train to Southall.

Overstepping great mounds of garlic and ginger, and glancing into shops filled with spices that even the most reclusive of taste buds would surrender to, Naina steered herself down The Broadway, in Southall – also known as Little India – with an overnight bag slung over her shoulder.

White people are the nomads of this town, where English is only used as slang. And if you want to get out, then first you have to get in; through the scrums of people or past the convoy of honking cars. Naina was already late for Sumita's, but not too late to stop her straying into each and every gold and sari shop.

Finally: '*Sat sri akal ji,*' Naina said, with hands

folded in front of her chest and her head bowed down slightly.

'*Sat sri akal ji*,' replied Sumita's mother-in-law. Her hair was grey, like a coyote's, and she had thick bifocal spectacles. She held the glass-fronted door aside to let Naina through, and pulled the tail of her light blue sari over her shoulder.

The slam behind confirmed her anger at Naina's late arrival.

'Sorry I'm late,' apologized Naina, turning to face the Battle-Axe. 'The train was . . .'

Suddenly, screaming from behind interrupted her lies. A two-year-old was having a tantrum. Anil was lying face down, crying into the patterned hallway carpet, promising to avenge the world for denying him sweets before supper.

'Sorry,' gasped Sumita as she gently pulled Anil to his feet. And she gave Naina a warm hug, while the young man sniffed with sparkly eyes. (Maybe Naina had sneaked in some sweeties.) Anil gave Naina a shy smile, then hid behind Sumita's legs, which were in turn hiding behind her violet satin shalwar.

'Sumita,' scolded Battle-Xxe. 'Give him his milk, you've got to give him milk if he cries.'

'Okay, Mama ji.'

Sumita and Naina exchanged looks, as they both headed into the large fitted kitchen. Mama ji scooped up Anil.

'Not too warm,' shouted out Battle-Axe.

'No, Mama ji,' replied Sumita, and punched the air with a two-fingered gesture to the wall. The gesture didn't sit well with Sumita's kind and generous face. But the Battle-Axe deserved it and that was that.

Sumita turned back round and the two of them giggled like kids.

'I'll have to show you those photos of you and Ashok; they came out really well. He's really good looking.' Sumita poured the milk into the tiny copper saucepan, and boosted the blue gas flame. 'Do you want some tea? Or coffee?'

'Coffee's fine,' Naina replied. 'I'm dreading marrying him, Sumita. Mum doesn't stop talking about him. Dad . . . well, he keeps congratulating himself at how well he's chosen.' She spoke quietly, 'He seems nice, but . . . oh I don't know.'

Sumita saw herself in Naina: the fear. The worry. The dread. 'It's normal to feel this way. You don't know him, but remember he doesn't know you either, and that's what will bond you together. The learning.'

Naina huffed. 'It's not that.' And speckles of tear dust glazed her eyes. 'I've met a bloke. He's white. I love him . . . not that he loves me. In fact, he's everything Dad tells us about white men . . . everything.' Naina stopped and looked at her shocked sister. She didn't know Sumita had fillings at the back of her mouth. 'I can't get him out of my mind and I can't marry Ashok knowing I love him.' And Naina removed the milk before it boiled over. This was a confession. Sumita's ears had been tampered with and the seal was now broken. Naina hadn't a clue why she had told her. Maybe she wanted Sumita to turn round and say, 'Go for it, save yourself the heartache of an arranged marriage, do what makes you happy.' Or maybe it was the guilt of not telling her sister something so very important –

they used to be so close, they used to tell each other everything.

Sumita had a hundred questions, but one charged through though, like a ramming bull. 'Have you slept with him?' Her eyes danced as her breath held.

'No.'

Anil ran in laughing with his model Eddie Stobart truck (named Anne-Marie) in his small hand. Naina grabbed him from the floor, his little legs still running in the air and gave him a raspberry kiss on his soft cheek.

'Naina,' Sumita's voice was a hoarse firm whisper. 'Forget him. It's not worth it. You go with him, you'll lose Mum and Dad. You know Mama ji would cut you out of the family as well, and then I'll never see you again. Do you want to lose your whole family? Do you want to shame the family? Hurt Mum and Dad? Do you want to wreck your whole life over a white man? You won't get better than Ashok, trust me.' She paused. 'It's not our way.'

'You're right.' Naina tried to sound confident and affirmative. But a shy mouse could have done better.

'What about when you have kids, half white, half Indian—'

Naina interrupted, 'He doesn't love me. I shouldn't have said anything. I know at the end of the day I will marry Ashok. I couldn't hurt Mum and Dad.'

Sumita stared at Naina.

Later that evening, when the men had returned home from work and they all sat in front of the TV with food-trays brimming with baigan, raita and rice; the air filled with chitter-chatter, Sumita stared some more. Naina was sure her lecture was far from over.

And lectures in any Indian household were part and parcel of life. You accepted them like you did the familiar surroundings. Forget Dolly the sheep, Indians began the cloning experiment first, each house being just like the other: decorative red or green/gold tissue boxes, pictures of Sikh Gurus, velvet flowery sofas, metal peacocks, AO-sized framed enlargement of sons' and daughters' degrees, suitcases atop your wardrobe filled with old saris and mothballs, and big bags of onions and drums of Hathi chapatti flour. Naina looked round the living room. It was all so familiar, right down to the old Indian mother-in-law battle-axe sitting in the corner, self-righteous and superior with a face as stiff as dirty socks. God, any second now she was bound to begin one of her famous speeches: Kashmir. Luckily Naina's mobile sang.

Unluckily.

'Naina, it's Dave. Fancy going down the pub? I'm feeling a bit lonely.'

The TV was turned down, all ears were on Naina.

'Hi, Leena,' Naina said as enthusiastically as she could. 'I'm in Southall, Leena. They've got a lovely new range of chappals. You must see them, they'll look lovely with your . . .'

'So a shag's out of the question. I'll catch you later.' And he hung up.

'Yeah, Leena, you should come with me next time . . . Oh, I know . . . Oh, I know . . . Okay then, bye Leena.' Naina smiled to the group. 'It was Leena.'

After excusing herself, she sat on the toilet and sent Dave a text message:

Go and sprain a wrist
I've rubbed you off my shagging list
Swalk.

Then she returned to the sitting room, smiling.

Kalvinder had worked hard all day, he needed a shot of Captain Morgan rum. The father-in-law had worked hard all day, he needed a shot of White Horse whisky. The women had worked hard all day, they needed a shot of Fairy mild to do the washing-up.

'And this is what you call clean, is it, Naina? Is this the hygiene Ashok can come to expect?' spat Battle-Axe, nearly throwing the plate back in the soapy bowl. 'Your mum should be stricter on you. Sumita came here all sloppy, didn't you, Sumita?'

'Yes, Mama ji.'

Later, Sumita dragged down the heavy heavy *heavy* duvet. The one you have to pay extra for on the flight back from India. The one that's heavier than a fully grown elephant. The one your mum adamantly persuades you is better than the cheap muck they churn out in England. Fifty togs worth.

Sumita closed the door and sat with Naina on the blue velvet sofa.

'Look, Sumita, I know what you're going to say,' Naina began. 'You are right. He's not worth it, I'm just being stupid. I'm just panicking. I don't want to let anyone down.'

'I know, I know. Is it because you're worried about the wedding night? You know, being with Ashok?' Sumita didn't wait for a response. 'I was scared stiff. Mum never told me anything, but it's not *that* bad.'

They both stared at the blank fuzz of the TV. 'I'm not going to sit here and lie to you and say I wasn't worried about my wedding, because I was, and it was hard coming into a new family, trying to fit in. But keep your head down, don't answer back, and when you have children, things will come together. You'll see.' Sumita gazed at Naina. 'Just forget you ever met this white guy. Trust me, I know what I'm talking about.'

Naina fidgeted with the tassels on the edging of a matching blue cushion. 'He's called . . .'

'I don't want to know!' It was the definitive end to the discussion. Then, 'Naina, this love, this feeling you talk of, you must remember that it is only infatuation. Love is a far stronger emotion.' Her words stung.

As Sumita disappeared from the room, Naina was left to come to terms with some things.

Was it time to forget Dave? Had this journey run its course? She thought about how much Sumita had changed. How much Sumita had been changed. Before her wedding, Sumita had been just like herself. Banging on about the latest fashions, going out, staying out, and even smoking once or twice. She couldn't cook, or sew, or speak fluent Punjabi. Now, Sumita was the perfect Indian wife and God did she seem unhappy. Not being who she wanted to be, but a clone moulded into what was expected of her. She was chained and she was trapped and she wasn't the sister Naina remembered so fondly, the one who never stopped smiling. That Sumita was flying around, up in the temple rafters, waiting for the real Sumita to come back. There must be more to life than clearing up after Indian men, there had to be.

Naina wondered if there had ever been a time when Sumita herself had been 'infatuated'. In some ways she hoped there had.

And in some ways, she hoped there hadn't.

Chapter Thirty-six

Every time Dave bought himself a new car, he would have to christen it. From the blue Ford Escort with its black vinyl roof where he had pounded Faith in the back of the Co-op car park, to the red Astra GTI, where Lesley was pushed to the point of near exhaustion, to the silver Calibre where Lucy – his ex-fiancée – was subjected to a quick impromptu shag while he waited for his fillet of fish to be cooked in the McDonald's waiting bay no. 2, to his black BMW 540i sport, where Rachel became the baking oven to his cookie stick, on a very cold night in November. And now to his swanky new sports car: a black BMW M5, £52,000 worth of power. The most expensive car so far. And this one needed a piece of class with no peers, a woman with no equal, a beauty without an heir, a stunner, a wonder, a sex-mad babe with perfect features and an all-in-one bag of sexual tricks up her sleeve, a dream, a lust cushion, a knockout and knock me down, a coast-to-coast breathless sigh of unkempt utter unforgiving unmatched God damn it shut up mind boggling dazzling entertaining and totally cock hardening babe. For the asking price, he thought the garage might have supplied her – he did ask.

Dressed in black, he drove out of the BMW garage, sniffing the pure magic of new-car smells, and smiled his Dave smile. This brand-new gleaming machine needed to be put through its paces. So, 0–60 in 5.2 seconds he scarpered up the road, burned the rubber, and 0-60 in 5.3 seconds he was back at the BMW garage.

'It is unleaded, isn't it?' he asked. And it was.

There was only one place to go: A505, England's autobahn. And with the miles sweeping under the metal, and the air-conditioning on full blast, Dave shunted his way up the six-gear wonder and felt the pure energy rush of ignited speed. And on the horizon lay the future, unclear and misleading in its promises. And the chilled energy threw him forward, charging through the passage of time. Racing the miles of hours, then days, and the next time we find him, he's . . .

Getting out of his sparkling black BMW, three whole months later, in June, dressed in a tight red Versace T-shirt, black combat trousers, black Nikes, Davidoff, and the cleanest, most honest look a man could have. Naina waited by the entrance to her office, unimpressed with Dave's skid mark on the gravel, and definitely unimpressed with his late arrival. He should have been there an half hour before.

'Well?' Naina said, getting into the passenger seat.

'Oh sorry, about that. I'm not going to lie, but I had this really nervous feeling in my stomach about taking the normal route, I thought there might be a crash or something so . . .'

'Leave it. Well?'

'Well, what?' Dave replied, checking in his rear-view mirror, noticing a rather attractive-looking woman on her own by the main-door entrance. Nice legs, nice face, splendid curves.

Naina looked at him severely. 'Did you tell Alison?'

'I haven't seen her since last week and I'm not intending to. Honestly, I don't know why you're so het up about her.' Dave's eyes couldn't tear themselves away from the lonely woman by the door.

Naina noticed Dave's wandering eyes. 'I'm not het up about her.' She paused. 'Are we going to stay here all day looking at that bimbo? Or are we going?'

'What?' His attention was still directed at the entrance door. 'Naina, do you know her? Does she work with you?'

'She's pregnant, Dave.' And the car sped off 0–60 in 4.1 seconds.

Three months had seen some changes. Although she still genuinely felt that underneath all Dave's boisterous womanizing, there lay the man she wanted, it was proving to be a stubborn, gritty challenge to try to change the proverbial leopard's spots. Since her so-named 'three ifs plan' had been born that day in Pizza Hut, Dave had just got worse. She'd tried depriving him of her body. She'd tried various methods of getting him to see that he didn't need more than one woman. She'd tried jealousy, talking about men at work and how they made her go all gooey. She'd explained that maybe Ashok was her dream man after all. She'd tested theory after theory. And he just got worse. Alison was a little worrying though: he found her sexy, intelligent, funny, and he'd already been on four dates with her. And to quote Dave: 'If I go on more than three dates with the same woman, then I may as well be fucking married.' As far as Naina was aware, since Lucy – his ex-fiancée – he'd never been on more than three dates with the same woman. Worse still, he talked about this Alison constantly. Yes, Alison was a little worrying.

Stiltskins, a family-run bar-come-restaurant, lay on the Grand Union Canal jetty appearing as if it was wading in the green algae-infested water. Bar tables perched up on the embankment with red and white canopy umbrellas still marked with the former name of the restaurant in faded black writing: Barge Thru Us. Dave and Naina took their pints over to them and sat, ushering along a few roaming geese which haggled for titbits of food from the ploughman lunches served in the afternoon. The sun bared its teeth, gave a huge smile, stretched out its clouds, giving the first day of decent weather that June.

Naina, dressed in a loose lavender dress, matching heels, matching nail varnish, watched with Dave as a battered old canal boat, *Soothsayer*, plodded past through the waters, with a daft-looking skipper at the helm in a pin-striped shirt, khaki shorts, white canvas shoes and hat, puffing on a French stick cigar, struggling to balance on his captain's deck chair up front. Who was steering the thing was a mystery, but somehow it stayed on course, leaving a faint ripple in its wake, and disappeared round the corner of the canal, out of sight. The seemingly peaceful pace of life was once again wrecked by Dave with a comment regarding sex.

'I finally christened my car last night, Naina,' said Dave, beaming a hearty, reminiscing smile. 'Three long months I've waited, just to find the right woman to do that car justice. I was getting to think that my car was going to remain a virgin.' He lit a fag. 'I thought I was going to end up asking you to get the damn thing over and done with. Honestly, Naina, it's been a fucking nightmare of three months. A classy car like that needed a classy woman.'

Naina, used to Dave's ongoing car saga, was a tad keen to know who this classy woman was. 'Go on then, tell me: what does she look like? How big her tits are, how much she moaned and groaned, how . . . have I missed anything?' She slurped on the lager.

'Well, you know who it is. It's Alison. She passed my vetting procedure, she's clean, she's supple, she's—'

Naina interrupted, 'You just told me not fifteen minutes ago that you haven't seen her for a week and you're not seeing her again.' She was seething. 'Didn't you?'

'Did I? Oh, why did I say that? Couldn't you feel the car purr today, Naina? Like it was thanking me. No, I'm definitely seeing her again, I'm cooking for her tomorrow night.'

Naina stood up. He'd never cooked a meal for *her*. Unless you class digestive biscuits smothered in jam as a romantic meal. 'That will be six dates, Dave; you're a liar. What is it with you and your dick? I'm going; I'm sick of you and your lies.'

Dave rose up, casting his eye to the few non-paying sideshow watchers. 'Eat your manky cheese ploughmens, you nosy tossers.' Then looked at Naina. 'Come on, what's eating you up?' Naina was halfway up the canal side. Dave gulped down the remains of both of their lagers as quickly as he could. 'Wait up, I'll give you a lift: you're miles from home.'

Naina turned round. A boiling ball of jealousy came out of her lips: 'I'm never getting in that car again. Not after you banged that bitch in it last night!' The words were like slaps to the face of the nosy listeners. They'd not heard such language in a long time. And Dave was totally confused, yet again.

Naina's figure disappeared round the corner of Stiltskins as Dave scrambled to catch her up, carelessly tilting the nosy listeners' table on the way. 'Sorry, you cretinous old farts,' he muttered, as the drink dripped on to their legs and blankets. The ploughman bread rolls lived up to their name and rolled off the wooden tables into the waiting mouths of the geese.

Round the corner, huddled against the old red brickwork of the restaurant, Naina let the tears trickle down her cheeks, little splinters of salty jealousy. She'd not even met this bitch Alison, and she hated her with relish. What had Alison got that she hadn't? And she'd been waiting for the last three months for Dave to ask *her* to be the minx who gave the BMW its purr.

'Naina, what's . . .' She was crying. 'Naina.' He gently swung her round, put his forehead to hers. 'What's wrong, tell me?'

'I can't talk to you any more, Dave, we just don't

391

communicate any more. Just leave me alone, please.'
And she pulled her head away from his and walked
off. Whose bloody idea was it to fall in love with a
womanizer in the first place? He was a lost cause. This
was the end. She could take no more. She needed to
get away from him for good.

Dave leaned against the wall. He knew that tone in
her voice, no use trying to manipulate her. He lit a fag,
really bemused, totally and utterly confused. What
the hell was going on? What had he said this time? He
went through the conversation word for word in his
head. And honestly, with his hand on his heart, there
was nothing, not one thing he had said, that could
possibly have upset Naina. Women.

Chapter Thirty-seven

Alison was due in twenty minutes. Dave studied the instructions written on the side of the beef and tomato Pot Noodle. Four minutes and dinner would be ready, leaving sixteen minutes to light the candles. He smiled his Ainsley smile.

The sound of 'Kim' by Eminem ripped through the foundations, as Dave dimmed the dining-room lights and lit four red scented candles, placing them on the chunky mahogany table. He wanted this evening to be perfectly romantic. A nervous tune played in Dave's stomach. Rarely would a woman delve so deep as to steal his nerves. But she did; she was as beautiful as nature would allow. The first time he had seen her in MK Art Gallery (a dead cert for picking up pretty women) he prayed to God that she wasn't *happily* married. With looks that could turn a tide, and a jolting beauty that wasn't borrowed from her make-up bag, he knew that if he wanted her, there was no room for mistakes. He would have to be the perfect gentleman. He was going to have to enchant her.

Dave sat with his black Nikes resting on the glass table in front of him, fag, glass of white wine and an intense look as he watched a calf being born on the Discovery channel. He flicked the TV to MTV: the ending ceremony to a Britney Spears concert; he flicked back the channels and watched the afterbirth instead.

Before the first 'Moo' the intercom buzzed and he unlocked the entrance door, then quickly switched off the TV, popped in a CD – The Four Seasons – guzzled down the wine to batten down the nerves and chucked in an Orbit while he opened the front door to greet her.

Happy hour. She was a knockout. The little black number she wore – a tight Gucci dress with winking sequins on deepest satin – and the black suspenders that encased her delicious legs, finishing on desperately balanced high-heeled shoes, etched the image into every fibre of Dave's lust-filled mind. Her glossy, cocoa-coloured hair glided down to her bare shoulders setting off her hazel eyes – she was beautiful.

He kissed her on the cheek, thanked her for the wine, hung her coat on the brass closet hook and led her by the hand into the living room.

'Sit yourself down, Alison. What can I get you? Glass of chilled wine?' he politely asked.

'Whatever you're having. Something smells *divine*.' Her eyes spotted a book on the glass table *Impressionism* with about ten book marks slotted inside. This man's devotion was incredible.

Dave returned with two crystal-cut glasses and a bottle of chilled white wine. Alison was glancing through the marked pages.

'Some of my favourites, Alison.' He placed the wine down, sat beside her, and helped flick through to various marked pages. 'That one especially I love, it gives me chills of frosted exhilaration.' He pointed to a picture: *Woman Bathing in a Shallow Tub*, by Edgar Degas. 'Edgar was a *bloody* genius.' When Dave had looked at it not two hours before, for the first time in his life, he thought the brown pottery jug beside the tub was a massive pooh – Edgar was a sicko. 'It's cunningly sentimental and discreetly pornographic,' he stated, wishing that she would just put the damn book down – it was so frightfully boring.

Alison took a thimbleful-sip of wine. 'It's so exciting being in a new relationship, learning all each other's little quirks and such.' She paused. 'Not that I've been in many relationships, well, I can only count one true one and you know all about my nine-year stint with Thomas.' Another thimbleful. 'I was beginning to wonder if I would ever get over him.'

Dave, trying desperately not to gulp the wine, sipped it like snobby Alison. 'It's so painful breaking up. When I split up with Bridget, I became absorbed by depression.' He racked his brains to come up with more lies, and coughed. 'I rested a red rose on the pillow where her head used to lie, and I hoped and prayed every night she would return, until the rose wilted and finally died. And when I buried it in the garden, I knew,' and he looked at Alison, trying to squeeze out a tear, 'I bloody well knew that it was over. Six whole years of my life – gone.' Dave's head slumped forward and Alison's sympathetic arm came to his shoulder.

'I understand, Dave, fully.' And Alison really did. They were connecting on a higher level.

Their embrace was short-lived, spoiled by a thumping knock at the front door. Dave pulled away. 'Back in a sec.'

He opened the door, grinned. 'Hello.'

Leena shot him a smile, stepped in the entrance, flung the door shut behind her and smothered Dave with thickest red stolen-lipstick kisses all over his grinning face. Barging past, she clomped through to the living room, spotted Alison, magnified her smile, then turned around to face a lipstick-coated stunned Dave.

Her brown eyes sparkling, Leena untied her mac strap, and let the blue mac fall to the floorboards.

'Play it cool Dave. Can't believe English women are so loose.' . . . *Sod off Danny Zuko, this is damn serious.*

There before him stood Leena. Leena the thief: in only a red lacy bra and knickers. Red suspenders. Red stockings. Red high-heeled shoes. What a body!

Dave's mouth moved but nothing came out. What the hell was happening? Alison agreed, what the blinding hell was happening? Who was she?

Leena *could* speak and she did, 'You've been a bad bad boy, Dave, yet again, and I've come here to punish you.' Her seductive voice was both husky and alluring.

It was at times like this that Dave wished his brain wasn't half devoted to sex, then he might have been able to think of something to say; alas, he could only think of what he wanted to do – with Leena. His manhood rose to the occasion, and you could say this was a defining moment in Alison's life – nothing like this had ever happened to her before.

Leena moved in closer to Dave and continued, 'Sex, Pint, Football, Lies. You just keep upsetting Naina, don't you?' Closer still. 'You just use her. I'm not sucked in by you, pig Dave. You don't treat my friend like that.' And she whacked him round the face. 'I'm your slap-a-gram!' She turned to Alison. 'And you, you'd better ask him how many women he's slept with,' and she shouted the next bit, 'and I mean just this week!' She picked up her coat, bowed to the mesmerized audience, looked at Dave. 'Not a word to Naina, darling.' And she was gone.

Dave tried to laugh. 'I know what you're thinking, Alison: jealous, revengeful, bitter Bridget.'

She wasn't thinking that at all.

Outside, Leena giggled towards Pete's 4×4 Range Rover, climbed up, and sat next to Kate, who was already in stitches. The Range Rover rolled out of the car park, with all three bursting with laughter.

'What happened? Was she there? Tell me, Leena, tell me. Did he have his clothes on? Leena? Tell me,' Kate eagerly ordered.

Leena tried to calm herself. 'I think I've hurt my hand. I can't believe the adrenaline rush: it was better than stealing, way better.'

'Did Dave take it well?' Pete asked, feeling like a Judas.

Leena, as best she could, explained what had happened.

Even though Pete had been cajoled and roped into this little saga with threats of a sex ban by Kate, he still couldn't recognize the purpose of it all. Everyone knew what Dave was like, including Naina.

'Stop the car, Pete, you moron!' demanded Kate. He stopped. 'You still don't grasp it, do you?' Pete shook his head. 'Look, I hate Dave, Leena hates Dave, you love Dave, Naina loves Dave. Do you get it now?'

'Well, why doesn't she tell him? Hang on, I don't fucking love Dave, he's just my mate.' He paused. 'I still don't get it.'

Leena tried. 'Look, Pete, it's really simple. Even though we all agree we all hate Dave—'

'I don't,' interrupted Pete.

'Shut up, will you; Kevin Costner would have got it,' said Kate. 'Go on, Leena.'

Leena continued, 'We all hate Dave, except for Naina who is our best friend. So we are going to wreck all of his relationships until he realizes that Naina is the one. Alison was upsetting Naina. Simple. Get it now?'

Pete thought about it for a second. 'Why doesn't Naina just tell him? That's far simpler.'

Two long sighs from Kate and Leena. Kate spoke, 'If Naina tells him, then Dave will run off to Tenerife. You know he will.'

And Pete finally, sort of, nearly, not quite, got their strange women logic, and was sworn to secrecy not to tell Dave. Plus, Naina must never find out; she would die if she knew.

'And besides,' continued Kate. 'It's loads of fun. He deserves it, no matter what the outcome. You shouldn't treat women like he does. Pig!'

But as the 4×4 dropped Leena off outside her house, Pete thought to himself: if they were helping Naina

along, then he, as a good mate, would help Dave
along, it was only right.

Supper simmered as Alison boiled while Dave
marinated in lipstick. Admittedly, Leena's exhibition
was a good one, anyone could have seen that. But
with the good so often comes the bad. And the bad in
this case was: 'How the hell am I going to talk my way
out of this one?' He tried to think of a way that would
make Alison look the guilty party here, so she would
end up having to apologize to him and come begging
and crawling, desperate to receive Dave's forgiveness,
desperate to take all her clothes off and prove how
sorry she was that Leena had intruded on their private
moment and wrecked the evening. Then Dave realized
that this was the real world. He needed a blasphemy,
a few swear words, a few verbs and a massive lie.

'Jesus fucking Christ, Alison. I ordered a serenade-
a-gram not a slap-a-gram. You know? Violins, the
sweet song of a tenor's voice. This was supposed to be
so special and then they send me a slag.' He held his
face in his hands. 'I am so embarrassed.' He peered
through his fingers – was it working?

Alison pondered the explanation. 'She seemed to
know you, though. Why would she say all those
things about how many women you've slept with?
And who is Naina?'

Dave rose up, and dramatically stared at the
window. 'That's the point of a slap-a-gram, they
make things up, they try to ruin your life.' He sat
down again next to Alison. 'Look, we've got
something special here, can't you feel it? Or is it just
me?' She was about to answer, but he put his finger to

her lips. 'Shh, this needs to be said. I would be lying if I said Bridget didn't mean anything to me – she did – and when I lost her . . .' Dave stared into her hazel eyes as his 'upset face' emerged. 'I thought my soul had died. But it hadn't, Alison, it was only sleeping. You woke it up.' And he kissed her on the lips. Sorted! And just to prove how much he wanted his shag, Dave told her to wait there, rushed out of the flat, came back after five minutes, told her to close her eyes and two minutes later led her to the bedroom.

'You can open them now,' he said, and dimmed the bedroom lights.

There, resting on the plumped-up pillow, was a solitary yellow rose, thorny and wet.

He continued, 'My rose has come back.' And she nearly cried.

Where was the challenge in that, thought Dave; she'd believe fucking anything.

Chapter Thirty-eight

Dave flicked through the glossy pages of his *Private* porn magazine, resting his head on four duck-feathered pillows. She must be the prettiest Alison in the world, he thought, glancing over at her lying by his side. He flicked the pages harder, and bounced up and down on the bed. Finally the sleeping beauty awoke – not with a kiss from a Prince, but tsunami on the mattress. A two-second reality check, a rub of her eyes, a sharpening of her focus, and she recalled: another fabulous night with her gorgeous new boyfriend, Dave. Not only was he irresistible and genuinely shy, rich, sensitive and honest, but he knew how to please all of a woman – every square inch, it was almost enough to make you want to be fat.

Alison unplugged her arms from her sides, sat up and leaned in to kiss Mr Perfect. 'Morning. What's that you're reading?' she asked, admiring his chest muscles.

Here goes, thought Dave. 'Uhm, it's *Private*,' he replied, eyes fixed to the magazine.

The word 'private' is a funny old word. To men it means: private. To women, it tends to mean: I own you, tell me, you no longer have any confidentiality.

Alison snatched the magazine. 'No secrets, Dave, remember.' She looked at the two-page spread of a woman bending over.

Synchronized facial expressions now took place: Dave's lifted to a face-breaker of a smile, while Alison's dropped like a face without a parachute. Page after page of naked women. Horror struck her face, surely there was an explanation: well? Dave still grinned as Alison threw the magazine across the room in disgust. 'What do you need that dirt for?'

He scampered out of bed, strode over to the magazine which had landed like a small tent, picked it up and opened it to 'Tania' centre spread, and held it up in full view. 'Look at her, and now look at you. No comparison, hey?' And he flung it to her, but Alison had a good backhand and the dirty filth flew diagonally back across the room. 'Ally, I can't put up with your fucking snobbiness any more; you're driving me nuts.'

Snivelling now. 'If you wanted to finish with me, you could have been man enough to admit it, rather than humiliate me with that.' She pointed to the magazine.

'Well, excussssse me for being original.'

Plenty of times Dave had sat and watched women in a frenzy, packing their stuff, cursing him under their breath, and always always always, they forget something, come back a minute later, then say something like: 'You may have looks and money, but you are a NOTHING.'

And Alison slammed the front door and left. The fact that the blue-varnished door was still on its initial set of hinges was a testament to the quality of the building – or builders. Dave reminded himself: must e-mail Ronseal and congratulate. It does exactly what it says on the can – withstands a woman's scorn.

Dave sighed with relief. She was gone. He tucked into breakfast – Rusks. When he was about six, he would equip himself with an empty Farley's Rusk packet under each foot and slide down the hall carpet as if they were skis. Nowadays, he just ate the contents, as he was doing now, sitting there on his blue sofa, listening to Coolio while he munched his way through baby biscuit number three. The protein content was fairly high, the carbs were good, fat was minimal and they tasted superb. What better way to end a relationship and still keep hold of your six-pack?

'OOzing,' said Pete as he entered Dave's flat.

'OOzing,' replied Dave, offering Pete some of his joint.

'Bit early, Dave, but sod it, cheers.' And Pete sat down, puffing like a trooper.

Cold refreshing Carlsberg was dished up, together with a bowl of mini Easter eggs, and a packet of pickled onion Monster Munch each.

Pete could never fathom the tidiness of Dave's flat. It was so unlivable. How could a man relax without the firm knowledge that there was at least one pair of smelly socks on show, a pair of washed underpants hanging off the radiator and at least thirty magazines strewn across the floor? It was unnatural.

'How's Kate?' Dave asked.

'Fine, talks too much though, bit of a handful.' He swigged the can. 'It's wedding talk nonstop at the moment. What with Jingle and Melody, and then there's Naina's.' He looked at Dave. 'I hope she don't go getting any ideas, 'cos I'm off to Tenerife if she does.'

Dave laughed. 'I can't believe Jingle's getting married. Poor cow.'

Pete wanted to get back on to Naina talk – his duty. 'Two months and Naina will be married, you'll miss her.'

Dave lit a fag in the other hand to his joint. 'She just doesn't stop crying these days, I can't say a thing right. The other day, right, we were having this healthy discussion about me shagging Jackie in that old barn off Cliff Avenue, you know the one? Where we used to drink cider?' Pete nodded. 'She suddenly asked me if there was ever a woman that I haven't lied to just to get into bed. I said of course not, and she ran off crying. Women, hey.'

Pete nodded his head. 'You're a wanker, Dave. Maybe she was hoping that you might have the sense to say there was one, and it's you, Naina.' He looked for a facial expression to indicate that Dave had understood. He didn't get one.

'What are you on, mate? I haven't shagged her for two months, she won't let me. She said, "I'm not sharing you with every other woman in MK." Her loss, hey, mate. Good stuff this, hey?' And Dave slouched back on the sofa, breathing a huge cloud into the air above. 'But I will miss her badly though, she's one of a kind.'

Pete thought back. Dave hadn't changed much since Hillthorpe School. He was reminded of the time in sex education, when the teacher had informed the class that sperm only has to travel a few inches to get to the woman's eggs. Dave, who was quite serious at the time, had stood up and said, 'Miss, what if she lives a few miles away? Does it catch a bus?' He was told to stand outside the classroom, and Pete could remember seeing him through the small glass window mouthing the word 'frigid'. He hadn't changed much. Sex was always getting him in trouble.

Dave continued, 'She shouldn't be marrying this Ashok. I wish I could just get it in her head, I have tried.' He passed the spliff across.

'Kate's tried as well. But, mate, maybe if she finds the right bloke, then she might pull out of it, that's what I think,' said Pete, clinging on to the joint, which Dave was trying to steal off him already – he'd only had one puff. 'Anyway, I shouldn't be saying this, I swore to Kate that I wouldn't say, but I'll tell you in a roundabout way, so I won't be breaking my promise.' Dave looked interested. 'There's this one woman, not mentioning any names, she's beautiful, Indian, her name ends in NA, she's one of Kate's best friends, you know her well, she's head over hills in love with you, mate. So wake up and sort it out. And don't let her go.'

Dave stood up and paced the room, flipped on a Puff Daddy CD. 'I bloody knew it; that explains everything.'

Pete was very pleased with himself. 'So, I didn't tell

you. I kept my promise. You thought about this all by—'

Dave interrupted, 'Say no more, Pete, say no more. This is perfect, un-fucking-believable.' And he came up to Pete and handed him the joint. 'I should have known, the way she looks at me sometimes. I can't believe how thick I am.'

'Yeah, mate, right under your nose and you, Mr Knows-women, couldn't even see it.'

As Pete rambled on about the Internet, Dave sat, Nikes on the glass table, with a smile that filled the room. It all made sense now. Leena the thief, in her frustration, had come round last night, dressed as heaven itself. Oh thank you, Lord; you do work in mysterious ways. I can't wait to work some mysterious ways myself – on Leena.

Chapter Thirty-nine

'Naina, my Indian beauty was right under my nose, I wish you had told me. Can you pop round before you go to work? I hope you're all right, Dave . . . I could kiss you all over.'

Naina listened to the phone message one more time outside the entrance to Dave's flat. Her heart was like an Aero bar, all blistered up with vacuums of bubbles. Big juicy bubbles of worry. Was this what she really wanted? Did she really want Dave now that she could have him?

'Go away, Mr Taxi driver', thought Naina, she wanted to check out her reflection in the entrance-door window. Finally he put down his *Sun* newspaper, threw out his fag stub and took off to his next call. She had made a special effort, and also taken the whole day off work, and she looked casually beautiful in black leather trousers, tight white fitted T-shirt, small black jacket and black chunky boots. A minute later she was standing on the living-room pine floorboards waiting for Dave to have a shower.

Moments passed and her mind knew of only one antidote to steady her nerves – food. She wandered into the kitchen to explore the silver Smeg fridge: surprise surprise, bacon, tomato, Utterly Butterly, and one Florelli's boxed apple pie, inviting and whole. She'd missed the taste of 'once tasted never forgotten' Florelli's apple pies. She brought out the cardboard box to the living room, sat down on the blue sofa and, with a fork, applied the antidote, wonderful mouthful by wonderful mouthful.

Dave's shower-singing voice could be heard – 'The Tide is High' by, she thought, Blondie. She hated to say it, and maybe it was because of the nerves again, but Dave carried the tune rather well.

Half a pie later, he was out of the shower and standing in front of her, generous smile, dripping wet hair, and that's about it – he had no clothes on, except a half-damp white towel – in his hand. Her nerves melted away: he was truly gorgeous, sumptuous, ravishing. She could have fucked him right there and then.

'You look fucking beautiful, Naina. Any chance of a shag?' he said, drying his muscular thighs.

'Depends.' The reply came out and Naina held on to the 's' like the noise of a low-powered over-used vibrator.

Suddenly drying wasn't important. He looked up, half bent over. 'Depends on what?' he threw in quickly, before she changed her mind.

'You know.'

'And you promise you won't go all moralistic on me

if I shag you first, then shag Leena later?' And Dave chuckled; promise, eastern promise.

Whatever Naina had been expecting Dave to say, it was not that.

'And what makes you think that Leena wants *you*?!' She stood and, squared up to him. 'She can't stand you. Are you trying to wind me up?' she screamed.

Easy now, easy, woe woe woe, woman on hormonal emergency ejection, stand clear. Dave took a step back and guarded himself with the towel. 'If she hates me that much, tell me why she stripped off for me last night,' he laughed. 'Gorgeous, she was unfuck—'

Dave's comment was cut off like a guillotine as Naina threw the apple pie; he ducked, it hit Ben Hur's chariot on the wall. He noticed that the fork was still in her hand. She shouted, 'Why are you doing this to me?' Then broke into a cry, 'Why are you being so cruel?' Dropping the fork on to the wooden floorboards, she picked up her jacket and rushed to the front door.

Dave ran across and grabbed her by the arm. 'What the fuck is going on?' His face was covered in confusion. 'Naina,' his voice was soothing as he hugged her as tight as he could. Why was his best mate having a nervous breakdown? 'Is it Ash-cock?'

Naina pulled away, repelled by the idiocy of the man. 'No, it's not bloody *Ashok*. It's you . . . *you* . . . you.' And each 'you' was punctuated with a long fingernail in bright cherry-red, prodding at Dave's tautly muscled chest. 'And will you get rid of that hard-on?'

He wrapped the towel round his waist, and tried hard to think of Maggie the traffic warden in a red G-string, bending over.

Naina resumed her tearful outburst, fumbling around her deserted mind, ignoring the Post-it note stuck on the inside of her head – 'Never tell Dave' – and betrayed her sense and reason. Her voice was raised, angry, and direct: 'I'm not particularly proud of this. In fact I'm quite ashamed of it, Dave. But, the truth is . . . the truth is, and don't you dare freak out, the truth is, Dave . . . the truth is . . . don't freak out.' And she whispered the next bit: 'The shit was you, always has been you, I love you.'

'Sounds like she wants to have a baby, Dave. I'm outta here.' Danny Zuko disappeared and Dave told him to get back and help him out – the double-dealing T-bird. Where the hell was his passport?

Get a grip, Dave, he thought, get a grip, act cool. He walked to the sofa. 'You can't . . . you can't . . .' He slumped.

'Love you?' She sat up close on the sofa.

'You can't, I'm immune to love. Simon Le Bon was wrong. Love can't conquer all, it can't conquer me!' he stated, rinsing his lungs with a hefty portion of smoke. 'I'm *fucking* immune.' Then he turned to Naina. 'What d'you want me to say? I can't love you, I just can't. I'm a wanker, I'm a bastard, you deserve much better than me.' And he put his arm round her and kissed her on the cheek. 'Sorry, I'm sorry.'

'I know, I just wanted you to know.' Naina stood up. 'Don't take this the wrong way, I'm glad I met you, you're one of a kind, but I can't see you again.' And like melting snow, Naina's tears fell. 'Under all this, you're a really nice bloke, a diamond geezer. Find yourself a woman and settle down. You never know, you might like it.' An achy lump in her throat distorted her quavering voice. He stood up and hugged her. 'You're screwing my mind up, and I can't marry Ashok with a screwed-up mind, it's going to be hard enough anyway, so I want to say goodbye now.'

Dave's bare chest was peppered with Naina's tears. 'Don't marry Ashok.' He rubbed her neck, comfortingly.

'I've got to marry him. You should know by now, I'm a very traditional Indian girl.'

And if Cupid wasn't all drugged up with weed that day, he might have fired the arrow straight. But as it was, he missed, and he missed by a long way. Dave held Naina close.

He lifted up her teary head, and stared straight into her brown eyes. 'I hope it works out with you and Ashok. If there's anything you ever need, then you know where I am – even if it's just to slap me.' He paused. 'I'm going to miss you, Naina.' And they cuddled for a while, and then Naina left Dave with nothing but a fake smile. But there was nothing fake about the loss he now felt. It was miserable.

Chapter Forty

A cool June melted into a warm July, which became a sweltering August. Six weeks had passed. Only two weeks to go to Jingle's and Melody's wedding, and one week to Naina's and Ashok's.

Naina stepped out of the black taxi, dressed in a white vest, black short skirt and mules. The taxi driver stank of BO and it was a relief to get out. She tied back her hair, and headed up the short path to Froggy's house, noticing the Flymo out on the side with the orange cable draped from the front-room window. She lifted her shades on to her hair and knocked, breathing in the sweet smell of just-cut grass.

A voice. 'He's not in.' And Naina turned round to see Froggy lying in the bushes with a can of lager in his hand, no top on, and what looked like a spliff in the other hand – he hadn't even raised his head to see who was knocking.

She ambled over and kicked him gently to open his eyes. 'Wake up.'

The sun was a scorcher, 90 degrees, no breeze; just the stubborn heat from the midday sunshine. They trudged inside, Froggy nearly tripping over the cable, and in the kitchen he poured her a Carlsberg. The place was a tip: empty ready-cooked-meal plastic cartons on the side, overflowing bin, washing-up, dirty clothes on the floor and the wonderful smell of damp. A clue to its origin was a pair of denim jeans hanging half out of the washing machine with mildew on one leg. Sandra used to keep a tidy ship. Sandra was gone and her mother now had the cleanest house in Bucks.

As Naina let the chilled lager bite the back of her throat, Froggy made a daring attempt to tidy up.

'Don't bother, Froggy, I'm not here to view your house. So, how have you been?'

He dropped the bin liner. 'Oh, so so, not too bad, actually shit. What about you? Getting ready for your big day?'

'Yeah, only one week, until prison.'

Froggy laughed. 'So how's Dave? Still being a wanker?' He leaned back against the kitchen cupboard.

'I haven't seen him for about six weeks. He's what I'm here about actually.'

'Oh?'

They moved into the living room and sat on the orange sofa. Empty picture hooks remained where once musical pictures had hung, proving that once a woman leaves, a woman's touch soon follows.

Naina began, 'I know what Dave did was really

bad, but you two were once really good friends.'
Froggy listened. 'And he didn't send me here and I
don't want him to know I came round either, but
don't throw your friendship away. I'm not saying
forget it, but give him a chance. The friends you make
at school, if you manage to keep them like you lot did,
you never make again. Life won't allow it.' Naina
took a sip.

Froggy lit a fag, then stubbed it out. 'I quit.' Then
re-lit it. 'Fuck it, I just started again. Look, Naina, he
shit on me big time. Believe it or not, I used to look up
to him and trusted him totally. That was what our
friendship was based on – trust.' He blew out the
smoke, enjoying the rekindling of his tobacco
relationship.

'It just seems a shame, that's all. You don't want to
hear this, but he would talk to me for hours about how
shitty he had been, and this was way before you found
out.' Froggy's eyebrows moved very slightly. Naina
continued, 'I know there are three things he regrets in
his life. He regrets letting Grandma's dog out.'

Froggy laughed, he'd heard that one before. 'Go on,
and the other two.'

'Well, I know he regrets undoing the bolts on the
primary-school slide.'

Froggy laughed again, he'd heard that one before –
and seen the result.

'I know he regrets *porking* Sandra.' And this time
they both laughed. 'Look, I've sat up with him late
some nights, him going on about how much of a
bastard he's been to you. And I know he'll never do it
to you again. He *has* learnt, Froggy.' And Naina
finished her lager.

Froggy thought as best as a doped-up Froggy could. 'Thanks, Naina, you came here in a taxi just to tell me that; you're a top woman, you know that?'

Naina stood. 'Well, if you do decide to talk to him, keep him out of trouble. I'd better go, Leena's expecting me.'

Froggy jumped up. 'I'll give you a lift. You know, Dave's going to have a fourth regret, Naina.' He gave her a caring look. 'Letting *you* go, and I think he's going to regret that one the most.'

Naina waited for her heart to catch up the missed beat, then, 'Don't tell him I came here. Thanks for the lift, but Leena's only fifteen minutes away.' And she pecked him goodbye on the cheek.

Shortly afterwards, two cans of lager later, Froggy picked up the cordless phone.

'OOzing,' he shouted at the top of his voice, 'OOzing OOzing, mate.'

'I beg your pardon. Who's this?'

'Sorry, wrong number.' And Froggy wished he had an audience then, so he could laugh with them. After a few minutes laughing on his own, he tried again. This time he was lucky.

'OOzing OOzing, mate,' Froggy shouted.

'OOzing OOzing, mate, hang on a second.' Dave turned to beautiful leggy Helen. 'Off off OFF! *Get off me*, this is important.' A few moments later. 'Sorry about that, Froggy, she just couldn't keep her hands off me.'

Froggy laughed. 'Dave, you'll never change. *Thank God*.'

Chapter Forty-one

If you have to keep up with what's in and what's out, then there's no use looking in your wardrobe in despair and saying 'there's nothing to wear' because let's face it, there never will be.

'This is unbearable, Naina,' Kate remarked in disgust, holding up a designer number – £350 worth of satin – and threw it in the heap that was now developing on Naina's bed.

'Kate, it's only a nightclub, not the Queen's ump par par party,' Naina replied, standing directly behind Kate, watching with perturbed interest at her man-handling of her expensive items.

Sonia looked on with a quizzical expression – just wear black, it's so easy – and continued typing her short story entitled *The Tooth Devil*, a story for children, which she was hoping to get published, about a Devil who comes to children on the eve of their birthday and extracts all their teeth. Happy birthday, little kiddies.

Kate silenced her critics, she'd found the ultimate bash trash: a tight little black all-over-beaded halter-neck dress with no back, no length, no guesses. No guesses as to what red-blooded males would like to do with a woman who could carry a dress like that, let alone wear a dress like that.

Sonia muttered under her breath, 'Would Ashok allow you to wear a floozy dress like that?' And she mumbled louder, 'I don't think so.'

Kate threw a large red velvet cushion at her. 'Put some colour in your life, Sonia.' And it hit her in the face. 'She's got six days to life shutdown. That gives her five days solid to party with Leena and me; it's none of Ashok's business.'

And life shutdown meant: Miss to Mrs – floozy to sari – English Naina to Indian Naina – chips to chapatties – single bed to double bed. When the brakes on Naina's party life would be applied with an emergency stop, sending her flying through the windscreen of life into an Indian temple of rules and regulations. Where the Indian spirit of Guru Nanak would say, 'Naina, if you had worn an Indian seat belt and not drunk booze, partied, smoked pot and had sex, then you wouldn't have landed with such a crash.' Cramming in five days of parties until her wedding day on Sunday seemed like a good idea to help her forget the future that hadn't even happened yet. The trashy dress was just the start.

It was a hazy cloudless evening of sultry heat. Open windows, lazy cats, over-the-fence chats, heated rows with drunken husbands cooling themselves down with one too many lagers.

Kate's bluey-purple Corsa came to a halt outside

Pete's place in Willen Park. She wrenched up the handbrake – oh, how she loved that sound – and popped a glance at Naina, handing her the quarter bottle of whisky.

'Have a gulp of that, I'll only be a minute.' Kate opened the car door. 'Actually you may as well come in, you know what Pete's like, too much chat and not enough action.'

Naina swigged a quarter of the quarter and followed Kate up the front path. On Pete's front door was a varnished wooden sign which read 'Vortex', with an arrow pointing to the letter box, and a sea-grass welcome mat below with 'Buffalo New York' printed on it, ordered from the Internet.

Kate never knocked with a polite 'Rat a tat tat'; it was always 'Crash bang wallop', and Pete, rarely ever more than a second away from the door, answered, lager in hand, fag in mouth, *Waterworld* T-shirt, and a casual smile. His eyes flitted to Kate's, then stared at Naina until kicked by Kate's hoof. Naina was looking stunning tonight; Kate had done wonders. What with her loosely curled, highlighted long hair, 'hold-me-back-I'm-coming-through' dress, long, looong, bare willowy-toned legs, six-inch-heeled strappy black sandals: this was one thing you couldn't order on the Internet.

Kate removed Pete's fag, kissed him, then removed Pete's gawp. 'Did I leave my purse here last night?' She thoughtfully smoked his ciggie, and barged in, dragging Naina by the hand.

'Come in,' said Pete, closing the door. 'Do come in.'

Pete's home-built patio consisted of twelve square concrete nonslip pink slabs plonked on the lawn. His patio table was three stacked car tyres with a plank of wood on top, and his chairs were beer crates. It had taken Pete and Dave a whole week to build, it was crap. They had even argued over the colour of the beer crates – orange or brown. And they couldn't use the crates as chairs until they had drunk the beer. They were sitting on them after only two days – pissed as newts.

Conifer trees roamed skywards on either side of the garden, blocking out the neighbours and unfortunately also blocking out the evening sun. Sliding open the patio door, Kate stepped into the shade and on to the wobbling pink slabs.

Through a gap in the conifer trees, Dave was staring at next door's washing line, his head encrusted with furry pines. A marked expression of disgust as he viewed a medieval version of Hot-pants: leggings. He heard the patio door slide shut behind him. 'You've got animals living next door, mate, fucking animals.' Then he heard the expressive sound of stilettos on concrete and his instinctive Dave smile arrived – *women* were here. His head swung round, almost whiplashing his brain and knocking him sideways. It was like turning over an ace and getting a royal flush. Naina was the last person he had expected to see and for once he was lost for words – even an incey wincey swear word.

'Dances like a butterfly, stings like a bee, the world's greatest emotion is . . .' Love. And you can do the Ali shuffle with it as much as you like, but when the knockout blow comes, it leaves you dazed and gasping. Naina needed to compose herself for a second: she hadn't been expecting this either. It had been six weeks since she'd last seen him, and she couldn't handle another goodbye – she'd already thrown the towel in once.

Dave took a ten-second count while the surroundings blended to only Naina, then came forward and kissed her on the cheek. Her mix of wondrous smells: Obsession, shampoo, lotions, and a touch of whisky – bliss. He'd thought he'd never smell her again.

'How have you been?' he asked. Pete and Kate nudged each other, pleased at their romantic gamble.

'Fine. You?' answered in an icy tone, eye contact avoided.

'I've missed you.' Dave stared at Naina's lowered eyelids.

Kate barged in, 'Anyway, me and Pete are going down the pub, there's wine in the fridge, so . . .'

Naina gave Kate a 'don't leave me' look. 'But I thought we're going to The Sanctuary.' Her voice was feeble and desperate. She could be forgiven for not realizing quite what was going on, under the circumstances, as she watched Kate and Pete leave, sliding the door behind them and locking her in the garden. Locking her in an emotional wilderness.

'I was going to call you loads of times, but . . . I didn't,' Dave said, pulling out an orange crate for Naina to perch her bottom on.

Naina smiled.

He sat down opposite her in his summer wear: tight cerulean blue Valentino T-shirt, with cut-off sleeves, black shorts, Nikes, Davidoff and tan. If Orwell was right and the thought police really existed then even they would have had trouble deciphering what was going through Dave's mind right then. 'I'm extending the gym . . . Steve's arms are too big.'

Naina laughed and finally looked up. 'What have you been up to then? Keep it clean.'

'Well, nothing then.' He lit a fag. 'Seriously. Sunbathing, working, nothing really. What about you?'

'Left my job on Friday . . .' Naina stood up. 'Sorry, I can't do this.'

When two friends talk, being polite is just the garnish. At the moment the garden was like one massive salad; Dave was afraid to say anything that could upset Naina and Naina was afraid to say . . . anything. And you can't get full-up on salad.

'Naina, I've got you a wedding present. I was going to give it to Kate to pass on, but I would rather give it to you personally.'

'You shouldn't have.' She paused. 'Really, you shouldn't have.' She thumbed through some thoughts. 'Best give it to Kate, thanks anyway.'

'Yeah, I thought you might say that.' Dave threw the end of his fag across the lawn. Slightly pissed off. 'Why has it got to this stage? I hate being fucking civil.'

Naina took a swig of his lager. 'Look, you'll never understand, because you're immune to love. Pathetic.' Naina, never really good with hand gestures, began waving her arms about. 'You don't know what it feels like to love someone, and day in day out all they do is give you a breakdown of what they've been doing with numerous other women. It's hard to listen to.' Another swig. 'It's fucking hard. And I know it's not your fault, it's my problem.'

Dave looked around in vain for someone to tell, 'Don't be so nosy,' but no one was listening, it was just the two of them, on their own. 'Do you know what it feels like for me to let you go and marry some bloke that you don't want, hey? Let him put his hands over you, let him undo your buttons, let him touch you all over.'

'What do you care?' Naina said to the bushes, refusing to look in his blue eyes.

Dave shouted, 'Because I fucking do care. I fucking care that I'm never going to see you again. I fucking care that he might treat you like shit. I fucking care that you loved me and I let you go.' He stopped, sat back down, lit another fag. 'But if you think I'm going to stand here and make a fool of myself by saying I love you, then you can think again.'

Naina spoke, 'Non-commitment is for insecure people. I suggest you go and read through the pages of what you've written about me in your yellow Handy Honeys book, Dave.' She walked to the patio door, turned back round. 'Once Ashok puts that ring on my finger, then nothing is going to separate us. I'm his one hundred per cent.' And Naina left Dave catching flies in his open mouth, still shocked that nosy Naina had read his yellow bible.

Daylight was spilling into dusk, as Pete and Kate returned from the Ship Ashore pub to an all-alone, pissed Dave in the garden singing a Rolling Stones song at the top of his voice.

'Where's Naina, Dave?' Kate asked, worried and disappointed that she hadn't found them in bed together.

Dave threw down Pete's strimmer, which he'd been using as a microphone. 'Naina? You want to know where Naina is . . . Naina is in Ashok's cold unbeating heart. She's one hundred per cent his. She didn't even leave a measly 1 per cent for me, the one she's meant to love.'

'Dave, did you tell her how you feel about her?' Pete asked, picking the strimmer out of the trees.

'She looked too,' and he stretched his head up so all the neighbours could hear, 'she looked too fucking gorgeous, and I couldn't even tell her. Ashok is a lucky man. *The wanker.*' And Dave fell over the crate. 'He stole her from me. She's my best mate. The best woman in the world. Why me, Lord? Why me?'

Pete and Kate nodded their heads in rhythm, helped him to his Nikes, marched him inside like puppet masters, walked him to the sofa, and sat him down.

Dave continued when really he shouldn't have, 'You know, well, actually you don't know, she's the only woman in the world that made me lose my erection because I was too nervous to fuck her.'

Kate knew. Pete's eyebrows raised – it had been noted.

Pete brought Dave a large Yogi Bear blanket, whipped off his Nikes, put his head on a cushion and turned out the light. He was about to be a true friend and tuck him in when – pop – Dave farted. Goodnight! And both Kate and Pete legged it up the stairs, giggling.

Naina kept the sleep at bay. A lamplight beside her bed shone down on memories of simpler times as she leafed through her photograph albums. She paused at a picture of Leena, Kate and herself on a school trip to Paris, standing by the Arc de Triomphe: it had been an excellent day of laughter, ice cream and sun. They were eleven years old. Kate loved cacti plants and butterflies, Leena loved angels and fairies, and Naina, she loved Rune-stones and Tarot cards. A fragment of times gone past, never to be retrieved, never to be the same again. Memories of bonding, of a friendship that rose above the fairies, runes and cacti, and tied itself together in something far stronger. And a tear rolled down Naina's cheek and dropped on to the photograph. She didn't want to be separated from them.

Naina placed the photo back in the laminated album, ignoring a picture of Dave and her picking the lion's nose in Trafalgar Square. How he had managed to talk her into shoving her hand up its nostril she'd never know. Then she realized, she wasn't ignoring the photo at all. The opposite, in fact. She pulled it out, and looked down to his good-looking face for a moment. Then she tore up the colour photo and chucked it in the woven-straw bin beside her bed. They do call them waste bins. *And* what a waste.

Chapter Forty-two

Summer seemed to just get hotter. Instead of the earth going round the sun, it seemed to be heading straight for it. Unfortunately one of the requirements for hotter weather was more alcohol. And just like the earth, instead of Dave going round the pub – avoiding it – he was heading straight for it, being pulled in by the gravity of cold refreshing pints of Stella. Froggy's text message was simple: *Windmill pub at twelve, let's get pissed, OOzing.*

After leaving Pete and Kate a scruffy note – 'Thanks for putting me up. By the way, heard you shagging last night, didn't last long. Felt a bit sorry for the both of you really. Seriously though, thanks a dozen' – he sped home, picked up his delivered *Woman* and *Woman's Own* off the mat, tucked into a challenging breakfast of Rusks, had a shower, a couple of aspirins for his hangover, and sat on his blue sofa with a blue towel round his waist, reading over the blue notes about Naina in his Handy Honeys book. Scribbled notes of what he would like to do with her were intertwined with notes of how much he liked her. It was almost a full-blown confession, and he threw it across the room in disgust. And the one comment that cleared his hangover completely was: 'when I made love to Naina'. Normally it would be 'when I porked' or 'when I shagged'. How many pints of booze had he drunk that evening to actually think, let alone write, the word 'love'? He didn't want to go down that road of mediocrity – only average men fell in the trap of love – real men porked. Simple.

Dave parked his black BMW next to Froggy's grey BT van. The gravel car park led precariously close to the expanse of Eleanor lake, which virtually surrounded the Windmill pub and restaurant. Apparently the windmill sails had stopped turning on 16 December 1901, and every year ever since, they used the same old publicity stunt to get people into the diner at Christmas: 'Will this year be the year the sails start to turn again?' Yeah right, thought Dave, like no one knows the sodding thing was only built twenty-five years ago, and the sails were just decoration.

Dave met up with Froggy at a shaded wooden table overlooking the lake. Two pints of Stella were already waiting for him with a packet of Planters peanuts, and pork scratchings.

'OOzing.'

'OOzing,' Froggy replied, head all gelled and spiked up, wearing shades, pale indigo short-sleeved shirt and a ferocious smile. 'Mate, this place is crawling with summer muff.' Froggy sparked a fag, tossed Dave the lighter. 'I think I've found the sweet spot of Bucks.' Dave lit a fag. 'And, mate, in a way, and this ain't the drink talking' – he pointed to the two empty pint glasses before him – 'but you did me a big favour getting rid of that slag. It will be just like the old days, you and me on bush patrol.'

Dave laughed, removed his Armani shades and, eyes squinting, clocked the various women at the various tables. Froggy was right, this place was bush country. Dave turned back to Froggy who was gulping like a man in the desert. 'So, you're not working today, Frog?'

'Fuck work, I'm sick. Those twats in Mursfelley village can do without their phone line for another week. Bloody hill-billies.' He belched.

Dave sipped his drink, and got to the point quickly. 'So how did you know when you loved Sandra?'

Froggy pondered. 'When I went past this woman in Tesco's and she was wearing the same perfume as her and I thought, *cheeky* bitch, that's Sandra's perfume.'

But nearly every woman in Bucks wears Exclamation Mark!, thought Dave. No, this was not about perfume. He looked out at the tranquil lake, watching rubber-clad windsurfers trying to catch what little wind was out there, performing all manner of twists and turns with their bodies until the momentum of their boards and the contortions of their muscles could take no more and they plopped into the water, only to try again five minutes later. It wasn't much of a spectator sport; if only there were a few ravenous sharks about. Dave looked back to Froggy who was nodding his head.

'What?' Dave enquired.

'I can't believe you, mate. Did you not see her? She was only two feet away.'

Dave was somewhere else: '*Once Ashok puts that ring on my finger, then nothing is going to separate us. I'm his one hundred per cent . . . I'm his one hundred per cent.*' Then an unwelcome vision: Ashok on the bed with Naina. Pulling her long soft hair to one side and kissing her neck, then pulling off her knickers and . . .

Dave stood up. 'I'm not going to let another man fuck her, Froggy, I can't!' His voice echoed across the water. 'She loves me, mate, she loves me.' And then Dave felt stupid, put his shades back on, covered his head with his hand and sat down again.

Froggy watched Dave light a fag. 'Do you love her, though? Or is this because you don't want anyone else to have her? I know you, Dave, this is all about your ego, nothing more.' Froggy was sure.

'I saw Naina yesterday, and it was *boom*, I felt something. And today I filled the car up with petrol and normally my eyes are everywhere, you know, checking out pump 1, pump 2, pump 3, pump 4, for a beautiful woman, but all I could think about was Naina. It's unhealthy.' Dave paused, inhaled his smoke. 'I love her, Froggy, I'm so sorry, it caught me.' And Dave looked away ashamed – his immunity all gone.

Three loud quacking ducks stopped by their table and Dave threw down some pork scratchings.

'They don't eat pork scratchings, mate, they eat bread,' said Froggy.

'What, are you a duckologist? When was the last time you read a duck's menu, you twat?' And the ducks ate the scratchings and Dave smiled. Sorted!

Froggy carried on regardless, 'I'm going to be a bit truthful here, mate, and don't take this all wrong, but Naina is far too good for you.'

'I know.' Dave stared at Froggy. 'Maybe I should just let her go. If I tell her, you know, how I feel, and if she decides to pull out of the wedding, then she loses her family. I can't do that to her.'

This was a bit heavy for Froggy, but he tried nevertheless. Dave really needed Matt at a time like this.

'Do you think you'll let her down?' Froggy refrained from laughing, of course Dave would let her down. 'Well? Once you've got Naina for two months, days, or even hours with you, and a stunning woman smiles at you, then what? No, you're right, you wouldn't be able to say no and you can't screw Naina's life up. Let her go, accept defeat—'

Dave interrupted, 'Excuse me, Froggy, but can I get a word in here?'

'Go ahead.'

Dave smiled. 'I love her, Froggy, and I'm not going to let her down, no matter what. I'll tell you why . . . you don't hurt the one you love.' Dave lit up two fags and smoked them both, while he illuminated Froggy with his words. 'I get women telling me how much they love their boyfriends or husbands, and next thing I know they're sucking on my cock, and I think: "stray dog on lower deck". Honestly, mate, people throw that word round like it's a Frisbee; at least when I finally said it, I meant it.'

Froggy took stock. Dave was actually making sense. Sandra had said she loved him countless times, when she wanted a new dress, when she wanted a new kettle, for example. But if she had really loved him, then she wouldn't have done the nasty and cheated with Dave. Dave had a good point – unfortunately.

'Frog, I'm gonna do it, I'm going to tell her.' He stood. 'I'll catch you later, mate, and thanks.' He took in a huge gulp of tobacco, as if it was his last, and threw the half-finished fag in the empty life-jacket box.

Froggy watched with an air of camaraderie: 'I hope he gets what he wants,' he murmured to himself, and then got angry at the ducks for not taking his pork scratchings. What had Dave got that he hadn't? Soon afterwards, while he sat there in solitude, a beautiful brunette sat down beside him on the long wooden bench. She smiled at him and then taught him how to dunk pork scratchings in beer so the ducks *would* eat it. And Froggy all of a sudden knew that with Dave it was all about tricks. It had nothing to do with Dave's good looks and perfect blue eyes and unbelievable body and money and car and posh flat, one liners etc. etc. Froggy grinned; the grin didn't last long . . .

'That gorgeous bloke that you were sitting with, is he married?'

Froggy stood up, smiled. 'He's in love.' And walked off thinking, 'That's my mate Dave, the lucky lucky *lucky* bastard.'

The lucky bastard paced up and down his flat floor, his nerves undone and scattered all over. Nothing compared to this feeling, this strange lonely feeling. All he wanted was Naina. And this want was all-consuming, something that ran rampant and knocked over all the solid rules he had applied to his life up until now. For fuck's sake, he was about to ask the only woman he had ever fallen in love with, to drop her wedding and move in with him. Oh fate, how you have teased me all my life and finally I see where you are coming from. This was meant to be. And he just wanted to hold Naina, be with her and who knows maybe even go to Tenerife with her. Naina was his soulmate and he knew it, as only a soulmate can.

A mile of walking later, here goes, he dialled her mobile, and she answered almost immediately.

'Naina, it's Dave, how are you?'

A long silence, then, 'Same as yesterday. You?'

'Naina, I love you, I love you so much,' Dave said, and meant it wholly.

'I know you love me, Dave, but you're too late, I knew you would be.' Naina's voice was masking nothing, no disappointment, no excitement, just a voice.

'What d'you mean, I'm too late? Didn't you hear? I love you, I love you. Is someone listening in? I love you.'

Another silence. 'No, no one's listening but me, and no one's really caring either. Thing is, Dave, if you were here in person I would give you a little red rosette for achievement, for finally admitting that you are allowed to love.'

Dave looked round the room, this was an unfair fight. 'Naina, can we meet? You're really confusing me here. I thought you'd be delighted. I love you, you love me, what's the problem?' Dave sounded like the women used to sound to him – desperate. 'Is this because I didn't let you christen the car? I'll get another one, a better one, a better model, you can do me in that, front, back, anywhere, Naina . . . Naina . . .'

'I'm still here, Dave; it's nothing to do with the car, but it's nice of you to offer. The fact is, I'm getting married on Sunday, to Ashok, and I don't want you.' The line went dead.

The mobile became nothing more than a piece of useless plastic, metal and silicon chips, as it fell to pieces when Dave threw it across the room. But the act of violence didn't make him feel any better. He wanted to destroy something more substantial than a mere phone. And then he sat down and realized – he already had.

Why had he thought he could have the best of all worlds? Naina, he had known all along, deep down, was the only one. He remembered his fiancée, Lucy, asking him to say the magic words: 'Tell me, Dave, tell me you love me,' and the best he could manage was: 'Lucy, I'll say this much, you are a bonus.' And then he had run off to Tenerife for six months with Froggy and the OOzing mates. But Naina was different: she was everything he ever dreamed of in a woman; yet still he went with numerous slaggy women who could never match up to her. Surely it wasn't all down to greed. It was for sex, that's about the size of it, sex.

Chapter Forty-three

When Naina was a little girl, Mum had explained an Indian wedding in all its glory, all its pretty colours, music and dancing, and she remembered thinking 'Wow' and she couldn't wait for it to be her turn, so that she could wear a beautiful sari and be the centre of attraction. As she grew older, however, it seemed so different. All so false and misleading. All so forced and pressurized. A pantomime which had no happy ending and relied on Prince Charming – Ashok – being chosen out of a lucky dip. Most girls dream of a white wedding and being whisked off into the sunset with the man of their dreams. Not Indian girls. They can only pray that the bloke picked out for them by their parents doesn't turn out to be a complete and utter bastard. That's it. It sort of takes the romance out of it all.

5 a.m. on the day of Naina's wedding. The house was still. Everyone who could sleep was asleep. Kate

and Leena, however, had been up since 4 a.m. nursing a very sorrowful bride-to-be. The morning darkness outside was a pittance to the darkness in Naina's heart, and as the radiant sunshine began to wake up, the realization that time was running out for the English Naina became all too apparent. The tears simply wouldn't stop; she wasn't handling the transition period well at all.

Kate sat with her arm round her downcast friend. 'Naina,' she whispered, 'enrolment is at 10.30; you've really got to try and pull yourself together. Look at you, your eyes are all puffed up.' And she picked out another tissue from the box and passed it to her.

Leena wasn't really much help, her best effort to cheer Naina up went along the lines: 'At least you know what your husband looks like, I won't know until my wedding day, when he steps off the plane from Delhi.' It didn't help much, but it produced a vague smile from Naina.

Naina snivelled, 'I want to see Dave. Maybe I was being too harsh; I was expecting too much from him.' And Kate and Leena looked at each other. 'Him saying I love you is probably like . . . like . . .' And she bawled out crying.

Since Tuesday's phone call from Dave, since his confession of his love, Naina just wanted to eat and get fat. Truth was she couldn't eat at all; her nerves were coated in barbed wire and tearing at her insides, leaving her in a constant state of nausea, pain and regret.

Kate crept round her words very carefully, 'You said yourself, if he really loved you, then he would keep trying. He makes one phone call, on a whim, and you don't hear from him after that; that doesn't sound like he loves you, Naina. Sorry, but you did right.'

'He's most likely lying in some drunken stupor right now, with a dirty slag by him, feeling sorry for himself, his ego all disintegrated. You did right, Naina, Kate's right, he's a loser,' said helpful Leena.

Naina felt robbed of comfort. 'You two haven't got a nice word to say about him. You can't even keep it shut just for me.' She wiped her eyes. 'You don't know what he's like with me, you just see his big act. You don't know half the stuff he's done for me.'

'Well, where is this saint then? St David. I'll tell you where he is, in fucking Amsterdam for three days with the OOzing lads, on Jingle's stag night. Let's see if he keeps his little cock in his Armani pants there; *doubt* it.' Kate felt better anyway.

Naina, predictably, began to cry. 'It's not little, it's massive.' And she sobbed into her pillow, '*It's massive.*'

Apart from Naina's room, almost every other room in the household was like a guest house in Cornwall when the eclipse came – chock-a-block with people – aunts, uncles, cousins, lost grannies.

Death, Damnation and Destruction had refused the offer of sleeping on the floor listening to farting aunties and wailing children, and decided to sleep rough in the garden, in a tent, under the stars. If the Devil wanted to take them that night, he only had to unzip their tent, load them onto his chariot of sin and let the four hooded horsemen gallop off into burning hell below. They were quite disappointed to wake up to vegetable samosas and tea. Bummer.

Naina worried. There was one thing that Dave

would never be unfaithful to – life, he was totally committed to that: living it up and enjoying it to the full. And that's what worried Naina the most – he would just forget about her; while ten, twenty, even fifty years later, maybe she would still be thinking back to what could have been; she just wished she had said goodbye properly and he had held her one more time.

'Dave wanted me to give you this.' Kate handed her two presents. 'He said open the envelope first, that's your original present. I think it's a voucher.' Kate and Leena watched with interest.

A blue envelope, with simply '*Naina*' written on it, and an extremely heavy oblong boxed shape wrapped in red-coloured metallic paper, with simply: '*Nothing lasts for ever, two hearts can't stay together, and life is just a phase.*'

Naina's hands, patterned in henna, her long manicured nails painted in red, shook delicately like a spider's web in the wind, as she gently tore the envelope open and pulled out a card: a picture of a monkey in a bright pink bikini mowing the lawn. Inside a note: '*Dear Naina, you know where I am if you ever need me. Hope it all goes well. Dave. I'll miss you.*' And the present: an open cheque.

Naina walked to the window and stared down on her street. Familiarity was a luxury that would soon be gone. Family and friends, her hometown and work, her shops, pubs, clubs, even Florelli's apple pie all gone; but most of all, Dave.

'Naina,' said a panicky Leena, 'open the other present, come on.'

'I don't want to.' For one small moment Naina

thought she could smell Davidoff in the room, and the smell invoked all manner of puzzling feelings. Then she sat back on the bed and picked up the heavy heavy present. Something under the red metallic shine was going to wreck an already bad day – she could just tell.

Naina looked to her two impatient friends. 'Sorry, Kate, Leena, I want to be on my own when I open this. Please.' And her two friends nodded understandingly and left her to it.

Naina unwrapped it, heart playing Jekyll and Hyde, gently pulling off the Sellotape, not wanting to rip the paper, undoing each corner methodically and nervously. Before her now, in her lap, a deep rectangular polished oak box. Two thick brass hinges shone as she carefully lifted the lid. Red tissue sat on top of a red velvet cloth and Naina, heart now sore, lifted the cloth up.

Gold. Naina lifted out the heavy block of 22-carat gold – the size of a small milk tray box. The slanting engraved writing was etched deep into the dazzling gold slab.

> *Sexy Naina,*
> *Far away in distant lands,*
> *The Amritsar Temple stands.*
> *You steal its gold, then leave behind*
> *Your sight now cursed, forever blind.*
>
> *Of which I am, I should have seen.*
> *My love for you, what could have been.*
> *I love you Naina, I always knew it.*
> *I've lost you Naina, trust me, I blew it.*

In my heart, in my dreams, in my soul
I don't want to let you leave and go.
But forget me now, and I shall die.
And all because we met, in life
Over apple pie.
Dave

Even tears of a thousand lost thoughts won't rust gold, and Naina wiped her sadness away and replaced the gold block in its holder.

Underneath a pile of tear-soaked tissues in her woven bin, Naina frantically grabbed the jigsaw remains of the only photo she had of Dave and her together and madly tried to return the photo to its primary condition, whole. Her tears fell silently as nothing seemed to fit, and with her temper gathering pace, she finally managed to put Dave's head back on his body and just stared down at him for what seemed only a second, but really was fifteen minutes, until there was a pestering knock at the door and Mum thundered in.

'Come on, we've got to get you ready,' Mum said in Punjabi, with uncontrollable excitement. 'You're going to look so pretty.' She hugged her daughter, kissed her softly. 'Don't cry, Naina, I love you.' And the moment was empty of anything but a mother's love for her child. Mum poked the corner of her eye, pretending to pick out dust. 'Ashok will look after you. You know we're always here for you. Your dad wouldn't let you marry someone who wouldn't take care of you. It will get easier, when you get to know him.' And they hugged for precious minutes until Naina's tears ceased, then Mum left.

Naina added the fixed photo to the oak box and

placed it carefully in her wardrobe under a pile of 'out clothes'. Leena and Kate, on the verge of orgasm, marched in, demanded to see the present, and nearly cried out loud when told, 'Sorry, no.'

'Well, what was it? Come on, Naina, we're your best friends,' ranted Kate.

'I don't want to talk about it and I don't want to ever talk about him again. I'm getting married today, and I can't let my family down.' Naina grabbed her lotions, readying herself for a hot bath. 'I just can't let my parents down.' And walked out.

'She's losing it,' Kate surmised. 'Big time.'

'It's just nerves, Kate; I wouldn't worry about it too much.'

And whatever bubble bath Naina used it worked wonders, because when she returned she was smiling like a bride, talking about Ashok and wearing a confidence only matched by the bright and cheery sunny day.

'What underwear do you think Ashok will want to see me in? Red?' asked Naina to her entourage of lingerie experts. 'Well, it will have to be, that's what I bought, and that's what men *like*.' Naina began to dress. 'And I'm sure he will want a shower before he fucks me, that's what men *do*.'

'Pete doesn't,' said a worried-looking Kate.

Naina continued, 'And I expect to find the bed sheets all clean, that's what men *do*.'

'No, Pete doesn't.'

'And,' Naina picked up her diamond choker, which Ashok had given her, 'and I expect him to roll a condom on with just one hand in three seconds flat. Men *do* that.'

'Pete doesn't, he takes for ever. I even have to help him, that's why I cut my nails short.'

They were interrupted as Naina's mum, her sister Sumita and two grumpy old hag-aunts took control of dressage and began to transform the English Naina to the perfect Indian bride. Forty minutes later, Naina stared at her reflection in the long mirror and nearly didn't recognize herself.

A red and gold sari, woven from finest silk, accentuated her brown skin, glowing with splendour. Gold rings on her fingers were joined like small pathways to gold bracelets that chimed together on her wrists. Her deep brown eyes were decorated above the brows with red and white dots of make-up. A small golden chain attached from her nose to her ear added to the eastern decoration that she carried so well, and you could be forgiven for thinking that she had just been plucked straight out of an Indian palace five hundred years ago. She was a queen and like a poet becomes his poetry, she became the wedding. Her beauty was matched only by her charm, which equally matched the occasion. Missing from these perfect ingredients for a bride was one thing that was strikingly clear – she had no smile. But still she would uplift even the heaviest of hearts. And surely only a man with no sense at all would have let her go.

Kate and Leena stood in their matching crimson shalwar kameez, tears welling. Their best friend was nothing less than a triumph of unbelievable beauty. Nothing shone as bright as Naina this day: not the sun, not the gold, not even the diamond choker.

'Naina, you are unreal,' Leena sniffed, 'stunning. Ashok's going to be knocked sideways.'

And Kate agreed, crying like a baby, mascara already making footprints down her cheeks. She knew, not that she had ever had any doubt, that this was going to be the hardest goodbye of her life, when Naina began her new life in Dagenham.

Naina stopped short of the door, glanced one more time at the bedroom she and Sonia shared, and knew that next time she saw this place, she would be a married woman. She smiled, reminiscing over times gone by, then turned to Leena and Kate. 'Come on, I'm finally getting married, let's go to the temple. I can't leave a gentleman like Ashok waiting.'

Chapter Forty-four

Like an imploding firework, a rainbow of colours from the M1, A1, M25, M6 and even a shanty town in Bahawalpur, congregated for the spectacle of Naina's and Ashok's wedding. Three hundred and seventy-five guests dressed in their bright saris, shalwar kameez, turbans and suits, all gathered outside the Sikh Temple in MK, like a field full of colourful frolicking flowers. From the clear blue perfect sky, the scorching sun shone down.

The mood was boisterously jovial, with happy faces, the music of laughter, proud parents, a ripple of beatitude sweeping through them all, and bustling women all trying to seek a glimpse of the star attraction – the bride, Naina.

Naina stood, head down, embarrassed by the swarming eyes. Leena at one side, Kate at the other, both desperate to have a gander at Ashok. Kate was overwhelmed by it all – her first Indian wedding – and felt every bit as proud of Naina as the throng of other guests. Leena too was proud, but mixed with her pride was a certain apprehension: this was almost a mock run for her own big day, her own arranged marriage, and there was no dispute in her mind that she too, come judgement day, would be bowing her head the same as Naina. It was enough to make you want to faint.

Ashok's handsome face appeared, smiling and confident. Dressed as Naina had expected he would be, as smart as humanly possible in a designer black suit, angel white shirt, scarlet red silk tie and gleaming black shoes. His heart galloped upon spotting Naina. She was exquisite; unbelievably beautiful and feminine: he could not believe his luck. And his imagination had not done justice to how he had visualized the diamond choker on her slender neck; it could almost have been made for her. He walked up, taking long strides, and stood as close as he was allowed, about two metres away.

'He's a bit of all right, Naina, not a bad looker. Sort of hunky in a refined way,' Kate whispered in Naina's dipped ear. 'He wouldn't cheat on you; he looks too kind.'

Leena spoke, 'And he's a gentleman. You can just tell, not rough at all. I bet he doesn't even swear. I can't ever see him getting pissed and losing his car.'

Naina sighed, still refusing to look up. 'I like my men rough. I don't care if they swear. What's the use of a creep of a man who does everything right when you've got a man that speaks his mind and isn't false? Ashok's all surface, he is, he could be a rapist under all that charm, and he's definitely not as good looking as . . .' Naina stopped. Then started again. 'I bet his body's a disappointment. I bet he hasn't got a flat stomach, let alone a six-pack, and why should I have second best? Who have I ever hurt in my life to deserve this?' Naina looked up to see Ashok smiling at her. She feebly smiled back, put her head back down and started up again. 'Did you see that? He's a murderer, I can just tell. Don't be surprised if I'm in the newspapers tomorrow, found dead in my sari in a forest in bloody Dagenham!'

Kate whispered in Leena's ear, 'Don't dare dig at Dave again. I can see this wedding going pear-shaped. She's quite scary when she gets going.'

Naina leered at Kate. 'Fucking heard that. And you tell that Dave when you see him, I'll be thinking of him when I fuck Ashok, you tell him that word for word.'

Whether it was the heat or the mass of collective faces, but the kids were all behaving and were totally disregarding the rules of weddings – that kids must cry and be annoying. Handshakes were taking place left, right and centre; what everyone was waiting for, no one really knew. Maybe the temple wasn't quite ready, maybe a few relatives were late arriving, who knows? Naina just wanted it all over and done with. Kiran looked on. He had had worrying doubts about his sister and that white piece of shit, but that was all sorted now, and like the rest of the family he now stood with a coating of love and pure proud contentment for Naina – he only wished Kaz and Nass would remove those embarrassing saffron bandannas, they were making him look stupid.

Finally the last guest arrived. And the three hundred

and seventy-five people who had merged on the temple lawn, turned their heads to the zealous arrival of the sparkling black sports BMW, Guns n' Roses blaring from the car speakers, almost rattling the insides of the now-shocked guests. Who could possibly have the audacity to turn up to a wedding, skid their car on the grass verge, and blast the airwaves with 'November Rain'?

The car door flung open, the music still played, and a chic man in a black Versace suit, white shirt, blue tie, a pair of shoes, fag in mouth, dark mysterious shades and a blue chrysanthemum in his buttonhole, holding a wrapped present, emerged, sensing all eyes on him.

Dave scanned the hordes of guests, smiled his Dave smile as he picked out the obvious groom – and, ignoring the deep mutterings of confused voices, headed straight for him.

'Ashok, this is for you and your beautiful woman.' A few voices went. 'Ahh, that's lovely' as Ashok reluctantly accepted the gift. Dave looked him up and down, not bad. Couldn't pick his own woman though, could he? Oh no. Mummy and Daddy had to help him. That's not a man, that's a cretin. Nice shoes though. Obviously got a bit of money. But money won't satisfy Naina in the bed department. You don't get many orgasms to a pound these days. Dave glanced to Ashok's crotch, Naina would have been disappointed.

Ashok politely peeked down to the present and back up to Dave. 'Thank you, er, and you are?' Ashok tried to think if he knew him or not.

'Dave. Nice Gucci suit, mate.'

'Er, thanks. You've left your car running,' Ashok stated, looking to the half-parked car, door open, music still blaring.

'Yeah, I've just come to collect someone.' And he threw his fag end at Ashok's gleaming shoe. 'No hard feelings, mate.' Dave turned round to catch Naina's eyes, as he smoothly walked towards her inert form. *Un-fucking-believably beautiful.* How could he ever have let things get to this stage? He should have had the foresight to tell her, she shouldn't have had to go through all of this.

Dave stood opposite her, a few inches away from her face. 'Naina, I love you, I can't stop thinking about you, I want you.'

Naina ignored a sense of suppressed anger filtering through the crowd, ignored the restless movement of Indian men moving towards her and Dave. 'Take your shades off, look me in the eyes and tell me.'

He whipped off his Armani shades. 'Naina, I love you, I want you, I *fucking* love you.' And he stretched his right hand towards Naina's. Instinctively, she grabbed his warm hand, the hand that felt ultimately right. Bright, generous, and honest, his killer blue eyes held hers in a gaze that unlocked a chain of feelings inside her. There was nothing misleading about them at all; he loved her, he was here to prove it and somewhere in her hidden closet of hope, she had known he would come, she had known he wouldn't have let her go, but even she didn't think that he would leave it this late. For Christ's sake, any later and he would have had to jump in bed with her and Ashok and kick him out. But that's Dave. Loves to make it memorable.

Dave smiled his accomplished smile, then became aware, amongst a cocktail of angry Indian voices, of someone shouting in English, 'Don't bloody touch her!' Naina's parents stood close by, looking on with an appalled expression, as Naina pulled Dave back. She hurriedly kissed her mum first, then her dad. 'I'm sorry, so sorry, but I love him. I'm sorry.'

Dave squeezed her hand. 'Run as fast as you fucking can, let's get the hell out of here!'

And then they legged it across the dry grass lawn, Naina's red heels digging into the turf; and they both jumped into the car, and skidded off before realization dawned on the disillusioned crowd, realization that a thousand years of tradition had been broken by one of their Indian girls in the name of *true love*. Their strict system had fallen flaw to a force of nature that nothing can truly bind. And Ashok, the one that this would hit the hardest of all, just watched as his beautiful bride vanished with a white stranger before his very eyes. But in a way, he had never really had her in the first place. Let's face it, he didn't even know his bride's favourite chocolate bar, or music, film, or favourite colour, he knew one thing and one thing only – she was beautiful and she was gone.

Kate and Leena, along with Sonia, were the only three who smiled, their eyes following the car as it screeched up the road, leaving a tyre-marked scar all the way from the temple to the traffic lights two miles away. Maybe only those three really had realized that this was what Naina had wanted all along.

'Jeez, I'm only surprised he didn't turn up in a turban,' said Leena. 'That man will do anything.' And they both laughed.

Kate took Leena's arm. There was nowhere to go but away from here. The tension was enough to curdle milk. They strolled down the road with the burning sun on their hair.

'Any guesses what they're doing right now?' said Kate.

And both together said, 'Porking.' And carried on up the road.

'It's probably his sick fantasy to shag her in a wedding sari anyway,' remarked Kate. And from her leopard-skin handbag she brought out her quarter bottle of whisky and both swigged it, toasting Naina and Dave: 'Good on them.'

Both Dave and Naina watched the miles cruise under the axle. There were no words between them; they simply listened to *Estranged* by Guns n' Roses, letting their over-active hearts beat once again at less than 200 b.p.m. Naina, hands trembling, lit two fags, passed Dave one and coughed through one herself. She knew she'd done right – this time.

As the car revved forward, Naina reverted back into the English Naina. Already half her jewellery was off, make-up wiped away – using man-sized tissues – and her hair let loose, blowing from the open window and sunroof. Dave quickly glanced across at the woman who now had his heart spellbound; he knew the tears would come soon now; first tears of sadness, then relief, then *hopefully* tears of joy.

'Dave, can we go to Kate's? I need to get out of this sari,' she urged. 'I need to get into some normal clothes. I need to wipe this whole fucking wedding out of my mind.'

He switched the stereo off, steamed his way back round the large Redmoor roundabout and headed towards bitch Kate's, as Naina began to unravel herself out of the heavy laden sari. Dave had read many articles in *Woman's Own* over the years, but he had never seen any about how to bring a woman's emotions back to equilibrium after you have ransacked her wedding and stolen her from her groom. He wondered why. He'd have to improvise. He took hold of her still-trembling hand and reassured her not to worry; things have a way of sorting themselves out. And with a voice as calm as Valium, he told her, 'Naina, me and my dick won't let you down.'

Naina's face broke into a smile, and then, 'What did you give Ashok?'

He drew up outside bitch Kate's flat, turned the engine off and faced a questioning Naina. 'I thought if he was going to have anything to remember the wedding by, then it might as well be a memory of the bloke that messed it up.'

Naina's face drew a blank. They both stepped out of the car, Dave immobilized it, and came round to take Naina's hand.

Finally, she spoke, 'Well, what was it?'

There was a sense of not wanting to tell her in Dave's eyes. There was an equal sense of not wanting to know in Naina's. She reached up to a hanging basket full of dead flowers, retrieved a spare key wrapped in muddy cling film and they both headed up the carpeted stairs to the flat entrance, with Dave carrying a thought: Would Danny Zuko have been able to gatecrash a wedding and come back with the bride, in style? Doubt it.

Kate's bedroom was now completely covered with Kevin Costner posters; *The Bodyguard*, *Perfect World*, *Robin Hood*, and *JFK*. Dave sniggered, totally tasteless. Metal wind-chimes tinkled softly by the small open window, a pile of make-up was scattered on the butterfly duvet, fresh-cut red tulips were arranged in a Dumbo vase with the flowers flowing out of its trunk – like it had a nose bleed, and a half-drunk bottle of vodka sat on her cluttered dressing table.

Naina was standing in her red underwear, searching through Kate's cramped wardrobe, the sari at her feet. Poor Ashok, thought Dave, didn't even get to see that much. Naina, almost clairvoyant, spoke with her back to him, 'Don't even think about it.'

He carefully pushed the heap of make-up to one side and lay back on the lumpy double bed. 'I gave him a large bottle of Davidoff,' he said casually.

Naina instantly turned round, holding a light blue summer dress on a padded pink coat-hanger. 'You gave Ashok a bottle of Davidoff? Are you sick?'

'I know, what a waste.'

She slipped into the perfect fitting dress, sat on the bed, and he eagerly pulled her down to join him. She lay on top of him, both looking into each other's eyes. Without words, a promise was made right then: 'No matter what, no matter who, even if things don't go well or smooth, there is no way that either of us will ever miss an episode of *EastEnders*.'

Dave kissed her softly on the lips. 'Naina, I love you, move in with me.'

She placed her hand on his forehead. His temperature seemed normal, there was no rash, even his breathing was steady. 'This was what I was afraid of with you, Dave. We go on barely three dates, next you want me to move in, then it will be marriage and babies. Sod it, I'm off to my dingy cave in Tenerife.'

Dave laughed. 'Words of an insecure person.'

Naina could hold out no longer. Her mehndi-decorated hands swiftly undid his blue silk tie, frantically undid the handcrafted shirt buttons, tossed it over the bedside. Meanwhile Dave was frantically lifting her cotton dress over her head and that too was tossed to one side.

'Wait! I bring bad news,' he announced. 'No sodding condom, I've got no condom.'

Naina pulled his trousers off and slid down his black Armani boxers. 'That's a first, you with no condom.' Nearly tripping over herself, she threw out most of Kate's messy drawers, chucking them on the yellow carpeted floor. 'There's got to be one here.' And then she found an opened box. 'There you go.' And span it to Dave's more than welcome hand.

Naina lay back on the dipping bed, naked. Dave, one-handed, began to roll the condom on, standing over her. 'Naina, I'm going to do you so bad.' His legs wobbled on the doughy mattress. 'It's been over three dreadful long months since I gave you one.' And he began to lower himself.

The varnished bedroom door hesitantly opened. Kate and Leena staggered in, mouths open, not quite believing what their eyes were showing them, but still they came in further, right up to the bed.

'Oh . . . my . . . God,' Kate slurred. 'Get a load of this, Leena.'

Leena held on to Kate's arm, steadying herself. 'Jeez.'

Naina harshly pushed an unwilling Dave off, looked at her two friends. 'I told you it was massive.'

All four stared to Dave's . . .

Dave smiled his big smile, put his free hand up. 'Ladies, this bod is no longer for lease, I no longer cater for foursomes. So Kate and Leena, sling your hook!' Sorted!